The Beginning

Caspian Stone:
HIS FATHER'S SECRET

MARCUS FULLER

ESQUIRE CONSORTIUM

Published 2016 by Esquire Consortium

ISBN: 978-0-99350-490-7

For Nevaeh & Megan

I:
HIS ESTRANGED FATHER

Of all the small villages and towns within the British Isles, the inhabitants of Little Bickham were by far the nosiest, most meddlesome, and intrusive little community in the entire country. With the total residents numbering just over two hundred, almost all of whom were busybodies with an insatiable hunger for the juiciest morsels of gossip, it was next to impossible to keep a secret from spreading through the rural hillside village like wildfire.

Take for example when Mr Jansen of number six Arnold Row had a spot too much of his favourite ale at the local village pub, The Old Dark Horse, one summer's eve. Rather than make it home that night safe and sound to crawl into bed beside his rather domineering wife, she had instead discovered him the next morning, fast asleep in Mrs Tilby's cabbage patch. This particular titbit of embarrassing information was common knowledge to the Little Bickham populace before a rather hung-over Mr Jansen had finished his first sobering mug of coffee.

On the morning that our story begins, however, Mr Jansen had not been found in Mrs Tilby's cabbage patch, nor in any other patch of home-grown produce for that matter. This mild autumn day, all village-based gossip involved the young boy who lived in the little house beneath the viaduct with his mother.

It was, of course, absolutely no secret to the neighbourhood that the boy's mother, Elizabeth Stone, was very ill. Her once long dark hair had fallen out many months ago, and after each monthly treatment she would stay inside her home for days on end, never setting foot outside until the side effects had ceased.

But during recent weeks Mrs Doddington, of number eleven Thorpe Lonsdale Lane, had reported the more frequent comings and goings of the doctor – in fact, no less than on *four* occasions last week! Nobody had approached Mrs Stone about her health directly as they didn't want to seem like they were prying, but everyone on the lane had their suspicions as to why the doctor's visits had increased and the general consensus was grim.

Caspian Stone was thirteen years old.

Thirteen is a difficult age for a boy. The body begins a metamorphosis from its adolescent structure of youth into the shape of the man it will maintain for the rest of its life. As this change occurs, the brain is flooded with hormones to which the effect could be likened to a superhero learning to control his newly developing superpowers: the body suddenly starts doing the most unthinkable things at usually the most embarrassing moments, resulting in an obstacle course of awkward experiences, uncomfortable situations, and mostly bad decisions – often involving the opposite sex. If teenage boys were superheroes, teenage girls would be their kryptonite.

Caspian had been forced to grow-up a lot quicker than most boys his age. His parents had separated when he was still a baby, and he really had no memory of them ever being together. His mother had never re-married or met anyone else, so in the last year when she had been diagnosed with her sickness he had naturally slipped into the role of her carer. On the days when she was too ill to get up he would do the shopping, the cooking, and the cleaning, whilst looking after her. And where as many young boys would begrudge such responsibility being thrust upon them, Caspian shouldered these burdens long-sufferingly.

He sat in a seat by the window, his mind an odd mixture of emotions as he looked out at Thorpe Lonsdale Lane in the early morning light. He was the first up in the little house this morning, but he'd heard Mother get up and rush to the bathroom a few minutes ago where she was probably being sick. This had become her morning ritual over the last week, as had the show that would follow, its purpose to give him the impression that nothing was wrong, that all was normal.

And in a strange sense it was.

Caspian had become accustomed to looking after his mother and the reversal their roles had taken. With each motherly task that she was no longer capable of doing, he would inherently start doing it for her.

Sometimes he caught a pained look in Mother's blue eyes, like *you shouldn't be doing that, I should.* But then she would get tired and have to sleep, especially after her monthly trips to the hospital for treatments; "Going to see my friends," she referred to them with intentional irony.

After a few minutes more she came and joined him by the window, caught his eye, and offered him a loving smile. She was a beautiful woman, but now that she struggled to keep her food down her weight loss was becoming more evident.

'Well, today's the day,' she said. The smile was still on her lips, but there was no happiness in her eyes this morning. 'Is everything packed?'

'I packed last night,' he replied as cheerfully as he could muster, although she seemed to sense it was only a façade.

'What is it, Cas?'

'I don't want to go live with him. I don't want to leave you alone.'

'I won't be alone, silly,' Mother said. 'I'm going to a place where they can keep a much closer eye on me. My "friends" will be with me every day.' She gave him a playful wink.

'But why do you have to go at all? I could have looked after you *here*?'

That pained look he knew too well briefly crept into his mother's eyes again, as though it had always been there hiding behind a screen. 'You shouldn't have to, Cas,' Mother said regretfully. 'You're a young man who should be out playing with his friends and meeting girls, not staying at home to babysit his mother.'

'I don't mind, Mom,' Caspian said honestly. 'You'd do the same for me.'

Mother smiled. 'Yes I would, because that is *my* job, not yours. You should be living your life. Just think, soon you will see London! You will be able to explore the streets of one of the oldest and greatest cities in the world.'

He smiled back at her, but his face was not a true reflection of how he felt inside. He did not share his mother's fascination with the nation's capital, and he certainly did not agree with her plan to send him there to live with his father, a man he knew barely any better than a stranger.

'London's so far away.' He couldn't bear the thought of being that far from her, especially whilst she was having one of her bad turns. London felt like a million miles away from where he ought to be.

'These days, the country is a much smaller place than it used to be,' Mother reassured him. 'It's only a few hours by train. You can come and visit me as often as you like. And plus, it's only whilst I get back on my feet.'

'Is it really going to take so long, though?'

'I can't answer that, Cas,' Mother replied. '*I* certainly hope not, but the doctor said it will take a month before they can tell whether the new treatment is having any effect, and then they will have to adjust what they are giving me in accordance. It could take a very long time, but you never know, I might even be on the mend by Christmas.'

'So why can't I stay here then? I could stay with Jess,' he suggested.

Jessica Ravenwood was his neighbour, and his best friend. They had been neighbours on Thorpe Lonsdale Lane for their entire lives, and friends for as long as he could remember. She was another reason he didn't want to leave Little Bickham.

'Tom and Wendy's house is not much bigger than our own,' Mother answered. 'They only have two bedrooms, and you are getting a little too old to be sharing a room with Jess,' she added with a raised eyebrow.

'Mom, Jess and I are just friends,' he answered, denying her implications. 'We're not going out or *anything* like that.'

A smirk crept onto Mother's face. 'Which is why you both need your own space. You know what the people in this village are like; just imagine what rumours would spread were you two to share a bedroom.'

Caspian felt his ears flare red.

At school they had been teased that they were "in love." Some of his classmates just couldn't grasp the simple concept that it was possible to be friends with a girl without feeling any of that romantic nonsense toward them. In his eyes, Jess was the sibling he had never had, and he was certain Jess saw him the same way.

'The arrangements have been made,' Mother continued sleepily. 'Your father has already prepared a bedroom for you, and he has managed to get you into a very respectable school…'

A least Jess wouldn't be teased anymore. On Monday, when everyone returned to school from their half-term holidays, he wouldn't be there.

Mother closed her eyes for a moment. Her sickness drained her, especially when she was having a bad day. Caspian watched her, feeling a mixture of love and sadness in the pit of his stomach. He was worried. Although she had had bad turns before, none of them had been as bad as this. They had never been bad enough to have to send him away.

Instinctively he reached out and placed his hand on top of hers. She responded by giving his fingers the weakest of squeezes, but a smile formed on her lips.

'I'm going to miss having you close, Cas,' she whispered with her eyes still closed. 'You are my brave boy, my little pillar of strength.'

He felt his throat go dry and tears welling up behind his eyes. *No*, he told himself. *I must be strong. She needs me strong. I mustn't cry.*

'You *are* going to come see me, aren't you?'

'As often as I can,' he replied. The words felt too big for his vocal cords, as if the emotion he felt was throttling his neck.

'Then we'll be okay, Cas,' Mother replied so softly it was barely audible, and with her eyes still closed she smiled her beautiful smile. 'We'll be okay.'

The big clock on the train station chimed eleven.

Caspian sat on a bench beside platform two, watching the rail track trail off endlessly into the distance. He was average height for a boy his age, having just finished a growth spurt. Following his sudden increase in height, his body had yet to fill out to the correct proportions and so, despite being the same height as many in his class, he appeared awkward and lanky. His hair was dark like his mother's, before it had fallen out, and he looked no different to any other regular teenage boy in his year, apart from one particular feature: his eyes.

Unlike most people, whose eyes are matching in colour, both of Caspian's were completely different. Whilst his left eye was deep blue, like his mother's, his right was a vibrant shade of hazel that in bright sunlight glimmered like gold.

This peculiarity in his appearance had brought him much unwanted attention over the years, and was often the focal point for a lot of spiteful comments. What Caspian found strange was that whilst some noticed that his eyes were different coloured, others didn't realise at all, until someone else pointed it out.

Beside him on the bench sat Jessica Ravenwood, her long dark hair in the corkscrew curls it stubbornly resorted to, no matter what she tried to do with it. They hung beside her pale face and emerald green eyes, slightly swaying in the midmorning breeze. Her parents, Thomas and Gwendolyn, had left them at the platform after making an excuse that they needed to query the cost of a rail ticket to Scotland. Both Caspian and Jess knew what they were really up to; they were giving them the opportunity to say goodbye.

'How is your mom doing?' Jess asked to break the silence that had fallen between them since their initial greeting when the Ravenwoods had collected him from his home. Mother was not well enough to come to the station with them, and so he had said his final farewells at home.

'She pretends that everything is fine, that all this is just another setback to overcome,' Caspian answered, his eyes still fixed on the rail track in the distance. 'But she's worse than I've ever seen her before.'

'Sometimes people need to get worse before they get better,' Jess suggested.

This was why he liked Jess. She had a kind of sensitive optimism, but not the over-the-top-and-unrealistically-optimistic optimism held by those with a blind faith. No, she just offered a positive grasp on the situation at hand – and hope. She always seemed to offer hope.

'Thanks,' Caspian said, finally looking at her.

'For what?'

'Just for…' he began, unsure how to put the gratitude he felt for his friend into words. 'Well, I guess for the last thirteen years.'

To his surprise, Jess burst out laughing. Then, as he saw how ridiculous his answer had been, he started too. It wasn't like they were never going to see each other again.

'You're still planning to come back for Christmas?' Jess asked.

'Yeah, of course.'

'And I'm still coming to stay at your father's in February, right?'

'I hope so,' Caspian replied. 'But I might have gone out of my mind by then.'

'It won't be that bad. How long's it been since you last saw him?'

He didn't need to recall for he clearly remembered the last time he had seen his father. 'It was just after mom was diagnosed. I haven't spoken to him since then.'

His father's visits were exceptionally rare. Caspian felt that his father had left them one day and had never looked back. That had been the day after his first birthday; so long ago that he couldn't even remember it.

Since then he had missed every birthday Caspian had ever had, sending only a simple birthday card, each year with the same uninspiring message inside:

Dear Caspian,
Many happy returns
Your Father

It always arrived late. If nothing else, his father was certainly consistent.

There was no real animosity between either of them, nor was much love shared. In actual fact, they both regarded one another with a mutual state of apathy. The silence between them had lasted as long as it had simply because neither had felt compelled to contact the other.

His father being a technophobe did not help this lack of communication. From what little Caspian knew about his father, he knew that he had never taken a liking to computers, mobile phones, or any of the new gadgets and technological advances that flooded the market every day. He wasn't even certain that his father owned a television. The man had surrounded himself with antiques, so much so that he was starting to become one.

'Maybe this is the opportunity you've needed to get to know him?'

'I guess,' he shrugged noncommittally. He really had very little interest in getting to know this man. They hardly knew each other at all and did not share any common interests that Caspian was aware of. When he was younger he had been more curious to know who his father was, but after it became clear that his father was not interested in getting to know him he quickly lost interest. These days they were essentially strangers, connected by blood alone.

Jess' parents returned to join them. Mrs Ravenwood was a tall, slim woman with hair like her daughter. She was good-natured, but could occasionally be a bit of a fusspot. Jess looked more like her mom than she did her dad, but she was more like him in terms of personality, who was a lot more relaxed and down to earth.

'You'd better make sure you have everything, Caspian dear,' Mrs Ravenwood fussed. 'You're father will be here soon.'

The suitcase at Caspian's feet was packed to the point of bursting. His father had insisted that he only bring the bare essentials as everything else would be provided when he arrived in London, but when it came to packing he found that everything felt like a bare essential.

'I'm sure he has everything ready, my dear,' Mr Ravenwood said beside her, giving Caspian a sly wink. Thomas Ravenwood wrote for the local newspaper, *The Bickham Observer*, and had his own column where he commented on political and business events. Unfortunately, most of the Observer's readership was far more interested in what local gossip had been reported rather than business news, but Mr Ravenwood always had an educated opinion on current affairs.

He was a stout little man with light brown hair, and he made quite a contrast to his wife in both personality and appearance. *Opposites really do attract*, Caspian thought, but then he thought just how different his parents were.

'Well, his train will be here in a matter of minutes,' Mrs Ravenwood continued on to her husband. Jess rolled her eyes and made a face of irritation that made Caspian smile. He would miss the Ravenwoods, all of them.

At eleven-eleven, Caspian's father's train pulled into the station and came to a halt at platform two. Not many people alighted the train, as Little Bickham was not the most "happening" of villages in the land, but of the few that did Caspian's father was the last.

This was typical of his father. He was a man who arrived at his own pace, never early and rarely with haste. Even now, he walked leisurely down the platform towards them as though time was not of his concern.

His visits to Little Bickham were infrequent, and so much time would pass between them that Caspian could almost forget what his father looked like. But each time he saw him, his father had hardly changed at all from how he remembered him.

Caspian's father's name was Edgar, which was a rather old-fashioned name. He was a tall man with smart dark hair, and his face was always clean-shaven. He was always immaculately presented and meticulously tidy. Today he wore a bowler hat, which was an exceptionally uncommon thing to be seen on anyone in the Little Bickham area, and yet worn on his head it seemed the most normal thing in the world. He was dressed in a tailored suit of expensive design, and on his feet he wore a pair of polished leather shoes that clicked loudly on the platform with each slow but deliberate step towards them.

As he drew closer, Caspian could clearly see his father's eyes. Just like his own right eye, his father's eyes were the same shade of vibrant hazel. It was the eyes that he remembered, that he always remembered, those golden eyes that seemed centuries older than the face that wore them. It sounded silly, but when Caspian felt those eyes upon him he felt like they were penetrating his thoughts, like his mind was one of the large city tabloids they were so accustomed to reading.

Those same golden, piercing eyes that were on him now.

'Good morning,' his father said, his eyes lingering over Caspian a little while longer before moving to the rest of the group. 'Tom. Wendy. How have you been?'

Caspian watched his father make idle chitchat with Mr and Mrs Ravenwood, feeling a contradictory mixture that he was being disregarded whilst on the other hand wanting to be left alone. Jess seemed to pick up this vibe and accompanied him in silence as they followed the adults over the bridge that linked platforms one and two, whilst he clumsily hauled his suitcase behind him.

Annoyingly, Father had left the tightest of gaps between his train arriving and their train departing. True enough; the trains to London did not stop at Little Bickham station very often, but even so, surely they could have caught a later train. Wouldn't Father have liked more time to catch up with Mr and Mrs Ravenwood, them having once been very good friends? Wouldn't he have liked to visit Mother? Caspian couldn't understand his father's rush to return to the city.

The train was already approaching in the distance as Caspian and Jess reached the bottom of the steps onto platform one with his luggage.

'Time to say goodbye,' Father called over to him.

Caspian still couldn't believe all this was really happening. He really *was* leaving, but his brain could not accept it to be true. He looked at Jess, found her green eyes behind her dark corkscrew curls, and searched for the words to say farewell to the one person he had shared every experience and every adventure with over the last thirteen years.

Thankfully he didn't have to as Jess threw her arms around him, hugging him close to her. 'I'm really going to miss you, Caspian,' she said, her voice slightly squeakier than normal. 'Little Bickham's not going to be the same without you.'

'Thanks, Jess,' he replied, pulling out of the embrace, his cheeks burning red.

'Call me and let me know what London is like.'

'I will,' he answered.

'Come on then, Caspian,' his father said. 'You'll see her again at Christmas. It will be here soon enough.' Father waved goodbye to Tom and Wendy Ravenwood, thanking them for bringing Caspian to the station, and then boarded the train leaving him to carry his own luggage on board.

'Bye,' Caspian waved awkwardly as he heaved his suitcase into the carriage.

'Good luck,' Jess called to him.

He joined his father at the seats reserved for them. As the train pulled out of the station, the Ravenwoods were at the window waving to him encouragingly. He tried to smile the most genuine smile he could forge with his face, but his eyes were fixed on Jess as the distance between them became greater and greater and greater.

Soon she was completely out of sight, like everything else that had ever been familiar to him. Little Bickham drifted away until it became a speck in the distance, leaving him ominously alone with no one but his estranged father for company.

II:
RED WAX

Caspian was used to trains, having lived in his little house under the viaduct that was frequently shaken by them passing overhead day and night, however he had never travelled in a first class coach before. His father, on the other hand, seemed quite accustomed to travelling in this particular manner, as he relaxed in a slightly larger chair than those allocated to anyone travelling in economy class, reading his large broadsheet newspaper from the city.

First class left Caspian feeling somewhat befuddled as the only real noticeable differences he could ascertain between first and economy class, other than the slightly larger seats, were the addition of a reading lamp and a curtain – neither of which he had much use for in the middle of the day. It was only when a trolley came round offering free sandwiches, pastries, teas, coffees, and cakes, that he could really appreciate his promotion in seated social status.

His father made no attempt to make conversation with him, which suited Caspian who had nothing that he wanted to say, not to his father anyway. This mutual silence persisted throughout most of the journey whilst his father thoroughly paged through the large broadsheet he held in front of him.

Neither happened to be particularly good at instigating conversation with one another, and Caspian was more than content to watch the world outside go rushing passed the window.

After the first hour of the journey, the train came to stretch of track that passed through a couple of tunnels. Each time the train was submerged in darkness, the interior lights allowed him to see the inside of the carriage reflected in the darkened glass window.

On one of these occasions, Caspian realised his father was watching him over his newspaper. Rather than meet his father's eyes directly, he pretended not to notice he was being observed but continued to watch him in the reflection, his heart pounding nervously in his chest. Why was his father spying on him? What was he thinking behind those calculating eyes?

As the train came out of the tunnel, Caspian snuck a glance back, but his father's face was hidden behind the newspaper he had returned to reading. A chilling thought entered his mind: Had his father been sneaking glances at him before now?

Feeling like he was now under a microscope, the rest of the journey became very uncomfortable. He continued to look out the window, but never again caught his father watching him, and slowly the countryside began to be replaced with urban areas as they drew ever nearer to their destination – London.

The cathedral of St. Paul had once dominated the city's skyline, back in the age before industrialism. Now, skyscrapers made of concrete, metal and glass reached up towards the sun as though they were designed to pluck the very stars from the sky, or part the clouds like knives slicing through butter.

Caspian had even heard that the American skyscrapers of New York dwarfed over the manmade pinnacles of London, but for what New York had achieved in height it could not match London for age or history. This was more than a city; this was a living, breathing organism that over time had grown to endure whatever the world had thrown at it. It had evolved to survive fires, wars, plagues, and more recently, economic recession. Like a garden left unattended, London's vine-like growth had rapidly engulfed the surrounding settlements until it became one of the world's largest metropolises. Its roots reached so far into the earth that, no matter what, it could never truly die.

Seeing the sheer expanse of the city that grew before him, Caspian suddenly felt a very long, long way from the little village he called home. Long gone were the familiarity he had become accustomed to, those familiar places and friendly faces. He was entering a world to which he was a stranger, an outsider; a world to which he didn't belong.

Why was everyone in such a rush?

As soon as Caspian set foot on the platform at St Pancras Station an elderly woman, who reminded him of Mrs Doddington, barged passed him, almost knocking him over.

He soon found that everyone in London moved with such haste, almost tripping over one another to get to their destinations and not worrying who they collided with in the process, be it man, woman, or child.

There were *so* many people. He had never seen such a large number of people in one place. London was said to be the home to more than eight million people, which was mind-boggling. You would have to take the entire population of Little Bickham and multiply it by forty thousand to even get close to that figure. Caspian couldn't even begin to imagine a place that was forty thousand times more populated than his home village.

And yet, everywhere he looked he could see masses upon masses of people: tourists, businessmen, old people, young people, families, builders, and office workers. There were people from every country he could imagine: Chinese, American, Polish, German, Spanish, Russian, Italian, and more. There were people driving black cabs, there were people on bikes. There were people driving black cabs shouting at people on bikes. There were people crowding onto big red double-decker buses that were so full they seemed like they would tip over when they turned a corner.

He also couldn't believe how many police officers he saw, many armed with large guns and wearing bulletproof vests. There were only two policemen in Little Bickham, and they both belonged to the same family. They didn't need to wear bulletproof vests or carry guns, as the most heinous crimes they ever dealt with were occasional vandalism or, every so often, a missing cat.

Caspian kept close behind his father amongst this pandemonium, carrying his suitcase behind him. Unlike everyone else rushing around, Father carried on at a comfortable pace, anticipating the crowd and moving amongst them so smoothly it was as though he were a ghost that could just pass right through without them even noticing.

By the time they arrived in Chelsea, where his father lived, Caspian was exhausted. His suitcase seemed to get heavier and heavier with every step he took, and not once had his father offered to help him carry it. In fact, they hadn't said a word to one another since they had left the train.

Old Church Street had clearly been named after the decrepit church that towered gloomily over the rest of the street. Over the years the building had not been well maintained and it seemed to have deflated into a defeated hunch. The spire no longer stretched upward towards the heavens as an unyielding monument of the Lord, but instead reached up wearily like the jaded arm of someone in need of being rescued. Its walls were so strained by the weight they bore that they seemed like they would collapse with exhaustion at any moment. If walls could truly talk, these would only moan.

Father's house stood beside the church, it's rear overlooking the graveyard behind. It was the last house on a row of three storey houses that lined both sides of the road, all of which seemed to lean further in the higher they got, making the entire street feel oppressively claustrophobic.

The ground floor of many of these houses had been turned into shops, and his father's home was no exception.

Turner & Stone Antiques had been established long ago by one of Father's relatives and someone called Alfred Turner. Nowadays, Caspian's father, who collected and sold all manner of rare objects, pieces, items, and artefacts from antiquity, solely owned the shop. Mother had told Caspian that his father ran this shop alone, and from time to time it would close for weeks on end whilst he travelled the world to buy a particular piece, or offer consultations and valuations to other antique buyers and collectors. This, in part, accounted for his father's constant unaccountability.

Caspian put down his suitcase outside the shop front, whilst his father fished in his coat pocket for the keys to the door, and stared in through the window at all the old and strange objects concealed within. Beyond the front door was a small porch with two further doors; one that led into the shop and the other which led up a flight of stairs into his father's house above.

Father led the way into the porch and bent down to collect an envelope that was lying on the doormat before unlocking the next door. Caspian couldn't help eyeing the envelope with curiosity as it had been sealed in a very strange way. Usually one would lick the gummed lip of the envelope and fold it over to stick it shut, but the sender of this particular letter had dripped red wax to form a seal over the folded lip and then impressed upon it some kind of embossed design.

Caspian had seen these kinds of seals in history shows on television, designed so that if the seal was broken the recipient could identify whether the letter had been read by anyone other than the sender, but never had he seen this kind of practise used in real life.

'That's a strange way to seal a letter,' Caspian commented.

Father turned and gave him an odd look, before placing the envelope in his jacket pocket and ascending the stairs into his home, leaving Caspian at the bottom with his heavy suitcase.

'Our dinner has been left on the stove,' Father announced as Caspian finally arrived at the top of the staircase, breathing heavily from the exertion he had just experienced. 'The two of us will be eating alone this evening as Mrs Hodges has the night off. Your bedroom and the bathroom are on the third floor, so feel free to leave your case up there and freshen up before we eat.' Father disappeared back into the kitchen from where he'd come, leaving Caspian to look despairingly at yet another flight of stairs.

Caspian had not given the matter much thought, but he had always presumed his father to be reasonably well off, being that he lived in London and owned an antique shop. Still, he had always assumed that Father lived in a small house, but as he explored where he would be living for his immediate future, he realised his presumptions may not have been entirely accurate.

Father's home was easily twice the size of Caspian's, tucked neatly under the viaduct back in Little Bickham. The rooms were not overly big, but they were numerous. The lower floor consisted of a kitchen, his father's study, and the sitting room, which looked more like a library than a normal person's living room. There was also a small guest bathroom and a dining room that seemed to double as a room for entertaining guests. On the upper floor the main bathroom could be found along with three bedrooms; the first belonging to his father, and another to Mrs Hodges – Father's housekeeper. The third bedroom, which would henceforth be Caspian's, had been a guestroom prior to his arrival, but it was so empty and cold that he suspected it had never been used for its intended purpose.

The floor in his room was solid oak, the floorboards creaked and moaned when he stood on them as though he were doing them some kind of injury. Quite a few of these were not secured down and when Caspian dumped his suitcase at the bottom of the bed one of the smaller boards sprang up like the end of a seesaw. He quickly pushed this back into place and then slid his suitcase on top to conceal it.

Once he had showered he joined his father in the dining room for dinner. His father's dining table was made of an expensive dark wood and large enough to seat eight people. Father had laid the table so that they both sat down the same end, opposite each other. The room itself was luxuriously decorated with more dark wood furniture, a leather chair, and a large framed picture on the wall that depicted a woman in a red dress standing in the rain.

Their meal consisted of beef bourguignon – a dish Caspian had never been able to pronounce – and fluffy white rice. He pushed the food around his plate with his fork, his appetite spoiled by all the cakes he had eaten on the train, as an awkward silence accompanied their meal.

Whilst Father ate he took from his pocket a small, leather bound diary and placed it on the table beside him. Caspian quickly spied the small pile of mail that had been neatly placed between the pages, particularly the distinctive red wax on the letter his father had retrieved upon their earlier arrival.

'Do you get a lot of letters?' Caspian asked.

Father was carefully opening an envelope with a silver letter opener. He removed the letter from within and placed it beside his plate. 'That depends,' he replied flatly, before taking a mouthful of food, his eyes not leaving the page as he read.

'That depends on what?'

'What do you perceive to be a lot,' Father replied, 'when it comes to letters, that is?'

Caspian shrugged. 'I don't know. More than a few, I guess. How many do you receive a day?'

'A few less than a lot.' Father moved the letter he had been reading to the side and carefully opened the next, revealing the envelope with the red wax seal that had been lying beneath it.

Caspian eyed the strange letter. From where he sat, he could see the design imprinted in the wax seal in more detail. In the very centre was a looping design that looked like a large propeller with four evenly sized blades. Encircling it were a string of words that he couldn't read, but they looked like they were written in Latin. 'Are many of them sealed like that one?' Caspian asked.

Father looked up from the letter he was reading. 'No,' he answered, and he placed the second letter on top of the first he had read. The third letter was the envelope that Caspian was so curious about. Father opened this one the same way he had opened the previous two, sliding the letter opener between the fold of the envelope and splitting it along the seam, leaving the wax seal intact.

Caspian watched eagerly as his father removed the slip of paper and began to read its content. 'It's just, you don't see many letters sealed these days with wax,' he persevered. 'What is the letter about?'

Father glanced at him with a steady look. 'It is of no concern to you. The letter was sealed thus to make it attractive in appearance. Its content is for my private attention. Now leave the subject alone, I will hear no more of it.'

Caspian dropped his eyes back to his dinner and continued making his rice run laps around his plate. Father turned the page in his diary to tomorrow's date and scribbled a note at the foot of the page. Caspian was certain it was something to do with whatever had been written in the letter with the strangely sealed envelope.

Neither he nor Father spoke a further word for the duration of the meal.

By the time Caspian climbed into bed it was almost midnight. Father had knocked on the door about an hour ago to say goodnight, and Caspian had spent the time since perched on the corner of the bed looking out of the guestroom window.

He had so many thoughts running through his head he didn't think he would sleep a wink this night. As he climbed beneath the covers he felt a rumble of an Underground train, somewhere far beneath the house where its tunnel must run, and thought of home – his *real* home, underneath the viaduct where trains gently shook the house as they passed overhead; where he and his mother were only separated by a few walls instead of so many miles.

Somewhere far beneath the house the rumbling faded away; the gentle rumbling that could have so easily been a train passing over a viaduct above, just like he was used to. And with that thought in mind, he finally drifted off to sleep.

III:
BREAKING AND ENTERING

That night Caspian was tormented by nightmares, the worst of which saw his mother standing on the platform where the Ravenwoods had stood to wave him off. Instead of waving, his mother was trying to tell him something but he could not hear her.

As the train started to pull out of the station Mother was running along side it, still trying to make him hear her. Caspian was running too, passing through the carriage as he tried to find a door, but the carriage was never ending and the door never came. When Caspian looked out the window again his mother was gone.

When he went downstairs the next morning he was grateful to see the familiar face of Mrs Hodges smiling at him from the kitchen where mouth-watering aromas were emanating as she prepared a large breakfast.

Irene Hodges had been a housekeeper for the Stone family for longer than Caspian had been alive. Father had employed her as housekeeper before he met and married Mother, and when he left he took Mrs Hodges with him. She was the ripe old age of seventy-two, but seemed to have the energy of a woman twenty years younger.

Being that his mother's parents had died when he was too young to remember them, and his father's long before he was born, Mrs Hodges was the closest thing Caspian had to a Grandma. She would make the journey up to Little Bickham a couple of times a year to see both him and his mother, much more often than his father did. After losing her husband, without ever having children of her own, she had likewise come to regard Caspian as her Grandson.

He watched her fondly as she darted around the kitchen, conducting the pots and pans like a culinary orchestra. 'Good morning, Caspian,' she greeted him kindly. 'Did you sleep well?'

'Yes, thank you,' Caspian lied, not wanting to talk about his nightmare or upset Mrs Hodges.

'Sorry I wasn't about to see you in last night. I was long overdue a catch up with an old friend of mine, and she insisted I stay the night rather than travel all the way across London.' She opened a fresh carton of orange juice and poured a glass for Caspian. 'How is your mom, dear? I'm sorry to hear that she's taken a bad turn.'

'The doctors will look after her,' Caspian replied. 'I think her new treatment will help.'

'Me too, dear,' Mrs Hodges said positively, however there wasn't much conviction in her eyes.

He took the juice she passed him and mulled over the meaning behind her expression whilst he took his seat at the breakfast bar. There was no reason not to be optimistic, was there? Mother had been ill before, but she had always pulled through. Why would this time be any different? Yes, she was worse than ever, but sometimes people needed to get worse before they got better…

'Are you looking forward to tomorrow?' Mrs Hodges asked as she loaded the large toaster with bread.

The impending doom that was tomorrow was Caspian's fast approaching first day at his new school, and the more he thought about it the more anxious he became. He had of course started new schools before, but never had he started one that none of his friends were attending, let alone in a completely different county.

And to make matters worse, all of his new classmates would have completed their first half-term together, allowing friendships to be made and groups to form. Caspian would start for the second half of term as the new boy whom nobody would recognise or know.

After breakfast, as promised, Father had organised for Mrs Hodges to take Caspian into the city to buy anything he would need for the school year ahead. On the way to the Tube station Caspian had asked Mrs Hodges which Underground line he had heard last night as he drifted off to sleep.

'Underground?' Mrs Hodges replied. 'Oh no, dear. It couldn't have been an Underground train. There are no train lines that go beneath Old Church Street. Maybe it was a car pulling away, or a dream perhaps?'

Caspian didn't think it was. It had certainly felt like the rumble of a train, and he was certain he hadn't dreamt it either, but he didn't push the matter any further. They reached Oxford Street and they searched for the items he required.

He needed a new sports kit, as it seemed his school were heavily competitive when it came to Games. The school had also provided Father with a long list of books Caspian would need for various subjects, and judging by some of the titles he was going to be studying a completely different syllabus to what he would have been studying in Little Bickham.

Caspian looked at the pile of English literary classics with dread as the bookshop cashier placed them into a large carrier bag. He didn't mind reading, but it was the over-analysis of the language used that seemed fundamental to English Literature classes that really put him off. For example, having to explain in what context *blunt* is being used in a sentence, or justifying the intended symbolism behind the author's usage of the word *blunt*, or perhaps explaining the impact that using and repeating the word *blunt* too many times in a paragraph tends to have on the reader. On the whole, it seemed pointless.

When they arrived home, his father was working in his study so Caspian carried all his new belongings up to his room and spent most of the afternoon idly paging through the books, far too distracted by his own thoughts to take in any of the words written on the pages.

As evening fell, so did the rain.

Caspian was seated alone in his father's ornate living room, directly above the shop front. He had settled into a large and uncomfortable antique-looking chair that was positioned facing outward through the room's large, rain-streaked, bay windows. A few people could be seen outside, hiding beneath umbrellas; however Caspian's attention was far from the activity on Old Church Street below.

Mrs Hodges had retired to her room for the evening – the only room in the house with a television set, Caspian had discovered rather begrudgingly – but his father had left earlier that afternoon to attend to something he'd described as "business related," yet Caspian couldn't shake the feeling that this was concerning the note he had made in his diary after receiving the mysterious letter. Whatever the significance of this letter was, Father was keeping it very close to his chest.

This was not unusual behaviour for Edgar Stone. In fact, it was how he dealt with everything, so it was of little wonder that Caspian had found his father to be a complete mystery on those rare occasions that he had spent time with him.

Father had left without saying goodbye, but that was understandable considering what had happened a few hours before.

Earlier that day he had knocked on Caspian's bedroom door.

'My apologies for spending the entire day burrowed in my study,' Father had said apologetically. 'There has been a lot of correspondence that required my urgent attention. In fact, I will need to go out this evening to settle one particular matter.'

It's about the letter with the wax seal, Caspian had been sure of it, but he knew asking would only get him in trouble.

Instead he tried to act like he didn't care and gave a simple shrug of indifference. He returned to one of the textbooks he had been glancing at, but not really reading, and pretended to be interested in the page in front of him, aware that his father was still loitering in the doorway.

'I was wondering whether you would like to see the shop?' Father asked after a moment.

'Erm…okay.' Caspian responded, caught off guard by his father's unexpected attempt of bonding. He stood and followed his father downstairs to the entrance of Turner & Stone Antiques.

The tour was short, but Caspian marvelled at some of the wonders his father had collected over the years. One particular piece caught his eye and he felt himself drawn to it.

An elaborately made medieval broadsword was fixed to the wall, hanging by its hilt from a mount. It was not in pristine condition, having been crafted many centuries ago, but it was still in better condition than those Caspian had seen in museums. The price of such a piece was unimaginable.

Without thinking, he placed both hands on the hilt and lifted it down. It was heavier than he had anticipated, but he lifted it towards him. To think that hundreds of years ago, knights and men-at-arms would have carried such weapons onto battlefields; some of those men only a few years older than he was now.

Caspian was in awe of such men, especially as he could barely lift the sword to point it at an enemy, let alone swing it back and forth with power and precision amidst the heat of combat.

'WHAT DO YOU THINK YOU ARE DOING?' Father bellowed, making Caspian jump. 'Put that back, NOW!' He was furious.

Caspian quickly lifted the sword to return it, but his arms had tired from the broadsword's weight, which now seemed twice as heavy to what it was when he'd lifted it down, and he no longer had the exertion to return it. The tip of the sword knocked against the floor with a mighty *clang*. He panicked, desperate to return the sword as quickly as possible, and lifted it higher whilst trying to walk forward, his arms straining and muscles burning as he tried to replace the hilt onto the hooks of the wall mount before him.

'CAREFUL!' Father shouted, but it was too late. As Caspian reached the wall he stumbled slightly under the weight of the heavy weapon and staggered sideways. Once again the sword *clanged* against the floor and Caspian's hip involuntarily slammed into a display case as he tried to regain his balance, causing the cabinet to let out a horrific creak.

For a terrifying moment he thought the antique display cabinet was going to collapse as its contents rattled and rolled around inside like a china tea set in a washing machine. That nothing broke was a miracle, but something must have come loose as out of the corner of his eye Caspian glimpsed a golden glimmer shoot across the floor and vanish beneath another piece of antique furniture.

'I told you not to touch anything,' Father said disapprovingly, bearing down on Caspian and snatching the sword from his grasp. 'These pieces are very old and fragile, and some of them are worth a lot of money to the right buyer. Either way, these are important historical artefacts that should be treated with respect, not as toys. When I ask you not to do something, I expect my instructions to be complied with, unconditionally. Do I make myself clear?'

After that, his father had removed him from the shop and locked the door behind them. Caspian had then returned to his room and kept out of his father's way until dinner, when avoiding him became impossible. Mrs Hodges had prepared a large roast chicken with all the trimmings, but when she had tried to strike up conversation at the table neither Caspian nor his father made much in the way of contribution. Then Caspian helped Mrs Hodges clear the table before she retired to her bedroom whilst Father headed out, leaving him to entertain himself, alone in a house with no television or access to the internet.

After an hour of moping around he had eventually settled in the seat at the living room window and stared blankly out at the umbrella-wielding occupants of the city, shielding themselves from the rain.

Caspian was angry at the way Father had reacted in the shop. He knew that he should have asked his father's permission before taking the sword down, but he had not meant any harm, only to inspect the sword closer. Had Father not shouted and made him panic he would never have tried to hastily replace the sword, thus avoiding the disastrous consequences that had followed. It still struck him as a small miracle that nothing had been broken, and the only damage caused was that something had dropped out of the cabinet and rolled across the floor.

Father had not retrieved whatever it was. He had been so angry and determined to remove Caspian from his shop before more damage was done that he must have forgotten. Perhaps he hadn't seen it fall. After all, Caspian had only just caught a glimpse of gold as it disappeared underneath another display case.

He began to wonder what the little golden object had been.

Whilst his mind wandered, a raindrop on the window slowly joined another droplet and they merged into one. This drop joined another, and then another, and another, each time growing bigger and bigger as gravity pulled it down the surface of the window, gaining momentum as it did so, until it eventually raced down the glass leaving a trail of tiny droplets in its wake.

Caspian's curiosity was like that initial raindrop; just an innocent and isolated speck of water on the glass. But once it began to grow, it began to move quicker and quicker, gravitating towards a needing to know what he had displaced until it eventually consumed him.

With Father out for the evening, and Mrs Hodges in her room, who would notice if he snuck downstairs to the shop and tried to find what had fallen? Moreover, he was certain he knew where the key to the shop was kept. After inviting Caspian to see the shop, Father had gone back to his study. Knowing how meticulous his father was for returning things to where they belonged, the chance that he had replaced the key inside was high.

Caspian left the seat by the window and started along the corridor towards his father's study. Now that he was up to no good, the whole house seemed unnaturally quiet as though it were conspiring against him to emphasize and exaggerate the slightest sound he made. And even though Mrs Hodges would probably think nothing of him moving about the house, it was still better to exercise caution than entice interest.

At the study door, he carefully turned the knob and slipped silently into the room. Large bookcases peered down at him from all sides, and in the centre of the room a large wooden desk was positioned facing him. He carefully crept round the room to the desk drawers and one by one began to open them in search of the key.

The top drawer contained neatly organised notes and sales receipts for the various items and curios Father had either sold or purchased last month. Trying not to disturb the way his father had organised it, he rummaged around inside the drawer for the key, but to no avail. He slid the drawer silently shut and opened the next, and was instantly rewarded with what he sought.

Caspian left the study and snuck down the staircase to the porch, once again exercising caution, and wondering just how much stamina caution had. There, he slipped the key into the lock and turned it, hearing the lock release. He tried the handle and the door swung open. *I'm in!* He thought with excitement.

Earlier, upon first stepping inside, Caspian had felt as though he had entered a wizard's workshop. He had been intrigued by all the fascinating, strange, and magical looking devices that were scattered around the room, or lining the shelves and display cabinets; some of which he could guess their use, whilst others seemed to have a purpose beyond anything he could imagine.

Now, however, in the gloom of twilight the shop took on a more sinister appearance as the street lamps outside cast strange shapes and twisted silhouettes across the walls and floor. Not wanting to attract any attention from outside by turning lamps or lights on, Caspian had to navigate his way around the shop in an insipid orange glow.

After a short while he found his eyes had adjusted to the lack of light and he made his way over to where his father had replaced the large broadsword on its wall mount. The little golden object had rolled quite easily across the hard floor without making much sound, but he had seen where it had gone even though he couldn't know exactly where it had ended up.

He knelt and peered under the display cabinet where the object had rolled and reached his arm under. His hand felt blindly across the cold floor into the darkness beyond, but he could find no trace of whatever had fallen.

Remaining on his knees, he crawled around the cabinet and headed along the trajectory the object would have taken, hoping to follow it to its final place of rest. He came to a strange table carved out of dark wood that almost seemed green in the low light. The table itself was circular, but its legs had been carved to resemble vines reaching out of the floor and holding onto the table, rooting it to the spot. It was a very odd looking table indeed, and Caspian had never seen a piece of furniture like it before, but then there were many other curios in his father's shop that the same could be said about.

If the object had not been altered in course it would have rolled right under this table. Caspian started to crawl under the table when he saw a glimmer of gold on one of the table legs. Sure enough, it belonged to the item he'd been searching for, but he was surprised to find it hanging from the carved table leg rather than laying on the floor.

What the item actually *was*, however, was even more surprising.

Hanging by a couple of its many legs was an intricately crafted metal spider. Careful not to damage it, Caspian released the legs and held it in his palm to inspect it. The spider's body was roughly the size of a wristwatch, but with the legs it was about as big as a tennis ball. It must have been quite old as in many places the golden coloured metal from which it was constructed had dulled, or in some spots started to turn green.

When he turned it over he made an even more astounding discovery. Each of the legs had tiny pistons attached, and these in turn were linked with miniscule sets of gears and cogs. The underside of the spider had a small glass window, just like an old-fashioned pocket watch, allowing him to see even more gears, mechanical components, parts and pieces, each precisely and delicately positioned inside this little device.

Could this spider move? Caspian wondered, but when he searched the little arachnid for anything that resembled a winder or an aperture for a key he found nothing. *Father would know*, he thought bitterly. Were he to ask about it Father would know he had been in the shop without permission.

'I'd better put you back where you fell from,' Caspian said quietly to the spider, wishing he could know more about this mysterious find. 'No doubt Father will tell me off if he finds you missing.'

He was about to climb out from under the table when he heard a scraping sound coming from the door. It sounded like a key being turned in a lock. His heart skipped a beat. Was Father home already? He ducked down further into the shadows and tried to sneak a look at the door, thankful he had pulled the shop door closed behind him after he'd entered – at least Father wouldn't immediately notice something was amiss.

But when he managed to get a look at who was outside, he realised it wasn't his father at all. Standing in the doorway before the porch was a figure wrapped in a dark cloak. In the poor light and wrapped in the hooded shroud it was impossible to discern much at all about this mysterious figure, but judging by the stranger's build Caspian guessed it was a man.

Whoever the hooded man was, he was trying a number of keys in the door lock, systematically taking one out from beneath his cloak, trying it in the lock, then replacing it and trying another. The sinister nature of this figure made Caspian nervous. Why was he trying to get inside, and what did he plan to do when he did?

I can't stay here, Caspian thought, but where else could he go. The hooded man was standing at the doorway that Caspian needed to pass to run upstairs. If he were to shout to raise the alarm, the hooded man would see him inside the shop. Either way he would be discovered, but he couldn't just hide. Mrs Hodges was upstairs and probably fast asleep by now. And what if this person was armed? What then?

Caspian realised that he was so tense he was squeezing the little spider in his hand, so he slipped it into his pocket to prevent him breaking it. On the other side of the door, the cloaked man was trying another key whilst the rain still beat heavily down against him.

Think, think! But Caspian couldn't see a way out of this without putting himself in danger. He crawled out from under the table and moved round behind a large display cabinet, ensuring at all times he was out of view of the door and shop windows. When he was a little closer to the door he stopped and took a deep breath.

There was only one thing for it. He would have to stand up and face whoever was trying to get in, and hope that he startle them enough to either scare them off, or allow him time to run up the stairs and call the police. He took another deep breath to try and calm his nerves, but his heart was pounding rapidly.

Quickly, he stood up from behind the cabinet and turned to face the door. No one was there.

Where had he gone? He had heard him trying keys only seconds before, but now there was nobody at all standing in the doorway. His heart was still beating hard in his chest as he approached the door to see if he could see anyone outside, but there was no one there. Whoever it was had gone.

That was when Caspian heard another sound. It was only very distant, but steadily it grew louder as it drew closer. He couldn't place why this sound had registered in his mind, a slow but steady clicking of footsteps against the pavement: *click ... clack ... click ... clack.* Why had this person's approach disturbed the cloaked stranger's plans?

And then, suddenly it dawned on Caspian why the sound had registered. It was the unmistakeable sound of his father's shoes. How would it look were Father to reach the door and discover Caspian in his shop? He would never believe him that someone had been trying to get inside; it would look as though he were lying to cover himself.

Without a second thought, he ran for the shop door and fumbled with the key to lock it behind him before his father reached the doorway. Then he slipped through the door before the staircase and quietly closed it and clicked the latch, just as he heard Father stop outside the door and the jangle of keys in his hand.

He made it halfway up the staircase as silent as a ninja when he heard Father's key slide into the staircase door and turn the latch. *He's already in the porch!* He jumped the last few steps and burst through the top door, closing it just as his father came through below.

He was not out of the woods yet.

With his heart in his mouth he dived into Father's study and slid open the top drawer of his father's desk, slipped the key back inside, and shot back out of the room a nano-second before Father opened the door atop the staircase and came through.

His father stopped, removed his hat, and frowned at Caspian, those golden eyes alert and full of suspicion.

'Caspian?' Father asked.

'Good evening,' Caspian answered as coolly as he could manage, trying to hide his fluster from running and panic.

'What are you doing at the door?'

'I heard you come in,' Caspian answered, suddenly feeling inspired. 'I want to apologise for earlier.' He felt his palms go clammy whilst he watched his father consider this pretext, and he suddenly became awfully aware that he had not replaced the little golden spider but that it was still in his pocket.

Father's eyes lingered for another excruciating moment before his brow raised and he gave Caspian the slightest nod of approval. 'Very well,' he answered simply, before hanging his hat and coat on a hook.

Caspian wasn't sure if his father's reply meant the apology had been accepted, or whether his ruse had worked, but he tried to carry on as casually as he could. However, he felt compelled say something about the hooded figure who had attempted to get in – but how could he bring this up?

'When you turned onto the street,' Caspian began carefully, 'did you happen to see anyone?'

'Was there someone particular I should have seen?'

'Not really,' Caspian replied, trying to be nonchalant. 'It's just I was in the living room before you came in and I thought I saw a strange looking person outside wrapped in a cloak.'

Father's reaction changed so rapidly it was like a firework had been thrown into a bonfire. 'What hooded person? When?' Father rounded on Caspian.

'Not … not long ago,' Caspian spluttered. 'Outside in the rain.'

Father's look was so intense Caspian thought it was going to cut him in two. 'I'm sure it was nothing,' Father said suddenly. 'Probably just the rain playing tricks on your eyes. Now, it's late and you should be in bed already. Tomorrow you start a new school, or had you forgotten that?'

Caspian felt so bewildered it was as though something had knocked him on the head. What did his father know about the cloaked stranger that he wasn't sharing? Why had he changed the subject so abruptly?

He looked at his father, spellbound, not knowing what to say.

'Then this is goodnight, Caspian,' his father said definitively.

'Goodnight,' he muttered in return and Father left him by the door. He reached his bedroom and found his hands were trembling slightly, although he could not tell whether this was from fear or exhilaration – maybe both.

First the strange letter, now the hooded man. Something very peculiar was going on, Caspian thought. 'Just when I thought things couldn't get any more complicated,' he said quietly to himself as he took the golden spider from his pocket.

And, as if in agreement, the spider leapt out of his hand and scurried across his bed, causing Caspian to almost jump out of his skin in surprise.

IV:
LOST

Caspian jumped backwards so quickly that he collided with the wall beside his bed. He knocked his head heavily, making a terrible thud, before collapsing onto the mattress, holding his crown whilst tears blurred his vision.

He reached blindly in front of him, anxiously trying to regain his senses, whilst his heart pounded frantically in his chest.

Confused, and slightly concussed, he tried to get to his feet, but this only brought about a wave of dizziness that swept his legs out from under him, dropping him to the floor where spots danced before his eyes.

He lay there for a moment, feeling sorry for himself, when something cold nudged against the back of his hand. Instinctively, he pulled his hand away, but when he looked he found the little mechanical spider had been trying to nuzzle him, its gears and cams spinning.

Caspian gave the spider an inquisitive look, and then wearily he let the mechanism nudge his fingers affectionately. 'This is … *impossible!*' Caspian said, and in response the spider rolled over onto its back like a puppy beckoning for a tummy rub.

Cautiously at first, he began to stroke the spider's glass underside. 'Who made you?' he wondered out loud. He had never heard of a mechanical creation being so advanced – so lifelike.

As Caspian caressed circles on its underside, the spider let out a gleeful purr reminding him of the sound a digital camera makes when zooming in or out. *This is amazing*, he thought, finding it hard to suppress the smile that crept across his face.

'It's late, Caspian. Lights out!' his father's voice ordered from the other side of the door, making him flinch suddenly with surprise.

'Okay...' he replied and hastily scooped up the spider before flicking out the lights. But he lay in bed for many more hours, letting the little mechanical spider clamber over his bed sheets, until he eventually drifted off to sleep.

The next morning Caspian woke with a start. What a strange dream he'd had, it had seemed so real. But of course it was just a dream, wasn't it? Clockwork spiders don't exist, and they certainly can't come to life as if by magic.

Instinctively he reached for the top of his head and winced.

'Ouch,' he said as his fingers tentatively touched the tender spot where a lump had appeared over night.

But if *that* was real...

Sure enough, on top of his duvet and curled up in a ball, there lay the little golden spider, presumably asleep. His movement seemed to cause the little mechanism to stir. It slowly uncurled its feet, stretched, and then crawled over to nuzzle his arm before rolling onto its back for another belly rub.

'If you want to keep having your tummy rubbed, you'd better stay out of sight today,' Caspian told it, unsure whether it could understand him or not.

In response, the spider purred happily beneath his fingertips.

Caspian wolfed down his breakfast whilst his father watched him curiously.

'How are you feeling this morning?' Father asked, clearly attempting to gauge whether his son's enthusiastic appetite was brought on by the excitement of today being his first day at his new school.

It was not.

He was keen to get back to his room and check whether the clockwork spider had understood his instruction to find a place to hide – just in case Father was the sort to check his room whilst he was at school. The last thing he wanted was his father to find the spider and return it to the shop.

As it happened, there was no sign of the spider when Caspian returned to his room to collect his school bag. He wanted to call out to it, but realised he had not yet given it a name – something he would have to rectify, he mentally noted.

Either way, the spider must have heard him as it came scurrying out from beneath the loose floorboard at the foot of the bed. It eagerly crawled into Caspian's hand and as he bent down to give it a stroke it jostled around excitedly.

'I'm sorry,' Caspian said. 'I can't take you to school with me.'

The clockwork spider made a sad sound. It had probably been cooped up in Turner & Stone Antiques for years before Caspian had accidentally knocked into the cabinet and set it free. Now it was clearly looking forward to an adventure outside of the house, but Caspian didn't want to risk losing it.

'Don't be sad,' Caspian said to it. 'I'll be back before you know it, and then tonight we'll go outside together.'

This offer seemed to satisfy the spider, who began to perk up.

He carefully placed it on his bedside cabinet and gave it an affectionate pat. 'Wish me luck,' he said, and then added, 'and don't get caught.'

The spider chirped merrily in response, but suddenly Father's voice sounded from the doorway. 'Have you got everything ready to go?'

'I think so,' Caspian replied, quickly positioning himself between his father and the bedside cabinet. 'Do you think I should take my sports kit?'

'I would. You should be issued with a locker today, so even if you don't have Games you can still leave it there ready for when you do. Shall we go? I'd like to get back to the shop before nine so I can open on time.'

'Okay,' Caspian agreed. 'I just want to double check I've packed everything, and then I'll meet you in the hall.'

As Father nodded and left, Caspian turned to check the cabinet and breathed a sigh of relief to see that the spider had taken the opportunity to hide. He zipped up his school bag, took his sports kit from the wardrobe, and hurried downstairs after his father.

Father escorted him on his first day to his new school, Hogarth House High School, leaving him at the school reception. He couldn't help thinking that from outside the old Victorian building resembled a prison more than a school. The only thing the tall white stone walls lacked were sentry turrets and razor wire atop the cast iron fences.

The receptionist informed him that he was going to be in Mrs Scrudge's tutor class; 9E. She didn't, however, give him clear instructions on how to find his new tutor class, which is how he ended up wandering the school corridors like a lost puppy. He wanted to stop and ask someone where he had to go, but no one was willing to help him, and most of the other students simply ignored him.

By eight forty-two, Caspian had still not found his form class and began to panic. The corridors were emptying quickly, as the other students herded into their tutor groups ready for the morning registration at quarter to nine, and there was almost no one around to ask.

Caspian felt hopeless, when all of a sudden a short boy appeared around the corner ahead and came sprinting towards him. He was black with very short hair and a wild look of panic in his eyes. Caspian didn't know what to make of him.

When the boy was level with Caspian he dived towards a room to the left, but the door was locked.

'What's the matter?' Caspian asked.

'A long story,' the boy said quickly, trying to regain his breath. 'Cover for me! Please!'

'Cover for you? From what?'

The answer presented itself in the form of two large boys who came rushing round the same corner from which the boy had appeared moments before. They were clearly older than both Caspian and the boy, and judging by their different uniform they were probably sixth formers.

They looked particularly angry, especially the taller of the two whose trousers were covered in water as though he had wet himself.

The short boy backed into the alcove of the doorway, pressing himself against the locked door, out of sight of these older boys, but not for much longer if they kept approaching. Caspian could feel the boy's eyes pleading for him to help.

'Hey you!' the taller boy shouted to Caspian, who stepped forward so that he was further blocking the boy from being seen. 'Which way did he go?'

Caspian pointed away from where the boy hid, down a corridor going off to the left.

'Thanks!' the second boy said.

'Let's show him what happens when he pulls stunts like that in the sixth form bathroom,' the taller boy said as they darted off down the corridor.

When they had gone the boy stepped out of his hiding place. 'Thanks,' he said, looking relieved. 'I owe you one.'

'Why were they after you?' Caspian asked.

Now that the panic had dissipated from the boy's face, Caspian noticed how mischievous he looked. 'Last term they were making fun of my friend's sister,' he answered. 'So, I promised this term I would give them a taste of their own medicine.'

'What did you do?'

'Just a little trick with a roll of cling film and the sixth form toilets,' the boy chuckled. 'That will teach them to take the p-'

The bell rang interrupting him and signalling the start of registration, and Caspian realised he still didn't know where his classroom was.

'Today's my first day,' Caspian said desperately. 'I can't find my form room.'

'Whose class are you in?'

'Mrs Scrudge's.'

'Then, not a problem,' the boy said extending his hand. 'My name's Billy Long, I'm your classmate. Follow me.'

Billy led the way to the classroom, but they still arrived five minutes late. Mrs Scrudge, his new form tutor, was the Head of History and a very scary looking woman, who seemed like she had climbed straight out of one of the historical time periods she taught about.

She reminded Caspian of a stereotypical headmistress from Victorian times; her wiry silver hair was pulled into a tight bun behind her head, small wire rimmed spectacles sat on her tiny nose, and she had the posture that can only be achieved by years of having a broomstick shoved up the back of your blouse. Her face wore a constant expression of disdain that, considering her considerable age, made it resemble an old sheet in need of a good ironing.

'Registration begins at oh-eight forty-five, gentlemen,' she said sternly as they entered the room. 'The classroom is unlocked from oh-eight thirty. The inability to be punctual is the flaw I will tolerate the least, so could you explain the reason you both see it fit to begin a new term with a late mark beside your names?'

'It wasn't our fault, Miss,' Billy replied. 'Caspian wasn't shown where our classroom is, so I was showing him the way.'

'It was quite convenient that you were available to lend your expertise to this matter,' Mrs Scrudge said unimpressed. 'Perhaps this afternoon you could show Caspian a *quicker* way to registration?'

'Yes, Miss.'

'Now take your seat,' Mrs Scrudge instructed. 'No, not you, Caspian.'

Caspian froze and watched Billy take a seat near the back of the class, yearning to swap places with him at that moment. Everyone in the class was staring right at him, making him feel deeply uncomfortable, but one person made him feel this more than the rest.

Sat to the far right was a boy with neatly styled blonde hair and a jawline so defined it could easily have been chiselled out of marble. It was ridiculous how handsome this boy was and no doubt every girl in this class, no – *every* class, probably swooned at his every whim. Although the same height as Caspian, he had filled out much better and was clearly on a sports team of some sort. His eyes were an icy blue and they were staring at Caspian with a curiosity so intense it could kill a cat with single glance.

'This is Caspian Stone,' Mrs Scrudge was saying. 'He has transferred to our school and will be joining our class as of this half of term. Please at some point throughout the day introduce yourself to him.' She turned to Caspian. 'Now, take a seat, please. I believe there is an empty place next to Billy.'

He quickly made his way through the class to his seat, trying not to meet the eyes of all those watching him. Thankfully, Mrs Scrudge immediately continued with the announcements she had been making prior to their arrival, taking the attention off him. 'Mr Dent is still off sick and will not be returning until after Christmas…'

'Thanks for covering for me,' Billy said beside him in a hushed voice whilst Mrs Scrudge had her back turned and was writing something on the board.

'Like wise,' Caspian whispered back.

'Welcome to the strictest class in Hogarth House.'

'Thanks,' Caspian grinned. He looked over at the blonde boy who had been staring at him, who now faced the front of the class listening to whatever Mrs Scrudge was explaining.

'You got your timetable for today?' Billy whispered.

Caspian took out the folded slip of paper the receptionist had given him before sending him blindly into the corridors. He nodded *yes*, not wanting to get in trouble with his disciplinarian form tutor.

Billy pointed at the first lesson of the day and whispered, 'me too.'

'Mr Long!' Mrs Scrudge barked from the front of the classroom where her back was still turned. 'If the excitement of returning from half-term break, coupled with the addition of a new classmate who has had the misfortune of being sat beside yourself, is too overwhelming for you, then maybe the thought of spending your first evening of this term in detention might encourage you to keep your mouth *shut!*'

'Sorry, Miss,' Billy said, giving Caspian a sly "I told you so" look.

'In fact,' Mrs Scrudge continued, 'maybe it would be better to have someone who causes less disruption to lessons act as Caspian's guide. Who else has mathematics first period and wouldn't mind showing Caspian the way to Mr Chang's classroom?'

'I'll show him, Miss,' said an assertive voice to Caspian's right, and the boy with the ice blue eyes turned and gave Caspian an award-winning smile.

'Caspian,' the handsome boy said, extending his hand toward him as they met by the door to their form room. 'My name is Hayden Tanner, nice to meet you.'

Caspian felt a confident grip as they shook. 'Nice to meet you too,' he replied.

They started down the corridor together, Hayden setting the pace. Everyone they passed seemed to be looking at Hayden, but then Caspian realised with a start that they were also looking at him.

'You're not from London, are you?' Hayden asked.

'No,' Caspian replied. 'I'm from Little Bickham.'

'I've not heard of Little Bickham,' Hayden said, but not unkindly.

'Not many people have,' he confessed, and Hayden smiled. 'Why were you staring at me?'

'When?'

'When I came into the classroom.'

'*Everyone* was staring at you,' Hayden pointed out.

That was true. The whole class had looked at Caspian, wondering who he was and what he wanted. Was it just the intensity of Hayden's blue-eyed stare that had stood out?

'So what made you move to London?' Hayden asked as they passed the science block. There was a strong smell of bleach and ammonia in the air, which was not particularly pleasant.

Hayden's question was stifling, not because the answer was difficult to find but more that it was difficult to admit, let alone explain to a stranger. Why had he come to London? Because his mother was severely ill and nobody knew when she would be getting better.

Caspian didn't want his new classmates to know this. Back at Bickham High, his classmates mostly knew about his mother's condition. After all, it was next to impossible to keep something secret in his village. They had all treated Caspian pretty much the same as they had treated him before, but there was no way of knowing how a group of strangers might react to this information. He certainly didn't want to be pitied, and he didn't want people feeling uncomfortable about how they should talk to him because of this news. In fact, he really didn't want to think about this nasty business at all, not whilst he was at school anyway.

'I moved down here to live with my father,' Caspian eventually replied, trying to be as vague as he could.

'During half-term?' Hayden asked him with a frown.

'Yes,' he replied guardedly. 'It was a spontaneous decision.'

'I see,' Hayden said, as though this answered some unasked question he had in his mind. His eyes flicked between Caspian's left and right eye; he was looking at the distinct difference in colour between them, although he didn't mention it.

'What about you?' Caspian asked. 'Where are you from?'

'I've always lived in London,' Hayden shared openly. 'My father is CEO of City Power, one of the biggest suppliers of energy to the city. My mother works in the world of corporate banking, in one of the tall buildings in Canary Wharf. They both have excellent jobs and, needless to say, their expectation for my own success is ... quite irrational.'

Caspian smiled. Despite seeming a little full of himself, Hayden Tanner was turning out to be refreshingly self-deprecating.

They arrived at their first class, which unfortunately for Caspian who was awful at sums, was double mathematics. He sat beside Hayden at the side of the classroom, and noticed that Billy had taken a seat next to a blonde-haired girl from another class he seemed to be friends with.

On the way there, Hayden had confirmed Caspian's suspicion that this school had once been a prison. This explained why the basement, where Mr Chang's classroom was located, was dark, windowless, and felt very much like a medieval dungeon. After the prison had been renovated and turned into a school it had been named Hogarth House – not after the famous painter William Hogarth, as many assumed, but actually after Lord Horace Hogarth who was supposedly the last prisoner to serve a life sentence within the prison walls.

This might seem an odd choice of individual to name a school after, however Lord Horace's final words before dying an old man, still imprisoned for his wrongdoings, perfectly summarised the aspirations for the newly renovated building. "After a lifetime locked within these walls, never has a much more truer lesson been learned." Evidently, this lesson hadn't been English grammar.

His rather ominous final phrase was engraved above the entrance to the school hall to either inspire the students to achieve greater things, or to give them the foreboding impression that their education would last their entire existence.

Mr Chang, the mathematics teacher, ended any conversations by ploughing straight into setting algebra based tasks that involved showing the relationships between two sides of some very tedious equations using inequalities – something Caspian didn't have a clue about!

Hayden, however, seemed to be as equally gifted with his mind as he was with his good looks, and together he and Caspian managed to complete the tasks. The lesson seemed to drag on and on, not much helped by the lack of natural lighting.

More than once a couple of classmates would look over towards Caspian and Hayden, and then whisper something to each other. At first he thought he was being paranoid, but then he caught Billy and his blonde companion doing the same thing.

'Why does everyone keep looking at us?' Caspian asked Hayden quietly.

'Don't worry about them,' Hayden said friendlily. 'Here, look at this equation. You can do this one.'

Caspian looked hopelessly at the next equation that Hayden was sure he could solve, but he really didn't think he could. It was then that he noticed something golden moving on the floor before him.

Suddenly he felt a cold sweat come on, as though he was about to have a panic attack. Crawling across the cold stone floor of the mathematics classroom was the little clockwork spider he had thought to be safe at home.

He cursed himself for not checking where the spider had hid after his father had barged in on him in the morning. Had he taken an extra minute to check, he would have discovered that the place where the spider had chosen to hide was his school bag. Now it was loose and halfway across the classroom, moments away from being discovered.

'It's not that bad,' Hayden was saying next to him, wondering why Caspian had seemingly frozen at the sight of the equation.

The spider was now directly under a girl's chair. Were she not busy sneaking peeks at a glossy magazine with her friend she would have seen it as it crawled under her foot.

Where is it going? Caspian wondered. He desperately wanted to run over and put it back in his bag, but he knew that were he to draw attention to himself he would also draw attention to it, and then his little secret would be known to all.

It scurried underneath a row of tables making it hard to see. He occasionally caught sight of it as it passed between desks, and he felt himself willing with all of his might for the little spider to come back.

'Are you okay?' Hayden asked, his ice blue eyes now intensely curious.

'Huh?' Caspian said. 'Yeah, sorry, the light is not great down here.'

'See what I mean about this being an old prison?'

'Uh-huh,' Caspian murmured.

The spider was now near where Billy sat, who was clearly enjoying solving equations as much as Caspian had been. When he spotted Caspian looking his way he acknowledged him with a slight nod.

Caspian was obviously not hiding his concern very well, as Billy immediately started looking around where he was sitting to see what Caspian was looking at. He leaned down and peered beneath his desk, but when he looked back he was quite confused. 'What?' Billy mouthed silently across the classroom.

Checking that Hayden hadn't seen, Caspian subtly mouthed back, 'nothing.'

But it wasn't *nothing*. In fact, something was very wrong. Literally a split second before Billy had looked under his table, Caspian had seen where the little spider had crept.

Sat beside Billy, the blonde girl was working hard on solving the equations. She was completely oblivious as to what had just crawled inside her rucksack.

V:
CAUGHT BETWEEN A BAG AND A BOOKCASE

The remainder of double mathematics passed so slowly it felt almost as though it lasted a decade. Caspian found it impossible to concentrate on anything Mr Chang said, but was instead fully focused on the rucksack that belonged to the girl sat beside Billy. Somewhere inside that bag was the little clockwork spider, and he had been watching it keenly just in case it decided to come crawling out.

So far it had not.

After Mr Chang had set a large amount of homework, which Caspian knew he would struggle to complete on his own, the lesson drew to a close. The bell rang, signalling break time, and instantly the calm of the class erupted into a chaos of papers being shoved into bags, chairs screeching across the floor, excited conversation filling the air, and a crush of students all trying to leave the basement classroom in one go.

'Come on, Caspian,' Hayden Tanner said. 'I'll show you where the canteen is and introduce you to my friends.'

Caspian looked at Billy and the blonde girl, whose name he had found out to be Clarissa Green. They had both been sat closer to the classroom door than he and Hayden and had already shouldered their bags and squeezed through.

'I'll catch up with you,' he said distractedly. 'I need to go see someone.'

Hayden gave him a look he didn't fully understand – a mixture of disbelief and irritation – but he hadn't the time to digest its meaning as he was more concerned about catching up with Clarissa Green and her bag.

'See you later,' he called and charged through the door.

Once out of the classroom he turned left and right, but there was no sign of either Billy or Clarissa. Not knowing which way to go, and with no other choice, he took a gamble and headed back the way Hayden had led him earlier that morning.

Again, he passed the science block, another part of the old prison basement that had been converted to suit the school's needs, which now housed gas taps and sinks, creating a strange ambivalence of contemporary furnishings built into historic architecture. In fact, with all the various vials and test tubes in the wall storage, it closer resembled a secret laboratory rather than a classroom.

He turned corner after corner, tried corridor after corridor, but there was still no sign of Billy or Clarissa.

Where are they?

It was beginning to look bleak. Caspian couldn't even find his way around the school, let alone find two students he barely knew. He continued to wander the corridors, trying to piece them together in his mind like a mental map.

Finally, when he'd reached the top floor with no idea where he was, he chanced upon them entering a room with a pair of worn old doors. He followed them through, wondering where the doors led, and found himself in the schools extensive yet somewhat decrepit library. Many of the books that lined the tall bookcases must have easily been written over a hundred years ago and, judging by the layer of dust that covered them, had not been opened for almost as long.

He found Billy and Clarissa sat at a small table. Billy was leaning back in his chair with his feet planted on the table, much to the obvious disgust of Clarissa who was trying to wipe away some of the grime that covered it.

'This place really should be cleaned,' she said, finally content that the spot she had been cleaning was sanitary enough for her to rest her bag. 'It's no wonder that nobody uses this place with all this dust and filth.'

'It's probably more to do with the internet,' Billy answered. 'Who needs books when everything is available online?'

'Not everything is available online.'

'Yeah, it is: books, television shows, movies, the lot. That's why the library doesn't get used anymore, so what's the point in cleaning it? It'll only get dirty again.'

Clarissa scoffed. 'If that's your philosophy on cleaning, the matter of your personal hygiene is highly suspect.'

Caspian stepped out from behind a bookcase before any further exchanges could take place between them. He had no idea how he was going to get the spider back without either of them seeing it, but he had to try.

'Caspian?' Billy said, surprised to see him. 'I thought you'd be with your new best friend – Hayden Tanner.'

'Err, no,' Caspian replied, not sure how to take Billy's remark. 'He was going to take me to the canteen but I wanted to find you. Why are you up here anyway?' It was certainly an odd place to spend their break, and they seemed to be the only ones in the library, other than the old librarian who seemed almost as decrepit as her books.

'It's a good place to come for peace and quiet,' Billy replied.

'And to hide from irate sixth formers who don't appreciate being made to look like fools,' Clarissa complained.

'You didn't see them on your way here, did you?'

Caspian shook his head. 'Mind if I join you?'

Billy gestured for him to join them at the table, from which he made no attempt to remove his feet, further infuriating Clarissa. Caspian sat, and Clarissa removed her bag from the table and placed it on the floor between him and where she sat. All he had to do now was unzip her bag without her noticing.

'I thought I heard voices,' a girl said from behind Caspian. 'How are you, Clarissa?'

'I'm good, thanks,' Clarissa said, rising to greet her friend. 'How was your half-term?'

Clarissa chattered to her friend, and Caspian couldn't help but notice how attractive this girl was. Her hair hung in long blonde curls that flowed from her head like a river of gold. She smiled a lot, and when she did two dimples appeared beneath her cheeks. He did all he could to not stare at her with an open mouth, but she was without doubt the most beautiful girl he had ever seen.

'I love your bracelet,' Clarissa was saying, referring to the silver charm bracelet that hung from the girl's slender wrist whilst she carried a small pile of books.

'Thanks,' the girl replied. 'I better check these out and get down to the canteen. I don't want to upset anyone…' she said with a wink. Then she waved goodbye to Clarissa and disappeared behind a bookcase.

'Who was that?' Caspian asked Billy as nonchalantly as he could manage.

Billy gave him a knowing smile. 'That's Rose Wetherby, from 9C, Ms Dalton's class. You got a thing for her, have you?'

'No,' Caspian replied, a little too quickly.

'I don't blame you, mate,' Billy said. 'She is beautiful.'

'Who is?' Clarissa asked as she took her seat again, and Caspian felt his cheeks suddenly burning.

'Rose,' Billy replied. 'Caspian likes her.'

'*Really?*' Clarissa asked excitedly.

Caspian sighed inwardly. 'I don't know. I only just saw her.' He really didn't want to be the subject of playground gossip in his first week at the school. 'I didn't even know she existed until a moment ago.'

Something else then dawned on Caspian. The prime opportunity to reach into Clarissa's bag whilst her attention was diverted had just presented itself, but he had missed it having been as equally distracted by the appearance of Rose Wetherby as she had.

'Well, you wouldn't stand a chance with her,' Clarissa said bluntly.

'Oh, thanks very much,' he replied sarcastically. 'And why is that?'

'Because she already *has* a boyfriend,' Clarissa explained as though it were obvious, dashing Caspian's hopes before they had even risen.

'Rob Harper,' Billy weighed in. 'He's killer at sports and has been scouted to play in major league football.'

'Supposedly,' Clarissa added.

'Yeah, well he's part of Hayden's *in*-crowd,' Billy said. 'Funnily enough, I bet had you gone with Hayden to the canteen you'd have probably been introduced to him, instead of seeing his lovelier other half. Personally, I think you still have a chance with her.'

'How do you figure?' Caspian asked. Rose had barely acknowledged him. 'How do I stand a chance if she already has a boyfriend?'

'If Hayden has taken a shine to you, sooner or later everyone will be interested in his protégé. Do not underestimate the influence of Hayden Tanner.'

'What is it about this guy? It's like he's a celebrity or something.'

'In his own way, he is,' Clarissa said. 'Hayden is by far the most popular boy in our year. I would even go as far as to say that he has become the most popular boy in the school. The upper years respect him, the popular kids gravitate towards him. He is just the right mixture of charm, intelligence, humour, and understanding, not to mention always setting the trend for what is *in*.'

Billy finally removed his feet from the table and leaned conspiratorially forward. 'The thing is, Hayden Tanner *normally* attracts people to *him*. He has never made an exception to this, except with you.'

'What do you mean?' Caspian asked.

'I mean that what he did this morning was unprecedented. He marked you as one of his own.'

'As one of his own?' Caspian laughed at the ridiculousness of what Billy had said. 'He did look a bit miffed, mind you, when I told him I was going elsewhere for my break.'

'I'm not surprised,' Billy laughed. 'He's probably never had that offer turned down before.'

If what Billy and Clarissa said was true, at least all the sideways glances and whispering in his maths class made sense, even if Hayden's motives did not. Billy had carried on talking on this subject, giving examples of other popular kids who had joined Hayden's ranks last term. Whilst both he and Clarissa were distracted, Caspian started to ever so slowly undo the zipper to Clarissa's bag so he could reach inside.

'The funny thing is,' Billy continued, 'that even though he is one of the popular kids, *everyone* likes him.'

'Well, that is generally what *popular* means,' Clarissa pointed out.

'Yes, but I mean *ev-ry-one!*' Billy retorted. 'Not only do all the other popular kids like him, but all the sports guys do, and the geeks and unpopular kids too. Heck, even the teachers like him – now, *that* is not normal.'

'Billy, you can be so–' Clarissa stopped mid sentence and her eyes widened as she looked at her bag. 'Caspian, what do you think you are doing?'

Caspian froze.

'What's going on?' Billy asked.

'Caspian has his hand in my bag!'

'It's not how it seems.'

'I think it's pretty clear,' Billy replied loudly, getting up from his seat.

'No shouting!' the old librarian shouted from somewhere amongst the bookcases.

'You don't understand,' Caspian said, trying to defend his actions. 'There is something that belongs to me inside.'

Clarissa looked like she was about to explode with fury, but somehow she kept her voice to a whisper. 'You are caught with your hand in my bag and you have the audacity to accuse *me* of stealing!?'

'I didn't accuse you of stealing it.'

'So I suppose whatever you think is inside climbed in by itself, did it?'

Exactly, Caspian thought, but he didn't know how to explain. Clarissa snatched the bag from him and started undoing the zip. 'Wait!' Caspian hissed. 'I need to talk to you before you let it out.'

Clarissa froze and her eyes widened, even more than they already were. 'Let *what* out?' she said uncertainly. She suddenly began to regard the bag as if it might explode.

'Look,' Caspian said gently. 'It will be easier to just show you, but I need you both to make me a promise before I do. The thing that is in your bag was not supposed to come to school with me today. I wanted to keep it secret.'

'So why did you bring it?' Billy asked.

'I didn't. It … *fell* into my bag before I left my father's house.'

'I'm not promising anything until I know you are telling the truth,' Clarissa said, still sounding a little worried as to what had joined the contents of her bag.

'Fine,' Caspian replied. He held out his hand towards Clarissa. 'Let me show you.'

'You are not putting your hands in my bag,' Clarissa snapped. 'If anyone is going through it, it's me!'

'Okay, okay,' Caspian said in a hushed tone. He didn't want the librarian coming over to tell them off for making a raucous. It would be one thing getting Billy and Clarissa to swear to secrecy about the spider, but quite another to keep an adult's mouth shut. 'Maybe it would be better to open the bag and leave it on the table. It will probably come out on its own accord.'

The colour left Clarissa's face quicker than a chalk drawing in a downpour. 'It's an animal!' she quietly exclaimed, viewing the bag with renewed fear. 'A *dirty* animal!'

'Sort of,' Caspian replied as reassuringly as he could. 'It's not really an animal, so to speak, and it is quite clean. Just put the bag on the table.'

Clarissa set the bag down, undid the zip at arms reach, and stepped back. Billy, eyes alight with excitement, did the opposite and leaned in, curious to see what was inside.

They all became quiet with anticipation. They waited and waited, and Caspian began to wonder whether the spider would come out at all – or worse, whether it was even still inside.

Eventually, however, they caught sight of a golden glimmer moving about inside the bag, heading for the exit. Clarissa had to clamp her hand over her mouth to prevent her screaming out. Billy, on the other hand, was absolutely beaming with delight, and as the mechanical arachnid climbed out of the bag he declared it was the coolest thing he had ever seen.

'Sshhh…' Caspian hissed, worried that the excitement would attract attention, but there was nobody else around to see. The spider crawled anxiously across the table, moving its little head as if it were sniffing the air. Then, when it finally noticed Caspian, it danced merrily over to him and chirped with excitement. Caspian hissed again. 'I told you to stay at home.'

In response, the spider lowered its head and made a sad whirring noise.

'Is it voice activated?' Billy asked. 'Where did you get it from?'

'It's a long story,' Caspian answered.

'What is it called?' Clarissa asked, gingerly putting her hand towards it. The spider gave her an affectionate nudge and she giggled.

'I don't know?' Caspian replied. 'I haven't thought of a name yet.'

'Is it clockwork?' Billy asked. 'Look at all those gears and sprockets.'

'I think so,' Caspian said. 'Hey, that would be a good name.'

'What would?'

'Sprocket,' and the spider chirped happily in agreement. It really did suit the little clockwork device.

The bell rang signalling the end of break. 'Meet us for lunch,' Billy insisted. 'I want to know all about how you found it.'

'Okay, but you've got to promise to keep it secret.'

Billy laughed. 'What, that you have a mechanical spider that either runs on clockwork or by magic? Who is going to believe us anyway?'

Caspian nodded. That was a good point.

VI:
NO GOOD DEED GOES UNPUNISHED

During the period before lunch, Caspian had English Literature, which was number one on his list of worst lessons – coming just ahead of Mathematics, which in turn was followed by Music Theory.

Hayden Tanner was not in his English class, and neither was Billy, so he sat at a table with Clarissa and a girl with exceptionally greasy hair by the name of Julie McFadden. Julie seemed a little too interested in Caspian for his liking, asking him question after question about how he was finding his first day at school.

'I've a great idea for an article,' she said, taking a worn looking diary from her bag and scribbling notes in it.

Clarissa informed him that Julie was hell bent on becoming a journalist and that she had been trying to get something published with the school paper all last half-term. 'You've got nothing to worry about,' Clarissa whispered to him at one point. 'No one ever reads it anyway.'

Still, Caspian wasn't so sure he wanted to be featured in an article for the whole school to read, which already Julie was giving the hasty title: *How Intimidating Can a First Day Be?* In answer to that, he thought it would be a great deal less intimidating if he were not subjected to such interrogation.

The lesson itself was a mitigated disaster. All the work was based on a book that the class had been given to read over half-term. Having only purchased it the day before, Caspian had not even opened the cover until now, and was forced to spend the entire lesson nodding along and pretending he had the faintest idea as to what the teacher and his fellow classmates were talking about.

Further to Julie's constant distractions he discovered to his horror that Rose Wetherby, the beautiful girl from the library, was in this class and constantly found himself glancing at her. At the back of his mind was also the paranoid thought that Sprocket might attempt another excursion from his bag, despite being safely zipped in one of the side pockets.

On top of all this, it turned out there might also have been credit to Billy's postulation that Hayden would have wondrous effects on his popularity. It got quite out of hand as at times his classmates would interrupt other interruptions to introduce themselves as though he were some kind of celebrity, making him feel extremely uncomfortable.

Lunch break came as a welcome relief.

Caspian and Clarissa met Billy, and then the three of them headed for the school gates. Students were allowed out of the grounds during lunch hour; however severe punishment awaited those that did not return in time for afternoon registration. Mrs Scrudge's punishment was probably the most unpleasant of all. Billy joked that she had brought back the cane – that, Caspian could easily believe!

Billy showed him a sandwich shop he and Clarissa often frequented before heading to a small park a couple of blocks from the school. It was a dry, but cold November's day, so not many of their classmates had ventured out at lunch and they were almost the only group in the park. They sat on a bench, with the exception of Clarissa who first used enough antibacterial wipes to sanitise, pretty much, her entire surrounding area.

'Why do you have a fixation on cleanliness?' Caspian asked as he watched her clean both her hands with a separate wipe.

'It's hardly a fixation,' Clarissa replied defensively. 'It's just good sense. My mother says that germs are absolutely everywhere. You probably don't even know where your hands have been.'

'I know where *my* hands have been,' Billy piped up.

'In your case, that's probably just as bad,' Clarissa answered. She watched in horror as Billy ripped open his sandwiches and took one out. 'Don't you even want to give your hands a quick wipe seeing that I already have them out?'

Billy only shook his head in reply, being that he had already stuffed his mouth full.

Caspian unzipped his bag pocket and let Sprocket out to clamber across the grass, where it stumbled and tumbled happily through a jungle of green blades, and then he took an antibacterial wipe to appease Clarissa and lessen her look of utter disgust.

Whilst they ate, Caspian told his story as to how he came to find the spider in Turner & Stone Antiques.

'Are there more like Sprocket?' Billy asked.

'I don't really know,' Caspian replied.

'You haven't been living with your father long, have you?' Clarissa observed.

'How did you know?'

'In the library, you referred to where you live as your "father's home," so you obviously haven't lived their long enough to feel attached to it.'

Caspian nodded. That was an astute observation. He was certainly not even close to considering his father's house his home. In fact, he was hoping he wouldn't be living there long enough for that to happen.

'Why did you move in with your father if you don't want to be there?' Billy asked.

'It wasn't by choice,' Caspian admitted.

'Why not?' Billy persisted, but Clarissa gave him a disapproving shake of her head.

'It's okay,' Caspian reassured her. He went on to tell them both about his mother's illness. It was really difficult for him to put into words to begin with, but with the help of Clarissa's patience and Billy's not so subtle prompting he eventually found that he was talking openly about the whole subject with ease, and that once he had started he could not stop until it had all been said.

Eventually, when he finished his tale, Clarissa gave him a sympathetic look. 'I didn't know that that is the reason why you came to our school.'

'Nobody does,' Caspian answered, 'and I'd rather it stays that way.'

'I don't think anyone would judge you for it, Caspian,' Clarissa said. 'But I understand why you want this.'

'Do you?' Billy asked, unsure whether he himself understood.

'Yes, Caspian wants to be able to deal with this in his own time, and if half the school know then he wouldn't be able to get away from it.' She looked at Caspian to confirm whether this was the case, and he gave her a nod.

For once, Billy looked completely serious. 'Don't worry, mate. We won't tell anyone. Your secret is safe with us,' he gestured to the clockwork spider crawling at their feet, 'both of them.'

'Where did the spider come from?' Clarissa asked, watching Sprocket happily playing.

Billy rolled his eyes. 'From his father's shop, or weren't you listening?'

'I meant before it ended up in the antiques shop. It must have belonged to someone before Caspian's father found it.'

Caspian had wondered the same thing that previous evening whilst he had played with the little golden spider on his bed. Who had made him? How long ago? Were there others, or was he unique? How had he come to end up in an old cabinet in Turner & Stone Antiques? To all of these questions, Caspian didn't have an answer.

'You could ask your father where he found him,' Billy suggested.

'Use your brain,' Clarissa said harshly. 'If he asks his father about Sprocket, then his father will know he was in his shop and that he took something from it.'

'I know, but his father must know where it came from,' Billy continued.

'I only found him because I knocked into the cabinet,' Caspian said. The spider had not been on display, he was certain. 'In fact, maybe Father won't even notice he is missing.'

'I can't believe it hadn't sold,' Billy said. 'I would have bought it straight away if I saw it for sale.'

'Your father could have made a lot of money by selling Sprocket, but instead he left him at the back of a cabinet,' Clarissa pondered. 'For an antiques dealer, your father has an odd sense of worth.' Caspian was inclined to agree.

'I'd love to have a look in your father's shop,' Billy said. 'I bet there is a ton of cool stuff there. I mean, if this little guy was hidden away in a draw, imagine what else must be inside!'

Caspian thought back to last night, when he had been alone in the shop and had seen the dark shape of the hooded stranger standing at the doorway. *He* had wanted to get inside also. Father had been quick to dismiss that the cloaked man existed, but there was definitely something his father wasn't telling him.

Actually, there are a lot of things Father doesn't tell me, Caspian thought as his mind wandered to the reason his father had left that night – the letter with the red wax seal.

In fact, the amount he didn't know about his father greatly outweighed the little he did, and this didn't change as the week passed by. After returning from school he would see more of Mrs Hodges about the house than he did his father who, when he wasn't in his shop, would spend many hours of the evening beavering away in his study. Other nights, once trading hours were over, he would disappear off to who-knew-where, not returning until close to midnight.

But the comings and goings of his secretive father had become the least of Caspian's worries. With each passing lesson his evening's homework pile seemed to become increasingly more mountainous and there seemed no end in sight to this avalanche of assignments. In geography they graphed globalisation, and in chemistry they considered compounds. Physics focused on forces, whilst the horrific holocaust inhabited history, and anamorphosis was on the agenda in art. In each subject more homework was set. Finally by Friday afternoon, Caspian had music, followed by biology. He suspected that to complete the weeklong theme of alliteration he would be studying Mandel, Mendelssohn, or Mozart until Monday morning.

That, however, was not to be the case.

'Seory is at zee heart of all muzic,' his music teacher announced from the front of the classroom in a loud baritone voice. 'Muzic is bascht on sie rules, and rules are zeer to be followed, *ja*?' Hogarth House's music teacher was a big German man, called Herr Trommel. He had big red cheeks and a very large bristly moustache that hung over his lip like a sly fox trying to conceal the opening to its burrow with its great bushy tail. 'Wizout zee rules, zeer can be no muzic; only noize ant disorders.'

Herr Trommel drew a range of notes on the board and started identifying them. 'Zis is a quaver, zis a semi-quaver, and zis von is a crotchet. Now, vee count and follow zee rules.' He gave them a piece of sheet music and asked them to play the melody, but no matter how much Caspian "followed zee rules," he felt that reading music was beyond him. Instead, he memorized the correct notes and tried to play these in the correct order without needing to follow sheet music, which probably defeated the object of the task.

After music they had biology with Mrs Plumb, a squat little woman who almost exceeded in width what she lacked

69

in height. She had a reputation for drinking hot chocolate to the extent that an elephant drinks water. The amount that she had consumed over the years could not be held to blame for her immense girth, although it probably hadn't helped.

Caspian's biology class consisted of all those he had met throughout his first week at Hogarth House. He sat beside Hayden, whilst Billy and Clarissa were sat together, and Julie McFadden was off to one side, scribbling notes in her diary as always. Rose Wetherby was sat near the front of the class beside a rather stocky built boy whom Caspian had been disheartened to discover was her boyfriend – Rob Harper.

Rob had a sportsman's physique, even at the age of thirteen. He was tall, had large powerful arms, and his bulking chest gave his torso a triangular shape. He was almost a complete contrast to the beautiful and slender figure that sat so delicately beside him. Caspian had initially wondered whether Rose was attracted to Rob's muscles or his mind, but it had quickly become obvious that Rob Harper was thicker than a field of fudge.

'What's wrong with your eyes?' he had asked Caspian one lunchtime.

'Nothing,' Caspian had replied. 'They have always been this way.'

Rob had grinned. 'So you were *born* defective?' he said meanly. Caspian had known there and then that they would never get on, especially as Rob was romantically involved with the girl of his dreams.

'This afternoon,' Mrs Plumb announced after taking the register, 'you will begin your first practical task.' The class fell silent in anticipation. They had already noticed that she was dressed in her white lab coat and a pair of rubber gloves, and a practical session was usually much more enjoyable than a session of theory. 'In pairs, we are going to dissect pig hearts,' she said, to the cheer of most of the boys in the class. The girls were not so enthused, especially

Clarissa Green who looked absolutely mortified at the thought of the task ahead.

They all put on lab coats and were told to remove jewellery and watches. The girls had to tie their hair back, and then they all put on surgical gloves. Caspian could see that Billy was very excited about slicing open a pig's heart, unlike his lab partner who had turned a colour very similar to her surname.

Mrs Plumb waddled around the classroom with a large polystyrene box placing the pig hearts on a cutting board in front of each pair of students. As she did this, she explained that the reason they would be using pigs' hearts was because they are closer in size to a human's than a cow's heart, which is considerably larger. 'In your pairs, you have been issued with a scalpel, a pair of scissors, and a set of tweezers. Ensure that these sets are complete at the end of the class as nobody will leave this room until they have been returned.'

Caspian looked at the pink organ that lay on the board before him, awaiting instruction. Once again, he was glad to be sat beside Hayden who was hopefully as skilled at practical work as he was with mental arithmetic.

'If you look carefully,' Mrs Plumb began from where she demonstrated at the front of the class, 'you will see a layer of membrane that protects the heart, called the pericardium – please stop stabbing it, Billy. It is already dead and you are making Miss Green feel sick. Maybe you should sit down, dear?'

Clarissa nodded and sat, looking faint. Caspian couldn't suppress the smile that slid across his mouth.

'The structure of the heart is related to how it works,' Mrs Plumb continued. 'The left side of the heart has evolved to be more muscular than the right – this is because the right side only has to pump blood the short distance to the lungs where it collects oxygen. The left side, however, has to pump the oxygenated blood around the entire body. Now take your scissors and start cutting into one of the blood vessels.'

Mrs Plumb held up her own pig heart to demonstrate. 'This is the vena cava. Be careful when cutting, you might find it quite tough because of the cardiac muscle surrounding it.'

Hayden handed the Caspian the scissors.

He was initially anxious that he was going to cut the wrong part and ruin the dissection for both of them, but soon he realised he was actually doing pretty well, especially when he noticed the table beside them had cut into completely the wrong blood vessel.

Eventually the whole class were at the same stage, and even Clarissa had managed to pull herself together and regain a more natural colour in her cheeks. 'Very good everyone,' Mrs Plumb appraised. 'What you should now be able to see is the right atrium, one of the valves, and then below that, the right ventricle.'

She then had them take out their notebooks and sketch a diagram of the heart, labelling the ventricles, arteries, aorta, and other parts of the organ. It was only after they had packed up that Caspian became aware that Rose Wetherby was looking particularly upset. She kept checking under the table and all around her as though she had lost something.

Beside her, Rob Harper was completely indifferent to her anxiety, too engulfed with a conversation about the school's rugby team to even notice that his girlfriend was troubled. In fact, Caspian could tell by the way that Rose kept glancing at Rob that she was afraid he *would* notice that something was wrong.

She reached under her table to check in her bag again, and that was when Caspian realised what she had lost. Rose's silver charm bracelet was no longing slinking round her wrist – she must have removed it when they had been told to take off jewellery and watches whilst they got ready to dissect the hearts. With all the movement of the class, returning lab coats and dissection sets, it could have been knocked off the table and ended up anywhere. He empathised with Rose, remembering how he had almost lost Sprocket on his first day.

Determined to find it and be the hero, he scanned the floor with his eyes but could see no trace of the bracelet. Mrs Plumb was setting more homework to steal away his weekend when he finally spotted it lying beneath one of the hand-wash basins at the side of the classroom.

When the lesson ended he made his way over where it lay, but it was not easy going as he was now moving against the tide of classmates pushing passed him towards the door. Finally he reached the washbasin, feeling giddy with excitement. He had found it! She would remember him for this, he was sure.

'What have you got there?' said a voice from behind him. The voice was silky smooth, and belonged to Hayden Tanner.

Not knowing what else to do, Caspian showed the bracelet to him. 'I know who's this is,' he said helpfully, snatching the bracelet out of Caspian's grasp before he could react. 'Hey, Rose. I found your bracelet.'

Caspian's face fell. *I found the bracelet, not Hayden.* But now Rose was looking at Hayden with appreciation and thanking him. She threw her arms around his firm shoulders and said, 'Thank you so much. I thought I'd lost it.'

'I won't tell Rob,' Hayden replied with a conspiratorial wink.

'Thanks. He'd kill me if I had.'

Bewildered by the speed in which his glory had been snatched from his very fingertips, Caspian was rooted to the spot. He wanted to say something, but what could he possibly say?

'What's up, Caspian?' Hayden asked, but before he could respond Mrs Plumb began congratulating Hayden on his find.

'It's those keen eyes of yours,' she said with a smile. 'You have the eye of a biologist there.'

'Thank you, Miss,' Hayden replied. 'I'm just happy to return it.'

But I found it! Caspian fumed. He felt like not only had his praise been passed onto the wrong person, but that it had been stolen altogether. He couldn't keep silent any longer.

'Mrs Plumb, I was the one who found the bracelet,' Caspian said.

'Now, now, Mr Stone,' Mrs Plumb said disapprovingly. 'If there is one thing that no one likes, it's a liar.'

'But I'm not lying,' he insisted. 'I found it, and Hayden took it.'

Hayden frowned. 'I didn't *take* it,' he said.

'Either you are lying, Caspian, or Hayden is,' Mrs Plumb said. 'But Mr Tanner has proven that it is not in his character to lie, so I strongly recommend against you ending your first week's tutelage at Hogarth House by labelling one of its model students as a liar and trying to steal his thunder.'

'But I'm not–' Caspian protested.

'Enough! That is the end of the matter, Mr Stone,' Mrs Plumb said with a tone of finality.

Caspian gave Hayden one last look and then, feeling severe injustice, shouldered his bag and stormed out of the classroom.

'What's up with you?' Billy asked when they met at their lockers.

'Nothing,' Caspian snapped grumpily, not wanting to discuss it.

'Okay,' Billy said. 'You'll never guess what just happened.'

Caspian really wasn't in the mood for guessing games and simply shrugged. He couldn't shake the feeling that his opportunity to impress Rose had been stolen and that

Hayden had betrayed him. 'What?' he muttered as he emptied his locker of homework and textbooks.

'Remember Knoles and Fraser?' Billy asked in hushed excitement.

'No.' Caspian had had to learn so many names this week he couldn't remember everyone's. 'Which lesson do we have with them?'

Billy shook his head. 'They were the two sixth-formers you saved me from on your first morning. Well, Jon Knoles just came over here.'

'And?' Caspian asked, suddenly anxious for his friend, but Billy smiled at his concern.

'And he shook my hand and said sorry.'

'What?' Caspian asked, bewildered. '*He* came to apologise to *you?*'

'Yeah,' Billy grinned. 'This morning in geography Hayden asked why Knoles and Fraser were looking for me. I told him what they did to Clarissa's sister last term and he convinced Knoles to come and make a truce, rather than bash my head in.'

Was there no end to Hayden's good deeds? Caspian thought bitterly. 'And how is it he knows them?' he asked infuriated. 'They're in the sixth-form.'

'Yeah,' Billy shrugged. 'Turns out Knoles' father works for Hayden's dad. Guess I owe Hayden one now. I wish I were as pally with him as you are; he's a good guy to know.'

Caspian slammed his locker shut.

'Seriously. What's up, mate?' Billy asked.

'I've really had enough with being told how wonderful Hayden Tanner is,' he replied and shouldered his bag. 'If you want him as your friend, you are welcome to him.'

He barged passed Billy and headed for the door. Billy called out but he didn't stop. He just wanted to get out of this school, away from Hayden and his fan club. Things started out well at his new school, but now he felt sour about the whole experience. He missed Jessica, he missed Little Bickham, he missed his mother, and he missed his home.

VII:
THE ASSOCIATE

It had been a week since he had tried to enter Turner & Stone Antiques under the cover of nightfall. His associate had failed him. All the fool had to do was acquire the keys, but instead he had tried to pass off a false set as the real ones and then disappeared: he had not gotten far. Now he lay on the floor, wriggling pitifully in pain as the poison coursed through his veins; it wouldn't kill him, but he certainly wouldn't want to experience it again.

'You failed me,' the hooded man said to his associate as he convulsed, 'and you failed *him*.' He, whom he referred to, his master, grew stronger every day and would not be as tolerant of failure. His return was imminent, and all that those who opposed him could do was bide their time.

'No, I didn't know,' the associate murmured weakly from the floor, his words barely audible through the breathing apparatus that covered his mouth. His voice was a high pitch squeak.

'No?' The cloaked man said darkly. His associate's hands and feet were bound, and rope secured him in position. The fat little man was trussed up like a turkey ready to roast in an oven.

He flicked a switch that made the bulky piece of equipment on the table beside him hum to life. On hearing it, the associate began to wriggle and squirm. A hose, attached to the machine, was secured to the mouthpiece that had been taped to its victim's face so it couldn't be shaken loose.

He unscrewed another vial of poison and poured it into the cup-like container atop the machine. Once released, the machine would vaporise the liquid poison in the canister and, over the course of the five to ten minutes that followed, his associate would breathe the vapour into his lungs causing an insufferable agony.

The associate watched him wide eyed. One press of the release button and the pain he had felt a few minutes before would start over again.

'The key,' he repeated. 'What went wrong?'

'I couldn't get it,' the associate whimpered.

'You assured me you would get me a copy.'

'It wasn't as easy as I thought. Edgar Stone is very cautious.'

'Do not speak to me of caution,' the hooded man growled. His face itched, but it always itched. The burning sensation had never gone away and he had learned to live with it, condemned to a life of constant aches and sores. The torture his associate was experiencing was nothing compared to what he had known. No, compared to what his master had done to him, this was akin the punishment an owner bestowed upon his disobedient dog.

'You tried to deceive me. You tried to deceive *him*,' he accused.

'No, no,' the associate squealed. 'I would never try to deceive *him*. I got Edgar out of the house, with that letter. He was out so you could get in. I didn't think you would need the key. I thought you would just break in.'

'And make Edgar Stone aware of our plot?' he hissed at him. For a man of his stature in society, the associate was not an intelligent one. 'You said yourself; Edgar Stone is a cautious man. One false move and all will fail.' He lifted his hand over the release button and paused menacingly. 'Or was this your plan?'

'NO!' the associate wailed pitifully. 'I'll send him another letter. I'll get him out of the way. I'll get you the key, please.'

'One can only cry wolf so many times before the village grow wise to a ploy. A letter is no longer a sufficient ruse to keep him from his beloved shop. Too much is dependant on us finding what he has hidden, and you are not even sure the shop is where he keeps it.'

'It has to be there.'

'No. It *has* to be found!' he snapped. 'Edgar Stone is all that stands in The Master's way.'

The fat little man looked at him meekly from the floor. 'What of the Council?'

'Without Stone, the Council will fall,' he said. 'Remove the foundations and the house will crumble. Now will you do as I say, or do you need further persuasion?' He let his hand fall to the release button. The poisonous liquid in the canister began to vaporise into a fine mist and the machine began to pump it down the hose towards the associate who let out a blood-curdling scream.

'I will, I will,' he bellowed, 'just turn it off!'

'Obey me,' the hooded man hissed, 'and my master will reward your subservience. What is it *he* can do for *you?*'

The fat man was writhing about on the floor, shaking in agony as his lungs filled with poison gas, undoubtedly feeling like they were about to burst into flames. At worst, he would be left with a nasty cough that would dissipate in time – but he didn't need to know that.

'I…' he began, tears streaking down his face as he sobbed. 'I just want to live.'

'We have been hiding in the shadows for too long. Soon comes the day when we once again see the light.' He turned off the machine and pulled back his hood to reveal his face. As the associate cowered away from its hideousness, he allowed a small smile to form. A smile uses a lot of facial muscles, and moving his facial muscles hurt like hell.

This smile was not a pretty smile, but it was the last thing the associate saw before unconsciousness took him. It was always the same, the hooded man thought. When it came down to it, in the end they all begged for the same thing.

But none of them would live forever.

VIII:
DAZED AND ACCUSED

The graveyard outside Caspian's bedroom window seemed bare and barren. The crimson leaves that had once formed a canopy of red over the restful dead had fallen from the trees that Mrs Hodges called Bloodgood maples. As November drew to a close, even the sunniest day seemed dark and grey.

During the weeks that followed, Caspian's reluctant rise in popularity continued. By the end of term, pretty much everyone at Hogarth House knew who he was. After taking credit for finding Rose's bracelet, Hayden Tanner had apologised for the "misunderstanding" and had been even friendlier to him, which absurdly had only further strengthened his popularity around the school.

Everyone greeted him when he arrived in the morning, waved to him as he walked down the corridor, or asked if he wanted to sit with them in classes. It had been flattering to begin with, but the gratification had quickly worn thin. Caspian quickly found the esteem that he was held in to be empty and shallow, unlike the reverence of his real friends.

Billy forgave Caspian for the strop he had thrown. Jessica had called a couple of times to find out how he was settling in, and as the shops began to glitter and shine with decorations he found himself counting down the days to the Christmas break when he would return to Little Bickham to see his mother and his best friend.

Caspian was feeling anxious about his mother, and the sooner he could see that she was all right, the better. For the first time he'd ever known, contact with his mother was beginning to dwindle. The regularity of phone calls had decreased, and Mother would often be sleeping when he did call, or when she answered she seemed confused and disorientated.

There was one particularly painful phone call when she didn't seem to remember who he was. 'Caspian who?' she had asked after he'd told her who was on the phone. Eventually, with his help, she had seemed to snap out of the stupor that had taken her and apologised profusely. Mrs Hodges said it was probably the effect of her new medication that was sending her "a little queer," but that offered little comfort to Caspian that Mother's condition had seemingly worsened in the brief time since he had left.

Father had started checking in on him, but their relationship had not much improved. Mrs Hodges was the only one who tried to bring them both together other than at meal times, but on each occasion the conversation quickly dried up and the atmosphere became very awkward.

Caspian instead spent most evenings alone in his room, watching Sprocket scurry around or coaxing him into chasing his hand across the bed, whilst he should have been attempting to complete the impossible volume of homework he was being set on a daily basis. Billy and Clarissa had both kept their word and Sprocket remained their little secret. Caspian allowed the little spider to travel to school with him, but only after he had made it promise not to repeat its inquisitiveness of that fateful first day.

On the final day of term before the Christmas holidays, he and Clarissa were sat in the school hall for their lunch break, awaiting Billy to join them. When he eventually arrived he had a sparkle in his eye that usually suggested he was either planning to do, or had just done, some sort of mischief.

'What have you been up too?' Clarissa asked suspiciously when she saw the familiar roguish expression on her friend's face. He looked like he had received an early Christmas gift.

'Me? Nothing,' Billy said with as much innocence as he would ever be likely to achieve, but an impish grin crept across his face. 'It's what I've just read,' and he promptly unfolded a piece of paper from his pocket and begun to read aloud. 'An Owe to Arlington,' he announced in his finest broadcasting voice. Then he read:

'When our eyes meet, our souls intertwine,
Someday I long that you could be mine
To love and to cherish, to have and to hold,
To live life together from young until old
Your smile is alluring, your eyes they glisten,
Yours is the voice I forever could listen
My love is an Arlington with only one name,
Whispered in secret, my darling, my James.'

Billy fell to the floor with laughter as he finished.

Clarissa snatched the piece of paper from him and looked at the poem. 'This is Julie McFadden's.'

'I know,' Billy said, still rolling with laughter. 'That makes it all the funnier,' and he rolled his head back and laughed even louder.

James Arlington was one of Rob Harper's friends; a quiet boy, but sufficiently handsome that he drew enough attention to be enrolled in with the popular group. Julie, with her long greasy hair and spotty complexion, couldn't be further out of his league, which made the whole affair even more tragic.

'How can you tell?' Caspian asked.

'It's her handwriting, and it is quite obviously a photocopy from a page of her diary,' Clarissa explained.

Caspian thought about Julie and her diary, the way it went everywhere with her to detail her every thought, along with her ad hoc interviews.

'This is awful,' Clarissa was saying.

'Isn't it,' Billy agreed, and then in a bad imitation of Julie McFadden he recited, 'your smile is *alluring...*'

'No. I mean it is awful that someone has done this to Julie,' Clarissa clarified, giving Billy a scalding look.

Even though the poem itself was awful, Caspian felt sorry for Julie. She wanted to get noticed for her proficiency as a journalist, but instead she had become the subject of a playground scandal with her most intimate thoughts and feelings circulated for all to see.

After lunch was double History with their form tutor, Mrs Scrudge. Julie McFadden was also in the class and her face was visibly pinker when she entered, especially as the class erupted into jeering and making snide comments. Fortunately, she was spared one embarrassment, and that was that James Arlington, the subject of *An Owe to Arlington*, was not in their History class.

As she took her seat she looked at Caspian and gave him a look so full of scorn it seemed like she was willing him to burst into flames before her eyes.

'What was that about?' Billy whispered.

'I haven't a clue,' Caspian answered honestly.

The class groaned as they were asked to take out their homework diaries at the end of the lesson. Everyone had been hoping for a break from homework over the holidays, but it seemed like all the teachers had gotten together with intentions of spoiling these dreams.

Mrs Scrudge in particular seemed adamant to keep their enjoyment of the festive season to a minimum. Next term in History they were going to be studying Victorian London, however she seemed willing to inflict this subject on them early by having them do research over the Christmas period.

'You will then write a two-thousand word report,' Mrs Scrudge explained sternly, 'and be warned; this report will form one of your main pieces of coursework of the year. You may decide which aspect of Victorian London you want to write your report on.'

Caspian listened carefully and made notes as Mrs Scrudge went though the criteria that their reports had to meet, including a ten minute presentation to the class of their findings. He glanced over at Billy, who looked particularly worried by the latter.

'You shall do your presentations and submit your reports at the end of January,' Mrs Scrudge continued. 'Even though we live in the modern age of computers, apps, and internet, as a historian myself I can tell you that some of the best material can still be found in books, so do not disregard the school library in which books are abundant.'

Father didn't have the internet, so the books in the school library would be Caspian's best source of information. He could head there straight after the bell went and take some books out to look at over Christmas. As the lesson finished he collected his bag and was about to head in that direction when a fierce looking Julie McFadden obstructed his path.

'I know it was you!' she hissed accusingly.

'What was?' Caspian asked confused.

'I know it was you who took my diary, photocopied it, and passed it around the school to make me a laughing stock.'

'Why would you think that?' Caspian asked, but Julie was too caught up in her own anger to hear him.

'Everyone thinks you are another Hayden Tanner, but I see you for what you really are, Caspian Stone,' Julie continued. 'You are just a mean boy, hiding behind your good boy reputation. But trust me; people will see the truth eventually, I will make sure of it!'

'I was nothing to do with it, Julie,' Caspian said honestly. 'I didn't know anything about it until I saw the page myself.'

'You are a liar, Caspian,' Julie said, tears forming in her eyes. 'Just give me back my diary and leave me alone.'

Caspian was dumbfounded. 'I...I don't have it,' he said, but she seemed to get even crosser until she burst into tears and ran out of the classroom.

He kicked his chair in under the table and stormed up to the library with Clarissa and Billy in tow. Why did people keep accusing him of being a liar when he was telling the truth? First Mrs Plumb, and now Julie McFadden.

He was so angry he could feel his ears burning.

'Don't worry about it,' Clarissa told him as they ascended the staircase. 'She's just looking for someone to blame, but she'll realise you are innocent eventually.'

'What are you going to do your report on?' Billy asked, trying to change the subject.

Caspian did have a really good idea for his report. It was during the Victorian times that a lot of work was done under the city of London. The sewers were completely renovated and the London Underground transport system was installed. 'I'm going to write about the subterranean progress made in the city at that time,' Caspian said.

'Good idea,' Billy said. 'I'm going to do mine on the thieves and pickpockets who robbed and stole so they could survive.'

'Sounds like you would fit in with them,' Clarissa joked. 'You're a regular Artful Dodger.'

By the time they reached the library it was teeming with their classmates, scrambling to find books before they were all taken. The poor old librarian seemed overwhelmed by the sudden demand for history books, and she passed from bookcase to bookcase telling her excitable customers not to shout.

All the books on the Victorian era had gone, and Caspian looked at the bare bookcase feeling downhearted. He had been foolish to think himself the only one to have the idea to come here straight from class, especially after Mrs Scrudge's not so subtle hints. He left the library with no books at all and headed down to his locker, but it seemed Caspian's bad luck had not yet gone home for the holidays.

Waiting for him at his locker was the bulky figure of Rob Harper. 'Alright, Two-eyes?' Harper said when he saw Caspian.

'Everyone has two eyes,' Caspian pointed out.

'Yeah, but theirs' are the same colour,' Harper replied with a grin, clearly pleased at his use of wit – or in his case, half of it.

'What do you want, Rob?' Caspian asked, trying to get round him to his locker.

'I need to have a word with you.'

'You already are.'

'Well, I need to have some more,' Rob replied. 'Do you think it's funny what you did to Julie?'

'I didn't do *anything*,' Caspian insisted. 'Who said I did?'

Harper lifted up his chest, enjoying one of the few moments in his life when he knew something that nobody else did. 'That's not the point,' he grinned. 'You can't come into this school and start picking on girls.' He gave Caspian a little shove with the last remark.

Caspian couldn't help thinking about how he had witnessed Rob treating Rose throughout the term. He certainly didn't seem to be treating her very well and he had seen her crying on more than one occasion, almost always because of something Rob had done or said. And when she had thought she'd lost her bracelet, she had been so scared of what he would do if he found out…

'That's fresh, coming from you,' Caspian blurted out before he could stop himself, usually knowing better than to insult someone with more muscles than brain cells.

'What do-ya mean by that?' Harper said, grabbing Caspian by his bag strap.

With the Christmas holidays officially begun, the corridors of Hogarth House were alive with excitement, but now a different kind of excitement sparked in the locker area like an electrical charge. A fight was about to break out and everyone wanted to see who would strike first and, more importantly, who would win.

'I'll tell you what,' Harper said with a smile, looking at all their classmates gathering around them. 'Why don't we settle this once and for all?' He pushed Caspian against his locker, whilst at the same time pulling the bag from his shoulder.

Thrown off balance, Caspian could do nothing to prevent the physically stronger boy taking his bag from him.

'Give that back!' Caspian shouted.

'Why?' Harper replied suspiciously, playing up to the audience. 'Do you have something to hide?'

Yes, Caspian thought. Sprocket was in his bag, safely zipped in one of the side pockets. He knew if Harper found him he would never see the little spider again.

'Perhaps a diary belonging to a certain young lady,' Harper continued, misreading the fear in Caspian's eyes as guilt. 'I think we all should see what is hidden in here.'

Harper unzipped the main compartment and started taking out Caspian's school books, homework diary, pencil case, and whatever else he could find, throwing them on the floor at Caspian's feet whilst he watched on helplessly.

'Innocent so far…' Harper said, but his hand was moving to the side pocket's zip; the side pocket where Sprocket was concealed. 'What have we got in – '

'Give me that!' To Harper's surprise Clarissa came out from behind him and, just in the nick of time, pulled the bag from his grip.

'What's your game, Green?' Harper snapped.

'You are not the law of this school,' Clarissa said bravely, but Caspian could see she wasn't feeling as brave as she sounded. 'It is not for you to decide who is guilty and deal out the punishments. Caspian should be given a chance to either deny or confess to taking Julie's diary, not searched on the spot by you.'

Clarissa gave Caspian back his bag and stood beside him. Billy came forward and stood on the other side, although he didn't look particularly pleased to be standing up to Harper.

'So be it,' Harper said, once again performing to the amused audience. 'Can you prove that you didn't steal and photocopy Julie McFadden's diary?'

'I can prove I don't have it,' Caspian said, slinging his bag over his back again, making sure he put his arms through both straps this time.

'Go on then,' Harper encouraged.

Caspian took his locker key from his pocket. 'You saw for yourself that it wasn't in my bag. The only other place I could have it would be here,' he said as he pulled open his locker door, exposing its contents to the crowd.

There was an audible gasp of disbelief; Harper wore a triumphant grin. There, in the middle of his locker, was Julie McFadden's stolen diary.

'Explain that,' Harper challenged.

But he was so shocked to see the diary in his locker that no words came to him. How could he explain it? How could the diary have ended up in *his* locker? Billy looked equally as surprised, and Clarissa looked disappointed. 'Oh, Caspian,' she said shaking her head. Hayden Tanner had appeared also, looking at him the same way.

'Someone must have put it there,' Caspian said out loud, but he could see by their faces that nobody believed him. After all, students only had keys to their own lockers, so who else could have been in Caspian's locker other than Caspian?

Harper stood over him now, looking him in the eyes with a menacing grin on his face.

'You think you are so big, being the popular boy who came from far away,' Harper said quietly. 'But you are not so big, Caspian Stone. You are nothing.' He reached into Caspian's locker and snatched Julie's diary, holding it up in the air like a trophy. 'Don't take things that don't belong to you,' he said louder and slammed Caspian against the lockers with all his might.

The wind was instantly knocked out of him as he crashed against the locker door, feeling the bag strapped to his back crunching on impact.

Rob Harper leaned in and put his mouth next to Caspian's ear. He whispered, 'And stay away from Rose. I've seen the way you look at her, and I don't like it. She would never be interested in someone like *you*.' He punched Caspian hard in the stomach, but his last insult dealt a heavier blow.

The audience let out a cheer as he fell to the floor clutching his gut, before they burst into laughter at Caspian Stone: the boy who had quickly risen to the height of popularity – and even quicker taken a fall.

IX:
EXERCISE IN TRUST

Humiliated. Accused. Framed. Innocent.

Caspian reached the front door to his father's home feeling like the whole world were not only sitting on his shoulders but also whispering behind his back.

It was already dark outside and the coldness in the air cut at him, making him pull his coat even tighter to keep in what little warmth it held. The twinkling lights and the decorations that sparkled from almost every home and shop window didn't fill him with the joy that the spirit of Christmas should, but instead he felt cold and bitter, just like the weather that made him snivel.

'How was school?' Father asked with the same lack of interest he always showed.

'Normal,' Caspian shrugged sulkily as he hung his jacket in the hall. He wondered whether Father realised, or even cared, what constituted as a "normal" day at school, or whether he was completely oblivious as to what his son was going through – probably the latter, Caspian decided.

After the earlier events of the day, his only real solace was that soon he would be returning to Little Bickham for Christmas, and hopefully Mother would give him the good news that she was on the mend. Then he could return home and continue his life as though he had never had to come to London, never attend Hogarth House High School, and never met Rob Harper.

'I need to have a word,' Father called to Caspian as he was about to head upstairs.

'Okay…'

The look that Father was giving him told him this was not going to be a positive conversation. 'It's about Christmas,' he said. 'There has been a change of plans.'

Caspian didn't like the sound of that, but surely today couldn't get any worse. 'What do you mean?'

'The doctor called. He was hoping your mom would be showing sign of improvement by now, meaning that they could discharge her for Christmas. Unfortunately, this has not proven to be the case.'

Caspian didn't say anything, but he felt his heart sink.

'I'm sorry, Caspian,' Father said. 'I know you had your heart set on returning home for Christmas, but I'm afraid you will not be able to.'

'But Mom wants me to be there,' Caspian argued.

'Yes, she does,' Father said steadily, 'but, she also knows this will not be practical with her current condition. She has agreed that you would be better off spending the Christmas holidays here. There will be plenty of time for you to see her once she is in a better state.'

'But I don't want to,' Caspian quarrelled. 'I don't want to be here.' And before Father could say another word he stomped upstairs to his room and slammed the door. He slumped onto the bed and placed his bag beside him. With a sinking feeling, he reached into the side pocket. When Rob Harper had pushed him against the locker he had felt his bag crumple under his weight. Now what he'd both feared and suspected, but sincerely hoped wasn't the case, turned out to be true.

Sprocket had been in that pocket, but now in his hand lay the intricate pieces of golden metal: the brass cogs, the copper wheels, the tiny gears and levers that had once been the clockwork spider, now nothing more than broken parts.

This was the final blow. The first tear ran down his face and he wiped it away, but soon more came flooding out. Everything was going wrong. Mother was not getting better, everyone at school would believe that he was responsible for taking Julie's diary, his new found friends probably wouldn't want to be his friends anymore, and the marvellous mechanical spider he had discovered was now broken.

He carefully placed all of Sprocket's parts in a white handkerchief, checking his bag pocket over and over to ensure he had not missed even the tiniest of pieces. At first he had delusions of fixing the spider himself, but he knew nothing about clockwork mechanics and there were easily over a hundred tiny components to reassemble.

Finally defeated, he placed the handkerchief in his pocket after securing it with an elastic band. Mrs Hodges knocked on his door twice to inform him dinner was ready, but Caspian didn't feel like eating and eventually she left him alone.

Some time around seven o'clock there was another knock on his door, except this time it wasn't Mrs Hodges.

'Caspian?' Father said softly.

He didn't answer, hoping his father might believe he'd fallen asleep.

'Caspian, open your door,' Father instructed.

Over the last month Caspian had thought that his father had pretty much forgotten about him, remembering he existed only when their paths crossed, like a piece of furniture from his shop he just couldn't rid himself of. But now there was something in his father's voice that he had not heard before. His father was concerned.

'Come on, Caspian,' Father persevered. 'Open the door. I feel we are long overdue a chat.'

When he opened the door he met his father's golden eyes, but they were not the intense probing eyes he had come to know, like the watchtower lights in a prison always on the lookout for no good. Instead he saw in them something familiar, something he had seen in Mother's eyes the morning that he left Little Bickham: a painful sadness.

'Come with me,' Father said solemnly, and led the way down the stairs to the hall. At first, Caspian thought he was taking him to the living room where the Mrs Hodges had decorated a Christmas tree with fairy lights that reflected off the large bay windows, but Father continued down the stairs leading to the shop and unlocked the door.

Inside Turner & Stone Antiques, Father took a seat at the counter near the rear of the shop – a small table with little else on it other than an old fashioned cash register, an antique abacus that was probably just for display purposes rather than actual use, and a flamboyant looking brass lamp with an emerald green lampshade of tinted glass.

Caspian sat opposite his father.

The shop counter was the only area of the shop that was not covered with stone flooring. Varnished oak floorboards, that echoed as he'd walked across them, had been laid so that they slightly raised a perfectly circular area like a small stage. Only a spotlight was missing.

Both he and his father sat in silence, neither quite knowing how to begin. Finally Father started. 'We have not been fair to one another, you and I,' he said sombrely. 'I know that you were not keen to come here to live with me, nor are you enjoying it. And, I suppose, everything considered, why should you?'

For the first time Caspian saw sadness in his father's face.

'The circumstances that have brought us together are not ideal,' Father continued. 'But if we are to continue living together under one roof we need to resolve the matter of our relationship.'

'It's not that easy to fix,' Caspian said. 'I used to go months without hearing from you, sometimes years without seeing you. I know *nothing* about you.' Suddenly all the feelings Caspian had managed to keep bottled up for years, many he hadn't even realised he had, floated to the surface and once he'd starting letting them out he couldn't stop.

'You always miss my birthday, we never spend any time together, and you rarely came to visit. You want to *repair* this relationship?' Caspian said loudly, almost shouting. 'We haven't got a relationship.'

Father merely sat in silence until Caspian had laid out all his accusations. Once he had finished he leant forward. 'Is that truly how you feel?' he asked softly.

Caspian nodded, feeling his throat tighten like a tennis ball was lodged in his larynx.

'And would you like to change this?'

Caspian nodded again.

'So would I, Caspian,' Father said sadly. 'I have reasons to justify why I have acted the way I have over the years, and we will get to all those in due course. The truth is, I am a man of many flaws with many secrets, and I have spent a long time trying to fix those flaws so that I may share those secrets.'

Caspian wondered what secrets a man as mysterious as his father must keep.

'You see,' Father continued, his golden eyes fixed on Caspian's. 'Trust – or more precisely; not being able to trust – is one of my biggest flaws. Without trust, how can a relationship begin and grow?'

'You don't trust me?' Caspian asked. The thought that his own father didn't trust him made him feel very sad indeed.

His father gave a little smile. 'That is a more difficult question to answer than it seems. There *are* people who I trust, but they are very few and very far between. Your mother, however, is one of that minority. But to answer your question honestly, no, I do not trust you – at least not yet. And you also clearly do not trust me, after all, how could you if you truly meant every word you just said?'

Caspian couldn't keep looking into his father's intense eyes and so he found himself staring at his own hands.

Everything Father had said so far was true. 'But if we don't trust each other, how can we begin to?'

'With honesty,' Father replied. 'Honesty is the soil in which the seeds of trust must be sown. Without this fundamental element trust quickly turns to distrust and deception, and the relationship wilts and dies.'

Father reached across the table and placed his hand gently on Caspian's shoulder. The unexpected contact made him jump involuntarily.

'I would like to propose that we make a fresh start, a clean slate. Let us leave what has happened between us in the past and move towards a more positive future, built on honesty and trust.'

Caspian liked the thought of that. For his entire life his contact with his father had been practically non-existent. Now, his father was reaching out to him, and although he felt hesitant about the offer, he too wanted to reach back. But being sat in the shop made Caspian feel a pang of guilt – this was where his first deception to his father had begun. He had broken into this very shop despite being told not to come here on his own. If they were truly making a fresh start, now was the time to come clean.

'I have something to confess,' Caspian said after a few moments of silence.

Father took his hand off Caspian's shoulder and looked at him strangely.

Caspian swallowed, but he seemed to have nothing to swallow. His throat had gone drier than a desert, but Father sat in his seat and patiently waited for Caspian to find the courage to continue.

'When I first came to stay …' he began, but then he seemed to lose all confidence. What could he say? He snuck into his father's office and stole the shop key? He broke into the shop and took the clockwork spider?

The sheer thought of Sprocket, broken and wrapped in the handkerchief in his pocket, only made it harder for him to continue. Another thought crept into his mind: if he admitted what he had done, Father would likely take Sprocket from him and he'd never see the little spider again.

Caspian sighed. He knew he was being selfish. If he kept Sprocket secret, he may never get him repaired and he owed it to the little spider to do whatever it took to have him mended, even if that meant losing him for good.

'I know what you did, Caspian,' Father said steadily, but instead of the expected harshness that had been in his voice on the day the sword had been removed from the wall-mount without permission, his voice was full of warmth.

'How could you know?' Caspian said bewildered, uncertain that Father really did know. When he looked at him a small smile had appeared on his mouth.

'I said I have many flaws,' Father began, 'but a slow mind is not one of them.'

Father recalled how he had arrived home that night to find Caspian at the door, out of breath. 'I cannot say that my suspicions were not aroused there and then,' Father said, 'but I decided to leave the matter alone. However, upon sitting in my study later that evening to deal with a few correspondences before I turned in, imagine my wonder at discovering that the key to this very shop had miraculously materialised in the top drawer of my desk, contrary to the fact I *always* keep it in the drawer below.'

Caspian's mouth fell open. He had not since thought about how he had ran up the stairs that night, trying to beat his father through the door so he could replace the key without being caught in the act.

'Most mistakes are made in haste or whilst under pressure,' Father stated. 'I can assume that my return home caught you off guard, and in your hasty retreat you made the mistake that would ironically lead you to being caught regardless.'

'I'm sorry,' Caspian apologised. 'You had gone out and I just wanted to see what else you had here.'

'You mean, what secrets I had here?' Father wryly suggested.

'I guess so,' Caspian hadn't really thought about it that way. He had just felt an unquenchable yearning to return to the shop.

'Secrets are funny things, aren't they?' Father said with a smile. 'The purpose of a secret is to keep something hidden, to keep it safe. And yet all a secret truly desires is to be told, to be shared.'

'I think I found one of *those* secrets,' Caspian said cautiously, and he reached into his pocket. Father looked on with intrigue as he carefully took out the handkerchief, removed the elastic band, and revealed the contents.

'Ah, so this is what happened to him,' Father said after studying the tiny pieces for a moment, as if some great mystery that had been bothering him for a long time had finally been solved.

'I didn't mean for it to get broken,' Caspian said sadly.

'I believe you,' Father said warmly, picking up one of Sprocket's legs. 'This little fellow would have known the risks when he found you.'

'What do you mean; he *found* me?' It was Caspian who had found the clockwork spider, not the other way round.

'You are not the first person he has become attached to,' Father replied thoughtfully. 'Over the years, only he has chosen to whom he will reveal himself.'

'But where did he come from? Who made him?' Caspian had so many questions about his little clockwork companion and there had been no one to ask until now.

'He was made long ago from a technology almost completely forgotten today,' Father answered mysteriously. 'But think not of this little spider as merely a gizmo or clever contraption. He is much, much more. Treat him well and you will have a friend for life, but abuse him like his previous owner did and he will abandon you forever.'

Caspian looked despairingly at the pieces of metal and tiny parts. 'What have I done?' he said sadly.

Father watched him for a while and then seemed to come to a decision. 'he has seen much worse days than this.'

'Can he be repaired?' Caspian asked uncertainly. He'd not known his father to fix things, but then he didn't really know his father at all. Maybe he knew someone in the antiques trade who would be able to help them.

'If all the parts are here, I think I can,' Father said with a smile. 'Stay where you are.'

Father stood and walked over to the back wall of the shop where he lifted down what looked like a large metal winding key. It was the same sort of key that would be used to wind a clock, except the clock mechanism to require a key this size would have to be massive.

'I want to show you something,' Father said as he returned to the raised platform.

'Okay…' Caspian said, watching his father with curiosity as he slotted the key into a hole, which Caspian had not noticed before, in the very centre of the raised platform where they were sat.

'What are you doing?'

'An exercise in trust,' Father explained, and then with both arms he began to turn the key. Instantly a loud clinking sound started beneath them as unseen gears began to whir. Caspian felt a rumbling and he realised that with each turn of the key the whole circular platform was descending into the ground, taking them with it.

X:
THE REFLECTORY

Caspian felt as though he were being lowered into a large stone well, except this well seemed much deeper than any he had ever imagined. Down and down, and further still they went, like the earth was trying to swallow them whole. And when, after they had descended a few metres and the mouth above them closed, all that remained to be seen was the interior of the extensive stone gullet that was slowly ingesting them.

The loud sound of clanking gears beneath and inside the walls around them made it nigh impossible to question his father as to what was happening and where they were going. The only light they had came from the lamp on the shop counter, which had illuminated as soon as the top of the shaft had shut them off from the world above.

How deep were they going?

Who had built this strange lift?

What was its purpose?

But he could do nothing more than sit and wait, looking up towards the endless darkness above him, hoping for the answers to the questions he sought to emerge.

After a while the curved walls had begun to glisten with moisture and the air became noticeably damper. He couldn't recall from when it had first appeared, but he became intrigued by an angled ledge that slowly circled the wall of the shaft forming a channel, corkscrewing all the way down as they descended. Presumably, this was to collect the drips of condensation as they dribbled down the walls, carrying the droplets downwards in a controlled manner.

Two to three minutes later, the platform suddenly came to an abrupt stop with a loud *clonk*. There was the sound of water trickling, as the runoff from the channel dripped into a gutter that disappeared into the wall, and only added to the sensation that this was the bottom of a mighty well with its cylindrical walls stretching upwards above them.

As the platform had come to rest they had come level with two doors. Father gestured for Caspian to follow him through the door to the left, carefully carrying the handkerchief containing Sprocket's broken components.

Beyond the door was a passageway that vastly contrasted the cold stone of the strange cylindrical elevator. The floor was laid with an expensive looking cyan-blue carpet, the skirting of which was fixed under polished brass plates that curved into the walls. Strangely, the first thing Caspian wondered was; who cleans down here? Did Mrs Hodges' duties extend beyond the cleanliness of the house above them?

The walls themselves were covered with elaborately carved dark wood panels. Each panel was engraved with a different design depicting various achievements throughout the industrial age: Newcomen inventing the first steam engine, the Wright brothers and their powered flying machine, the large structure of Big Ben being built, and many more wondrous achievements captured in these ornate engravings.

A row of small lamps, which had burst into life as Father had opened the door, gave off a warm light that bounced off all the polished brass whilst emphasising the detail that had been painstakingly inscribed into the dark wood depictions.

Caspian wanted to stop and look at each illustration, marvelling at how beautifully intricate each carving was, but Father insisted they move on.

At the end of this corridor of pictures there was another door, but this one was very different to any door Caspian had ever seen before. Unlike the solid wooden door that they had passed through to enter the decorated corridor, which had been heavy and thick like the sort one would expect to find in an old church or castle, this particular door was made of three separate layers. The innermost layer was mirrored glass that had blackened over the years due to the outer layers making cleaning it impossible, even for the diligent Mrs Hodges. The middle layer consisted of a visibly complicated locking mechanism that was protected by an elaborate outer layer of decorative golden vines and branches, weaving and winding in such a way that the doors innards were visible but utterly tamperproof.

Right at the very centre of this ornate protective layer was an emblem that looked to Caspian like two snakes, twisted together in a strange knot, each biting the other's tail. With a start he realised that the shape they made was very familiar, however the last time he had seen the emblem it had been imprinted in red wax on a certain mysterious letter rather than fashioned from gold and decorating a door.

'What is this?' Caspian asked, unable to contain his curiosity any longer.

Father, mistaking the subject of his son's question to be the door itself rather than the symbol at its centre, answered, 'This is an Armadador.'

'An Armadador?' Caspian repeated. 'It sounds Spanish.'

'No, not an Armadador; an *Armada* door,' Father explained. 'In the sixteenth and seventeenth centuries, strongboxes, called Nuremburg chests, were built and designed to safe keep officer's valuables, soldiers' wages, taxes, and so on. Instead of having a singular locking bolt, these chests had multiple bolts that moved in different directions making them some of the most secure contraptions ever designed.'

Father pointed out the locking bolts along all four edges of the door. 'This was built with that design in mind.

There are twenty-four locking bolts on this door, all controlled by the same mechanism.'

'*Twenty-four*,' Caspian said in awe, looking more closely at the intricate assemblage of pins, rivets, cams, springs, connecting links, bolts, clips, rods, locking levers, and release levers. With all these elaborate moving parts, he couldn't help thinking that he was looking at the innards of an ancient machine – perhaps he was.

Father slipped a key into the centre of the two looping serpents where a small cavity was formed – a concealed keyhole. As he turned the key with ease, Caspian watched with amazement as the parts of the lock began to move, slide, twist, or contract. The whole mechanism seemed to clench like fifty fists of fingers and thumbs, independently rearranging themselves, and yet each movement intrinsically imperative to the overall objective. Twenty-four bolts, moving in unison, slid back into the unlocked position and the brief but brilliant shifting and shuffling lock assembly was dormant once more.

And if the door at the end of this passage had not fascinated Caspian, then what lie beyond was purest wonderment. As the door slowly opened, he felt his mouth drop and his eyes widen in shear stupefaction of what they perceived.

'What is this place?' he whispered.

'This is a reflectory,' Father replied with a smile.

Caspian had no idea what a reflectory was, but it put him in mind of the inside of a submarine as would have been depicted in the writing's of Jules Verne. The room itself was a perfect octagon in shape, covered from ceiling to floor with large polished mirrors. When the Armada door closed silently behind them, he saw that it too was covered by mirrored glass, just like the other seven walls – were he not careful it would be easy to forget which side the door actually was. Four ledges had been built into four sides of the eight sided room, housing levers, gears, peculiar buttons, and all manner of strange devices the likes of which he had never before seen. Whatever the purpose of this room was, Caspian could not divine it from the mysterious objects that were its occupants.

'What *is* a reflectory,' he asked, looking about him. 'I've never seen a place like this before.'

'Well,' Father replied, 'think of an observatory, built up on a high place designed with the purpose of observing the outside world, specifically the stars and the sky. A reflectory is the opposite, built deep underground away from all that might distract, it provides a place where one can look into their thoughts, to sit, think, and reflect – hence its name.'

In the centre of the room, above a large golden octagonal table, hung a strange looking chandelier that had illuminated as the door opened, just as the small lamps had done in the adjoining corridor. The light reflected off the mirrored walls making it easy to believe that this strange room was many, many times larger than it really was, and gave the impression of walking into a honeycomb built of brass and glass.

Father rolled up a large detailed blueprint that had been covering most of the table, and moved some of the other objects that had been cluttering it to make space for them both to sit. 'Place the handkerchief with all the spider's parts on the table,' he instructed Caspian.

'His name is Sprocket.'

'Sprocket?' Father said, raising an eyebrow. 'I'm certain that never before has this little spider been given a more befitting name. So be it, please place Sprocket's parts on the table.'

Caspian did as he was told whilst his father lifted one of the strange devices from a surrounding ledge and placed it carefully in front of them. The device was made of polished brass and iron, and had three large glass lenses, each the size of a plate, that could be manoeuvred into position over the other to allow varying levels of magnification. It seemed to be a strange version of a microscope.

Father sat in front of the magnifying device and with nimble fingers began to separate the different parts and pieces of the clockwork spider into individual piles. 'These are gears or cogs, and these are wheels and axles.'

Caspian felt torn between watching his father work and letting his eyes wander about the strange and unusual room he was sat in. He would occasionally glance over at some of the strange devices on the shelf, or at the rolls of paperwork that were stacked to one side. It was during one of these lapses in attention that his father caught his eye and asked him what he was thinking.

'I was just wondering, who built this place?' He was almost certain they had descended below sea level, which had probably accounted for the moisture forming on the stone walls, but he just couldn't fathom who could have built a place like this *and* kept it a secret from the world?

'It was built generations ago by like-minded thinkers as myself,' Father answered, his golden eyes seemingly massive as they stared through the glass magnifying plates.

'But the things you have here,' Caspian continued, looking about the room, 'I've never seen anything like them.'

'Yes, you have,' answered Father. 'Even though the technology here comes from the time Sprocket was conceived and created, all of the theory behind these contraptions has been distilled into the design and mechanics of modern machine.'

'But Sprocket is the most advanced mechanical device I have ever seen, and yet he seems to be a hundred years old, or more.'

'That may well be the case,' Father said distractedly as he took a tiny pair of tweezers and examined one of the minuscule cogs more closely. 'Technology moves with discovery. Electricity started being manipulated in new and useful ways, and scientists began to understand how tiny components interacted with one another to form our world. Travelling through the skies was no longer a fantasy but a reality, and travel beyond our atmosphere into the depths of space was becoming increasingly more plausible. Is it any wonder that some aspects of mechanics are out-dated and replaced before they have been truly perfected?

'Technology like this little clockwork spider was overshadowed by new advances and innovations in other areas and eventually it was forgotten completely, save from those who found traces of it to have survived the passing of time.' Father sat back and looked up from the magnifying device. 'I am glad to report; Sprocket doesn't seem to have been damaged beyond repair. It will, however, take some time to get him up and running again.'

'How much time?' Caspian asked.

'That is hard to say, but it might be a few weeks at least,' Father replied. 'My time is already distributed between the maintaining and running of the shop, advising clients, and attending auctions. But I promise you I will devote as much time as I can to getting this little fellow moving again.'

'Thank you,' Caspian said, feeling genuinely grateful.

'Oh, do not thank me yet,' Father said with a wry grin. 'We must first discuss rewards and punishments.'

'Rewards and punishments?' Caspian repeated, confused.

'Yes,' Father answered. 'You broke into my shop and my study, and you took something from both without permission. For those deeds you need to be punished.'

Caspian felt his shoulders sink. He had been enjoying the new relationship he and his father were beginning to establish, but despite what had been said it seemed that Father wasn't really offering a completely clean slate after all.

'But,' Father continued before Caspian could offer anything by way of protest, 'I must take into consideration your honest confession, for which you should also be rewarded. After all, the scales of justice require balance.'

Father carefully positioned the handkerchief containing Sprocket's pieces before them. 'So, as a reward it seems only fair that you become the rightful guardian of Sprocket, providing he is happy with that.'

Caspian's heart leapt. Ever since admitting the discovery of Sprocket to his father he had feared that this would be the last he would see of the little spider. But now Sprocket would truly be his to look after, as long as Father could fix it, and as long as it forgave Caspian.

'But if I were you,' Father continued, 'I would not tell anyone about him.'

'I already have,' Caspian said guiltily. 'He didn't leave me much choice. On my first day at school Sprocket climbed into my friend Clarissa's bag. I got caught trying to retrieve him and had to show him to her and Billy. There was no other way, but they promised not to tell anyone about him.'

'And I presume they have kept this promise?' Father asked, to which Caspian enthusiastically nodded. 'Very well. Sprocket is your secret now, Caspian. It is up to you with whom you share such a secret, as it is to decide who can be trusted with such information.'

Caspian nodded in understanding.

'Your punishment,' Father said, pausing afterwards for effect, 'will be this: you will assist me in repairing Sprocket, helping you to understand how he works and what literally makes him tick. After all, he will be your responsibility now, and thus you must take his upkeep seriously.'

Caspian was overjoyed. That didn't sound like punishment at all. 'Yeah, sure,' he said enthusiastically. 'Not a problem.'

Father seemed to be watching his reaction to this news with mild amusement, when all of a sudden the sound of a telephone ringing filled the room and made Caspian jump with surprise.

'You have a phone down here?' he asked his father, who was about to lift the receiver. 'I thought this place was for thinking without distractions?'

'Sometimes there are things that mustn't be ignored,' Father replied. 'This is an internal line and only Mrs Hodges knows the number, for which she has been instructed only to use in cases of the uttermost importance.'

Father held the receiver to his mouth and pressed a button beside the telephone before speaking. 'Mrs Hodges, what necessitates this phone call?'

Mrs Hodges voice sounded tinny and mechanical as it came out of the phone's speaker. 'I'm sorry to disturb you, Sir, but unexpected company has arrived.'

'Company?' Father enquired. 'Who is it?'

'It is Mr Smeelie, Sir. He is adamant that he speak to you right away and is most persistent about it.'

'Thank you, Mrs Hodges,' replied Father. 'Please take his coat and offer him a drink, and kindly explain that I will shortly be up to collect him from the entertaining lounge.'

'You wouldn't rather I send him down to the shop?' Mrs Hodges asked.

'I would not.'

'As you wish, Sir,' Mrs Hodges said and the line went dead.

'Come on, Caspian,' Father said. 'I'm afraid we must cut this session short tonight for it seems I have pressing matters to attend to. Leave Sprocket, we will pick up where we left off tomorrow night.'

Father pulled a lever that made the Armada door slide quietly open. They then made their way back to the cylindrical elevator and took their places – Caspian in the seat at the counter and Father by the winding-key.

The loud noise began again as they ascended towards the surface. Caspian sat and patiently watched as they rose towards the ceiling. When they were close to the top the cover slid open and the platform came to a halt in its place.

'Caspian,' Father said seriously. 'I want you to do exactly as I tell you to, and please do not ask why; there isn't time to explain.'

'Okay,' Caspian replied.

'I want you to find a place in the shop, out of sight of the counter, and I want you to hide,' he instructed calmly, but Caspian noticed a tone of urgency in his father's voice that seemed alien to his personality. 'It is imperative that the person I am about to bring down to the reflectory does not see you. Once the cover is in place and we can no longer be heard, I want you to go up to your room and stay there until my guest has departed.'

'Okay,' Caspian said again, feeling a little bewildered.

'Good lad,' his father said, and then as an afterthought he took his watch – a large old fashioned timepiece – out of his pocket and handed it to Caspian and with no further explanation he said, 'look after this for me.'

Father promptly turned and headed for the door whilst Caspian followed his father's instructions and found a dark spot behind a large astrological globe to conceal himself. Father's footsteps slowly faded as he went upstairs to fetch whoever Mr Smeelie was.

Caspian waited in his hiding spot, wondering what was going on.

A short while later he heard his father's footsteps coming back down the stairs followed by another's.

'It is most unlike you to turn up out of the blue, Ponsonby,' Father was saying.

'This is hardly out of the blue,' Mr Smeelie replied, his voice much higher in pitch than Father's. He coughed a couple of times, and it sounded to Caspian that Mr Smeelie was unwell. 'What were you doing in the reflectory?'

'Reflecting,' Father answered dryly. 'But I also needed to repair my watch. What is a horologist without his timepiece, besides unfashionably late?'

'Quite,' Smeelie replied distractedly.

Caspian looked at the watch in his hand. It was working fine. What was his father talking about? Then he realised that they had left Sprocket on the table in the reflectory and Father was misleading Mr Smeelie as to what it truly was.

'I have to say, Edgar,' Smeelie continued, 'I expected to hear back from you concerning my letter. I presume you followed it up?'

'I looked into it,' Father replied steadily. 'It was little more than a loose end, and certainly didn't require impetuously sealing it with the insignia of the Council.'

They were talking about the letter with the red wax seal! Caspian couldn't believe it. So the strange symbol was the emblem of a council. Was this Ponsonby Smeelie a member of a mysterious council? Was he, along with Father, involved in a secret society of some sort? In any case, it seemed that he was the sender of the letter. Despite his father's instruction, Caspian now felt compelled to get a look at this man.

'Do you think there is any risk?' Smeelie was asking in his squeaky voice.

'No,' Father replied calmly. Caspian heard footsteps on the wooden platform near the shop counter. They were about to descend down to the reflectory. This was his last chance to catch a glimpse.

Being dreadfully careful, Caspian poked his head out ever so slightly so he could see Mr Smeelie.

Ponsonby Smeelie was a portly man who had clearly over indulged in the nicer things in life. His round cheeks were red and his features seemed like they had been squished up in the centre of his face. He wore a top hat and a smart suit – although, try as he had, the jacket did not do up over his rotund belly.

'I just think that with all this activity going on,' Smeelie fussed, 'maybe it isn't best for just one of us to know the location of the weapon.'

Caspian frowned, wondering what they were talking about. What weapon?

'The Council voted that it was to be placed in the hands of one of us, to keep it safe from *his* grasp,' Father said sternly.

Smeelie burst into a coughing fit. He sounded weary once it had passed. 'Might I remind you that not all of us voted that way, Edgar?'

'You needn't remind me,' Father replied steadily, although Caspian thought he detected something in his father's tone to suggest he didn't really like this man.

'What if he is truly ready to return?' Smeelie continued regardless. 'You must know he will be searching for it.'

'This is not conversation for the shop,' Father calmly interrupted.

'No,' Ponsonby Smeelie agreed. 'I suppose we cannot be too cautious.'

Father started turning the large key and the platform once again disappeared into the floor. When the cover shut a few seconds later the noise of the gears turning was almost completely muffled, sounding instead like an Underground train passing beneath the streets.

What is going on? Caspian wondered. He stood there for a moment, thinking about all the questions that had arisen with the appearance of Ponsonby Smeelie, before deciding he'd better do as he was told and hurried upstairs.

XI:
AN EARLY GIFT

The next morning was Christmas Eve, and Caspian awoke feeling a certain ambivalence towards it. On the one hand, it was the day before Christmas, and even at the age of thirteen he still couldn't help getting excited. But the more excited he got, the guiltier he felt that he was not back in Little Bickham.

During the day he went to the supermarket with Mrs Hodges to help her carry all the ingredients she was buying to build a Christmas dinner worthy of her culinary reputation. Last Christmas, Caspian had gone to the local supermarket in Little Bickham by himself to do the food shop, but in London he quickly learned why this was a two person job.

The supermarket was heaving with customers, all shoving so many items into their trolleys it seemed more like the apocalypse was approaching rather than Christmas Day. At one point both he and an elderly lady reached simultaneously for the same packet of Brussels sprouts, to which she promptly knocked him on the head with her walking stick and scarpered down the aisle waving the sprouts above her head victoriously, leaving Caspian in a state of utter bewilderment. Worse still, were he to believe in coincidences, he was sure she was the same elderly woman that had barged passed him when alighting the train after arriving at St Pancras Station on his first day in London.

They carried the shopping home, and Caspian couldn't believe how much food Mrs Hodges had bought. There was only going to be the three of them for Christmas, but it seemed like she had bought food to feed twice this amount.

Caspian didn't mind though; if Mrs Hodges Christmas dinners were anything like her normal dinners, he would happily eat twice as much.

They only had a simple dinner that night and whilst Mrs Hodges wrestled with the pots, pans, roasting tins, and baking trays in preparation for tomorrow's main event, Caspian and his father retreated to the shop and took the lift down to the reflectory. There they spent the next couple of hours painstakingly working side by side, Father supervising whilst Caspian learned all about clockwork mechanics.

After they had eventually finished one part of the mechanism that controlled leg movement, that took meticulous concentration to complete, they had a break and Caspian could no longer contain his curiosity.

'The man who came yesterday,' he began, as nonchalantly as he could manage. When he glanced up, Father's golden eyes were fixed intensely on him. 'Who was he?'

Father seemed to weigh the question carefully before answering. 'Ponsonby Smeelie,' he said. 'An acquaintance.'

'I overheard some of what he said.'

'So I gathered.'

'Who was he talking about?' Caspian asked. 'He said someone was ready to return.'

Father frowned. 'Mr Smeelie does not always have a good grasp of the facts. He is also an irrational worrier, and a chronic hypochondriac.'

'Yes, but he sounded rather worked up,' Caspian continued. 'And he came to speak to you specifically about it.'

'He did,' Father replied. 'We spoke. I reassured him and he left.'

'You're not going to tell me any more than that, are you?' Caspian asked, but he knew the answer already. His father was evading answering his questions with the mastery that a martial artist avoids his opponent's blows. Were he not so invested in the past, Caspian imagined his father would do particularly well as a politician.

'At this juncture, I am afraid I cannot,' Father told him. 'And please don't ask me why, Caspian. When the time arises that I can share this with you, be assured that I will.'

'I suppose you also can't tell me why I had to hide last night.'

Father gave him a sympathetic look. 'My sincerest apologies, Caspian: all in good time. Speaking of which, look how late it is!'

Caspian looked at his father's pocket watch, which showed it was ten minutes passed midnight.

Father said warmly, 'Merry Christmas, Caspian. Would you like one of your gifts?'

'Shouldn't we wait until morning?' Caspian asked. He'd never been allowed to open his Christmas presents before he'd gone to sleep on Christmas Eve before.

Father smiled, 'Shouldn't you *not* want to wait?' he countered. 'Besides, it is only one gift, after all, and it isn't wrapped anyway.'

'Okay,' Caspian replied, looking about the reflectory for anything that might be said gift.

'I know that you had your heart set on going back to Little Bickham for Christmas, and unfortunately that has not been able to happen. I may have, however, found a compromise.'

'A compromise?' Caspian asked, not entirely sure what his father was getting at.

'Yes. I have been speaking to Mr and Mrs Ravenwood about the possibility of bringing forward Jessica's visit.'

'And…?' Caspian asked, eager to hear the outcome.

'And they have agreed,' Father said with a smile. 'I have covered the costs for her rail tickets, and she will be coming to stay with us.'

'When?' The thought of seeing Jess sooner than February eclipsed everything he had been feeling since the last day of term.

'She will travel down on the twenty-eighth, and travel back on the second.'

'The twenty-eighth? Of *December*?'

'Yes.'

Caspian couldn't believe it. 'That's this Friday!'

'I know,' Father answered with amusement.

'That means she'll be here for New Year's Eve.'

'Yes, it does.'

'Brilliant!' Caspian threw his arms around his father and gave him a hug. Father, who was rather a taken back by the sudden gesture, gave him a hesitant pat on the back.

'Right then,' Father said, trying to regain his composure. 'Enough excitement for one evening, I think. Let's call it a night.'

Caspian leapt out of bed on Christmas morning, still full of the joy that his best friend would be spending New Year's Eve with him in London. He couldn't believe she hadn't told him – was she in on the surprise, or were her parents keeping it as a surprise for her? Either way, he was so excited he almost forgot that there were other presents to give and receive.

They all ate bacon rolls for breakfast around the Christmas tree in the living room whilst they opened their presents. Caspian spoke on the phone with his mother who, in spite of her illness, sounded full of Christmas cheer. Then, whilst Mrs Hodges set to work in the kitchen, Father brought out a beautiful hand-carved wooden chess set and they spent the rest of the morning trying to defeat one another.

After Caspian had lost two out of three games, Mrs Hodges declared that dinner was ready to be served. Caspian had never seen so much food on one table before. There were honey-glazed parsnips, herb roasted potatoes, buttered carrots, broccoli, cauliflower and Brussels sprouts. There was a large turkey with juices and mouth-watering aromas still pouring out of it. There was homemade stuffing and surely hundreds of pigs in blankets. The gravy was like silk, dark brown in colour with a tint of red, and smelled like no gravy he had ever tasted before. There was bread sauce, cranberry sauce, and even a pot of butter that had been clarified so it tasted even richer than normal.

They pulled crackers and ate until their bellies were so full they might explode, and then to ensure successful detonation, Mrs Hodges brought out the desserts, and then she followed with a cheese board. By mid afternoon Caspian was lying across one of the chairs in the living room feeling like he would never need to eat again. The evening was passed with playing games. Mrs Hodges surprised Caspian with her talent at charades, whilst Father was unbeatable at Trivial Pursuit.

Caspian was by far the best at Pictionary, and he fell about with laughter when they played a game called one hundred questions – this involved having a small note stuck to your forehead with a name written on it by another player. You then took it in turns to ask questions to determine who you are, before another player guesses their own identity.

Father wrote the name to go on Mrs Hodges' head as *Ms Piggy* from the Muppets. After ascertaining that she was a famous female actress with curly blonde hair, she kept insisting that she *must* be Marilyn Monroe.

After Christmas had passed Caspian was literally counting down the days until Jess' visit. On the day of her arrival, he went with Mrs Hodges to collect her from the station.

'I can't believe people can be so fickle,' Jess commented as they boarded the Underground. Caspian had been filling Jess in on the events that had caused the dramatic shift in his popularity at school, turning him from one of the most popular boys to the contrary. 'You should be treated as innocent until proven guilty.'

Mrs Hodges, who was sat opposite, was far too distracted by the gardening magazine she had bought at the station than to pay any attention to their conversation.

'Her diary was in my locker,' he reminded her. 'In my situation, I think it's guilty until proven innocent.'

Jess laughed, 'Yeah, I guess it is.'

It had been almost two months since they had seen one another, and yet seeing her now made it feel like it were only yesterday. Having Jess here to talk to and to laugh with made it feel just like old times again.

She wore her dark corkscrew-curls tied back today, so Caspian could clearly see her reaction to London as they travelled through the vast city. *Did I look that lost when I first arrived?* Caspian wondered when he saw the disorientation on his friend's face.

If the hubbub of central London had not disorientated her enough, Jess had certainly become bewildered by the time they alighted the Underground.

'How do you know which way to go?' she asked, looking at the spaghetti-like Underground map as though it were written in ancient hieroglyphics.

Caspian grinned. 'I know,' he agreed. 'At first it feels like you are just blindly following the crowd and if you arrive at your desired destination it is purely chance, but believe me you pick it up surprisingly quickly.'

That morning a frost had lain and everything was touched with a glistening sheet of silvery-white, which in the golden glow of the winter's sun looked magical, the city resembling a greetings card.

They called into the shop to see Father, before taking Jessica's luggage up to Caspian's room where she would be sleeping – he would be spending the next few nights on an impromptu bed on the living room floor.

'Your father really doesn't seem as bad as you've made out,' Jess commented.

'Well, things have changed.'

'Oh, really?'

'Yeah.' Since he and his father had sat down and had a heart to heart, Caspian had not had the opportunity to speak to Jess about it. 'We were too busy talking about your visit when we spoke after Christmas, but on the last day of term we talked about making a fresh start.'

'That's great,' Jess enthused approvingly. 'How is it going?'

'Really well, actually. He's more relaxed than he was when I first arrived, and we've been spending a bit of time together too.' In fact, they had spent almost every evening together since that first visit to the reflectory, and they were now beginning to make real progress with Sprocket. Caspian had learnt a great deal from his father, who had a precision and steadiness of hand that must have taken decades to perfect.

He wished the little spider had already been repaired because he would have loved to see Jess' reaction to his clockwork pet, but unfortunately there was still work to be done before Sprocket would move again. Having Jess stay meant that he couldn't take trips down to the reflectory, and so repair work on Sprocket had come to a halt.

One unexpected result of the new relationship Caspian shared with his father was the impact it had on mealtimes. The awkwardness that had once hung over the room, with the same electric tension a storm creates between the flash of lightning and the rumble of thunder, had completely vanished – a development that Mrs Hodges was particularly pleased by.

'So, what have you got planned for tomorrow?' Mrs Hodges asked that evening whilst the four of them were sat at the dining table.

'I ... er ...' Caspian stuttered.

'You must have some idea as to where you want to take Jessica.'

'Well … er …' he continued.

'We were thinking about a museum,' Jess answered, coming to his rescue.

Father looked up, 'Which were you thinking about?'

'We haven't decided yet,' Jess replied pleasantly. 'Which would you suggest?'

'I would suggest visiting them all, were you not so constricted by time,' Father answered with a sly smile. 'Each has its own merits and provides the opportunity to learn from the past. I am, however, rather partial to the Science Museum.'

That evening, after dinner, Caspian and Jess stayed up late talking. 'Museum, huh?' Caspian said with a smirk.

'Like you had anything better planned,' Jess retaliated. 'You are rubbish at organising.'

'In my defence, I didn't know what you would want to do,' he shrugged.

'Oh, good point,' she said sarcastically. 'In which case, you couldn't have possibly organised a single thing.'

'Exactly,' Caspian grinned.

'Fine, I take it back,' Jess smiled. 'You are not rubbish at organising. You are just rubbish.'

In response, Caspian picked up a pillow and threw it at her head.

'Anyway,' Jess said, knocking aside the feather-filled projectile, 'I thought it would be both fun *and* beneficial.'

'How do you mean?'

'Haven't you still got a report to write?' Jess asked. 'My money says that you haven't done any work on it since it was set.'

'That was the last day of term,' Caspian argued, 'and all the books were taken out of the school library.'

'You live in London!' Jess pointed out as if he were an idiot. 'There are hundreds of libraries. But anyway, I was thinking we could go to a museum that has an exhibition on your subject matter. That way we can spend the day at the museum, and you won't have to spend the evening reading books for your report.'

That did sound like a much better idea, Caspian thought. 'But this is supposed to be your holiday.'

'It's meant to be a chance for us to hang out together, plus I love museums,' she said with an air of finality. 'So who else can come tomorrow? Will I get to meet these new friends of yours?'

Caspian felt a knot in his stomach. He hadn't told her that he had also fallen out with Billy and Clarissa over the diary incident.

'What's wrong?'

'Nothing,' Caspian said as naturally as he could. 'I expect they'll be busy.'

Jess frowned. 'You can still ask them, though. I'd really like to meet them, especially if they are replacing me.'

'They're no replacement for you,' Caspian answered, hoping she would drop the matter.

'Substitutes, then. Anyway, give them a call.'

'No, I'd rather not.'

'It's because of this stupid diary thing, isn't it?'

Caspian shrugged vaguely, not wanting to openly admit she was right.

'You're being ridiculous,' she told him. 'Go phone them now, I bet they'll come. And if they don't, then they'll miss out.'

'Miss out on what,' Caspian snubbed, 'a day at the museum?'

'Yes,' Jess smiled, 'and a chance to spend a day with me and my disorganised friend.'

XII:
THE OFFICE OF PONSONBY SMEELIE

The Museum of London told the social history of the city's inhabitants through time, from prehistoric all the way to modern day, in a range of galleries arranged in chronological order, including an area that recreated a section of Victorian London. It was built beside a still standing portion of the London Wall; however the museum building itself was contained within a tall circular wall, forming the central island of a busy roundabout in Barbican.

Rather than take Father's suggestion of the Science Museum, the Museum of London's *Victorian Walk* seemed more beneficial to Jess' objective of forcing Caspian to do his homework. She had likewise succeeded with her other objective and, with her encouragement, Caspian had spoken to Billy over the phone. To his surprise Billy was keen to speak to him and didn't seem to hold any grievance over what had happened outside the lockers. He also didn't seem phased by the evidence implicating Caspian for the whole Julie McFadden prank, but in actual fact he thought it was absolutely brilliant – although he had not wanted to say so in front of Clarissa.

'I told you I wasn't anything to do with it,' Caspian had argued.

'Which makes the whole thing even more genius if what you say is true,' Billy had replied. 'That would mean whoever *did* come up with such an elaborate prank successfully got away with it by pointing blame at you. You've got to admit, now *that* is brilliant!'

'Yeah, I'm in awe,' Caspian replied sarcastically, not sharing Billy's enthusiasm. 'Look, my friend Jess has come over to stay for a few days. She'd really like to meet you and Clarissa, and we are going to the Museum of London tomorrow. Would you like to join us?'

'Definitely!'

'Really?' Caspian asked surprised. He had not figured Billy as the sort who enjoyed museums.

'Absolutely,' Billy continued. 'I mean, I'm sure the museum will be dull, but we can liven it up a bit.'

Ah, there we are, Caspian thought to himself as Billy expressed his true intent. 'What about Clarissa? Do you think she'll come?'

'Why wouldn't she?' Billy asked, but then figured out that Caspian was inferring to the incident with the diary. 'Look, mate. The thing about Clarissa is she is rather highly opinionated. She just felt let down because she stood up for you in front of everyone, and then it turned out the diary was in your locker after all.'

Caspian went to protest but Billy interrupted him dismissing his defence. 'Hey, whatever, it's all in the past. But you know how Clarissa gets when she is wrong about something. Heck, once she confused Newton with Einstein in a Physics lesson and was unbearable for a week.'

'Great,' Caspian said derisively, seeing that an end to the feud over those unproven allegations against him was not in sight.

'But the point is,' Billy continued, 'she got over it. Just give her time, and the opportunity to hang out. She'll eventually get over this too.'

They met outside the museum the following morning, and even though Clarissa was awfully standoffish with him he was glad that she had agreed to come. Thankfully Jess quickly befriended Clarissa and soon the mood lightened, and whilst the girls were getting to know one another Billy discretely quizzed Caspian about Sprocket.

'*You* are fixing him?' Billy exclaimed after Caspian had updated him. 'Do you even know how?'

'I'm learning,' Caspian replied. 'My father has an amazing knowledge of clockwork machines.'

'I suppose he would as an antique dealer, as otherwise if a clock broke down he wouldn't be able to mend it and sell it.'

'It's not just that,' Caspian said. 'His understanding of the inner workings of these devices goes far beyond mending clocks. I'm learning so much from him.'

'Have you shown Jess yet?' Billy asked, referring to Sprocket. 'She seems pretty cool.'

'She's great,' Caspian agreed, 'but I haven't told her about it. I thought it would be easier to explain once he's been mended. You know, it'd be a bit more … believable.'

Billy gave a knowing nod, and then he spied a replica of a fossilised mammoth tusk and began pretending to play it as though it were some sort of prehistoric saxophone.

'He seems a bit of an idiot,' Jess commented when the girls joined Caspian.

'You're not wrong there,' Clarissa replied.

They were all surprised by how diverse and interesting London's past actually was, and Caspian could see why his mother was so enthusiastic about seeing the city. There were elements about the city's history he had never considered, like why the Roman's had decided to build their settlement in the place that they had.

A tour guide was explaining this point to a group of visitors and Caspian overheard some of what was said. It turned out that they had chosen to build their settlement at the point where the banks of the Thames were narrow enough to be bridged, deep enough to handle seafaring vessels, and yet still be influenced by the tide.

'Why was the tide important?' a visitor beside Caspian asked.

The guide pointed to a series of slides that showed how the shape of the Thames Valley had changed throughout history. 'The modern river is much faster flowing than the

Thames of Roman times. The tide was an important factor for ship captains in those days, who would ride the rising tide upstream, or travel towards the sea on the falling tide, using tidal direction to their benefit.'

Caspian was surprised to learn that there had once been an amphitheatre in Roman London, not anywhere as audacious as the Coliseum of Rome, nor as large as the Olympic Stadium in Stratford. He found it interesting, nevertheless, to think that it had been discovered buried beneath the Guildhall where it had been concealed for centuries. What other secrets lay hidden beneath the city's streets?

There had also once stood a large Basilica that would have been the centre of commerce in this region of Britain during Roman times. A detailed model of the Basilica was on display in the museum, giving the impression of how it would have looked before being buried by the sands of time.

They worked their way through gallery after gallery, travelling through Medieval, Tudor, Stuart, Georgian, and Regency London. Through plagues, fires, restoration, and industrial revolution, until they reached the Victorian era: it's gallery an entire area designed with replica shop facades that were so realistic Caspian felt as though he had stepped into the pages of one of Charles Dickens' novels.

Whilst the others looked around the gallery with fascination, Caspian found a section full of information he could use for his report. His planned subject matter was Victorian advances made *beneath* the city, and what better a feat to talk about than the underground railway – the first the world had ever seen.

A video explained that by the middle of the nineteenth century road congestion had become a major problem for the city. Additionally, London was encircled by more railway stations than any other city in the world, for which the construction of railway connecting these stations had cost around a hundred thousand Londoner's their homes between 1850 and 1900. Eventually, the solution to this problem was not to lay track along the streets, but beneath them.

Caspian was so immersed with the information in the video that he barely noticed someone walk passed him. It was only when this person coughed a wheezing cough that his attention was caught and he was taken aback by who he saw. A corpulent little figure, who was smartly dressed, waddled hurriedly through the Victorian Walk, passing Jess, Billy, and Clarissa who were peering through one of the shop windows.

'What is it?' Jess asked when she saw the expression on Caspian's face as he watched the fat man disappear round a corner.

'That's Ponsonby Smeelie,' he whispered furtively, forgetting that his friends had no idea of Mr Smeelie's relevance to him.

'Who's that?' Billy asked.

'He's the museum's curator,' Clarissa answered.

Caspian turned to Clarissa, surprised. 'You know him?'

'No,' Clarissa replied, confused. 'I know his name from the visitor information brochure. How do you know him?'

'I don't.' Realising that he was confusing his friends, but with no time to explain, he said, 'Come on,' and set off after Ponsonby Smeelie, not giving the others the opportunity to question why.

Something was definitely up, Caspian thought. Smeelie's squished up little face had been full worry and Caspian felt a compelling need to know what was making him so nervous. Father had described Smeelie as an irrational worrier, but the museum's curator had seemed beyond the point of worry and closer to tipping over the edge with panic.

Smeelie left the Victorian gallery and went down a staircase. Caspian followed, hanging back enough so that he wouldn't be seen; however Smeelie seemed in too much of a rush to notice.

'Caspian, what is –' Clarissa began, but he held a finger to his lips to silence her.

At the bottom of the staircase were a set of toilets, another gallery that was currently closed off whilst it was being prepared for a new exhibition, and another staircase that was gated off with a sign reading *Staff Only*.

Caspian hopped over the gate and was followed by Billy without question. Both the girls hesitated, but soon Jess decided to follow the boys and, not wanting to be left out, Clarissa came begrudgingly after.

They moved quietly down a long white corridor at the bottom of the staircase, somewhere in the museum's basement. Up ahead they could hear Ponsonby Smeelie's squeaky voice, along with an occasional cough, although what he was saying they couldn't be sure.

On either side of them were rooms full of cabinets and various pieces from galleries that had once been on display but since uninstalled, all covered with plastic dust sheets. Smeelie's voice was coming from behind a closed door; the sign on it said *Curator's Office*.

As they neared the door they heard footsteps coming close to the other side, and a menacing raised voice from within.

'Quick, in here!' Billy whispered as loud as he dared. 'Hide!'

The hooded man looked at the pitiful state his associate had worked himself into. He had been caught off guard by this surprise visit, but then intimidation always works best on the unprepared. At least he had given up on the idea of running away, and clearly just the mention of the nebulizer had caused memories of the anguish and agony that he had suffered to rise to the surface. Sweat trickled down Smeelie's fat little face, making his eyes squint and appear even smaller than they were. He wanted to laugh out loud at how pathetic this man was, but that would ruin the moment.

'I am tiring of your excuses,' he said coldly. 'The code is useless to me without the key.'

'I have tried to decipher it, but it isn't just simple alphabetic substitutions,' Smeelie squealed. He sounded terribly afraid.

'The Council appointed Edgar Stone and Edgar Stone alone to guard it, but he would have prepared for every eventuality,' the hooded man said, feeling himself losing patience.

'W…w…what…?' Smeelie stuttered.

He grabbed Smeelie by his podgy shoulders and heaved the heavy man against the office door, knocking it ajar as he dropped trembling to the floor. Standing over him, he said, 'Edgar Stone would have a contingency plan, just in case something was to happen to him. He would ensure it is safe, but never allow for it to be lost. So, *what* eventuality would Edgar Stone prepare for?'

'His death?' Smeelie yelped, barely audible through his terror.

'Yes,' the hooded man answered, curling his disfigured mouth with painful delight around the word. 'In the unlikely event of his death, he would have a plan.'

'Yes,' Smeelie nodded, but no further words came from his whimpering lips. Without warning, he stood on Smeelie's podgy little hand, crushing his sausage shaped digits with the heel of his boot. The museum curator yelled out in pain. 'He would leave a clue,' he cried. 'Something that would mean nothing to most people, but to anyone who knows what they are looking for…'

'It will be a sign,' the hooded man agreed, lifting his foot. 'You have known him for a very long time. Where would he keep this clue?'

'In his home,' Smeelie sobbed, holding his hand like a small delicate creature he was trying to protect from a vicious predator. 'I'm sure it is the only place he would keep it.'

The hooded man kicked Smeelie's hand away and pinned it down with his foot. 'And what will this sign be?'

'I don't know, I don't know!' he cried out. 'I really don't know. He wouldn't tell me. He really wouldn't.'

'But he told you when the event will happen?'

'No, he didn't,' the associate answered warily, clearly fearful of another assault. 'I can't be certain, but everything seems to point to the anomaly occurring in the month of May.'

'*Everything*,' the hooded man repeated cynically. 'You promised me answers, and yet all you have provided are little more than hints, theories, and codes that you can't solve.' He stood over the curator of the museum, his associate, Ponsonby Smeelie, and leant down so that their faces were so close he could smell the fat wimp's stench. 'Do you have any further use?'

'Please…' Smeelie grovelled, so afraid it was embarrassing to call him human.

'However, useless as you have proven to be, your cooperation will not go unnoticed. As agreed, you shall keep your worthless life for as long as my master deems fit. Your assistance is no longer required, so go clean yourself up and carry on about your business. I'm sure I needn't warn you, but should you utter a word about any of this our agreement is void.'

He pushed the office door fully open and stepped over where Smeelie still lay cowering. Without looking back, he quickly headed down the corridor, back towards the secret passage through which he had gained access to the museum's basement.

Caspian heard the footsteps fade. He could hear Ponsonby Smeelie groaning as he got to his feet, but he couldn't move from where he was hidden; he was still shaking. Clarissa had turned so pale it was as though she had been asked to dissect a pig heart again, and both Jess and Billy looked unnerved by what had just transpired.

But what *had* just transpired?

He had not been able to see much, but after the other man had thrown Smeelie against the door, pushing it partly open, he had heard everything and yet could make sense of none of it. He could only listen from his hiding place, paralysed by the overwhelming terror that had taken him.

As the other man left, Caspian had tried to see who he was but the dark hood attached to the long black cloak he wore concealed his head and identity. There was no doubt in Caspian's mind that this was the same hooded man who had tried to gain access to his Father's shop, and something about him struck Caspian with a fear deeper than he had ever known. How had Ponsonby Smeelie become involved with this man, and what were they looking for?

Smeelie whined as he got to his feet. Jess wanted to go and help him, but Caspian held up his hand to stop her. If they were discovered here they might never know what secret the hooded man was trying to find.

The door to the curator's office clicked shut.

'What the hell is going on,' Billy whispered.

All three of Caspian's friends looked at him for an explanation. 'You heard what I heard,' Caspian shrugged. 'I'll explain the rest when we are out of here, but I need to have a look in his office.'

'Why?' Jess questioned.

He looked at the closed door. 'Whatever that man is planning, it somehow involves my father. And I'm sure the answer is in there.'

'How do you expect to get in there whilst the curator is inside?' Clarissa asked, still looking awfully pale.

'You'll need a distraction to draw him out,' Billy said with a smirk. 'I can be of help there.'

'I'll help you search,' Jess said, 'but once we are out you need to tell us everything.'

'Okay, fine,' Caspian answered. 'Billy, how are you going to – '

But before Caspian could finish his question Billy was on his feet and dragging Clarissa unwillingly towards the curator's office door.

'No, wait,' Jess tried to say, but it was too late. Billy knocked loudly on the door.

'Who's there?' Smeelie's voice squeaked irritably from within, clearly not wanting any more visitors.

'What are you doing?' Caspian hissed.

'Just stay hidden,' Billy hissed back, and then turned to face Smeelie as he opened the door.

'What in the devil...?' the curator said with surprise. 'You two shouldn't be down here.'

Clarissa had gone as pale as a ghost again, but this all seemed part of Billy's mischievous plan. 'I think we took a wrong turn,' Billy said innocently. 'My friend is ill and I need to get her to the lobby.'

'Well, it isn't this way,' Smeelie snapped. He hadn't fully opened the door, and Caspian began to worry that he wasn't going to leave the office at all. 'You need to go back the way you came.'

That way would be back up the stairs. Smeelie was giving them directions, not the personal escort Billy was counting on. The plan was not going to work.

That, however, didn't seem to phase Billy who politely chirped, 'okay, thank you. Come on Clarissa, it's this way,' and he quickly dragged her down the corridor in the direction, Caspian realised, that the hooded man had just headed.

'Wait!' Smeelie panicked, undoubtedly realising the same thing, and came rushing out of his office. 'No, not that way.'

'Yes it is,' Billy replied dumbly. 'We just came from down there. I'm sure we'll find our way back the way we came.'

'I said, it isn't that way.' He gave an audible sigh. 'Come on, this way. I'll show you how to get back to the lobby. Come with me.'

Billy and Clarissa walked with Smeelie back towards the staircase they had followed him down, Billy talking loudly and constantly as they went. 'It's such a big building; we followed the sign to the toilets but obviously went to far. I thought the way out was this way too because we had passed the empty exhibition and then…'

As Billy's voice died away Caspian and Jessica darted into the office.

'What are we looking for?' Jess asked.

'I don't really know,' Caspian confessed. 'They said something about a code; let's see if we can find it.'

They quickly began to search filing cabinet drawer after drawer, looking through the contents, unsure how long Billy's ploy would keep Smeelie distracted. Each drawer they opened was filled with tedious museum records, but nothing that resembled any kind of hidden code.

Caspian broke away from searching the filing cabinets and started going through Smeelie's desk. These drawers were quite the contrast to his father's, who kept his methodically organised and scrupulously tidy. Smeelie's were a mess with rail ticket receipts, chocolate bar wrappers, opened letters, theatre brochures, and various other clutter.

He was about to return to the cabinets where Jess was still searching when he read part of the title to a book, half obscured on the desk by a pile of museum financial papers. Caspian moved the papers aside and read the title, *Cryptanalysis & Code-Breaking for Idiots, by Willy Solvitt & Betty Fales*. He opened the book on the page where a slip of paper had been inserted. 'Bingo!'

'Caspian,' Jess said urgently, 'you need to see this.'

'What is it?' Caspian asked, but he was more interested by his own discovery. Handwritten on the slip of paper inside the book were a series of random alphabetic letters. This had to be the code the hooded man had mentioned. Smeelie must have been trying to solve it, hoping the book would act as a reference.

'You need to *see* this!' Jess repeated, but suddenly Caspian's mobile phone started ringing. It was Billy. Caspian answered it.

'He's on his way back to you,' Billy said urgently. 'We kept him as long as we could but you have no more time. Get out of there.' The phone went dead.

'We have to go,' Caspian said, beckoning for Jess to follow. She looked torn between taking and leaving what she had found, but then returned the particular file she had been looking at and slid the cabinet drawer shut. They both rushed to the door and ran down the corridor back towards the staircase.

'Caspian,' Jess said as they got to the stairs. 'You need to listen to me.'

'What is it?' he asked, but before she could answer a very unimpressed looking Ponsonby Smeelie was glaring at them as he made his way down the stairs.

'More children?' he sighed. 'What am I paying security to do?'

'We were just looking for our friends,' Caspian said, trying to emulate the innocence Billy had so naturally conjured. 'A boy and a girl.'

'The girl is ill,' Jess added, 'and the boy – '

'Just won't shut up,' Smeelie finished, sighing heavily. 'Yes, they were here. I just escorted them to the lobby, which you will find at – '

'It's okay, we know the way to the lobby,' Caspian said, and they started up the stairs.

'Just one minute,' Smeelie said putting out an arm, blocking Caspian. He was looking at him with a strange expression on his face, particularly taking a keen interest in his different coloured eyes. 'What is your name?'

'It's Rob. Rob Harper,' Caspian answered without hesitation.

'You remind me of … ' Smeelie began, but he thought better of finishing. 'Never mind, get out of here. The sign says staff only. If you children spent more time reading than you do watching television…'

They shot up the stairs as quickly as they could and made their way back to the lobby to regroup with the others, not wanting to give Smeelie any more time to figure out who exactly Caspian had reminded him of.

XIII:
CONUNDRUM

'It started on the day I came to London. Mr Smeelie sent my father a letter because he was concerned that something my father was looking after was no longer safe.' Caspian, Billy, Clarissa, and Jess had all bought sandwiches from a café near the museum and were huddled around a table whilst Caspian told the story. 'At the time, I had no idea what this letter was about or who had sent it, but it was because of this letter that my father went out the following night. Whilst he was out someone came to Father's shop and tried to get in, but didn't succeed.'

'Who tried to get in?' Billy asked. 'Was it Smeelie?'

'No. It was the man who just threatened him. I saw him, wearing that same outfit, the night I snuck into my father's shop.'

'Do you think Mr Smeelie sent your father the letter to get him out of the way?' Clarissa asked.

'So that the hooded man could break in? Maybe.' Caspian had not connected the two events before, and why would he? Had they not stumbled across the encounter between the hooded man and Ponsonby Smeelie he would have had no reason to form a connection. 'But on the other hand, he also warned my father. Mr Smeelie came to see him on the last day of term. I was with my father, but he told me to hide and to make sure that the man who came to see him didn't see me. I hid, but from my hiding place I heard some of what they talked about. That was how I found out that Mr Smeelie had been the one who'd written the letter.'

Billy leaned in. 'Did they say anything else?'

'Mr Smeelie said that someone was ready to return, and that my father had been solely trusted to keep a weapon safe.'

'What sort of weapon?' Billy asked, rocking back on his chair with excitement.

'I don't know,' Caspian shrugged.

'Hey, here's a thought: maybe your dad's a spy, working for the government? Could be he's trying to keep this weapon out of the hands of the Russians.'

'A spy? Russians? *Really*, Billy?' Clarissa sneered. 'This isn't the Cold War. How would Mr Smeelie and the other man fit into that scenario? Caspian, what else did Smeelie say?'

'He thought there was a risk that someone was going to come looking for the weapon.'

'Well, it seems like he was right,' Clarissa said. 'But if Smeelie is working for that hooded thug, why would he warn your father?'

'Precisely,' Caspian agreed. 'It doesn't make any sense, unless he wasn't working for him at that point. The hooded man could have recruited Mr Smeelie after his first attempt to break into the shop failed.'

'Or he's a double agent,' Billy suggested.

'Seriously?' Clarissa rolled her eyes.

'Do you think the weapon is in your father's antique shop?' Billy continued as if he hadn't heard Clarissa's scoff.

'That wouldn't make sense after what we just overheard. He and Mr Smeelie were trying to crack a code instead of find a weapon.'

'Unless the code explains where it is hidden, just in case…' Billy trailed off.

'…In case something were to happen to my father.' Caspian took out the piece of paper he had removed from Ponsonby Smeelie's office and placed it on the table.

He stared at the encrypted words blankly, without a clue as to what they meant or how to decipher them. Was his father in trouble, or perhaps this was all some big misunderstanding? This weapon he was protecting, was his father really willing to risk his life to keep it safe?

```
FLYDKOJSWTW      KDTJJPSAZMT
TGPBUYYZJHI  QXRKUUWWSEE  JV
KGQHUDNLGEV      JSYDCHYWWAV
IKYKTLZFYOB      MWLQGYIAFNA
YGRX
```

```
YZJOKJWWYSB      MWDOUBLZYTW
YZJEXNWSAEA      IAIPNLDLFKM
NFYDOZXMGTT      JHQWILFEJSA
FYJEYONVIEV      NFFDOKIWSKM
JHXWQL
```

'Is it in Russian?' Billy asked hopefully, leaning back in his chair once again.

'No,' Clarissa sighed.

Caspian noticed that Jess hadn't said a word since their encounter with Ponsonby Smeelie on the staircase. Now, whilst the other two were fixated with the code, she was staring at him.

'What is it?' he asked.

'I think there is more to your father than we know,' Jess said bleakly.

From her tone Caspian knew that she meant more than the obvious. There was something else. 'What *did* you find in that filing cabinet?'

'There was an entire drawer, dedicated to your father,' Jess answered.

'What do you mean by "dedicated?" ' Caspian asked apprehensively. 'You mean that Mr Smeelie had been gathering information *about* my father?'

'Yes.'

Father had obviously known Smeelie for a long time, so who better to be corrupted into working against him than someone already within that circle of trust. But if Ponsonby Smeelie had managed to collect an entire drawer's worth of information it was beginning to look like Smeelie had been involved with the hooded man for longer than they thought.

'It isn't the quantity of information collected that I thought you should know about – it's the content,' Jess said solemnly. 'I had a look in a couple of the files in that drawer to see what information Smeelie was keeping – I actually thought that was where we would find the code. One of the files was full of pictures of your father, newspaper clippings, pages from the national records office and more. The thing is, they were all taken from a long time ago.'

Caspian shrugged. 'That isn't that surprising. If they were gathering information they would have to look at my father's past.'

'No, you don't understand,' Jess said firmly. 'When I say long ago, I'm not talking five, ten, or twenty years. The records on your father go back for *hundreds* of years!'

Jess' statement was suddenly punctuated with an almighty *CRASH!* The excitement had clearly overwhelmed Billy – and his sense of balance.

'What do you mean hundreds of years?' Caspian asked once Billy was back in his chair and all four legs were firmly on the ground.

'I was wrong: your dad's not a spy, he's a Time Lord,' Billy declared, his theory escalating from Dr. No to Doctor Who.

Caspian ignored his friend's comments. 'There must have been a lot of people named Edgar Stone throughout history.'

'But why would Mr Smeelie gather information about *other* Edgar Stone's?' Clarissa asked. 'He knows that your

137

father is the one keeping the weapon. It doesn't make sense?'

'There has to be a logical explanation for this,' Caspian said.

Billy muttered, 'Time Lord,' under his breath.

'And this doesn't give us any clue as to how we solve this code.' Caspian looked at the blocks of letters that appeared to have been generated at random. 'We have absolutely no idea what this is or how to decipher it.'

'Smeelie said there is a clue,' Billy said. 'He said it would be in your father's house, and that anyone who didn't know what they were looking for would miss it.'

'*We* don't know what we're looking for,' Clarissa pointed out. 'Do you have any idea what this clue could be?'

'Not in the slightest,' Caspian replied. He had lived with his father for a couple of months now, and nothing seemed to hint at being helpful to decipher the code before him.

'Let's see what we *can* tell from this code. Maybe that will give us a better idea as to what we are looking for.' Jess suggested. 'For instance, has anyone else noticed that most of these blocks of letters are eleven letters long?'

Clarissa leaned in. 'It would be difficult to make a sentence using only eleven letter words.'

'Exactly,' Jess agreed. 'So there might be a second level of encryption used.'

'What does that mean?' Billy asked.

'It means that even if we do decipher the code, there is a high likelihood that another form of encoding has been used to hide the message further.'

'That's not fair,' Billy protested.

'I don't think this information was meant to be easy to decipher,' Caspian said despairingly. 'No wonder Mr Smeelie was in such a state about cracking this; we don't even know where to begin.'

'Smeelie was working to the timeline of a psychotic man in a cloak – What's with that, anyway?' Billy asked. 'Point is, there's four of us, and we've got more time than Smeelie had.'

'What was it they said about an anomaly?' Clarissa asked.

'It's going to take place in May,' Jess replied, 'or so Mr Smeelie thought.'

'Yeah, but what is?' Billy asked.

Everyone looked blank. Considering all that they had heard, no one was sure what May might bring.

'So we have until May to solve this?' Caspian sincerely hoped it wouldn't take four months to solve. How long would it take the hooded man to crack? 'What if he solves it first?'

'Well,' Jess said uncertainly, as though she was dipping her foot into a hot bath to test the water. 'There is another option that might speed things up, but you probably won't like it.'

'And that is?'

'Tell your father what's going on.'

'Are you serious!'

'Completely,' Jess replied. 'He is supposed to be keeping this thing safe, and you have information that will help him to do so. If Mr Smeelie is working against him, and if that hooded creep is planning something too, he needs to know.'

This was the voice of reason speaking, but Caspian was sceptical about it being the best way to proceed. 'Do you know what happened when I told Father that the hooded man had tried to get into the shop? He dismissed the entire thing like I had imagined it, even though he knew I hadn't. Whenever I've tried to bring up the incident he shuts me out or changes the subject. He doesn't want me to know about *him*.'

'He's probably just trying to keep you safe,' Jess said. 'Look what happened to Mr Smeelie.'

'He also told me to hide when Mr Smeelie came to visit,' Caspian continued. 'He didn't want Smeelie to see me, and we've just bumped into him on the staircase after taking something from his office. How am I going to explain to my father that we followed Mr Smeelie because I thought he looked suspicious?'

'But *that's* the truth.'

'Not everyone believes the truth,' Caspian said bitterly. 'We have until May to crack this code. If we can get to the weapon before that shady guy does, we can move it somewhere else.'

'Why?' Jess asked. 'What good will that do?'

'I know next to nothing about my father,' Caspian answered. 'Apparently he is a member of some secret council. He is in charge of hiding weapons, which means he could be an arms dealer or a terrorist for all I know.'

'Or a spy, or a Time Lord,' Billy added.

'I just want to find out the truth, and if I see it for myself then I won't have to question whether it is true or not.'

Jess gave him a long look. 'Well, for the record, I think you're making a big mistake.'

'Does that mean you won't help?' Caspian inquired.

'No, I'll help,' Jess shrugged. 'But I won't enjoy it.'

Caspian smiled, knowing his friend too well. 'I bet that not only do you crack this code, but you enjoy doing it too.'

Jess looked at his outstretched hand like he was being conceited, but she shook it all the same, to which Billy let out a loud *whoop* with excitement.

The game was on.

For all his life, Billy Long had had to fight for every ounce of attention he could get whilst he was at home. He was the third of five brothers, separated by a four year gap on both sides. For a while he had been the baby of the family, but then along came Troy, shortly followed by Sam, at which point he had been forgotten about all together. Over the years he had found that there were other ways to get noticed and had excelled at being the biggest pain in the backside, which explained his obligation to wreak havoc everywhere he went; it didn't help that he really, *really* enjoyed doing it.

Working on breaking the code in Clarissa's living room had proven to be more than an exercise in self-control for poor Billy, whose attention span was more restless than a dog with a sore bottom.

It didn't help that Clarissa's older sister, Selena, kept walking in and out of the living room whilst she was setting the television to record various reality TV shows she was into. Selena was in the upper sixth and exceptionally beautiful, and on many occasions Billy was caught staring at her with his mouth open.

'Blimey,' Billy said after Selena had left the room. 'Now I understand why Devon fancies *her*.' Devon Long was the second eldest of the Long brothers, and he was in the same Year as Selena at school.

Jess just shook her head, but Clarissa gave that remark a particularly scornful look.

They spent most of the remainder of the school holiday round Clarissa's as Billy's household proved too distracting to get anything done, and they thought it best not to try deciphering the code right under Caspian's father's nose. Each evening though, Caspian and Jess would make a subtle sweep of his house, trying to find anything that could be considered a clue, hidden in plain sight, which might help to provide the answer. However, as most things in Father's home were a little unusual anyway there was really nothing that jumped out at them.

As well as being very clever, Jess was also particularly good at essay writing. With her help, Caspian crafted one of the best reports he had ever written for his History assignment. They managed to incorporate a lot of the information Caspian had learned at the museum, and backed it up with photographs taken at the time. He titled it "*The Expansion of Subterranean Victorian London*," and even Clarissa, who hated admitting other people's work was better than her own, agreed it was an excellent title.

New Year's Eve came and went, and soon it was time for Jess to return to Little Bickham and for the holidays to come to an end. Caspian and his group of friends had celebrated the New Year at his father's house, where Mrs Hodges had laid a fine spread of party food and cakes.

At ten to midnight, Jess had found Caspian standing alone, staring out the large bay windows of the living room, lost in thought about all that was happening, and all that his father was keeping from him in spite of his new policy of openness and honesty.

'I suppose I needn't ask if you have any New Year's resolutions,' she said quietly to him.

He gave her a knowing smile.

'Caspian, you have so much going on in your life right now…' She was referring to his mother's illness. They were still awaiting any positive news. 'I'm just worried about you,' she said softly. 'It's one thing to distract yourself from what is going on, but quite another to be consumed by it.'

'Is that why you think I'm trying to break this code?' he asked. 'As a distraction?'

'Is there another reason?'

Caspian sighed. 'I don't know anymore, Jess. Everything is becoming so blurred. All I want is answers and the truth, but everything seems to be wrapped up in lies, or kept at a distance.'

'I'm sure there is a good reason…'

'For my protection?' Caspian couldn't help sounding cynical.

'One minute to go,' Mrs Hodges chirped from upstairs. Everyone else had gathered on the upper floor where they would have the best view of the fireworks.

'Come on, Cas,' Jess said. 'Let's go join the others.'

'Okay,' Caspian agreed.

They all cheered and shouted as the entire sky above the city exploded in flashes of colourful light, enormous bangs and blasts thumping through the air like a God playing a drum solo.

As the fireworks glittered over the rooftops, Caspian still couldn't take his mind off the code, Smeelie's deception, and his father's secret. He thought to himself with determination, *I will break the code. I have to.*

XIV:
THE CRUEL METHODS OF MR DENT

Hogarth House High School had been built in an area of Chelsea where playing fields were not in abundance. To resolve this lack of recreational ground, the school bus ferried students to a large sports field that was shared by a sports facility in the area, where Games lessons were held.

Caspian had been in separate lessons to his friends for his first day back at school after Christmas, meaning that he was forced to face alone the ridicule and spite his peers directed at him in response to his supposed bullying of Julie McFadden. He was grateful Hayden Tanner was still treating him normally, but he was really looking forward to the afternoon when he would finally share a lesson with both Billy and Clarissa.

'Do you think it's true?' Billy asked as he plonked himself beside Caspian on the school bus. As well as being the first day back for all the students, it was also the first day back for someone else. 'I mean, Mrs Scrudge said he would be back after Christmas, but I didn't expect him to come back *today*.'

'Has anyone seen him?' Caspian asked.

'I haven't,' Clarissa shrugged.

'Well, in English before lunch, Joe Gibbons said he had him this morning. Apparently he's already made two girls cry.'

'Selena told me he is the worst teacher she has ever had,' Clarissa added.

'He can't really be *that* bad, can he?' Caspian asked.

'Devon said he was alright,' Billy commented.

'Devon was on the rugby team for two years,' Caspian pointed out. 'Everyone knows the only students he treats nicely are those that play for *The Hornets*.'

'Or any prospective Hornets,' Clarissa added.

There had been an unsettled atmosphere on the school bus that afternoon, as everyone had heard through one means or another that they would no longer be having the very timid Ms Weaver for Games as Mr Dent had returned. He had sustaining an injury during a rugby tournament last year, despite that he had actually been coaching rather than playing the sport. An altercation with another coach had escalated into more than just an exchange of words and resulted in Mr Dent damaging a pre-existing hamstring condition.

The class became even more unsettled, half of the students on the bus moved to the other side to get a better look at the man approaching them.

Mr Dent had once played professional rugby, but had been forced to retire early from the sport. Unable to play the game he loved, and forced into a job he hated, he became bitter and resentful, and his unfortunate students were made sentenced to bear his failings in life – mainly in the form of press ups.

The only group to escape his wrath were those who made the school's rugby team, The Hogarth Hornets, which he coached. You had to be in years ten or eleven to even tryout for the team, and it was composed mostly of the school's meatheads and thugs. Caspian knew without a shadow of a doubt that Dent would already have Rob Harper, Rose Wetherby's bullying oath of a boyfriend, in his sights for next year's team tryouts.

He was not a tall man; however, with a shaven head and arms that looked like huge sacks of potatoes, there was a psychopathic quality about him that matched perfectly with his psychopathic reputation. Mr Dent was renown about the school for being the meanest, nastiest, and most prejudice of all the teachers, and his return was by no means a reason to celebrate.

'Good afternoon, *ladies*,' Dent growled as he climbed aboard the school bus, gripping the handrail so tightly his knuckles went white. He winced with every step as he tried to support himself on what was clearly not a fully recovered hamstring, which only seemed to further infuriate him.

'What a bunch of *girlies* you lot are!' he sneered. 'It makes me wonder whether you have a Y chromosome between the lot of you. Every year the class seems to get weedier and weedier.' Dent dropped awkwardly into his seat at the front of the bus and called to the driver, 'Let's get this over with!'

'Well, he seems ghastly,' Clarissa commented.

'At least you only have him for this year,' Caspian said. 'Next year girls and boys have separate Games. You'll have Ms Weaver again, whilst we'll be stuck with *Corporal Punishment.*'

'Devon said he was one of Mr Dent's protégées when he was on the team. Maybe that will go in my favour,' Billy said hopefully.

'Maybe. Or on the other hand, his expectations of you might be much higher,' Clarissa pointed out.

'Oh,' Billy said solemnly. 'I didn't think of that,'

They arrived at the sports facilities and went to get changed into their sports kits. As Caspian set down his sports bag, he felt Rob Harper's menacing eyes upon him.

'Keep an eye on your things, guys,' Rob advised everyone in the changing room. '*Sticky-fingers* Stone might go through your bags if you don't watch him.'

Caspian balled his fist, but Hayden caught his eye and shook his head.

'Hey, back off, Rob,' Billy said, standing up for him.

'Why? What are *you* gonna do?' Rob taunted. 'Billy Long by name, Billy *Short* by nature.'

Many of the boys in the changing room laughed, making Billy feel even smaller than his lack of height had already accomplished.

'Don't worry, I'm not going to do anything,' Rob grinned. 'By the time Mr Dent's finished with you two, he'll probably make you get changed with the girls.'

More laughter followed from his flock of supporters.

'What's his problem,' Billy said to Caspian whilst they were getting changed.

'He's a dickhead,' Caspian replied. 'Don't you think it was strange that he knew I had that diary when even *I* didn't know I had it?'

'Yeah, I suppose so. Why? Do you think he set you up?'

Caspian nodded. 'He's had it in for me since I first met him.'

'Well, you do fancy his girlfriend,' Billy smirked.

There was no denying that, Caspian thought. 'It seems I'm not her type though.'

'What, big and muscular?'

'More like, big and stupid. Have you finished your history report yet?'

'Don't remind me,' Billy sulked. 'I've still got loads to do on it. Clarissa says she's done hers. I can't believe you've also finished already.'

'Already? It's due *tomorrow*,' Caspian said. 'Mine's in my locker, all set to present in the morning.'

'You're not making me feel any better.'

'I wasn't trying to,' Caspian shrugged, 'and how would that help, anyway?'

'Cheers mate,' Billy mocked, pulling his sports jersey over his head. 'What are friends for?'

'Having your back, and taking the piss,' Caspian laughed.

'Well,' Billy grinned, 'you certainly excel in the latter.'

The class lined up wearily outside whilst Mr Dent glared at the lot of them like a deranged drill sergeant intimidating his troops.

'Right,' he bellowed once everyone was ready. They all felt like they were facing a firing squad. 'No more mollycoddling for you, you bunch of babies. Playtime is officially over.'

'I thought games were supposed to be *played*,' Billy said wryly, which was a massive mistake.

'You!' Dent hollered like a shot from a gun. 'What is your name?!'

'B…B…Billy Long,' he stuttered.

'That's Billy Long, *Sir!*' The last word was shouted so loudly that more than half the class jumped, but then his tone altered. 'Long, hey? Are you related to Devon Long, by any chance?'

'Yes,' Billy said hopefully, giving Caspian and Clarissa a subtle I-told-you-so-look, before hastily adding, 'Sir.'

'Devon was such a disappointment,' Dent spat. 'It would seem this is your family trait. Well, *Billy.* For talking without permission you can start doing star jumps.'

'How many?' Billy asked.

'UNTIL I TELL YOU TO STOP!' Mr Dent roared. 'The rest of you miserable lot will be doing a spot of cross-country running. Get into same sex pairs and get running round the field – the whole field. If you don't run fast enough you will find yourself doing star jumps alongside Mr Long, here.'

Clarissa paired off with a girl from her class and Caspian paired up with Hayden Tanner. Mr Dent ran behind them shouting 'FASTER, *FASTER!*' at the top of his lungs.

'But what if we need to rest?' Someone asked.

'*But what if we need to rest?*' Mr Dent imitated in an exaggerated whiny voice. 'If you need to rest, then just sit down and rest.' A menacing smile stretched across his thin lips. 'But if you do, then your running partner must do press-ups until you have regained your breath.'

The grounds were decorated with Hogarth Hornet's banners as the school's rugby team used the facilities as their practice ground. The athletics field was roughly the size of four football pitches. By their second lap half the class were tiring.

'He's going to kill us,' Caspian said to Hayden as they overtook a pair of boys who were practically dragging each other onwards, trying earnestly to prevent each other from having to do press-ups. 'He's a maniac.'

Hayden shrugged his shoulders. 'But from a motivational perspective his plan is almost perfect. Look at those two we just passed. Neither will stop running for fear of torturing the other. Those who do stop will not stop for long, as resting comes with the price of guilt for making their partners suffer. Military academies have used similar tactics to form fellowships, encouraging each soldier to push themselves further in order to keep their buddy from punishment, all in the name of camaraderie.'

'But, this is a school,' Caspian pointed out, 'not the army.'

'Maybe so,' Hayden agreed, 'but then take a look at some of our classmates. The only exercise some of them do is lifting a fork to their mouths, and chewing doesn't burn off the amount of calories they ingest.'

'You can't be serious,' Caspian said, starting to pant. Hayden on the other hand was barely breaking a sweat – how was he so fit?

'I'm entirely serious,' Hayden replied. 'They need to get in shape, and in this world you have to be cruel to be kind – like the methods Mr Dent is employing now.'

Caspian was surprised to hear this coming from Hayden; it was a side of him he never knew existed. 'You said his plan was *almost* perfect,' Caspian said, breathing heavily. 'What did you mean?'

'I meant that guilt is not always enough to motivate someone. Would Mr Dent's methods work on someone of a selfish disposition who was less inclined to feel guilt? What happens if a malicious element is introduced into the equation?'

'I don't understand,' Caspian said, unsure where Hayden was going with this.

Hayden looked at him and smiled darkly. Then he stopped running and sat down.

Caspian stopped as well, surprised by the suddenness of his running partner's actions. His heart was pounding heavily in his chest now, and he appreciated the moment to catch his breath. 'What are you doing?' He asked Hayden.

'Resting,' Hayden replied as though it were the most obvious thing in the world.

'But you are not even tired!'

Hayden just smiled back at him. Mr Dent's Neanderthal-like commands boomed across the field like a cannon aimed at Caspian. '*You*! Press-ups! NOW!'

Bewildered by what was happening, Caspian dropped to his hands and assumed a press-up stance. As he lowered his chest towards the cold wet muddy grass of the athletics field he could see Hayden watching him with amusement.

By his fifth press-up, Hayden showed no intention of getting to his feet and instead commented, 'lovely day, isn't it?'

'Why are you doing this?' Caspian gasped, his back and biceps burning with exertion.

'I'm being malicious,' Hayden said casually. 'I thought that was clear.'

'But why?'

'Because I can,' Hayden replied. 'I have the power here – but you've already witnessed that, haven't you, even if you didn't realise it then. It took but a modicum of time to lift you to the peak of popularity and, when that became dull, well I just plucked that popularity from beneath your feet.'

'What?' Caspian asked, unable to add further words to what barely constituted a sentence let alone a question.

'This is all a game, Caspian Stone,' Hayden said coolly, 'and I'm willing to see how far you can be pushed before you break. My reputation precedes me at Hogarth High; I am the golden boy, the teacher's favourite, our classmate's idol. I am not being arrogant in saying this; I am simply being perceptive. But what *nobody* seems to have perceived is that *I* have managed to portray you to all of them as a liar and a thief.'

Caspian halted his press-ups and stared with disbelief into Hayden's ice-blue eyes. '*You?*'

Hayden smiled that charming smile of his. 'Yes.'

'It was you who stole Julie's diary,' Caspian deduced.

'Mmm hmm,' Hayden nodded.

'You photocopied those pages and spread them round school.'

'Along with the rumour that you had done it,' Hayden added. 'Don't forget *that*.'

'You two!' Mr Dent's voice roared toward them from across the field. 'Why have you stopped!?'

'You put her diary in my locker,' Caspian continued, feeling anger and betrayal bubbling in the pit of his stomach. When the missing diary had been revealed to be inside his locker he had seen Hayden in the corridor, looking at him with disappointment. But that wasn't real – he had been there to watch the show.

'And I let Rob know what you were up to,' Hayden smiled. 'After how upset you got when I took credit for returning Rose's bracelet, and how easy it became to make it seem like *you* were just trying to take the credit yourself, you allowed me to mould your image into someone who lies to look good, willing to steal and spread someone's most

151

intimate secrets to just gain and maintain your popularity. That doesn't sound like a very nice person, does it?'

Fire was coursing through Caspian's veins. He had been so certain it was Rob who had planted the diary that he never suspected the involvement of any other, but the clues had been there. How had Billy described the mastermind behind the diary prank? He'd said they were *brilliant*. Well Rob Harper could neither be described as brilliant, nor a mastermind, but Caspian had been blinded of the truth, all because he was jealous that Rose Wetherby was with Rob Harper instead of him.

'The thing with you, Caspian, is that you are easy to manipulate, like putty. You, just like everyone else in this *stupid* school, are easy to mould to my will, and believe me – you *will* mould to it.'

Caspian's anger was magnified by the devastating blow that Hayden, someone he thought he could trust, had turned out to be the sole conspirator behind the miserable time he was having at school. 'I'm going to get you for this,' Caspian vowed bitterly.

'Of course you will,' Hayden said serenely, getting to his feet and standing face to face with Caspian. 'After all, you are just so terribly predictable.'

'Am I really?' Caspian snapped at the handsome face that concealed such cruel intentions. He clenched his hand into a fist and pulled it back ready to hurl it like a sledgehammer at the chiselled features of Hayden's face. But when he went to swing, his hand remained where it was, locked in a vice like grip before it swung behind his back forcing him into a painful arm lock.

'Try to punch someone in my class, will you?' Mr Dent hissed venomously in Caspian's ear, holding his wrist so tightly it felt like he would snap it off his arm like a twig from a tree branch. 'You,' he said, pointing at Hayden, 'have had enough rest. Start running or the next person to try and hit you will be *me*, and I throw much quicker!'

Without hesitation, Hayden set off at a sprint. Caspian watched him go, welling with hatred. Not only did he now know the truth about Hayden Tanner, but he had also been manoeuvred into a trap. He was furious, his only desire to hold Hayden down and pummel him with both hands until that handsome fake exterior matched his bona fide rotten innards.

Mr Dent dragged him across the athletics field, still in an excruciating arm lock. They passed Billy who was now on the verge of collapsing – his star jumps more closely resembling sluggish flops – but despite his exhaustion he still managed a curious glance in Caspian's direction. Mr Dent shoved him onward and sent him to get changed, and then told him to sit on the bus and await the end of class. 'Wait here,' Dent instructed, 'and once we are back at the school we will decide just how *extensive* your punishment will be.'

Being forced to miss out on the rest of Dent's lesson turned out not to be an entirely bad thing, Caspian realised when his classmates limped and slumped onto the bus after the lesson, moaning of aches and pains. But despite being exhausted, weary, and many on the verge of tears, this didn't stop numerous mean words or hard glances being sent in Caspian's direction.

'Hayden told us what you said to him,' one girl said to Caspian as she took her seat. 'I hope they expel you.'

'If they don't,' Rob Harper added, 'you'd better watch your back.'

What lies had Hayden been feeding them whilst he was incarcerated in the school bus? Caspian was about to react when Clarissa took his arm and shook her head. Billy slumped into the empty seat on his other side, but lacked the energy to say a single word.

'Is it true?' Clarissa asked discreetly. 'Did you try to hit Hayden?'

Caspian nodded.

'But why?'

'Because he was the one who put Julie's diary in my locker,' Caspian said. 'He set me up to take the fall for it.'

Billy's eyes widened, but Clarissa was having none of it. 'It must have been a misunderstanding, Caspian. He wouldn't do that.'

'Wouldn't he?' Caspian asked. 'No, I suppose that would be completely out of his character. Where as I, on the other hand, am prone to publishing people's diaries.'

'That's not what I meant.'

'No, you are right,' Caspian said. 'It would take someone who is exceptionally clever to pull off the sort of scam I am implying.' He gave Billy a meaningful look.

Hayden was one of the last to get on the bus, ensuring there was a full audience to see his arrival. He gave Caspian a look of pity and shook his head before taking his seat. This little act for the benefit of the class made Caspian want to rush over to where he sat and try to punch him all over again, but thankfully he now had better control of his fists.

The school bus pulled up outside Hogarth House and the class filed back into the building to collect their bags from their lockers before leaving for the day. When Caspian stepped off the bus an irritable looking Mr Dent was there, waiting for him. 'Judgement time,' he grinned, and Caspian suspected that Mr Dent really enjoyed watching punishments being dealt.

He was escorted to the headmaster's office where he was told to sit and wait outside whilst Mr Dent went in to explain the situation – or at least the limited version of events that he understood to be the situation – to Headmaster Clay.

Eventually Caspian was called in and took a seat before the headmaster. Mr Clay, headmaster of Hogarth House High School, was a very slender and quiet man who more closely resembled a priest than he did a figure of discipline.

Known for being a kindly man, Caspian suspected he might not look as kindly upon boys who threaten to hit their classmates.

'That will be all, thank you,' Mr Clay said softly to Mr Dent, who had been lingering in the doorway with a horrible smile on his face.

The smile quickly vanished. 'You mean I can't watch … er … I mean … shouldn't I sit in?'

'I don't think that will be necessary,' the headmaster responded calmly. 'I won't be needing any protection, will I Caspian?'

Caspian shook his head.

'There we are, Donald,' Mr Clay said kindly. 'I will take it from here.'

Donald Dent! Mr Dent's full name suddenly made him seem a lot less threatening.

'It's *Don*,' Dent said through gritted teeth, before storming out and letting the door slam behind him.

'He does get awfully tetchy,' Mr Clay said thoughtfully. He leaned forward and tucked his long skinny limbs under his chin like a praying mantis. 'Now then, Caspian, I hear there were some issues over at the sports ground this afternoon. Would you care to elaborate on what happened?'

Like it matters what I say, Caspian thought. As Hayden had said, he had already been painted a liar and untrustworthy. Who would believe his word against "Wonder-boy" Hayden's?

'I'm sure Mr Dent has already told you what happened,' Caspian replied.

'Ah, but words are not really Mr Dent's strongest suit, especially when it requires taking a neutral perspective. He is much better suited to giving orders than he is giving testimonies, and I'd quite like to hear your version of what happened.'

Caspian tried to take a deep breath, but it were as though his lungs rejected the air he gave them. Deflated, he said, 'I tried to punch Hayden, but Mr Dent stopped me.'

'In my experience, the action is almost always preceded by provocation, and very rarely the other way round,' the headmaster said smoothly. 'So what, pray tell, did the good Mr Tanner do to deserve a thick ear being dealt?'

Caspian thought how he could answer. He so wanted to tell the whole truth, but the whole truth was so unbelievable that it seemed fictional. He sighed, 'He said some things to make me angry.'

'It sounds like he succeeded,' Mr Clay observed. 'Caspian, we need never use physical violence to solve our problems – it often causes more problems than it solves. The victor is not he who lands the first blow, but he who can walk away from the battle without landing any.'

'That doesn't sound like winning,' Caspian thought out loud.

'No, it doesn't,' Mr Clay laughed. 'But maybe one day you will understand what I meant by that turn of phrase.'

Caspian looked at the thin man sat opposite him. 'Aren't you going to tell me off?' he asked hesitantly.

'Should I?'

'I tried to hit someone,' Caspian shrugged, not really understanding why the headmaster was being so pleasant to him.

Mr Clay slid smoothly from his chair and walked over to his office window. He seemed much taller than Caspian had realised. 'We are not here to work against you, Caspian. Not all lessons in life can be learnt through punishment. No, we are here to work *with* you. I know that many of my faculty, like many of your classmates, are prone to taking sides and being biased towards the obvious truth, but sometimes the truth isn't as obvious as it seems.'

Caspian didn't know what to say. What was Mr Clay getting at?

The headmaster continued, 'I am aware of the circumstances that brought you to us, that you deal with silently every day.'

'Oh,' Caspian said, his throat suddenly drying up. He had tried so hard to keep school and his mother's illness separate, as they seemed so far from each other. But now Mr Clay seemed to be breaking down the walls that separated them.

'Of all the students in this school, you have a valid reason to be upset and angry, and we need to be able to support you. Where necessary we need to be able to make exceptions for you.'

'I don't want to be treated differently,' Caspian said quietly.

'Even the strong need someone to lean on from time to time,' Mr Clay said. 'And when the time comes, Caspian, we will be there to support you.'

'Okay.' Caspian didn't want to talk about this subject. He didn't even want to think about what Mr Clay was implying. Even having Mr Dent shout at him was more preferable than enduring this torturous matter.

'You can go now,' the headmaster said. 'Please think about what has been said here. And just so you know, my door is always open.'

'I'm not getting detention?' Caspian asked, somewhat disconcerted.

'No, Caspian,' Mr Clay smiled sadly, 'you will not be getting detention.'

'Am I not getting punished at all?' he asked, wondering to himself why he was suddenly so desperate for some form of punishment.

The smile faded from Mr Clay's saddened face. 'Unfortunately, there is no punishment I can give that is worse than that you already have to face.'

XV:
SHADOWS IN THE DARK

'I can't believe you got away with it!' Billy said as Caspian opened his locker.

'I didn't really get away with it.' Caspian had found Billy and Clarissa waiting for him after his encounter in the headmaster's office.

'Yeah, you did,' Billy replied. 'You tried to hit someone, got taken to the headmaster's office, and *didn't* get detention. *That*, by definition, is getting away with it!'

'Well, it doesn't feel like a victory.' He really wasn't in the mood to see Billy's positive grasp of the situation. He took his bag out of his locker and noticed that his history report and notebook were not there.

'It wasn't a victory at all,' Clarissa said snootily, interjecting with her opinion on the matter. 'There was no need to try and hit Hayden.'

'No need?' Caspian snapped. 'He lured me into attacking him. He lured me into a trap.'

'Hayden said it was a simple misunderstanding.'

Irritated, Caspian rooted through the folders in his locker. 'Of course it was,' he said sarcastically. His history report was nowhere to be found, and Clarissa's persistence was not helping his temperament.

'Maybe he's right,' Clarissa added. 'He said that you think he's out to get you.'

'He *is* out to get me,' Caspian retorted. 'He said so during Games.'

'That doesn't sound like Hayden.'

'Which is why he has the perfect alibi.'

'I don't know, Caspian,' Billy said. 'Hayden's popular and smart. He isn't a bully.'

Caspian laughed cynically. 'Yeah, he's smart all right. He's managed to use his popularity to pull the wool over your eyes, over everyone's eyes. He's cruel, and he's mean, and he always makes sure his plans can never be traced back to him.'

'You sound like you are talking about an evil genius,' Billy laughed, trying to lighten the mood.

'Maybe he is,' Caspian said bitterly. 'But I'd appreciate a bit more support from you two. Is that too much to ask for?'

'I'd like to believe you,' Clarissa said, 'but there just isn't any evidence to prove it.'

'So I have to prove it to you, do I?' Caspian said angrily. 'I have to *prove* it to my supposed friends.'

'I didn't mean it like that,' Clarissa replied, her voice suddenly high pitched.

'You won't believe me until you see proof, that's what you said.'

'I'm not saying I don't believe you,' Clarissa said defensively, 'I just think that maybe you want Hayden to be the villain. So much so that you are not seeing things clear – '

Caspian threw the contents of his locker onto the floor with frustration, interrupting Clarissa and making her jump back in alarm.

'What's wrong, mate?' Billy tentatively asked.

'My report,' Caspian said as he rummaged through the files on the floor. 'It's not here. I had it here this morning, but it's gone.'

'It has to be here,' Billy said.

'It isn't. I've looked a hundred times through these folders and it isn't here. It's gone.'

'But where could it have gone?' Billy asked. 'If you put it in your locker, nobody could have taken it.'

However, that wasn't true. Caspian flashed with rage. He knew who had been in his locker and taken his report:

the same person who had opened his locker before to incriminate him with Julie's diary. Only one person he knew could do this: Hayden Tanner.

Not only had Hayden expected Caspian to try and hit him, he had known that it would result in him being detained, allowing time to gain access to his locker and steal his report and notebook. Without it, Caspian would have nothing to submit or present in class tomorrow. The confrontation on the athletics field was a distraction, and this his master plan.

He looked at his friends, who now seemed to regard him as though he were a cross between a venomous snake readying to attack and a lunatic who had found a way to wriggle free of his straightjacket. He knew they wouldn't believe him if he once again blamed this on Hayden Tanner's doing.

'Caspian?' Clarissa said, as though she were handling an explosive device that had just been armed.

'Just leave me alone,' he muttered quietly as he started shoving papers, folders, and notebooks back into his rucksack. Clarissa backed away but Billy tried to help pick up his belongings. 'No!' Caspian smacked away Billy's helping hands. 'I said leave me alone!' he roared.

'Come on,' Clarissa said. As his friends walked off, Billy turned back as if to say something but Clarissa shook her head and they left Caspian alone.

He pushed the rest of his fallen schoolwork into his bag and left in the opposite direction they had taken, feeling absolutely furious as he walked home by himself. Once again Hayden Tanner had gotten one over him, but he was determined not to let him win.

Despite his notebook being stolen along with the report, he could remember a lot of the key points he had written. It would mean a long night, but with enough willpower and hard work he might be able to replicate the work he and Jessica had done.

I'm willing to see how far you can be pushed before you break. Hayden's words repeated inside his head. This thought galvanised his determination. He wouldn't let Hayden keep winning, but how could he beat him?

He tried to recall what Mr Clay had said to him; something about the victor is not the one who lands the first blow, but the one who doesn't land any and walks away. That was exactly what Hayden had achieved: he had walked away victorious every time, never leaving any evidence behind suggesting his involvement. Each time he had been able to manoeuvre Caspian to do exactly what he expected him to do to. *After all, you are so terribly predictable.* How was Hayden so astute to his every action?

By the time he was almost home, Caspian's mind had drifted from Hayden Tanner to his mother. Mr Clay's parting comment had left him feeling unnerved about his mother's situation, as though someone had pulled back a sheet to reveal a monster hiding in the room. The monster had been there all along, but whilst it had been covered up and out of sight it had slipped out of his mind.

He had last spoken to Mother on New Year's Day, and she had not sounded as joyful as she had when they spoke at Christmas. In fact, she had seemed quiet and not particularly responsive to what Caspian had told her, but at the time he had put this down to her probably just being tired. So distracted had he been with everything that seemed to be happening involving his father that keeping track of Mother's condition had slipped into second place.

Who have I become? Less than a year ago he wouldn't have dreamed of going more than a day without speaking to his mother. Now with each passing day he grew more and more disconnected with her.

His trip to the headmaster's office meant that he was thirty minutes later than normal when he turned onto Old Church Street. It was early January and the nights were still closing in early, so at this time the only light provided was that of the street lamps. But, as he turned and looked down the road where his father's home was located, there was no light from the street lamps at all.

That was strange, he thought, seeing that the lamps on all the other streets were illuminated. Had there been a power failure that was only affecting this particular road?

He started carefully down the dark street, which seemed strangely deserted for this early in the evening. He could barely distinguish the tops of the houses that leaned in over him from the darkness above; apart from the dull orange glow that light pollution tainted the sky.

The only light in the whole street poured out of his father's shop front, ignorant to the gloom surrounding it. As he drew nearer he could see his father still working inside, busy cataloguing an item. Just when he was about to step out of the black and into the light something moved on the roof opposite and he froze.

On the edge of his peripheral vision he had glimpsed something, black against the blackness. It had probably just been a cat moving across the rooftops, but his heart began to thump.

From where he stood the night consumed him as much as whatever else was out there with him. Even so, he backed against a wall and slid into the doorway of a neighbouring home.

Was he being irrational? Surely he was too old to be scared of the dark? Either way, something about this evening made him feel uneasy.

The light from Turner & Stone Antiques dimly lit the building opposite. Caspian scanned the house, floor by floor, bay window and balcony, searching for what he had merely glimpsed, feeling like he were chasing shadows in the dark.

Near the rooftop a dark silhouette flapped silently like the wing of a giant black crow. Caspian held his breath as he tried to distinguish what he had seen from what his imagination suggested it might be. Then, when it moved again, he saw it for what it truly was.

Peering down at the illuminated shop, its head hooded like a nightmarish wraith, its body a cloak as dark as the furthest reaches of space that starlight cannot touch. The mysterious figure, obsessed with the treasure Edgar Stone protected, now clung to the rooftop, motionless but for when the breeze took his shroud and caused it to twist and turn like smoke exploring the air about it.

There was no rain to blame for his vision tonight. The hooded man had returned.

Caspian found himself holding his breath whilst he focused on the dark ghostly shape, like a sniper keeping the target in his sight before he pulled the trigger. But Caspian had no weapon to defend himself and, regardless of the cover of nightfall, he felt terribly exposed standing in the uncovered doorway.

So far as he could tell, the man clinging to the rooftop had not seen him. He was probably watching Caspian's father as intently as Caspian now watched *him*.

Caspian wondered why he hadn't just gone into the shop and threatened Father like he had Ponsonby Smeelie? Was this strange man scared of Father, or did he just not want Father to know he was trying to find the weapon?

It felt like a long time that he stood there watching the mysterious watcher on the roof, not wanting to be seen himself, neither at roadside nor entering the shop. He managed to position himself behind a large plant beside the doorway where he hid; never taking his eye off his target for fear he might lose him.

Just as he began to think he might be stuck outside all night, the hooded man withdrew from his position and moved so gracefully across the rooftops it were as though he glided across an ethereal plain.

Caspian watched him go, wondering whether the hooded man had seen all he needed to see, or whether another clandestine rooftop stakeout awaited him. He knew he should really go and tell Father, but the dark figure was moving quickly and would soon be gone, along with the only chance they had of knowing where he was going.

Without stopping to reconsider, Caspian hurried quietly after the cloaked stranger into the dark streets of London: the darkened street lamps on Old Church Street flickered to life as they left.

The hooded man didn't stay on the rooftops for long, as even with his wing like cloak he lacked the ability to fly between buildings. Ahead of Caspian, he moved quickly, ducking and weaving between pedestrians along the main street forcing Caspian to hurry to keep up.

He followed him down a subway to an Underground station, trying to keep enough distance between them so that the cloaked figure would not realise he was being followed. He boarded the same train carriage the hooded man had climbed onto, which was heavily crowded with commuters beginning their journey home after a day at work. They made the perfect cover for Caspian, who was able to spy on the man in the dark cloak between other passengers.

Not once in the whole journey did the man show his face. The cloak always hung over it, preventing a glimpse at the man he was following. The train became busier and busier, and there were moments when it was impossible to see him at all.

Then, at Embankment, Caspian peered between two business men at the place where the hooded man had been to discover he had vanished. He spun and searched through the sea of people on the platform trying to get on the train, and amidst the flow he saw the black shape of the cloaked man heading for the escalator.

To the displeasure of many passengers, Caspian forced his way off the train and headed in the same direction. He hurtled up the escalator trying to gain on the hooded man's lead, his legs burning with each step.

'This is a customer announcement,' the PA system proclaimed. 'To avoid injury to yourself and others, running is not permitted on the escalator.'

Caspian knew the message was directed at him, but he had to push on. He couldn't lose the hooded man now.

At the top of the escalator he caught sight of him, just passing through the barrier. Caspian quickly followed and slipped in amongst a group of people heading the same direction to try and become more inconspicuous. He was now heading in the direction of Charing Cross and The Strand, but he really had no idea where this journey might take him.

'Where are you going?' he wondered quietly to himself as he followed the hooded man towards Covent Garden.

The district was abuzz with tourists and off duty workers meeting for an evening beverage in the many bars that populated the main square, surrounding the large 19th century piazza that housed three markets, a selection of restaurants, and a couple more bars that further offered the populace places to wet their proverbial whistles.

This area had been used long ago by Westminster Abbey as land for growing crops and orchards, known as *the garden of the Abbey and the Convent*. In the centuries that followed, the once arable land became an arcaded square surrounded by fine houses, a pleasure ground for playwrights, and finally developed into a successful market and area of commerce, renamed Covent Garden.

An urban myth, considered true by many Londoners, spread concerning this district's change of name. It suggested that Covent Garden was supposed to be called *Convent* Garden, however after a spelling mistake ensued without rectification, the misspelled version stuck.

This, the hooded man knew as he passed a convincingly motionless human statue, was utter nonsense. Covent was the old French and Middle English word for nunnery; a term that had spread with the Norman dialect into popular use in Britain during the time of the crusades. The city of Coventry was similarly named for its heritage, the early settlement forming around a Saxon nunnery. As for Covent Garden, the site of the Opera House was originally a nunnery attached to the Abbey of Westminster.

People these days were too eager to believe a half-amusing false truth over remembering a fact that formed their heritage. He understood why his master loathed society, and why now was the time for his return. If the average man knows not his ancestral roots, then what hope can be held for the legacy of his species?

A street performer was attracting a crowd in the centre of the street, forcing him to move round the group to avoid unwanted attention. He pulled his cloak over his face and moved to where a large glass shop front to his left exhibited the current winter fashion, manikins in the window as frozen and lifeless as the human statues who mimicked them.

In the reflection of such a window, he saw the boy was still following him. So it *was* more than coincidence, he thought.

The boy had first roused his suspicions whilst he travelled the Tube. A gangly boy of average height, dark hair, and no older than fourteen, he had sensed the boy's curious eyes upon him.

He could not blame the boy for curiosity; after all he was a particularly grotesque sight. However, British people are known for two distinctive traits: Firstly, their apathy – their reluctance to get involved in a situation unless they themselves are directly brought into it – and secondly, there was their palpable politeness. No one else in that carriage would have dreamed of the persistent staring that this boy had maintained, and despite his caution his own reflection had betrayed him.

Now, after a trek through crowded streets, he still followed – failing to be as discreet as he probably thought he had achieved. But something else intrigued the hooded man about his young pursuer: the boy's eyes were not evenly matched in colour, but in fact were completely different: one of gold, the other blue.

Many would consider this nothing more than a condition known as heterochromia iridum, a difference in iris coloration that could either be inherited or be as the result of disease or injury. He, however, suspected there was more to this particular boy's mismatched eyes than a mere anatomical state.

Without another glance at his young shadow, he moved towards one of the large throngs of spectators and ducked amongst the busy hustle of the crowd.

It seemed to Caspian like he had stumbled into a carnival. Human statues lined the streets, offering cheeky winks at occasional passers-by before returning to stone-like states, as if they were effigies of enchanted marble. Crowds gathered and cheered and cooed at street performers, gymnasts, fire-breathers, and musicians.

The cloaked man moved through the crowd, Caspian struggling to follow, until eventually he moved to the side away from the performers, making use of the clearer pathway beside the shop fronts and bars. This didn't last long; abruptly, he moved right into the crowd again, so suddenly and unexpected it shook Caspian from tailing him.

He tried to follow but soon realised it was useless: there were just too many people.

'Can I have a volunteer from the audience,' the performer at the centre of a large crowd nearby was asking. 'Hey, young man,' he said, pointing at Caspian.

Caspian shook his head and ducked into the crowd away from the unwelcome attention.

'Oh, come now, don't be shy,' the performer leered with a smile, playing to his audience. The crowd cheered encouragement, but Caspian pushed his way through them not wanting to lose the man with the dark cloak. 'You all scared him off,' the performer jeered behind him to his crowd's amusement.

Caspian looked around, trying to search the mass of people for the shadowy figure he had followed on a whim into the city alone, but he was nowhere to be seen.

The fire-breather stepped forward and made him jump as he released a jet of orange flame into the night sky. As the warm fire illuminated the ring of faces that watched from the surrounding crowd in a blaze of red and gold, Caspian saw the hooded man standing behind the fire-breather.

The crowd let out a cheer as the flames leapt from the breather's mouth, billowing into the air, but Caspian was deaf to it all. As he locked eyes with the face beneath the dark cloak he felt fear once again take grip on him.

Beneath that hood, the man's face had finally been revealed by the firelight, an ensemble of scarred flesh and twisted metal. One half scorched and scratched, disfigured by burns, blisters, and all manner of mutilation. The other was fitted with a half-mask of dull dark metal that looked like the work of a raving mad blacksmith. It even covered the man's right eye, his other was fixed on Caspian and his mouth turned in a nasty grin.

There was no doubt in Caspian's mind that the table had turned; it was his turn to run.

It all happened at the same time: A group of tourists stepped in front of Caspian to take a photo. Caspian turned and hurled himself into the unsuspecting crowd. The cloaked man pushed the fire-breather aside just as another flume of fire was expelled into the air, his hand groping at Caspian's shouldered backpack but failing to purchase.

He shook free and made a break for it, heading away from the market as fast as he could, not knowing where he was going. He tried to move fast, weaving through crowds and pedestrians alike, but it was no good – the agile hooded man was right behind him, an unremitting remorseless shadow.

As he hurtled across a busy road, taxicabs screeched their tyres and honked angrily at him, a few drivers' hurled expletives out the windows like verbal hand grenades.

On and on he ran, passing more shops, and more wine bars. He shouted for help as he ran, but those he ran passed just looked at him like he was trying to cause trouble. He crossed another road and was nearly struck by a large red bus, its tyres screeched loudly as the driver stepped on the brake. He didn't stop but just ran harder, hearing the commotion behind him – the hooded man must still be on his heels.

He turned onto another street, and then another, until he had no idea where he was at all. Finally he chanced a look behind him, and was relieved to see he had lost the hooded man.

He bent double, breathing heavily as he tried to regain his breath.

Am I safe, he wondered, when suddenly a hand from behind, as cold as ice, clamped over his mouth and dragged him into a dark alleyway.

Evidently, he was not.

XVI:
McCabre & Grieves

Caspian struggled, but the hooded man held him in such a tight grip he could not break free, his hands so cold against him he felt like he was in the grip of a dead person. His legs kicked wildly to no avail, and with the frosty hand over his mouth he could not call out for help. Futilely, he continued to fight but he couldn't see where he was being taken.

There was a loud bang as his captor kicked open a doorway behind him – a small bell above the door rang as he did so – and then he was bundled inside like dirty laundry into a washing machine. He fell to the floor and lay disorientated in the darkness as his captor released him and locked the door.

'What are you going to do to me?' Caspian asked, trying to get to his feet, partly not wanting to know the answer to his question.

'Do?' his captor's voice asked in a slow and confounded tone. 'I have already done what I was to do.'

Caspian looked for the man that had seized him, but the room was very dark and his eyes had not adjusted. Only a single beam of dim light shone down from the ceiling, but it did little in the way of lighting the room.

There was something about the tone of this man's voice that didn't match that of the hooded man. In fact, Caspian was now certain that he was not in the hands of that grotesquely half-masked maniac after all, but with somebody else entirely. 'Who are you?'

Very slowly the man edged out of the recess of the shadows and moved toward the light. His hands appeared first; those ice cold hands that had felt frozen against Caspian's skin, his long skinny fingers pale white in colour.

Then his torso appeared, dressed in an elaborate black silk shirt that was an extravagant amalgamation of ruffles and frills, wrapped in a long dark coat with deep red velvet innards.

Finally he was fully illuminated by the dim light, and Caspian could see this strange man's face. 'Are you unwell?' he asked, shocked by his pale complexion.

Like his pastel white hands, the man's face was colourless. Long dark hair hung straight down his back reaching below his waistline, and his eyes had bags so dark beneath them he looked like he had not slept in decades.

Between his lengthy digits he withdrew a long match and ran it along the striking surface of a matchbox.

'What are you doing?'

'It is better to light a candle than curse the darkness,' the man said in his solemn voice as he touched the lit match to a number of candles in the room.

In the candlelight, Caspian quickly saw that the windows had been blacked out to prevent any natural daylight from coming in. Looking around the room where he was held he took inventory of its strange contents: a till sat beside a ceramic pot upon a small table counter, shelves from floor to ceiling covered the walls, jars and jars containing funny looking liquids and very odd objects.

Was he in some bizarre kind of shop? And if so, was this outlandish tall and pale man the shopkeeper? Caspian was uncertain whether he was any safer in this shop than he had been out on the street with the hooded man.

Despite his brain telling him he was being silly, there was something oddly vampirical about this man. He mentally totted up what he had noticed: his hands were *dead* cold, his shop windows were sunlight resistant. In fact, everything about the man's appearance seemed to ooze vampirism. Except for the fact that vampires didn't exist, did they?

'My name,' the man drawled, his tone low and sombre, 'is Artemis Grieves. I'm sorry that I startled you. I was just out looking for a bite to eat,' he said dramatically, 'when I found you.'

Caspian shrank away as Artemis Grieves loomed over him, reaching inside his long black coat. 'What are you planning to … er … eat?' Caspian asked, fearing he might be on the menu. He decided to put his crazy vampire theory to the test. 'Will it be something garlicky?'

Grieves froze and flinched. 'No,' he moaned with disgust. 'We don't have garlic here. It does *terrible* things to me.'

'Like what?' Caspian found himself asking. He recalled stories that vampires didn't like garlic but he couldn't remember the reason why. He was sure it didn't kill them; no, that was sunlight, or a wooden stake.

'It doesn't agree with me,' Grieves replied slowly, pulling a half eaten baguette out from his inside coat pocket, 'and it makes my breath awfully smelly.'

'And…' Caspian encouraged, determined to prove to himself whether or not Grieves was truly a vampire.

Grieves shrugged, 'and I don't really like the taste.'

Caspian decided on a different approach. 'I bet you don't like stakes, either?'

'Oh, they are dreadfully bad for my heart,' Grieves declared before adding, 'I try to avoid steaks like my life depends on it. I'm trying to watch my cholesterol.'

Then he took down a jar from a shelf above the counter and unscrewed the lid. Reaching into the cloudy liquid with his bony fingers, he withdrew what looked like a pickled tarantula and snapped off a limb.

'Would you like a leg?' Grieves offered. 'Or, if you do not care for soused arachnid, maybe you would like a pickled egg.'

'I'm not hungry, thank you,' Caspian declined politely, still staring at the spider leg Grieves was waving about.

172

'I'm not surprised. I have a lot of trouble selling pickled eggs. My customers think they are disgusting.' With a shrug and a slurping sound, Grieves sucked the leg into his mouth and began to chew on it. 'What brings you to this part of London?' he asked as he swallowed.

'I was following someone.'

'Your generation must have a different meaning for "follow" than mine,' Grieves replied slowly and thoughtfully. 'From where I stood, it seemed like *he* was following you.'

'You saw him?' Caspian asked. 'Do you know who he is?'

'I'm afraid I do not, but then *your* name still alludes me, even after I have told you who I am.'

'Oh,' Caspian said, feeling very rude for not introducing himself. 'My name is Caspian Stone.'

'Cas-pi-an Stone,' the vampire-like man repeated lengthily. He turned and said to the shop counter as though someone was sat there, 'you see? I told you it was he. Edgar Stone's own flesh and … *blood.*'

The way Grieves said "blood" sent a cold shiver down Caspian's spine.

'Erm, excuse me, Mr Grieves. Who exactly are you talking to?'

Grieves opened his mouth in horror. 'How very rude of me! I should have introduced you earlier,' he said, gesturing toward the empty seat behind the shop counter. 'This is James McCabre, my business partner and good friend.'

Caspian could not see to whom Artemis Grieves was indicating. As far as he could see they were the only two people in the shop. 'I'm sorry, where is he?'

'He's right here,' Grieves replied, lifting the ceramic pot that sat on the shop counter. It was the same sort of urn that held the ashes of a cremated family member. 'Caspian Stone, James McCabre. James, meet Caspian Stone.'

'Um, Mr Grieves?' Caspian asked cautiously, not wanting to offend his host. 'Is your friend, Mr McCabre, deceased?'

'Obviously…' Grieves replied sadly. 'But he has not completely left this world, if you know what I mean.'

'I'm not sure that I do,' Caspian admitted honestly.

Grieves frowned and lifted the urn to his ear as if it were talking to him. 'Now, now, James. There is no need to be rude!' He turned and gave Caspian a remorseful look. 'My apologies, he doesn't get out much, cooped up in this urn all day long. It makes him a little irritable at times.'

A jar containing a strange greenish liquid beside Caspian spontaneously bubbled, making him jump. 'What kind of a shop is this?'

'McCabre and Grieves' Apothecary Supplies,' Grieves replied as he gently set James McCabre's urn back on the shop counter. 'Here for your alternative pharmaceutical needs, nine till five.'

The contents of the shop had to be the strangest collection of things Caspian had ever seen. There were jars of different coloured worms, strange plants, unusual reptiles, furry fungi, and balls of human hair. There were jars of snails and slugs, used tea bags, and a even a jar full to the brim with toenail clippings, sat beside what appeared to be a jar of liquorish allsorts.

Caspian looked at his watch. 'It's past five now. Shouldn't you be closing up?'

'Closing?' Grieves replied confused. 'No, I must get ready for when we open in a few hours time, and some of the stock need feeding.'

'A *few* hours?' Caspian thought it was more than a few hours before nine in the morning, and then it dawned on him. 'You mean this shop opens from nine at night until five in the morning?'

'Yes, *nine till five*. I fail to see how that was unclear,' Grieves replied.

'But who shops at that time?'

'Those who need these sort of things, for a start. Although, we do reduce our opening hours during the summer months to between eleven and four.'

'Because of the sunlight?' Caspian asked, assuming that the longer hours of daylight during the summer months was quite a big factor effecting a vampire's trading hours.

Grieves gave a noncommittal shrug. 'It's mainly because our supplies are in less demand during the summer,' he answered slowly. 'Our customers tend to grow their own when they can, you know, because of the current economic situation and all…'

'Mr Grieves, you said you know my father?'

Artemis Grieves shook his head. 'I did not say that. I made the observation that you are the son of your father.'

'Yes, but to know that you must *know* my father.'

'Not necessarily. One could know of him without ever knowing him. After all, your father's reputation is *dreadfully* well known in the circles I tread.'

The way Grieves used "dreadfully" made Caspian uneasy. What "circles" had his father been moving in? 'What do you mean by my father's reputation?'

Artemis glared at him with as much surprise as his vacant eyes were capable of. 'You do not know? Your father has done wonderful things for the free people of this world. If the rumours are true, then even now he is our last defence against an evil once vanquished returning to power.'

'You must be mistaken,' Caspian said. His father collected and sold art and antiques. He certainly wasn't capable of vanquishing evil.

Grieves shook his head. 'There is no mistaking what your father has done.'

'But if he really did what you say he did, surely everyone would know. He would be famous.'

'That is not the way of the world,' Grieves said slowly. 'Your news tells of the disasters that strike and the horrors that have occurred, but disasters averted sell less papers. How many disasters do you think your Government has prevented this year? What *has* happened is harder to deny, whilst what *might* have happened needn't unnecessarily worry the nation. Do you understand?'

'Yes,' Caspian answered. 'So very few people know about what my father did.'

'Correct.'

'Can you tell me?'

Grieves said nothing whilst he considered how to answer this request. 'If your father has not told you himself, then there must be a reason for it. The tale is his to tell.'

'Great,' Caspian said gloomily. Fat chance of Father telling that story, he thought. He'd have more luck transmuting lead into gold. 'What about this vanquished evil?' he asked.

Grieves reached over to a shelf and lifted what appeared to be a human skull. He held it so theatrically that Caspian thought for a moment he was going to perform his own rendition of Hamlet. 'Evil reigned on this world long, long ago – when the Dark Ages truly were an age of darkness. *He* mastered the five arts, and grew more powerful than that of any mortal man. With that power he could have created, but he chose to destroy.'

'But what happened to *him*?' Caspian asked.

'The power he lusted eventually crippled him.' Grieves stared at the skull as if it had once belonged to the evil one he spoke of. 'From time to time there are murmurs of his insurgence, that he has resurfaced to abolish those who inhibit his mend – like your father. Others believe he was never gone, but merely bides his time for the moment to strike.'

Grieves' story seemed more like a fairytale to Caspian. There couldn't be any truth in this, could there? 'How does my father fit into this? You said this evil was powerful in the Dark Ages, whereas we live in modern times.'

A small smile formed on Grieves' thin, slightly purple, lips but he said nothing.

Caspian hazarded a guess. 'Is my father protecting a weapon that the evil needs?'

'As far as rumours tell, yes.'

'And if they were true,' Caspian asked, 'what would happen were he to get this weapon?'

'Not to be over dramatic,' Grieves said histrionically, setting the skull back where it came from with a slow and precise movement, 'but probably the end of this world as we know it.'

'Oh,' Caspian said.

Quietness fell over the little shop like the whole room was holding its breath. Ever since he had stumbled across the mystery of what his father had hidden, one particular question plagued his mind. 'What is it?' he asked, anxious to know what this mysterious weapon was that his father had been charged with watching over.

'Cheese!' Grieves replied.

The boy was almost within his grasp when suddenly he darted across the road, narrowly being missed by a bus. Tyres screeched and the big red double-decker swerved, smashing into a parked car. The road was completely blocked, and traffic moving in either direction came to a halt.

The hooded man had no choice but to give up the chase. There were too many bystanders, too many witnesses. He couldn't chance drawing attention to himself, and his appearance was hardly inconspicuous. Sirens were already beginning to sound, and soon the Metropolitan Police would descend on the scene like vultures on field mice.

He ducked away, before anyone spotted him standing at the roadside. The appearance of the boy changed everything. If this truly was the son of Edgar Stone, as he believed it was, then his master needed to know. If the prophecy was correct after all, then this child posed a greater threat to their plans than Edgar Stone ever could.

He searched the streets near where he had lost the boy for longer than he should, but could find no trace of him. Either he was long gone, or had found somewhere locally to hide and bide his time. Whichever way, he could afford no further time to waste searching for him.

Finding the next piece of the puzzle would have to wait. *My master must be told of this*, the hooded man decided. There was still plenty of time to solve Stone's riddle before the deadline drew near, but now he would have to temporarily abandon his work in England to report this unexpected complication: one that could either work in their favour, or ruin everything.

Mr Grieves' enigmatic reply had come so suddenly that Caspian thought he must have misheard. 'I'm sorry, did you say cheese?'

'Yes,' Grieves replied. 'Would you like some? I just remembered that I have some round here, somewhere. It might be a little old, but my understanding is that cheese only gets better with age.'

'No, please, don't worry about it,' Caspian said, eager to return to the matter of the secret weapon.

'It's no problem, really,' Grieves replied, gliding across the shop to a set of shelves near the back where he started picking up jars, moving containers and various other receptacles whilst in search of this illusive cheddar of his.

'But I'd rather hear about the weapon,' Caspian protested to deaf ears. There was nothing more he could do but watch this strange man run his long fingers across the shelves, and patiently wait for his return. However, as he quietly waited, something took his attention on a shelf nearby.

An ornate box no larger than a matchbox, made of very dark wood and painted with faded and flaked white stripes to resemble a rib cage, lay beneath a thick layer of dust and cobwebs. A spider (not quite large enough to whet the appetite of Artemis Grieves) laid beside it, dead, its legs twisted and mangled at the behest of some callous torturer.

'Aha!' said Artemis triumphantly from the other side of the shop, but Caspian was far too curious as to what wonders were dwelling within this strange box than to celebrate his host's skill at cheese detection.

He cautiously lifted the lid off the box to reveal a hexagonal ring, carefully crafted from six small pieces of bone, placed on a very old piece of cloth within. 'What is this?' he asked, mesmerised by the strangeness of his discovery.

From the other side of the shop, Grieves continued on about the cheese whilst he replaced the jars he had moved to get at it. 'I should have known it would be between the verruca ointment and the jars of condensed wart pus…'

Caspian tilted the box so he could see the ring better in the candle light, and as he did the ring seemed to shift slightly, as if a tiny tremble had travelled around the ring through each of the bones and back to the start again. It was almost as though the ring had twitched.

He held it still, wondering whether it had been a trick of the flickering candlelight, but surely enough the tiny bones flinched once again before his eyes as they had done before.

Tentatively he lifted a finger to touch it. Was it really moving on its own accord, or was this an optical illusion?

'No, don't!' Grieves called out, urgency surfacing for the first time from his languid manner, but the warning came too late.

As Caspian's finger brushed the surface of the ring of bones he instantly knew it had been a mistake. Like a crack of lightning, pain shot up his fingertip into his hand, up his arm, and quickly spread to the rest of his body. It was so horrible, and so intense, that he dropped the ring and fell to the floor writhing about in agony.

Grieves dropped the cheese and darted over to a glass cabinet behind the shop counter where he rummaged about inside amongst the various bottles and vials it held.

The excruciating pain Caspian felt was too severe to focus on anything Grieves was doing. He could only hear the clinking of bottles whilst he lay on the floor, his eyes clenched tightly shut, and feeling like his bones were burning white hot from within. Unbearable anguish surged through every part of him, coursing through his veins and back into his bones, like tributaries of molten metal pouring into a river of volcanic lava.

He tried to move, but with each movement the pain intensified.

'Try not to wiggle,' Grieves said, kneeling down beside him. Caspian welcomed Artemis' ice-cold touch that opened his mouth and held a small glass bottle to his lips. 'Drink this, it will help.'

Caspian obeyed and took a gulp from the bottle, and then almost gagged at the foul taste of the liquid it contained.

'It tastes kind of nutty, doesn't it?' Grieves said.

Caspian thought it tasted kind of vile, but quickly the terrible pain began to subside. 'What is that stuff?' he asked weakly.

'*Sauerpott's Sore-Bone Remedy*: a blend of herring, grasshopper, almonds, and dog's milk, amongst other things,' Grieves explained. 'It's high in everything healthy bones need; such as calcium – and marrowbone jelly.'

Caspian wished he hadn't asked, especially when Grieves forced him to take another swig from the bottle.

Meanwhile, whilst he recovered from the pain (and the acquired taste of Sauerpott's Sore-Bone Remedy), Grieves used a pair of bolt tongs – similar to the sort a blacksmith might use – to pick up the ring and return it to its box.

'Did the ring do that to me?' Caspian asked from where he sat hunched on the floor.

'It is rumoured that the Ouanga ring is tainted with a Voodoo curse – a powerful dark magic from long ago,' Grieves carefully lifted the box back to its shelf and slid the lid back in place. 'Said to be crafted from the arthritic toes of a witchdoctor, touching the ring of bones will bestow agony enough to silence the living and wake the dead.'

'I think this rumour's been proven true,' Caspian said, getting unsteadily to his feet.

'It was once the prized possession of King Philip the Fair of France,' Grieves went on. 'How do you feel now?'

'Like every bone in my body was broken and used as kindling,' Caspian replied, but fearing that admitting this would result in Grieves prescribing another gulp of the revolting elixir, he quickly added, 'but the pain is going away. I feel better already.'

He tried to return the bottle, but Grieves shook his head. 'Keep it. The symptoms have been known to return sporadically over a period of six months after contact with the bone curse. Carry the remedy with you at all times, as you will regret it should the pain return when you are without it.'

'Thank you,' Caspian said, begrudgingly putting the small bottle in his bag and sincerely hoping he would neither have to suffer that pain nor taste the foul remedy again.

Grieves said thoughtfully, 'you might even find that if applied at the correct moment this makes for a wonderful *deus ex machina*.'

'I don't understand.'

'All will become clear at a later date.'

'Yeah, I get told that a lot,' Caspian commented cynically. Despite the taste of the horrid medicine, Caspian felt indebted to Artemis Grieves for curing him. 'I don't have much money with me, but could I pay you for the remedy?'

'Certainly not,' Grieves said looking offended. 'The son of Stone shall not pay for any item here, not after all his father has done for us. Speaking of which, you really should be getting home. He will be wondering where you are by now.'

Caspian wanted to stay and find out more from Mr Grieves, but after his ordeal with the Ouanga ring he was feeling weak. 'Okay,' he conceded. 'If you do know my father, please don't tell him what I was doing tonight. I don't think he would approve.'

Grieves gave Caspian an inquisitive look. 'Clearly, you *are* your father's son. You both live your lives governed by the secrets you keep,' he said, offering a toothy smile. And when he did, for the first time allowing Caspian to glimpse his teeth, it was impossible not to notice just how particularly sharp, exceptionally pointy, and extraordinarily fang-like two of those teeth appeared.

It was after seven in the evening that the boy stood outside the door to his father's house, keys in hand. He took a wary look over his shoulder, up to the rooftop where the cloaked man had last been perched, but now there was no one on the roof. With a sigh of relief, he turned the key and entered the building, locking the door behind him.

A smile crept across the unmasked half of the half-masked man's face as he watched the boy through the tinted glass window of his parked car. With his suspicions confirmed, he started the ignition and drove away. A long journey lay before him.

He would be greatly rewarded for this information, but there was only one reward he truly sought. He wanted his revenge against Edgar Stone, and the arrival of the child meant it was now even closer at hand.

XVII:
SUCKER PUNCH

Caspian barely slept a wink that night, but not because of the aches and pains he'd suffered as a consequence of touching the Ouanga ring. His sleeplessness came as a result of the large amount he had to achieve and the severe shortage of time in which to do it.

He couldn't really recall how he'd gotten home from central London, which was considerably concerning. He'd found himself standing at his doorstep with the key in his hand, some time after seven o'clock.

After clambering up the stairs he had asked Mrs Hodges where Father was. Caspian felt it was high time he brought his father up to speed regarding the dangerous man who had been watching them so closely.

'He's gone out, Dear,' Mrs Hodges explained. 'He took a phone call earlier this evening and went out straight after. He said he probably wouldn't be back until tomorrow morning.'

'Tomorrow morning?' Caspian exclaimed. 'Where has he gone?'

'You know your father,' the old housekeeper replied. 'He didn't say. I wish he wasn't so disapproving of mobile phones. It would make tracking him down an awful lot easier.'

Frustrated that his father had left before he could warn and tell him about what had been happening, he informed Mrs Hodges that he would be passing on dinner due to a dodgy stomach. His stomach wasn't as dodgy as he'd made out to Mrs Hodges, but Sauerpott's Sore-Bone Remedy (coupled with the memory of Grieves slurping down pickled

184

tarantula legs) had almost entirely abolished his appetite for the evening.

Before going upstairs to his bedroom to find the motivation to start his report from scratch, he tried calling his mother to see how she was feeling. The phone rang off with no answer, as it usually did when she was sleeping. Was it bad timing that he always managed to call her when she was asleep, or was she sleeping an awful lot these days?

He was both relieved and thankful to get a hold of Jess when he tried her number. By the time the birds started singing their wakeup chorus the next morning, he had botched together a passable version of his original report. He would just have to explain to Mrs Scrudge that he had lost his notebook and pray she was in a good mood.

'Jeez, you look bloody awful,' Billy greeted him as he walked in for registration, looking at the dark bags under his eyes. 'Did you go to bed at all last night?'

'Bed, yes. Sleep, no,' Caspian replied. 'Sorry for losing it with you yesterday.'

'No worries,' Billy sympathised. 'You were really stressed, it had been a long day.'

It had been a long night too, Caspian thought.

'Speaking of losing things,' Billy continued, 'how'd you get on with your report?'

'The best I could with only twelve hours, no notebook, and a headache so strong it would have been a blessing to be decapitated,' Caspian explained. 'I called Jess and she helped me rebuild it as much as possible, but compared to the original it's dog muck. Yours?' he asked, hoping that at least he wasn't the only one nervous about presenting his report.

'Cat poo,' Billy shrugged. He gave Caspian a concerned look. 'Are you all right though, mate, apart from being up all night, obviously, and losing your report? It's just, you seem a little off.'

Father still hadn't returned that morning, and he'd tried calling his mother before school but her phone didn't seem to be working. He felt uneasy that both his parents were now unreachable, and even though he was sure his father was fine, he couldn't prevent his brain from conjuring up scenarios where the half-masked man jumped him from behind and forced him to give up the weapon.

'It's nothing, just a lot on my mind,' he told Billy. 'Come on; let's take our seats. I had quite an interesting night last night and you're going to want to hear what I found out.'

This certainly took Billy's attention away from Caspian's mental wellbeing. 'What did you find out?'

'I found out what's so important about the weapon my father's hiding.'

'Really! How?' Billy's eyes were wide with excitement. 'Did your father tell you?'

'Yeah, of course,' Caspian replied with lashings of sarcasm. 'I said to him, "Dad, you know that weapon you've been asked to look after – the one that no one's supposed to know you have, including me? Well, my friends and I were wondering why it is so important?" '

'You know what?' Billy retorted. 'You were right; it would be a blessing if you were decapitated.'

Caspian laughed. They took their seats and waited for Mrs Scrudge to work her way through the register.

'So, come on, your killing me,' Billy whispered after their form tutor had finished calling out the names. 'What is *it* for?'

'Apparently it has the power to restore some sort of ancient evil.'

'Pull the other one,' Billy replied.

'I'm serious,' Caspian said. 'I have it on very good authority.'

Billy raised an eyebrow. 'Okay, saying any of this is true; when you say an "ancient evil," are we talking myths and monsters, or end of the world, here-comes-the-apocalypse sort of thing?'

'Probably the latter.'

'Well there's a cheery thought,' Billy said. 'Maybe I shouldn't worry too much about my end of year grades, then.'

Caspian smirked, 'I don't think you could possibly worry any less about your grades than you already do.'

'Hey, there's always room for improvement,' Billy winked. 'But on a serious note, you don't really believe it do you?'

Caspian thought about the unbelievable story Artemis Grieves had told him last night, and then he thought about his encounter with the paralysing Ouanga ring. He thought about poor Sprocket – still no closer to being mended – crawling across the classroom floor on his first day at Hogarth House. 'I'm beginning to think anything is possible,' he shrugged.

'It must have been a very reliable source to have you this convinced. Who told you?'

'Your going to think I'm mad,' Caspian sighed. 'It all happened last night, and it's a bit of a strange story.'

Billy grinned, 'with you, mate, it always it.'

Before Caspian could explain how he came to know the new information about his father's secret, Mrs Scrudge began with her announcements from the front of the class. 'In conjunction with your history lessons for next term, a school trip is going to be taking place in a fortnight. You all have the opportunity to visit the Tower of London, but I should emphasise that nobody will be going off site without a signed consent form.'

Alison Tyrell, a short girl with red hair, began passing out the consent slips at Mrs Scrudge's signal. As she made her way round the class Billy admitted, 'I've always wanted to go to the Tower of London.'

Caspian also liked the idea of seeing one of the capital's oldest tourist attractions. 'That's where they keep the crown jewels, right? You may have to be on your best behaviour.'

Billy gave a wry smile. 'I promise to try my hardest,' he pledged with one hand raised and the other across his chest, but an oath of best behaviour from Billy was about as reliable as the eyewitness testimony of a short-sighted compulsive liar.

The bell rang, signalling the start of lessons. Since Billy and Caspian's first lesson was in their tutor group's classroom, neither needed to move. Whilst those who had lessons elsewhere shuffled out, Billy asked again how it was that Caspian came to know more about what his father was hiding.

'When I got home last night,' Caspian explained, 'the hooded man was watching my father's shop.'

'What, the same hooded man who beat up Smeelie in the museum?'

'Yeah, of course the same one.'

'But how can you be sure?' Billy asked. 'He was wearing a cloak?'

'Look, it was the same one,' Caspian said impatiently. 'I'm a hundred per cent positive. Anyway, I followed him when he left.'

Billy's jaw fell open. 'You followed him?'

Caspian nodded. It made him sound brave, but Billy didn't yet know how badly things had gone that night, or how much worse they could have gone had Artemis Grieves not been out looking for a snack.

'I followed him all the way into London. I was trying to be really careful not to be seen, but in Covent Garden he spotted me.'

'You saw his face?' Billy asked.

'Sort of,' Caspian replied, thinking again of the brief but horrific glimpse he had had when the fire-breather lit up the crowd. 'It wasn't a pretty sight. He had this mask over half his face.'

'Like the Phantom of the Opera?'

'No. It was like a metal torture device strapped to his face, but that wasn't the worst of it. The uncovered side of his face was badly burnt and scarred, like he had been in a fire.'

'No wonder he wears that cloak out in public,' Billy commented.

Clarissa dropped her bag onto the table beside them and looked wearily at Caspian. 'How did you get on with your report last night?' she asked, treading carefully as to not get her head bitten off.

'Sod his report,' Billy butted in. 'No offence, mate, but I'd rather hear what happened next with the *Man in the Iron Mask*.'

'What man in an iron mask?' Clarissa asked.

Caspian recounted his tale of the previous evening to them both. He told how he had slipped away from the cloaked man and how Grieves had dragged him off the street.

'A vampire?' Clarissa repeated with scepticism when he told them about Artemis Grieves. 'I doubt he was a vampire. He was probably just a Goth. They dress like that and pretend to be vampire's as a kind of fashion.'

'I know what a Goth is,' Caspian replied, but he gave up trying to convince them. He also decided to leave out the part about the Ouanga ring, as if his friends didn't believe what he said about Mr Grieves, they certainly wouldn't believe that an old Voodoo ring had cursed him.

'Did he sleep in a coffin?' Billy said, making fun. 'Or, when he walked passed a mirror he had no reflection?'

'There weren't any mirrors, and we were in his shop, not his bedroom,' Caspian said.

'So what does a vampire sell then?' Billy goaded, enjoying giving Caspian a ribbing. 'Was it blood by any chance? Did he work in a blood bank?'

Clarissa shook her head. 'If only you were as applied with your schoolwork as you are at making quips and causing mayhem.'

'Yeah, but I'd be a lot less fun to have around,' Billy replied.

Caspian managed to finish explaining what he had learnt from Grieves just before Mrs Scrudge's shrill voice ended any further discussion. '*Mr Long!* What have I told you about leaning back in your chair? If you want to be on two feet instead of four I will happily remove that chair and you can spend the entire lesson standing. Do I make myself clear?'

'Unavoidably clear,' Billy mumbled as his chair dropped back onto four legs. Both Caspian and Clarissa supressed amused smirks.

'Shall we get started?' Mrs Scrudge asked rhetorically. 'We have a lot of presentations to get through, so to ensure we can get through them all the only person I want to hear talking is he or she who is giving the presentation. Seeing that Billy is unable to correctly use a chair, we'll start with him. Up you come, Billy.'

Like a puppy that'd just been told off for having an accident on the carpet, he plodded up to the front of the classroom with his tail between his legs. Caspian felt for his friend, knowing that soon enough he too would face the walk of shame.

As it happened, Billy had nothing to worry about. He delivered a wildly entertaining presentation about criminal life in Victorian London, giving elaborate demonstrations on how to pick pockets and cause all manner of trouble. The class thought his performance was absolutely hilarious; however Caspian sensed that Mrs Scrudge was not overly pleased that he had quite successfully promoted a life of crime to his peers. Billy, on the other hand, seemed quite happy with himself as he returned to his seat amidst the applause his japes and jokes had earned him.

The presentations that followed were much more educational and serious. From his seat at the back of the class, Caspian kept trying to build up the courage to go next, but each time he chickened out at the last minute, until he was one of the few left in the class who had not yet presented.

Amongst those left, Hayden Tanner was also included. Throughout the other presentations, Caspian had noticed Hayden glancing in his direction as if to gauge whether he were about to volunteer to present next.

This irritated Caspian. There was absolutely no doubt in his mind that Hayden had been the one who went through his locker and took his report. And worse, it was clear he *wanted* Caspian to know he had taken it, as otherwise he wouldn't have confessed on the sports field as being responsible for putting the diary in his locker.

As far as Caspian could see, Hayden was hoping for one of two things. He either thought he could irritate Caspian into causing a scene and blaming him for not having his report, or he wanted to see him struggle to present a rubbish report that he'd been forced to prepare the night before. Surely, seeing how tired Caspian looked, it must have been pure bliss for someone as sadistic as Hayden.

Well, I'm not going to give him the satisfaction, he decided, picking up the report he had cobbled together less than twelve hours ago. It might not be the amazing report he had prepared before, but he could still present the hell out of this one and show Hayden that he wouldn't be so easily beaten.

'Thank you, Melissa,' Mrs Scrudge said as Melissa Brundlewick returned to her seat with a sigh of relief. 'Who's next?'

Caspian stood, but before he could say anything another member of the class quickly called out, 'I'll go next, Mrs Scrudge.'

Hayden Tanner was already on his feet and marching towards the front of the class, leaving Mrs Scrudge with the unbelievable situation of two students wanting to present at the same time. 'Take a seat, Caspian,' she said. 'Hayden can go next, and then you can follow.'

'Great,' Caspian muttered quietly as he took his seat again and glared at his nemesis at the front of the classroom. Something didn't feel right. What was Hayden up to?

Hayden refused to meet his eye whilst he introduced himself to the class with his clear and confident voice, oozing with his trademark charm. Caspian watched him closely, like a child trying to fathom a magic trick by carefully observing the magician's hands.

Finally, Hayden Tanner's ice blue eyes met Caspian's and a broad smile that seemed to say, *I win*, danced across his lips.

'What's the matter, Caspian?' Clarissa whispered beside him, but he didn't acknowledge hearing her.

'My presentation,' Hayden said coolly, still looking directly at Caspian, 'is called *The Expansion of Subterranean Victorian London*.'

Clarissa let out a tiny gasp.

On the report laid out before Caspian, the title it bore was exactly the same. Not only had Hayden stolen his report, he was presenting it as his *own*. He felt his blood begin to boil with rage.

Billy put his hand on his shoulder whilst Hayden continued delivering *his* report word for word, as Caspian had written it. 'Don't,' he warned quietly.

'But that is *my* report,' Caspian hissed.

'I know it is, mate. You told me the title over Christmas,' Billy replied. 'But he probably expects you to make a scene.'

192

'And there is going to be one,' Caspian whispered angrily. 'What am *I* supposed to present? I've got a very similar report, only a shadow of the one I previously wrote – the one *he's* now presenting. I'm meant to go next!'

'Is there a problem, Mr Stone?' Mrs Scrudge asked quietly but sternly.

'No, Miss,' Billy answered for him. Once Mrs Scrudge's attention had returned to Hayden, Billy whispered, 'let him finish, and then we'll handle this together. I know you wrote that report.'

'So do I,' Clarissa added. 'I'm sorry we didn't believe you before.'

'That doesn't matter now.'

'No,' Billy agreed. 'You have witnesses. What evidence has he got that *he* wrote the report?'

Caspian nodded and agreed to wait until the presentation was finished, but he didn't relax. His eyes were so fixed on Hayden that it were as though he held a bow and was waiting for the right moment to loose an arrow. Hayden kept glancing in his direction, and smiling – obviously happy to see his victim stewing.

And every sentence that Caspian heard, he became angrier and angrier. His head was pounding as his mind raced between panic and rage, as though they were two contrasting personalities holding a debate: *What was he going to present?* Nothing, he would confront Hayden in front of the class. *What if Mrs Scrudge didn't believe him?* She'd have to believe him. How could she not?

Eventually Hayden brought the report to a conclusion and received a much louder round of applause from the class than all the prior presentations. Even Mrs Scrudge was clapping loudly.

'Does anyone have any questions?' Hayden asked coolly, slipping Caspian a subtle smile as his eyes glided over his classmates.

Caspian threw his hand straight up, but didn't wait to be chosen to speak. 'Yeah, I've got a question for you,' he said angrily. 'Why are you presenting *my* report, instead of one you've written yourself?'

'Boom!' punctuated Billy, by way of support.

There were gasps from around the class, but Hayden stood at the front laughing it off like some ridiculous joke. 'What are you talking about, Caspian? I've worked hard on this report for weeks.'

'And where's your evidence of that?' Billy asked.

'What is the meaning of this?' Mrs Scrudge said sharply, but nobody answered her.

Hayden gave his accusers a calm shrug. 'I have my notebook, full of all the research and notes I made in preparation for writing my report. Why, what do you have?'

'You know I don't have my notebook,' Caspian replied.

Mrs Scrudge summoned both Caspian and Hayden to her desk. 'What exactly are you saying, Mr Stone?'

Caspian showed her his own report with matching title. Her eyes narrowed behind the wire-rimmed glasses as she read the opening paragraph. 'He stole my report,' Caspian explained.

'I have no idea what he's talking about,' Hayden said smoothly. He laid the report he had just presented on Mrs Scrudge's desk before them, and Caspian saw that he had rewritten the entire report in his own handwriting. 'But it does seem odd that Caspian's report bears such a close similarity to my own.'

'Similar?' Caspian spat. 'You've copied it word for word. I had to rewrite it from memory.'

'You know that's not true,' Hayden replied. 'I leant you mine to give you some ideas, but I didn't think you would stoop low enough to copy it.'

'He's lying,' Billy said coming to join Caspian.

'That's enough,' Mrs Scrudge said grimly. 'One of you is either a thief, or a charlatan. Bring me your notebooks, the evidence will speak for itself.'

Hayden promptly spun and moved to his desk to collect his notebook, leaving Caspian standing at Mrs Scrudge's desk without a notebook to show her. His only hope of redemption was that Hayden's notebook would clearly not reflect the weeks of work he had supposedly put into his fabricated report, seeing that he had not possessed Caspian's report until yesterday afternoon.

But this hope dissipated as quickly as a wisp of smoke on a windy day. When Hayden returned he happily set his notebook in front of Mrs Scrudge and showed her the pages and pages of preparation he had done for the report. There were sketches of old maps of the original underground train lines, notes on the Victorian sewers and the Kingsway Tram Tunnel. There were photocopies of pictures taken near the end of the era, showing the grand scale of work undertaken to dig deep trenches along the street and to lay the rail track beneath. And there was page after page, and draft after draft of the final report – Caspian recognised it all as the weeks of research and hard work that *he* had put in, all convincingly copied into Hayden's own handwriting.

'But, how?' Caspian said as he stared blankly at the notebook before him, wondering how Hayden had created such a convincing counterfeit in so short a time. Beside him, Billy's eyes were wide with disbelief.

'I think it is obvious,' Mrs Scrudge said. 'Weeks of hard work and planning have gone into this, as was demonstrated by the presentation itself. I suppose you are going to tell me that you forgot your notebook?'

'No,' Caspian started, 'he took it when he –'

'That is quite enough, Caspian,' Mrs Scrudge bellowed. 'It is one thing not to do the work, but quite another to accuse a fellow pupil of stealing your own, only to offer up a slapdash copy yourself.'

'That isn't what happened,' Billy interjected.

'Go and sit down, Billy. This doesn't involve you.'

'But,' Billy protested.

'Sit Down!'

Caspian felt himself broil with anger, whilst Hayden looked on with imitation innocence. He wanted justice but, just as Mr Clay had said, Mrs Scrudge couldn't see the truth for the lies.

'Well, Caspian?' Mrs Scrudge said coldly, awaiting justification for his actions.

Caspian had no idea what to say. He felt like someone had knocked him to the ground with an unexpected blow, leaving him dazzled and confused. As all he had to offer was the truth, of which couldn't be sustained with evidence and was prone to being overlooked for the sake of favouritism, there was really nothing to say.

There was a sudden knock on the classroom door. The class, Caspian, and Mrs Scrudge all turned to see a very solemn looking Headmaster Clay standing in the doorway.

Caspian wondered what had brought the headmaster here, and even Hayden looked befuddled for once.

'My apologies for disrupting your class, Drusilla,' Mr Clay said. 'I'm afraid that Caspian needs to take leave, as of immediate effect.'

'What?' Caspian asked, completely surprised.

Mrs Scrudge's coldness and disciplinarian appearance suddenly washed away. 'Of course,' she said. 'Caspian, collect your things and go with the headmaster.'

Why had Mr Clay come in person to collect him? Caspian wondered as he returned to his desk, the class watching him in stunned silence. What had happened?

'Caspian…' Clarissa whispered as he picked up his bag. 'What do you think…?'

He shrugged. Had the masked man finally broke into Father's shop? He still hadn't seen his father since he had disappeared the previous night, had something happened to him?

'I'll call you later,' Billy said quietly, and Caspian nodded.

He walked through the classroom towards the door, and as his eyes met Hayden's he saw that same curiosity in his ice-blue eyes that had first met him when he'd joined the school.

Mr Clay gave him a warm smile as he reached the door and they headed into the corridor together. 'What is it?' Caspian asked. 'What has happened?'

Headmaster Clay frowned and looked at him sadly. 'Caspian, your father will be here to collect you shortly.'

'Why?' Caspian asked, but his headmaster didn't answer, leaving Caspian feeling like for the second time that day he were on the receiving end of a sucker punch to the head.

XVIII:
CALIDEUS

'I don't understand,' Caspian said as he walked alongside his headmaster towards the school office. 'Why has my father come to collect me?'

Headmaster Clay gave him the briefest of looks. 'He would be better to explain that than I.'

Caspian's mind was racing. He needed to warn his father about the half-masked man and his intention to steal the mysterious weapon. What if he had already found where Father had hidden it? Maybe he had broken into the shop and found the way down to the reflectory, or had something worse than that happened? Could it be that the evil Artemis Grieves was describing had returned?

He had so many questions already in his mind, but when he met his father outside the school gates he suddenly had a whole lot more.

Father was stood beside a black sports car like nothing Caspian had ever seen. He looked at it in awe, wondering how his father had come by what was probably a very expensive machine.

There was no manufacturer's badge or distinguishing mark that associated it with any car company he knew. Its chassis was low and its sleek body was painted matte black so it didn't reflect light but seemed to absorb it. The shape was almost insect-like, aggressive and predatory looking, like a wasp. The black angular and aerodynamic shape could easily have resembled the armour plating of a soldier ant. Large air intakes at the front and rear wheel arches, and cooling vents along the side, put Caspian in mind of a jet plane. This was a vehicle more akin to Batman than his father.

Father seemed to guess Caspian's first question, and answered, 'it belongs to a friend of mine.'

'Who's that?' Caspian asked, still staring in disbelief at the hostile machine in front of him, 'Bruce Wayne?'

'No,' Father replied, portraying no hint as to whether he knew who Bruce Wayne was. 'It belongs to your uncle.'

Uncle? Caspian didn't have any aunties or uncles. To his knowledge both his parents had no siblings, much like him. 'I don't have an uncle?'

'Yes, you do,' Father said, 'but he is not a blood relative. Now get in, we need to get a move on. I'll explain on the way.' Father seemed in a hurry so Caspian opened the door and climbed inside, slinging his bag onto the limited seating space behind him.

In as much as the car's exterior resembled no other, the same could be said for the interior. Although stylish and slickly designed, there was little sign of the instruments that came as standard in modern cars: no built in stereo, no satellite navigation, and no electronic dashboard. The interior was cold, metallic, and purely functional, with no additions to distract from this machine's only purpose: to be driven.

Father turned the key in the ignition and the engine roared to life like a lioness defending her cubs. They accelerated away with such speed that Caspian thought his seat was going to swallow him whole.

'Where are we going,' Caspian asked as his father weaved his way through the streets out of London. 'What's going on?' He had never known his father to do anything with haste, so seeing him drive fast made him anxious that something had happened.

'It's your mother, Caspian.'

'Is she okay?'

Father didn't answer immediately, as he weighed his words carefully. 'No, she is not.'

The world seemed to crumble down about him. 'But the doctor's said she was doing better.'

'They thought she was, but the problem with the kind of illness your mother has is that no one can know for certain which way it is going to go. It looked like she was getting better, but in the last week she has suddenly taken a turn for the worse.'

'But she could get better again,' Caspian said.

'I strongly believe that if anyone could, your mother would be where I'd place my bet. She has fought admirably, more than most could manage, but the truth, Caspian, is that she is now fighting a battle she can no longer win.'

Raindrops began to speckle the windscreen as the sky above turned a darker shade of grey. The road glistened before them.

Father was probably wrong, Caspian thought. He had to be. He didn't know for certain that Mother couldn't recover. 'Maybe there is another treatment they can try?'

'She is in a specialist hospital, the best that money can buy,' Father explained. 'They have tried everything they can, but they have no more options left.'

'There must be something they can do,' Caspian argued. 'They can't have tried *everything*.'

'They have done all that they can.'

How could Father be so certain, almost determined, that nothing more could be done for Mother? It was as though he had already given up on her. This made Caspian feel angry; why was he the only one still trying to keep her alive?

'You don't even care if she dies!' he blurted out angrily. 'You don't even care!'

'Yes, I do,' his father replied quietly.

'No, you don't,' Caspian shouted. 'You turned your back on her when you left us, and you never came back. When she became ill you never even came to visit. She didn't have anyone there to help her, except me, and I moved away too.'

Tears dripped down his cheeks as he felt his heart aching with guilt, anger, and sadness. He had moved away and she was supposed to have recovered, not gotten worse. 'It's not fair,' he said quietly to himself, and then he started punching the passenger door panel with his fist. 'It's not fair! It's not fair!'

He punched until his hand hurt, and his throat became so tight his voice was barely more than a whimper. Then he slumped back in his seat and stared out the window as the world rushed passed, crying quietly and not wanting to talk.

About an hour from Little Bickham the rain began to clear and they were greeted by the winter's sun, distant and cold in the sky above them. The cities were traded for farmer's fields, bare and barren where they had been ploughed, awaiting spring and the sowing season. Like the roads, Caspian's eyes were still wet but drying. His anger had faded, but was replaced by his increasing guilt.

Without the distraction of radio, they had travelled on in silence until Father eventually spoke. 'Your uncle Toby left me with the keys to this car, with the instruction to only use it when absolutely required. He is rather possessive of this vehicle.'

'I've never heard of an Uncle Toby,' Caspian muttered distractedly.

'That is because your mother has never really approved of him,' Father said with a small smile to himself at some private joke. 'Toby is the closest thing I have to a brother, and although we are not bound by blood he has always remained a loyal friend.'

'He must be very rich,' Caspian reasoned. 'After all, this car must be very expensive.'

'Despite all his ambitions, Toby is certainly not a wealthy man.'

'Then, how did he afford a car like this one? I've not seen another one like it?'

'That's because this is the only car of its kind. It's called Calideus, and Toby did not buy this vehicle, he built it by hand.'

'Built it?' Caspian exclaimed, looking about the car with new found wonder.

'Yes,' Father nodded. 'From the engine to the exhaust pipe, the axis to the chassis: he built, shaped, and crafted every inch of this vehicle. It was he who taught me almost everything I know about repairing complicated mechanisms, like Sprocket. Your uncle is known for two things, and one of them is his affinity for mechanics.'

'And the other?'

'His attraction to trouble,' Father explained. 'Hence your mother requesting he keep a distance from you. I think she thought you would follow him off on one of his adventures, or get caught up in the chaos that frequently follows him about like an anarchic shadow.'

'He sounds a lot like Billy.'

'Yes,' Father agreed. 'I'm not sure your mother would approve of Billy either.'

Caspian smiled; she definitely wouldn't. Out the window, the countryside blurred passed and he felt a strange sensation of déja vu.

'Caspian,' Father said, serious again, 'I want you to understand that nobody expects anything from you today. To do so would be unfair.'

'What should *I* expect?'

Father took a moment to answer and Caspian suspected he was working out what to say. Eventually he told him honestly, 'Expect to be shocked by how different your mother looks compared to when you last saw her. She might have difficulty breathing at times and has a respirator should she need it, but so far she is happy breathing without. You will notice a dramatic change in her weight due to her inability to properly digest food and her body trying to conserve energy. She might muddle information, things like names and places, or get confused about events that happened long ago but that seemed to have happened recently in her mind. She will need you to be patient with her.'

As Father told him this, Caspian had difficulty processing the information as reality. Part of him didn't want to believe it, rejecting it because maybe someone had made a mistake and it wasn't his mother after all. They could have looked at the wrong chart. Although highly unlikely, these sorts of administrational errors were not impossible in hospitals, but deep down inside he knew that he was just hoping for a mistake to save him from facing the unbearable truth.

'Thank you,' he said quietly.

Father glanced at him, his golden eyes full of surprise. 'For what, Caspian?'

'For being honest with me.'

XIX:
Loose Ends

They were sat in a small waiting room in the specialist hospital where Mother was being treated, a room that was unfortunately more often used to give privacy to family members receiving bad news. The doctor who greeted them looked about the same age as Father, although he was completely bald on the top of his head.

'Mr Stone,' the doctor said compassionately. 'I need to speak to you and your son about your wife's deteriorating condition.'

For the stupidest reason that Caspian couldn't explain, he was more affected by the doctor referring to Mother as Father's *wife* than mentioning her declining state. Perhaps this was because he had never experienced his parents as a conjugal couple and it was difficult to even imagine that they were once harmoniously married.

Now take Mr and Mrs Ravenwood: they were a *married* couple, the way a married couple should be. His parents on the other hand were just too different to one another; too incompatible to even contemplate that they could have once been in love. It was like imagining a lion in love with a lamb.

The doctor knelt down beside Caspian so they were both at the same level. 'So you must be Caspian,' he said warmly, as if some mystery had been solved. 'Your mother has spoken often about you.'

'She has?' Caspian replied quietly, thinking about the phone calls when sometimes she couldn't even remember his name.

'Yes, all the time. She is exceptionally proud of you.'

It made him feel uncomfortable to receive his mother's praise through her doctor. He stared at the floor, his hands fidgeting nervously.

'How much do you know about your mother's illness?' the doctor asked softly.

'Quite a lot,' he mumbled. 'She started getting sick, over a year ago.'

'And that sickness kept getting worse?'

'Yes,' Caspian replied, but the word caught in his throat. He felt uncomfortably warm and breathless. The doctor took the seat opposite him and patiently waited for him to compose himself. 'They tried radiation and different drugs. Sometimes she started to get better.'

He looked at the doctor with wet eyes. The doctor looked back sympathetically. 'It never lasted though, did it?' he gently encouraged, 'Her getting *better*?'

Caspian shook his head, his throat tight again, he couldn't speak.

'You see, Caspian,' the doctor said slowly. 'What your mother has been fighting has been very strong, and very resilient against everyone's efforts to stop it. Were your mother not so strong and resilient herself … well, she would not have fought for as long as she has.'

Beside him, he felt Father place his hand atop his shoulder. Caspian looked at him, meeting those golden eyes that usually shone like lighthouses across the sea, although they didn't shine so brightly today. They seemed fogged and hazy, like the lights were on but a mist had clouded the lenses, had taken away the shine.

'Our efforts have been to try and control her illness,' the doctor continued, 'to try and slow its progression, and even to make it go away. We have tried everything we can, but it has proven too strong, and it has now grown beyond the point that it can be stopped.'

The doctor paused and Caspian's heart leapt into his mouth. He already knew what the doctor was going to say before he said it.

'There is little else we can do. I'm afraid she will not be with us much longer.'

Father gave his shoulder a little squeeze. Caspian took a deep breath, but he couldn't force himself to meet the doctor's eyes. 'How much longer?' he asked, so quietly he wasn't sure the doctor heard him.

'I honestly cannot tell you,' the doctor replied, genuinely sad that he couldn't give him a more specific answer. 'She might stay until nightfall, however it might be sooner. When she is ready to go, she will.'

A teardrop splashed against Caspian's cheek. 'Is she in any pain?'

'No,' the doctor reassured. 'We are managing your mother's pain to ensure that she is as comfortable as possible. She won't feel anything bad.'

'And when it happens,' Caspian started to ask, his throat feeling drier than a desert plain, 'how will she … go?'

'Peacefully,' the doctor said with assurance. 'She is very drowsy now, but she will stay awake for as long as she can. Eventually, when the time comes, she will just drift off, as if she is falling asleep.'

'But she won't wake up again, will she?' Caspian asked.

'No, she won't,' the doctor said gently. 'She won't feel a thing.'

The doctor and Father stood, and Father thanked him for all they had done at the hospital. But Caspian couldn't see what they really *had* done; after all, if his mother was going to die they had not done their job. They were supposed to save her, to make her better again, but they had not done that.

Again, he found himself questioning whether this was really happening, like a dream within a dream he could no longer tell what was real. Only that morning he had been willing to face off with Hayden Tanner over the plagiarism of his history report, but now it seemed like the most trivial thing in the world. Even the mystery of the half-masked man and the weapon that connected him to Father seemed insignificant.

In the last few hours, the walls that held up his world had come crashing down, and Caspian found that he was not yet ready to accept that these changes could not be undone, nor face the devastation that would lie in their wake. And so, without a word or making a sound, he drifted unnoticed out of the waiting room leaving the doctor and his father behind.

He drifted down the corridor, tears gently trickling down his cheeks. He moved with no sense of purpose, as though he were on roller-skates and an invisible force was pushing him along with gentle shoves. The world around him felt cold and alien, as if he had become a ghost from the Shadowlands, slipping invisibly amongst the living. And as he passed people in the corridor they didn't look at him, they didn't speak to him, some didn't even seem to notice he was there at all. He could pass right through them, right through the walls maybe, and they would not even realise it. He could not be seen, he could not be heard. He was just drifting, alone.

'*Caspian…*' a voice called from behind, far away.

'*Caspian…*' It restrained him and stopped him going further, an anchor that prevented him from drifting with the tide, from being lost out at sea.

'Caspian…' the voice repeated, warm and caring.

He faced his father's solemn look. Before he could give explanation for his unannounced departure, Father gestured for him to sit beside him on a bench in the corridor.

They both sat, but Caspian found himself staring at a picture on the wall opposite of a boy flying a kite in the wind, rather than look at his father. 'I'm scared,' he quietly admitted, once he found the courage to acknowledge how he felt.

'So am I,' Father confessed.

'You don't seem scared.' It was difficult imagining anything that could frighten a man like his father.

'No?' Father replied. 'Some of us are better at hiding our feelings than others.' He reached inside his pocket and took out a small golden device, not much larger than a pocket watch. Caspian looked at it and instantly recognised it as part of Sprocket's main mechanism.

He gave his father a quizzical look, wondering why he would bring this of all things with him.

'One thing Toby taught me about fixing things is that it is a truly engrossing distraction.' Father idly turned the part over and over in his hand. 'All the time in the world,' he said sadly, 'and it is still not enough.'

'Why didn't they help her?' Caspian asked. 'They are supposed to be specialists here. They were supposed to make her better.'

He took Caspian's hand and placed Sprocket's part in his palm. 'Human's are not like clockwork devices, Caspian. When something goes wrong, our parts are much more complicated to repair. And sometimes, despite the valiant efforts of those around us, sometimes we just cannot be repaired at all.'

'But there must be something they haven't tried,' Caspian said quietly to himself. 'Why did this have to happen? Why *her*?'

Father gave Caspian a look of sadness the likes of which he had never known of him. Looking at him now, it was not impossible to see that his parents had once been a family. 'I have asked myself that same question, over and over,' he said. 'In this world there are none more deserving than your mother of a long and happy life – yet when disease, illness, pain, and misery are dealt, what is deserved is not a consideration.'

'But that's not fair.'

'You are right,' Father replied grimly, 'but neither is life. We just have to play the hand we are dealt and make the most of it. Like characters in a book, we don't know what is written on the next page, or how our individual roles play into life's complicated plot. What we do have are the interactions we share with one another, the memories we form, and the past we create.'

Caspian mulled over the meaning of this Father's words. He didn't favour the idea that his existence had already been inscribed before him, his every movement calculated like a piece in some colossal cosmic clockwork device, a slave to a predetermined path with a foreordained fate; the implication that free will and choice are merely illusionary, the result of conscious thought scrabbling at the rocks to carve its own path in the world.

'Don't weigh my words heavier than they really are,' Father said with a smile, observing his son's furrowed brow. 'I didn't mean to give reason to debate the meaning of life, only to offer an affirmation of hope. Pre-written or not, those choices *you* make, the challenges *you* face. Your perspective of life is entirely yours. As Descartes would put it: *Cogito ergo sum* – I think, therefore I am.'

'Meaning what?'

'Meaning your life is a gift that only you can experience and appreciate. Your mother is someone who truly appreciates life, who understands the importance of living for the moment for we can never know what lies around the bend.' Father smiled, 'That's one of the reasons I fell in love with her.'

Caspian pondered the emotion in Father's eyes. 'When the doctor greeted us…' he began, 'well, I don't understand; you and Mother have been separated for as long as I can remember. Why didn't you get a divorce?'

'This is going to sound confusing,' Father replied, 'but it's because we never stopped loving each other.'

'Love each other?' Caspian said with unintentional bitterness in his voice. 'If you really loved her, you wouldn't have left in the first place. How can you say that? You just packed up and went. If you loved her, why did you leave? It doesn't make sense.'

'You are right, it doesn't.' Father gave him a long penetrating look. 'I forget how fast you are growing up, and I guess I cannot shelter you from certain truths forever. Secrets have a tendency to rebel against their purpose.' Father gave a long sigh. 'But, now is not the time for you to hear this tale and my motives for having to leave your mother. For the time being, please accept that our separation was a necessity and not a choice either of us favoured.'

Caspian tried to consider what necessity could have forced a rift between his parents, after all the chasm he knew that separated them was dreadfully deep. 'Was it difficult,' he asked after a few moments reflection, 'leaving her and moving to London?'

'You tell me,' Father replied. 'Unfortunate circumstances meant you had to do the same thing, no?'

Caspian nodded, recalling the resentment he had felt at being sent to London, away from her. He thought he felt this alone, but it seemed he and his father shared a common bitterness.

'Choosing to live our lives apart was by far the singular most difficult decision your mother and I have ever had to make,' Father explained, 'but we were charged with looking after something very important to the both of us, something we are still trying to keep safe today.'

Caspian thought about the weapon, kept in its owner's hands to prevent him rising again to power. How had his family come to be caught up in this plot – no, not caught up; torn apart by it?

'My father once told me,' Father continued, 'that we are all droplets in the ocean, and that through the actions of our lives we create ripples that can be felt by, and have an effect on, all those that surround us. When you were born, I knew that you were something different, Caspian. You were no ordinary droplet, like my father described. I knew then that the splash you would make in your lifetime would have an impact on many. You, my boy, were not destined for making ripples; you were meant for making waves.'

Father gave Caspian a final nod to ascertain whether he was ready. In truth, he would never be ready for what was to follow, but here they were, stood outside the door to his mother's room. His father turned the handle and gently pushed the door open before gesturing for him to enter.

'Aren't you coming in?' Caspian asked quietly.

'Not just yet,' Father replied reassuringly. 'This time is for you and your mother. I'll be just outside the door.'

He entered the room and the door closed softly behind him. He was alone, just he and his mother who lay motionless on the bed before him, his heart in his mouth.

She just lay there.

The change since he had last seen her was indescribable; she almost looked like a completely different person. She had lost so much weight her emaciated body looked like a skeleton, a shell of the woman she had once been. Her hair had begun to grow back since they had stopped her radiotherapy, but it was thin and light, like a newborn baby's.

'Mom,' Caspian said gingerly. No answer. 'Mom?' he repeated, this time hearing the growing panic in his voice and fearing he was too late.

Her eyelids fluttered, she slowly turned her head and opened her eyes. 'Cas?' she asked weakly, 'is that you?'

He reached for her hand, feeling awash with relief, and felt her grip him back – she was so weak and cold. He sat beside her and held her hand between both of his, trying to transfer some of his heat to her.

'I knew you'd be here when I woke up,' Mother said. She looked at him with her blue eyes and smiled warmly. 'I knew you'd come.'

'Of course I came, Mom,' Caspian reassured her. 'I'd have come sooner, only I didn't know. I didn't know that–'

'It's okay, Cas. You are here with me, that is all that matters.'

'No it isn't,' he said emotionally, feeling a tightening in the pit of his stomach. 'I should have visited more often.'

'And what good would that have done?' Mother asked, but not unkindly. 'I've had some very bad days, Cas. Seeing me on those days wouldn't have done you any good.'

'I could have helped,' he said in protest.

Mother gave him a loving smile. 'And I know you would have. You would have given up all your time to stay and nurse me, but my ailments are beyond the skills of a thirteen year-old, even one as bright and mature as yourself.'

'There would have been something I could do, ' he continued, unsure as to who he was trying to convince.

'And what then?' Mother asked, looking at him sternly. 'What would have happened if you had stayed? We would have still reached this point, and where would that leave you?'

Caspian realised what his mother was implying and that he hadn't thought this all the way through. Had he stayed he would have still been at home, but who would be there to look after him and support him financially – he was too young to have a real job. He would probably have stopped going to school too, wanting to spend more time looking after his mother.

He had felt discarded by the way his mother had just sent him away to live with Father in London, but now he saw the bigger picture and the greater purpose to her actions. If she hadn't sent him away he would have willingly thrown away his life to look after her.

By doing what she had done, she was putting him first, even though she probably had actually wanted him to stay with her. Even now when she was the sickest she had ever been, and was only getting worse, she was still looking out for him – that's what mother's do.

'You knew you weren't getting better, didn't you?' Caspian said sadly. 'That you would *never* get better.'

An incredible sadness flooded Mother's face and she couldn't meet his eyes. 'Yes,' she confirmed in a pained voice. 'The doctor told me I was getting worse, but they were not sure how much time I would have. I wanted to tell you, but I just wasn't brave enough. I'm sorry.'

He squeezed her hand tightly and she eventually looked into his eyes. 'I'm sorry too,' he said. He had not meant to draw a confession from her; his question was purely rhetorical.

A teardrop leaked onto his cheek and as he looked into his mother's eyes he realised they had both started crying. 'I'm so sorry,' she whispered weakly.

'It's okay, Mom,' he said, 'I understand.'

'That is why you had to live with your father,' she continued. 'I needed you to start building a new life away from Little Bickham, away from the home we lived in, and away from me.'

Caspian spoke sullenly. 'But I don't want to forget the life we had.'

'I don't want you to either. We had such happy times together. I love those memories we've shared, but I can't have you associate them with loss. Living in our house surrounded by so many memories, they would eventually become tainted by pain and hurt.'

She held his hand for a moment, watching him with loving eyes. 'So,' she said eventually, trying to lighten the subject, 'what is London like?'

Caspian shrugged. He couldn't think of anything to tell her. 'There isn't much to tell.'

To his surprise his mother laughed. 'Cas, are you seriously telling me that our capital city, one of the busiest cities in the world, has nothing going on? If I were you, I would be out all the time, exploring the city, seeing the sights, losing myself in the diverse culture that surrounds me. What sights *have* you seen, or has your father been keeping you locked up in that little shop of his?'

'He'd probably prefer that,' Caspian said with a smile. He went on to tell his mother about his trips on the Underground, visits to Oxford Street, and his trip to Covent Garden (although he left out his meeting with the vampirish Artemis Grieves).

Mother listened with interest as he described each location, before asking him to try and see as much of the city as he could.

'I will,' he promised.

'I need you to do something else for me,' Mother said weakly. She looked very tired now.

'Anything.'

She closed her eyes but kept a loving grip on his hand. 'I need you to be brave for me.'

Breathing suddenly became impossible, like someone had just placed a clamp on his windpipe.

'You are a Stone, just like your father,' Mother continued in her sleepy voice. Caspian wondered whether the drugs she had been given to relieve any pain were taking affect. 'You are brave and strong, so strong. I'm so proud of you.'

He couldn't speak. Tears ran freely down his cheeks and dripped off his chin. He tried to wipe them away but they kept coming.

'Cas?' Mother said, barely audible now. 'Live that you may live forever.'

Then she was still.

'Mom?' Caspian whispered. 'Mom?'

He had not heard the door open and close quietly behind him, but his father must have slipped in at some point as he now stood beside Caspian, giving his shoulder a tender squeeze.

Caspian was overcome with dread, seeing his mother so seemingly lifeless before him. She had not had the chance to say a single word to Father. He swallowed, but couldn't find the words. He looked at his father whose face reflected the sadness he felt inside. 'Is she…?'

'No,' Father said gently. 'She is just asleep.'

INTERLUDE:
THE NINE SABRES

The wind pulled threateningly at his cloak, trying to haul him from the narrow stone staircase that barely provided footholds as it ascended along a sheer, unmitigated drop. Clouds battled across the night sky like thick black waves, frequently breaking over the moon and blotting out what little light it provided. The cliff face was cold, wet, and slippery from damp. These were all odds that encouraged a false move, but here a false move would be fatal. No one would find his body. No one would notice he was gone.

The hooded man, the half mask, the phantom; he who had not given his name, slowly and carefully made the climb up and up the Forgotten Stair. The winds howled and screamed like foreboding phantasms as they blew through the tall jagged teeth of rocks, known by locals as the Ni Sablene.

Five kilometres out at sea, due east of Ramberg, Norway, can be found the Nine Sabres, the tallest being Efterfalt. Local lore tells of how these points were once a young mountain that grew taller than its sibling mountain, Skottinden.

As the mountain grew taller and taller it also grew arrogant and proud, and as it reached up towards the heavens it began to boast of its superiority over all that it rose above. This angered the Gods of old and they sent a terrible storm to engulf the mountain. They focused the might of the storm – all of the thunder and all of the lightning – at this lone peak, rising high above the rest. With an almighty crack, the mountain shattered and fell into the sea.

When the storm had cleared, all that remained of the mountain were nine shards reaching out of the sea and up towards the highs from where it had fallen. Skottinden looked down on the broken mountain with pity, where pride had left it after the fall.

Local fisherman and villagers grew superstitious of the Nine for the sharp rocks wrecked their ships, gnawing at hulls of passing boats with sharpened stalagmites. They heard the groaning of the wind and they appointed this to the woeful wailing of the souls the Nine had claimed, forevermore charged with warding others away from Efterfalt and its deadly points.

The Forgotten Stair had been carved into Efterfalt hundreds and hundreds of years ago, each step carefully protruding from the tall shaft of rock, invisible unless you were stepping out onto it. This staircase wasn't so much forgotten than it was unknown.

A small boat had been stored in a hut on Sandbotnen bay, which he had taken at nightfall. It took the best part of two hours to circumnavigate the main outcrop of rocky terrain and ragged peaks that protruded between the trough of waves like a stony grey sea-monster poking its head up to strike. These waters were even more precarious by night, and no one would cross them by choice save for the hooded man for whom darkness was a necessity.

There was no place to moor a boat against Efterfalt – the crashing of the waves against the base of this rocky tower would smash a boat to pieces as though it were made out of egg shells, depositing another wreck to its collection beneath the surface. However, by approaching Svaktann, the smallest of the Nine, from the south it was possible to land a small vessel on the flat jut of rock that struck out from its base. He had landed here many times before but the winds were not in his favour tonight and he would need to line his little boat up perfectly, or he would be following it to the bottom of the sea.

The wind screamed at him, blew salt water in his face. Waves crashed against the steep face of Efterfalt to the west. He pulled the sail tight and adjusted the rudder. The lights at the front of his boat dipped down to face the black water, momentarily plunging him into darkness. He held tight, waiting to ride the wave in.

For a moment the air stilled and an unnerving calm hung over the nine rocks.

Then, with a terrific *boom*, the hull of the boat struck the submerged spikes that made the Nine so dangerous. Everything tipped violently sideways as the wave lifted the small vessel up and, with all the spite of the Norwegian Sea, slammed it against the rock.

Rain beat heavily against the coffin as it was lowered into the ground. Someone had once told Caspian that rain on the day of a funeral meant that those who had died were good people, and that the sky was crying that they had passed.

His mother had been a very good person.

The number of Little Bickham residents, friends, and family members who had turned out to pay their respects in spite of the weather reflected this. A very sober Mr Jansen, holding a large black umbrella, stood beside his wife who wept on his shoulder. Mrs Doddington and the rest of the Neighbourhood Watch Committee of Thorpe Lonsdale Lane stood in solemn silence; for once their waggling tongues were stilled. The Ravenwoods were there; Jessica stood at Caspian's side with his father on the other.

But all Caspian could feel was a numbness. There was an emptiness within him that he knew could not be filled, not for a long, long time.

During the service he had followed his mother's coffin down the aisle formed by those who had come to attend, sheltering under large black umbrellas, watching sadly as they made their slow procession to the front.

And all the time, Caspian had felt oddly detached from what was happening. Somewhere deep in his mind he had not been able to accept that it was his mother who was laid inside the coffin. His brain just wouldn't let him accept that someone he had loved his entire life was there with him, accept that she was no longer *there* with him.

It was only when the Minister started recounting words about Mother, and when her friends and those who had been close to her stepped up to the alter and shared memories with the congregation, that it truly hit Caspian.

Mother was gone.

Tears began to fall. For the strangest reason he felt ashamed to cry, but beside him his father gave him a sad smile, his own golden eyes wet with grief. 'Cry, Caspian,' Father whispered to him gently. 'There is no shame in grieving those you love.'

A fresh wave of sadness washed over him as he thought back to the night Mother had died. The final moment of his mother's life they had all been together as one family. There had been a happiness in his mother's eyes when she awoke to find Father in the room, a happiness the likes of which he had not seen in her since before she had first become ill.

He could not imagine how his father felt, having missed out on a life with his wife. And now it was too late. Now that she was in the ground.

'...earth to earth, ashes to ashes, dust to dust,' the Minister said over her grave, as water trickled from the umbrella his aid held to shelter him. 'In sure and certain hope of the resurrection to eternal life.' A brief bitter look passed over his father's face as the Minister read those last words, but Caspian couldn't possibly fathom why these words had created such a reaction.

The first shovel of soil landed on the coffin with a dull *thud*. Then the second, the third, the forth. Jessica held his hand tightly, and his father rested a hand gently on his shoulder. And soon the coffin was covered and they led him away whilst the rest of the soil was laid over where Mother would forever lay at rest.

The wind ripped at his dark cloak. He turned his head and looked about him. He had been lucky.

The hull was still intact with minimal damage to its structure. The wave had landed him on the ledge, just where he'd planned to make berth, but the underwater impact had turned the vessel so that it had landed sideways. Using the rope he kept onboard, he quickly began securing the small boat to the old iron rings that had been fixed into the hard stone of Svaktann, bored into the rock like miniature braces fitted to a tooth.

A small walkway was worn up the side of the rock, leading from south to northwest, from where he could look directly at the dark harsh rock face of Efterfalt. The gap separating the smallest and the tallest of the Nine Sabres was just about wide enough to squeeze a yacht between, but the water here frothed and foamed with the ferocity of a rabid dog. Crossing here was the only way to reach the first step of the Forgotten Stair.

A large turning lever was fixed into rock, which the hooded man gripped with both hands. It was heavy to turn, and difficult now his hands were cold and wet from the sea spray. Slowly the lever turned, and as it did it began to pull taut a chain-link bridge that had moments before dangled helplessly down the vertical rock of Efterfalt's base.

When the lever turned no more he locked it in position and began to climb across. As he stepped off Svaktann he felt the cold winds blow hard against him, and he saw the water churning below where more sharp rocks eagerly awaited a mistake.

The first time he had come here the Forgotten Stair had truly petrified him. He had climbed across the frothing churn below and clung to the side of the rock like a baby bird that had never taken its first leap from the nest. But the fear of that first journey could not parallel that inflicted by his master, confronting him over his anxiety to make the ascent: Those scars he still bore today and had sworn to never succumb to fear's paralysis again.

The Forgotten Stair scrambled upwards to a crevice cut into the great shard of rock after a climb of roughly a hundred metres. There was no handrail to hold onto. What handholds existed were too subtle, eroded away to leave nothing but the callous face of the rock, to offer support to any man who mistook his step.

Nearer the crevice the Stair was concealed and sheltered by a wall of stone, created when at some point in history Efterfalt had been split, a gaping crack that ran down the face of the rock like a deep scar. This shielded pathway ran the remaining distance to the crevice and, protected from the wind and the sea spray. The hooded man was always grateful to reach this leg of the journey. Even the stairs he climbed became more prominent and defined from this point on, making it easier to move quicker and with more confidence than before.

At the top of the crevice, he turned and looked down the path he had come, following it to the chain-link bridge, still pulled taut, linking Efterfalt to Svaktann. His eyes were more than adjusted now to the darkness that surrounded him, and he scanned the sea to make sure no other boats had followed his course from the mainland.

Completely certain that he was alone, he turned and ducked under an opening in the crevice, slipping into the walls of Efterfalt itself. For all the stories, myths, and legends that had grown about the Nine over the centuries, no one had ever suspected that the tallest of these was actually hollow.

XX:
THE INDECIPHERABLE CIPHER

After Mother passed away, Father had made the arrangements for Caspian to stay in Little Bickham until her funeral. During this time he had stayed with the Ravenwoods, sleeping on their sofa.

He felt ambivalent about not staying in his own room for this week. On the one hand he wanted to; it was after all the room he had slept in for most of his life. The only thing that stopped him was the thought of being alone in the house where his mother had always been. *We had such happy memories*, his mother's words repeated in his head. *I love those memories we've shared, but I don't want you to associate them with loss.*

In the run up to the funeral, Jessica helped him sort through the house, boxing up and putting away certain valuables, cleaning the house where dust had settled in the months it had been empty of living souls. They remembered the good times they had shared there; either together, or memories Caspian had of being with his mother.

It was quite a shock for Caspian to discover that his mother had left him the house during the reading of her will.

'The deed of ownership shall be signed over to you on your twenty-first birthday,' the solicitor had told him. 'Until you are of the correct age, number nineteen Thorpe Lonsdale Lane will be entrusted to Thomas Ravenwood and Gwendolyn Ravenwood, as per the agreement reached by both Edgar and Elizabeth Stone.'

Mr Ravenwood had said later once outside the solicitor's office that, 'as far as I'm concerned, Caspian, the house is already yours regardless of your age. You are welcome to come and use it whenever you like.'

'But you're also more than welcome to stay with us, dear,' Mrs Ravenwood had added in her fussy little way.

The funeral came and went. The following week was half-term break, leaving Caspian one last weekend in Little Bickham before he would have to return to London, and return to school. Billy and Clarissa had been on the phone to him regularly to see how he was doing, which he'd really appreciated. He had, by now, missed out on the trip to the Tower of London, but that had really been the last thing on his mind.

Father drove back to London early Saturday morning, having booked tickets for Caspian to travel back by train. Uncle Toby's car, Calideus, was certainly drawing a lot of inquisitive looks from the residents of Little Bickham, who shamelessly gathered around it with intrigue parallel to that that medieval farmers would have had over a modern day television set.

Caspian was glad to have one more weekend to spend with Jess, and as the rain had passed and the day was clear, although rather brisk, they decided upon taking a walk in the woods that surrounded the small village.

They ambled down a muddy track surrounded by evergreens on both sides. Nettles and shrubs lined the pathway; they died off and shrank back during the colder months, but come summer they would aggressively expand their hold on the territory.

For a while they walked in silence, content to just have each other's company. Caspian mulled over the mess of thoughts that lay strewn about the inside of his head as if his mind had been converted into a washing machine and everything inside had been tumbling over and over and over.

After a while they came to a small clearing where the pathway met the edge of a stream and sunlight breached the canopy above them. Caspian climbed up onto a large rock and let his feet dangle, watching the water trickle by beneath.

'There's something I've wanted to show you,' Jess said as she leant on the rock beside him. 'With your mom's funeral coming up there wasn't an appropriate time, but as you go back to London tomorrow… I've been doing some research about the code we found in the museum.'

'The code?' Caspian asked dumbly. How had she had time to even think about this? He had been spending time with her all week, seen her studying and doing her homework, when she wasn't helping him with the house. 'When did you have time to do research?'

'Every now and then,' she shrugged, 'and it's sort of been on my mind since we found it.'

Both Billy and Clarissa had continued to work diligently on it whilst he had been away, but each time he spoke with them on the phone they had made no progress. Caspian, on the other hand, had been happy for his friends to pick up the slack on solving this whilst his mind was being plagued with other thoughts.

'Any luck?' he asked, expecting Jess to say the same thing as the other two.

'I think I know what kind of encryption was used,' Jess replied smoothly.

'Really?' Caspian asked, feeling like someone had tipped a bucket of water over him whilst he'd been dozing in the sunshine. 'How?'

'I tried simple things to begin with,' she explained. 'You know, real basic code breaking. I first tried to find out if it was a substitution encryption.'

Clarissa had tried the same thing. They had all sat around the table in her home whilst she had painstakingly substituted each letter with another, one interval up: so *abc* became *bcd*. This was known as a Caesarian Shift cipher, named after the Roman emperor who supposedly used it to encrypt military messages by shifting the text three places.

They tried each of the twenty-five possible substitutions (with Billy snoring through the final ten), but each substitution shift they tried resulted in giving no solution to the code.

'The thing is,' Jess continued, producing a tablet device from her bag and turning it on, 'some of the words just don't allow substitutions because of how the letters in the words are structured.'

The tablet screen illuminated and she quickly ran her finger across the glass searching for the app she was trying to find.

'What do you mean?' Caspian asked, looking blankly at her.

Jess had opened a text file and immediately the frustratingly familiar letters of the code appeared.

FLYDKOJSWTW   KDTJJPSAZMT
TGPBUYYZJHI QXRKUUWWSEE JV
KGQHUDNLGEV   JSYDCHYWWAV
IKYKTLZFYOB   MWLQGYIAFNA
YGRX

YZJOKJWWYSB   MWDOUBLZYTW
YZJEXNWSAEA   IAIPNLDLFKM
NFYDOZXMGTT   JHQWILFEJSA
FYJEYONVIEV   NFFDOKIWSKM
JHXWQL

Caspian had begun to wonder whether the code was actually written in another language, which was why they had struggled so far to break it. 'Maybe we should consider that the code is not in English,' he suggested.

'I thought the same thing,' Jess nodded, 'so I also put *every* different result after a shift through an online translator to see if it made sense, but again nothing matched. What we have here is not a basic substitution cipher.'

'That's obvious now,' Caspian said. 'But if it wasn't encrypted using substitutions, then how do we solve it? Billy wondered whether it might be an anagram of some sort.'

Jess gave a derisive snort. 'Well, he can spend forever trying to make words by jumbling up those letters, but he'd soon find there are not enough vowels to make words out of all of them. And plus, using an anagram to encode such a large amount of letters wouldn't make sense as there is nothing to help the person decode the information and put the letters in the correct order.'

'So what are you saying?'

'For any code to be cracked there has to be a key,' Jess stated. 'The whole point of a code is to share secret information between only those who know how to decode it.'

'Yeah, I know that,' Caspian said impatiently. 'I'm not a simpleton.'

'Well, I think I know how it has been encrypted, which will make our search for the key much easier.' Jess couldn't prevent herself from looking smug. 'Have you ever heard of a Vigenère cipher?'

'Let's assume I haven't.'

'Well, a Vigenère cipher is much more effective than a Caesarian Shift cipher,' explained Jess, 'because to crack a message encrypted using a shift substitution system you can work through the shifts until the message becomes readable.'

'Right…' Caspian nodded, wondering when she was going to explain how this was relevant to the code in front of them.

'If you really wanted to encrypt something so it would be very difficult to decipher you would need to shift every letter of the phrase to *different* shift substitutions.'

'I thought you said this isn't a substitution cipher?'

'I said it isn't a *basic* substitution cipher,' she corrected him. 'The thing about having every letter shifted differently, well it makes the code impossible to crack unless you know the different substitutions to make, which is why the Vigenère is known as the indecipherable cipher.'

'Indecipherable,' Caspian despaired. 'How is anyone meant to decipher it if it is indecipherable?'

'That's just it,' Jessica said. 'To make the shifts easier to remember, and easier to pass to those who you want to understand the message, a key phrase is used. Look.'

She opened a simple spreadsheet showing a grid, constructed of alphabetical characters. The top-most horizontal line contained the alphabet written from left to right, whilst the left-most vertical line contained the alphabet written top to bottom. The rest of the grid was constructed so that each line of alphabetic sequence started from a different letter.

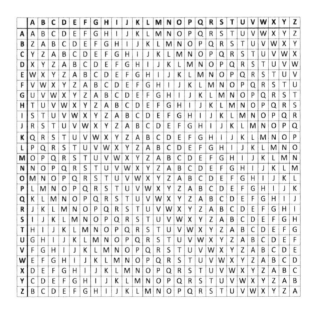

'This grid is the complete encryption and decryption tool,' Jess explained. 'But to encrypt or decrypt something we need a key.'

'What sort of key?'

'It can be anything you like: an individual word or a phrase. It's a reference that can be passed onto whoever is intended to read the encrypted passage.'

'Okay,' Caspian said, trying to come up with something inventive as a key. Immediately his mind emptied and he could think of nothing, but above him the sky was clear blue so he settled for that. 'Go with "blue sky," ' he decided.

'Blue sky?' Jess smirked. 'Manly.'

'Just get on with it.'

'Fine,' Jess shrugged, still smiling. She ran her finger down the side of the spreadsheet, removing rows from the grid and reshuffling them until the vertical axis spelt Caspian's chosen key phrase; *Blue Sky*.

'Let's encrypt your name,' she said. 'Think of the vertical axis as your key word or phrase, and the horizontal axis as the plaintext to be encrypted. Where the two meet on the grid is the encrypted letter.'

Caspian gave her a bewildered look.

'The first letter of our key is *B*.' Jessica pointed to the letter *B* on the vertical axis. 'The letter we need to encrypt is *C*.' She followed the row horizontally with her finger until she was under the letter *C* in the horizontal axis, and touched the letter it had landed on. The square went grey, highlighting a letter *B*. 'Do you see how it works?'

'I think so,' Caspian frowned. He tried to follow the same process she had just shown him. However, as the next letter of his name to encode was the letter *A*, he needed only touch the letter beside the one he had started from. 'Is that right?' he asked, unsure of himself.

Jess nodded for him to continue.

He did the rest of his name, each time starting from the consecutive letter of the key phrase until each letter of *Caspian* had been encoded. The seven greyed out letters on the grid looked like they had been picked at random. Caspian frowned again, not knowing what to do next.

	A	B	C	D	E	F	G	H	I	J	K	L	M	N	O	P	Q	R	S	T	U	V	W	X	Y	Z
B	Z	A	B	C	D	E	F	G	H	I	J	K	L	M	N	O	P	Q	R	S	T	U	V	W	X	Y
L	P	Q	R	S	T	U	V	W	X	Y	Z	A	B	C	D	E	F	G	H	I	J	K	L	M	N	O
U	G	H	I	J	K	L	M	N	O	P	Q	R	S	T	U	V	W	X	Y	Z	A	B	C	D	E	F
E	W	X	Y	Z	A	B	C	D	E	F	G	H	I	J	K	L	M	N	O	P	Q	R	S	T	U	V
S	I	J	K	L	M	N	O	P	Q	R	S	T	U	V	W	X	Y	Z	A	B	C	D	E	F	G	H
K	Q	R	S	T	U	V	W	X	Y	Z	A	B	C	D	E	F	G	H	I	J	K	L	M	N	O	P
Y	C	D	E	F	G	H	I	J	K	L	M	N	O	P	Q	R	S	T	U	V	W	X	Y	Z	A	B

'Read it vertically,' Jess hinted, 'the same way the key phrase is written.'

The letters spelt out *BPYLQQP* as he picked them out, descending row by row.

'See how both *I* and *A* have been encrypted as *Q*'s?' Jess asked and Caspian nodded. 'That's possible because both letters had different starting letters on the grid. The double *Q*'s give the impression of a double consonant encrypted by a Caesarian Shift cipher, but we know that both those letters are actually not the same. Is this making sense?'

'It is…' Caspian answered but not convincingly, least of all to himself.

'Okay,' Jess said patiently. 'Maybe this will make it clearer.'

Again she ran her finger over the spreadsheet, this time removing, copying, and shuffling columns rather than rows. Caspian tried to follow as she tapped a few of the squares to grey them out. Eventually she was left with a smaller grid; the vertical axis still reading Blue Sky, but the horizontal axis instead spelt his name in full.

	C	A	S	P	I	A	N	S	T	O	N	E
B	B	Z	R	O	H	Z	M	R	S	N	M	D
L	R	P	H	E	X	P	C	H	I	D	C	T
U	I	G	Y	V	O	G	T	Y	Z	U	T	K
E	Y	W	O	L	E	W	J	O	P	K	J	A
S	K	I	A	X	Q	I	V	A	B	W	V	M
K	S	Q	I	F	Y	Q	D	I	J	E	D	U
Y	E	C	U	R	K	C	P	U	V	Q	P	G

Now the greyed out squares made a diagonal pattern down the grid, and it was much clearer for him to see how the key phrase just repeated to encrypt his surname. He looked over at his friend who was smiling back at him, and he had to admit it was hard not to be impressed.

Jess tapped the screen and the text document appeared beside the spreadsheet. 'Look at the original code compared to what you have just encrypted. Even though they are not the same, you have to admit that they look similar.'

Caspian compared the two and he had to agree. 'So this was encrypted with a Vigenère cipher.'

'Yeah, I think so,' Jess said. 'But this does create a further problem.'

'Uhu,' Caspian agreed gravely, for the first time feeling on the same page as his friend. 'Without knowing what the key phrase is, we will not be able to decipher the message.'

'Exactly. Any ideas?'

'Not off the top of my head,' he replied. A man as mysterious as his Father would certainly not have a particularly easy key word to guess. 'What have you tried?'

'I've tried lots of things,' Jess answered. 'I've written them all down on a list at home, but I was hoping that maybe your father had mentioned a particular word or phrase that might have some relevance.'

'With my father, everything seems to be both relevant and irrelevant, and sometimes at the same time. I wouldn't know where to begin,' Caspian sighed.

'At least we know what we are looking for.'

Caspian smiled to himself.

'What are you smiling at?' Jess asked.

'I *said* you'd crack this and enjoy doing it,' he pointed out.

'I wouldn't consider it cracked, just yet,' she replied.

They spent the rest of the day trying different words and phrases in attempt to crack the code, but without luck. They tried important dates, types of antiques, famous artists, and anything they could think of that might relate to or be of interest to his father. After many fruitless hours, doubt began to creep into his mind. That evening whilst they sat in Jess' room staring at the Vigenère grid he began to wonder whether they were going down the wrong track.

'We're not going to crack this in a few hours, Caspian,' Jess told him. 'This sort of thing takes patience.' She turned her head as a thought crossed her mind, and the coils of her corkscrew curls bobbed up and down. 'Perhaps we are looking at this from the wrong perspective. We are trying to find a key based on something your father would use, but surely someone like your father would have a contingency plan to ensure that the key wouldn't be lost were something to happen to him.'

That made sense, Caspian thought. Father had the foresight to ensure that plans were in place were he to be incapacitated – or worse. He would have found somewhere secure that only a select number of people would know about to keep the key to this code. Father was, after all, a very cautious man.

Then it hit him.

'Billy was right all along,' he said dumbfounded.

'What?' Jess asked, unsure what he meant.

'I think Billy guessed where my father keeps the key to the code, although at the time he didn't know what we were looking for.' He thought back to the moment before Hayden presented "his" history report. 'In class, Billy, Clarissa, and

I were discussing where Father might hide such a weapon, and Billy suggested in his antiques shop.'

'You think the *key* is in the antiques shop,' Jess said thoughtfully. 'That was why the man in the hood was trying to get inside.'

'Yes,' Caspian said. 'But my father wouldn't leave something like that in the shop. He might, however, have hidden it *underneath*.'

XXI:
ALL HE SOUGHT

'I suspect that this was their point of entry,' Inspector Costard deduced rather obviously from the gaping hole where the door to Turner & Stone Antiques had been seemingly ripped from its hinges by a stampeding rhinoceros.

Whilst the inspector continued with his far from brilliant elucidations, two other members of the Metropolitan Police were inside dusting the ransacked shop for fingerprints. Unfortunately, considering the amount of dust that had already caked many of the antiques on display prior to the break in, the incompetent officers were essentially achieving little more than dusting.

This was the scene that met Caspian upon his return to Old Church Street on Sunday evening. Two police cars were parked outside the shop-front, which had been roped off by a line of police tape to prevent pedestrians walking into the crime scene. He had had to convince a rather suspicious police officer that he actually lived here and to let him through.

'What happened?' he asked, taking in the state of disarray that the intruders had left in their wake, although it was quite plain to see: the door had been kicked in from the outside, the shop turned upside-down whilst it had been searched. It was hard to assess the cost of the damage that had been caused to some of the ancient antiques his father had collected over the years.

Then another thought struck Caspian, 'Was anybody hurt?' he asked, wondering where Mrs Hodges and his father had been when the break in occurred.

Before Inspector Costard could replay his interpretation of events, Father explained that both he and Mrs Hodges had been upstairs. 'Subtlety was clearly not their intent. We were alerted by the loud crash of the door being kicked in and the noise they made in the shop. I came down to investigate whilst Mrs Hodges called the police.'

'Who was it?' Caspian asked, but he was sure he already knew the answer. The hooded man had returned and broken into the shop under the cover of nightfall.

'Whoever it was must have heard me coming,' Father said. 'By the time I came into the shop they had left, leaving this mess behind them.'

Inspector Costard flipped a page in his notepad. 'Probably youngsters, hooligans,' he said, making a note.

Or a masked psycho, Caspian thought, remembering the mad glare he had seen in the hooded man's eye after pursuing him across Covent Garden. He felt his eyes drift over to the small counter where the till sat, and more specifically the circular platform that formed the reflectory's secret entrance.

'They didn't get in there,' Father reassured him. 'I never leave money in the till after closing,' he added for the inspector's benefit.

Caspian could read between the lines. *He didn't get into the reflectory*. Relieved, he asked, 'Did they take anything?'

'It will take some time and sorting to be sure, but I don't think so,' Father answered. 'If they did, I doubt we will see it again.'

Inspector Costard gave Father a reproving look. 'You don't place much faith in the Metropolitan Police, do you Mr Stone?' he said. 'Now, where is that housekeeper of your's with the tea?'

The inspector was a tall thin man with an unusually spherical bald head which, when he stood upright, made him resemble a lollipop. He sported a large bristly walrus-like moustache that in addition to his other attributes contributed to a look of a lollipop that had been rolled in fluff.

Earlier that day, Caspian had said goodbye to Jessica and a rather teary Mrs Ravenwood before catching a train from Little Bickham to London – this time on his own. His mind had been a jumbled mess the entire journey back, flicking from the emotional weight of his mother's death to the discovery as to how the code was encrypted.

On top of it all was the anxiety he felt about returning to school the following day. Caspian knew that everyone would be awkward around him, not knowing what to say, or worse, feeling they had to give him special treatment like he was broken. Surely his nemesis, Hayden Tanner, was relishing the opportunity to lay into him about his mother's passing, especially as he'd narrowly escaped his previous devious snare. What lies had he been spinning in Caspian's absence? He dreaded to think.

As Caspian had rounded the corner on to Old Church Street he had seen the flashing blue lights of the parked police cars, and his stomach had done a somersault. The thought that the hooded man had broken into the shop was the furthest of his fears, instead he worried that something had happened to the only family he had left – his father and Mrs Hodges.

Suddenly, a blood-curdling shriek sounded from above them, followed by an almighty *crash*. Caspian, stood nearest the shop entrance, ran through the doorway and hurtled up the staircase, followed closely by Father and Inspector Costard. All three made haste towards the source of Mrs Hodges' screams.

Caspian found her sobbing with fear in the hallway; the tray of hot drinks she had been carrying lay strewn across the carpet at her feet. A look of overwhelming dread resonated from her eyes as she seemed to look right through Caspian and stared with trepidation at the staircase that led up to the second floor.

'Caspian, no!' Father shouted to him, but the words whistled passed Caspian having no impact.

Without a second thought he leaped over the mess of crockery and darted for the flight of stairs Mrs Hodges was anxiously eyeing. Behind him he heard Inspector Costard ask her what had happened.

'He went up there...' she answered, her voice shaking with fright.

As Caspian reached the top of the stairs he heard a scraping sound emanating from his father's bedroom. This had to be the way Mrs Hodges' assailant had gone. He crossed the hallway in pursuit and burst into the bedroom, just as Father reached the top of the staircase.

The door flew open and a blast of air gushed towards him. Two towering figures in crimson cloaks seemed to rush at Caspian out of the darkness, but then their hoods caught and they both lurched awkwardly backwards towards the window, tumbling and flapping as they went; the pair of large velvet curtains blew aside to reveal the bedroom window gaping wide open behind them.

Even in the dim light of the room, Caspian knew he was alone and the assailant had escaped.

Up on the rooftops of Old Church Street the hooded man moved northwards with soundless agility across the tiles and chimneys, his dark cloak black against the night.

He silently cursed himself for not taking into account the housekeeper. It should have dawned on him that Edgar Stone was the sort of man who considered himself too important to concern himself with the daily mundane chores that consume the average homemaker. That simple miscalculation had almost got him caught.

Had the old woman not screamed, Stone would have been none the wiser to my true intentions tonight.

Not that it mattered. The hooded man had found what he had been searching for. As soon as he saw it sitting innocuously upon the shelf he had seen it for exactly what it was: the key to breaking Edgar Stone's code.

Father instructed Caspian to look after Mrs Hodges who was still rooted to the same spot where her assailant had left her surrounded by broken teacups, a shattered teapot, and standing in a puddle of what Caspian sincerely hoped was nothing more than their contents.

'Where did he go?' Inspector Costard had asked after he and Father had followed Caspian into the bedroom, clearly not connecting the dots between the open window and the vanishing man.

'I didn't see him,' Caspian replied, 'but I heard him open the window. He must be on the roof.'

The inspector had rushed out of the room calling out instructions on his radio. He and another officer left to go in pursuit whilst a couple of officers remained to assist Father at the shop.

One officer wanted to ask Mrs Hodges a few questions about what she had seen however, considering her current condition, Father asked him to allow her a few minutes to recover.

'Please go and sit down, Mrs Hodges,' Father had asked her.

'But the mess!' she'd fretfully replied, 'I can't just leave the place in this state.'

Father gave her a warm smile. 'Mrs Hodges, I am more concerned with the state of my housekeeper than I am with the state of my floor. Caspian, escort Mrs Hodges to the reception room, and I'll send the police officer in shortly to speak to her. And Caspian, fetch her a hot drink to calm her nerves.'

'If it's to calm my nerves, I'd prefer a strong drink to a hot one…' Mrs Hodges mumbled to herself as Caspian took her by the arm and led her to a comfortable chair, although it did little to help her relax.

As they'd neared the room her eyes had darted from side to side, she whispered to Caspian, 'He was in here…' Her elderly hands were still shaking when he returned to her with a cup of tea and a blanket.

The tea seemed to do the trick, and after a few sips Mrs Hodges was a lot calmer, albeit still noticeably distressed. She sat staring straight ahead, clutching the hot cup between her faintly trembling hands as though she had spent the night outside in the cold.

Caspian felt a mixture of sadness and anger to see her in this state.

The break-in had clearly been meant as a distraction to draw the residents of the house down to the shop, allowing the assailant to search the house whilst everyone else investigated the disturbance. Unfortunately Mrs Hodges, who had been in the kitchen making tea for the officers, had still been in the residence when the second break-in occurred, under cover of the first.

'Mrs Hodges?' Caspian said quietly, trying not to startle her. He already had a very good idea as to who was behind tonight's misdemeanours but he needed the only witness to confirm it. 'Who was in here?'

She turned to him, eyes distant, her face had become much older. He knew Mrs Hodges was old, but he had never thought of her that way. She had always been such a sprightly character, full of life and energy. But now, sat before him with a blanket over her lap and a strange look in her eye, for once she seemed to show her age.

'I barely caught a glimpse of him,' she replied quietly. 'At first I thought I was looking at a shadow. Wrapped in a dark cloak, he was, to conceal his identity.'

Caspian felt his stomach twist, even though he had expected this to be the answer. The hooded man had been here, in his home.

The man beneath the cloak must have been watching the house, but why hadn't he tried this sooner? Surely he would have had better opportunity to try this whilst Father had been in Little Bickham for Mother's funeral?

In a sense, it was better it had happened this way, Caspian thought. It bear not thinking about what might have happened had he broken in whilst Caspian and Father were away. Poor Mrs Hodges would have been all alone in the house and this story might have ended quite differently.

'Had I not happened to glance in here as I passed with the tray of drinks,' Mrs Hodges continued, 'I doubt I would have noticed him at all.'

The street outside was becoming increasingly illuminated as more police cars arrived on the scene, their blue lights flashing and casting strange shadows on the buildings around them. The rumble of a helicopter could be heard overhead, searching the area from high above.

'It's okay,' Caspian tried to reassure her.

'No, Caspian,' Mrs Hodges said looking at him now. 'For the briefest moment I saw what he concealed under that dark hood of his, and I have never felt such fear. His face was twisted and scarred as though he had been dragged through all nine circles of Hell, and the hate that burned in his eye... I cried out, for I was sure he had come to send me to the grave.'

Caspian rested his hand on her wrist, but it seemed Mrs Hodges had found momentum now and wanted to let it all out.

'My cry must have alarmed him,' she continued, 'as he stopped what he was doing and ran towards me. That was when I glanced the other side of his face for the first time, and it was even more hideous than the one before. You wouldn't believe me unless you saw it yourself, Caspian, but it were almost as though he were part man, part machine.'

In an instant Caspian was back in the crowds of Covent Garden. The flames of the fire breather had illuminated the face beneath the hood and he was staring into the distorted metal imbedded into half of the horrifically scarred face, his singular visible eye alight with odium.

'He came through the door, and just when I thought my number was up he passed me and ran upstairs. Oh, Caspian! I sincerely thought I had served my last pot of tea!'

'I'm just glad you are okay,' Caspian said. 'You said he stopped what he was doing when he saw you?'

'I guess he didn't know I was in the kitchen,' she replied.

'But what was he doing?'

'He was looking at that.' Mrs Hodges gestured to one of the many bookcases that lined Father's reception room. This bookcase was filled with various reference books on all manner of subjects, but it was not the books that she had pointed at. On the very top shelf, between a pair of very odd carved stone figures that resembled giants, there sat a polished wooden plaque in the shape of a shield. It was decorated and engraved with what Caspian could only assume were his family's coat of arms.

'I don't know why he was interested in that old thing,' Mrs Hodges said. 'If he'd hoped to make a pretty penny selling it, he would have been better off stealing from downstairs.'

Amongst all of the interesting artefacts that decorated his father's reception room, it had been easy for Caspian to overlook this rather dull piece. But now as he studied it more closely he saw why it had peaked the hooded man's interest.

It wasn't the piece itself he had been after, but the words engraved upon it. The same words Caspian sought – the key to the code.

It seemed to Caspian that his father was avoiding him. He had waited until the police had finally left following the double break in before attempting to confront his father, but he was met by a torrent of excuses; he needed to tidy the shop, he had too much on his mind, he was awaiting an update from the police – the list went on.

But for Caspian, he felt an overwhelming urge to bring up a subject that had been shunned on that first fateful weekend in his father's house. Just before midnight, he found Father sat in his study deep in thought, and decided that he would no longer accept any excuses. This was too important not to discuss.

'Caspian?' Father asked, seeing him in the doorway. 'Is everything all right? After everything you've had to go through, I'm sorry that to cap it all off you've had to return to pandemonium this evening. But then, criminals are not known for their consideration.'

'This wasn't the act of merely criminals, and you know it,' Caspian blurted out, annoyed with his father's dismissal of the obvious truth.

The concern that had been in Father's golden eyes quickly dissipated, leaving a look full of suspicion. 'What are you implying?'

'Mrs Hodges told me what she saw. She told me who was in the house. It was a man wrapped in a dark cloak, the same cloaked man I saw through the window when I first came here who you dismissed as nothing.'

'A cloaked man?' Father asked sceptically. 'If this man was wrapped in a cloak, how can you be sure it was the same man?'

'She said he wore a half mask across his scarred face,' Caspian answered. 'There can't be two people wearing half masks over hideous scars.'

Father sat back in his chair. He placed his hands together, fingertips under his chin, and gave Caspian a long penetrating look. 'That first time you saw him, it was raining, wasn't it?'

'Yes.'

'You never mentioned half masks or scarred faces.'

242

'I'm sure I did…' Caspian said, feeling off balanced by the direction Father was taking.

'No, you didn't,' Father said with unshakeable certainty. 'That night, I did not dismiss what you saw. In fact, I was very interested by what you told me, but I didn't want to portray this to you for fear that you might do something rash – like following him on your own across half of London.'

Caspian's mouth dropped open. *He knows I followed him, but how?*

'What were you thinking?' Father continued, sounding a mixture of disappointment and perplexity.

'I wasn't… Hang on. You've been spying on me?' Caspian said accusingly.

Father leant forward. 'Quite the contrary, actually. Fortunately, it seems that chance put you in the path of an acquaintance of mine who delivered you from harm.'

Artemis Grieves! Caspian realised. 'So, Artemis does know you: he told me he didn't.'

'Mr Grieves is not one to lie,' Father answered. 'He has the habit of speaking quite literally. So much so, to ensure he answers correctly one must ensure of absolutely zero ambiguity in the question.'

'But if you knew what I'd done, why didn't you say anything earlier?'

'And be accused of spying on you?' Father said with a wry smile. 'Nevertheless, I did not want to incite any more curiosity in the matter on your behalf than you had already created.'

'But you know the hooded man is real! He is trying to find the weapon you have been hiding.'

At the mention of the weapon, Caspian noticed the slightest surprise register in his father's eyes. *He didn't expect me to know about that!* he realised.

'Artemis told you this?'

'Yes,' Caspian answered quietly, suddenly feeling like he had betrayed Mr Grieves.

'He should not have.' Father shook his head. 'I forget that that man has a flair for the overly dramatic. That secret was mine to keep, and mine to tell.'

'I'm sorry.' Caspian felt guilty he had asked Artemis Grieves. He had persisted in trying to get the information out of the mysterious man and now it seemed he had gotten him in trouble. 'But is it true? You are hiding a *weapon!* And this is what the hooded man is planning to use to resurrect his master.'

'His master?'

More irritation filled his father's eyes. Caspian suspected he was digging Mr Grieves a very deep hole.

'*That* master no longer exists, and has not for a long, long time.'

Caspian thought back to when he had hid in the shop to avoid being seen by Ponsonby Smeelie and had overheard some of what Smeelie had said to his father. *What if he is truly ready to return?* Could Ponsonby Smeelie and Artemis Grieves have been talking about the same person? It certainly seemed logical that they were.

'About the weapon,' Caspian said, trying to recall exactly what Grieves had said about it being needed to return the evil one to power. 'Can it be used to bring people back from the dead?'

Father gave him an odd look, as if a troubling thought had crossed his mind. He observed Caspian for a long while, trying to reach a decision. 'Did our good friend Mr Grieves actually tell you what this weapon is, what it is capable of?' he asked after a while.

'No,' Caspian said thinking back to the snippets of information Grieves had divulged. 'Nothing good.'

Father nodded slowly in agreement. 'Nothing good at all.'

'Artemis said it could bring about the end of our world as we know it.'

'Exaggerations and extrapolations are the core of Artemis' prestige,' Father sighed. 'But maybe in giving you the answer as to what it is I protect, you will no longer try to find answers by yourself?'

Caspian nodded in agreement.

'Then let me tell you a story,' Father began, gesturing for Caspian to sit down opposite him.

He took a seat, and the room seemed to suddenly grow darker and closer at the same time, as if all four walls had leaned in to hear what his father was going to say.

Father closed the book he had been working in and took out a matchbox. He struck a match and lit the large white candle on the edge of his desk. 'Back in the beginning, before the universe burst into life as the result of the big bang, a battle was waged. This battle wasn't fought by armies, nor by monsters or men, but between two of the purest opposing elements in our existence – light and dark.

'This concept has been used in every religion, culture, and lore of the human race since our species first perceived night and day as opposites, cementing the ideology of light and dark as a recognisable elemental representation of the battle between good and evil throughout the history of humankind. This eternal struggle between two opposing forces is perhaps best portrayed by the concept of the two flames.'

'The two flames?' Caspian frowned. 'I've never heard of them.'

'I'm not surprised, as very few have. One was named Incendium, the other Obscurium. Both burn with opposite results, forever locked in a battle to smother the other and gain dominance of the universe.

'Incendium burns hot and radiates light that we may see through the darkness. This is fire, as you know it, a familiar substance in our world. Obscurium however, the sibling flame, is lesser known. The dark flame draws in the warmth, feeds on the light, and consumes all energy and life it touches, extinguishing it from our world to leave nothing but the darkness whence it was borne.'

'So one feeds on light, and the other emits it?' Caspian thought about one of his Physics lessons at school. 'The way that they cancel each other out, it sounds a bit like you are talking about matter and antimatter.'

'That is a good analogy, as there is certainly a resemblance,' Father said with an appraising smile. 'However, in the case of a matter and antimatter collision both particles annihilate on impact leaving nothing behind but a burst of pure energy. These two flames do not cancel each other out but instead consume one another until the stronger flame endures.

'Is that what you have been keeping? The dark flame?'

'No. For many, many centuries the dark flame has been absent from our planet, thought to have been permanently extinguished a long time ago.'

'But anyone can light a fire,' Caspian stated, 'why can't the dark flame be relit?'

'It is not as simple as striking a match,' Father replied. 'Nevertheless, just like if left to burn unsupervised fire can burn fiercely, relentlessly, and grow out of control, the same could be said of Obscurium. If the dark flame were allowed to burn again, our entire planet could be consumed by the darkness.'

Caspian wondered how this tale of a dark flame that consumed all light and energy could be linked to the hooded man and the secret weapon his father kept safe. But before he could ask, Father continued with the story.

'Only once in human history has mankind managed to ignite the dark flame on Earth, and use it in a controlled manner. A single man of incredible intellect, a master of metallurgy among many other disciplines, achieved this miraculous task.'

'Was this the "Evil One" Mr Grieves spoke about?' Caspian asked.

Father nodded. 'Some believe he unlocked the secrets of the flame through his knowledge of alchemy, whilst others believe he found a way to bend the flames to his will. Whatever the truth, both sides agree that although the fire did not burn for long, it burnt long enough to achieve a purpose as dark as the flame itself. A sword of unusual strength and subtlety was forged in Obscurium, a Geldrin Blade, and the qualities of the black fire were impressed deep into the folded steel. The behaviour of the metal was forever reformed, assimilating the attributes of the fire used to cool it. To be touched by the blade would be a fatal act for *any* living thing.

'Why would anyone want to make such a weapon?' Caspian asked.

Father gave him a grim look. 'For the same reason that man has forged weapons since he first swung a stick or hurled a heavy stone: to dominate his fellow man.'

'But what about the involvement of the man in the black cloak?' asked Caspian. 'If the Geldrin Blade cannot raise the dead, then he can't be using it to bring his master back to life.'

'The path and purpose of this hooded man is shrouded in mystery,' Father said thoughtfully. 'However, wheels are in motion to ascertain his intentions and to prevent them from being achieved. The question we face is how he came to know so much.'

Caspian suspected he knew the answer to this. 'Over the Christmas break, my friends and I went to the Museum of London. Whilst we were walking round the museum and looking at the exhibits we took a wrong turn and ended up outside the museum curator's office.'

Father didn't react to this revelation, so Caspian continued on. 'I saw the hooded man threatening the curator into helping him find the hiding place of the Geldrin Blade –

although neither mentioned what the weapon was. I think the curator has been helping the hooded man, even if it might be against his will.'

'Do you know the name of the curator of the Museum of London?'

'Yes,' he answered slowly. 'His name is Ponsonby Smeelie.'

Father narrowed his eyes. 'And you have heard this name once before, haven't you?'

'Yes. When we first went down to the reflectory, he was the man who came to visit you.'

Father sat back in his chair and gave Caspian another long searching look, once again weighing some unfathomable decision. 'Ponsonby Smeelie has been an associate of mine for a very long time. Although he may not be the most agreeable type of man, I can vouch that he is not in league with this masked man, nor would he divulge sensitive information under duress.'

'But I heard him – '

'No, Caspian,' Father interrupted. 'You must trust me, you are wrong about this point. Drop the issue and leave it with me to deal with. I do not want to find you anymore involved with this, do I make myself clear?'

'But I can help,' Caspian protested.

'No, you must not.'

'But – '

'No more following people, no more hurling yourself into danger, and no more sneaking around trying to find out about the Geldrin Blade. Am I making myself understood?'

Caspian gave a hesitant nod.

'You are smart boy, but you are in over your head with something you don't fully understand. I have told you everything tonight because I want to quench this thirst you have developed, and I expect you to keep this entire saga secret.'

'I will,' Caspian swallowed, feeling rejected.

'You understand the importance of what I have said?'

'Yes.'

'And you promise?'

'Yes.'

Father's golden eyes watched him very closely for a while. 'And there is nothing else regarding this matter that you have to tell me?'

'No,' Caspian lied, 'that's everything.'

Except that I have cracked your code.

XXII:
RIDDLE ME THIS

Caspian almost ran to school the following morning. The anxiety and trepidation he had felt towards his return to Hogarth House had not fully disappeared, but his excitement and anticipation to share his discovery with Billy and Clarissa had easily outweighed the former.

He found them both waiting for him at the school gates. Clarissa threw her arms around him and said how sorry she felt for him (she had told him this pretty much every time they had spoken since he'd been excused from History on that fateful morning). Billy, on the other hand, settled for giving him an awkward pat on the shoulder.

'I'm okay,' Caspian told them honestly, 'but something else has happened.'

'What is it?' Clarissa asked looking worried that another terrible thing had occurred.

'It's not like that,' he said quickly to put her at ease. 'It's about the code: I've solved it, I know what it says.'

'Seriously?' Billy asked in amazement. 'But how did you solve it?'

Caspian quickly explained to them the progress that Jessica had made in identifying how the code had been encrypted – the Vigenère cipher. Clarissa was impressed and quickly grasped the concept of the key word or phrase, although it took Billy somewhat longer to understand how the cipher worked.

'So we needed this "password" to unlock the code?' Billy asked.

Caspian nodded. Then he told his friends about the break in.

Clarissa went pale and was concerned that nobody was hurt, whereas Billy seemed blissfully blasé that a psychopathic masked madman, who was not above committing acts of violence, had been sneaking around his friend's house with unknown intentions. 'He was in your home?' he asked excitedly. 'Did he see you?'

Caspian shook his head.

'What about the police?' Clarissa asked. 'Have they caught him?'

'Not that I'm aware of. It seems that after he climbed out of the bedroom window he just vanished without a trace.'

'You would think that someone with his features and unique dress sense would be easy to find,' Billy commented. 'What was he doing there?'

'Isn't it obvious?' Clarissa said. 'He was looking for the key phrase. We heard Ponsonby Smeelie reveal to him that the clue was hidden in Caspian's home.'

'Well, he found it,' Caspian said. 'And had Mrs Hodges not seen what he was looking at we wouldn't have known.'

'So, what was it?' Billy asked eagerly.

'It was three Latin words, engraved on a plaque displaying my family's coat of arms,' he explained. 'Vive ut Vivas.'

'It was your family motto?' Clarissa asked, surprised.

'Yeah. We'd been looking for the key, or the clue to solving the code, in the wrong way. I'd assumed that my father would have something cryptic as the key phrase, or would have hidden it in some secret compartment. Believe me, my father is a very secretive man,' Caspian shrugged. 'But above all things, he is a traditionalist. I didn't suspect for a moment that he would leave it out in plain sight, written on a tatty old plaque, but when I saw it I knew it was the key.'

'That, and the fact the hooded man was staring at it,' Billy said. 'More importantly, what does the code say?'

Caspian took the piece of paper he had written the decoded message on and showed it to them.

ATTHEHEARTO   FLONDINIUML
OOKFORTHEHA LFMOONRENEW ED
FOLLOWITBEN   EATHWATERAN
DSTONEUNTOT   HEGUARDIANS
TOMB

THESECRETST   HEYSOUGHTTO
THEIRGRAVES   DIDTHEYTAKE
INTHISSUBTL   EPLACEAMESS
AGEISHIDDEN   INAHIDDENKE
EPSAKE

'It still doesn't make sense?' Billy said, staring at the encrypted message.

'Yes it does,' Clarissa smiled. 'The words are all bunched together.'

She took the piece of paper from Caspian and after a few seconds of scrutiny began to read the message out loud. ' "At the heart of Londinium, look for the half-moon renewed. Follow it beneath water and stone unto the Guardians tomb. The secrets they sought, to their graves did they take. In this subtle place, a message is hidden in a hidden keepsake." '

'What does that mean?' Billy despaired. 'Is it a riddle?'

'Sounds like it,' Clarissa shrugged, 'but it could also be directions to finding where the weapon is hidden.'

'And the hooded man now knows the same thing we do,' Caspian added. 'As of last night we are now tied with him in the race to find it.'

'We need to work out what each phrase means.' Clarissa was still looking at the riddle. 'There must be hundreds of tombs in London, but I've never heard one referred to as the Guardians tomb.'

'There's something else I need to tell you,' Caspian said, before his friends got too engrossed with the meaning behind the words of the riddle. 'Last night, my father revealed to me the nature of the weapon he is hiding.'

'Yes!' Billy said with excitement. 'And…'

'It's a sword.'

'A sword?' Clarissa frowned.

'Yes.'

'All this just to hide a sword?'

'Apparently it is more than just a normal sword,' Caspian added. 'It's a special type of sword, known as a Geldrin Blade.'

Clarissa's eyes widened, her mouth fell open. 'That isn't possible.'

'What?' Billy asked, unsure what was going on.

'You've heard of the Geldrin Blade?' Caspian asked.

Clarissa shook her head as if to clear it. 'Yes, but it's a child's story. My grandpa told me the story once when I was young. It can't really exist.'

'How much do you know?' Caspian asked.

'He said that it was forged in a darkness the likes of which our world had never known,' she replied, her brow burrowing as she thought back to the story she had been told.

'That sounds ominous,' Billy quipped.

The bell rang, signalling the start of registration.

'So does that,' he added.

'We haven't got lessons together until this afternoon,' Caspian said, wishing he had more time to find out what Clarissa's grandfather had told her about the Geldrin Blade. 'This conversation is to be continued. See you at break time.'

Clarissa nodded, still looking spellbound and baffled at the news that the weapon they were looking for was featured in a story she'd heard as a little child. She left to go to her classroom, whilst Billy and Caspian headed for their own.

He followed Billy into their tutor room. His classmates, who had moments before been loudly regaling one another with how they'd spent their weekends, all fell quiet as he came through the door. Suddenly, he became acutely aware of the eyes of his fellow students on him and the excitement he had felt but moments before melted quicker than an ice cream in a volcano. It was just like his first day all over again, with all eyes on him, judging. However, the one pair of eyes he had dreaded the most, those ice blue eyes that so mercilessly calculated mischief were nowhere to be seen.

'Where's Hayden?' Caspian whispered to Billy, almost too hopefully. It occurred to him that he might have simply beaten Hayden to the classroom, however the last person to enter the room was Mrs Scrudge who immediately began taking the register.

'Daddy took him skiing,' Billy whispered back.

'I didn't think we were allowed to take holiday in term time?'

'When your dad is on the committee for the school, you can take holiday whenever you like,' Billy replied. 'He's off all week.'

Caspian breathed a sigh of relief as he wouldn't have to face his nemesis for another seven days. Maybe his first week back wouldn't be too bad after all.

As the morning passed almost everyone in his class came over to acknowledge his loss. At first Caspian didn't know how to react to their condolences, but in the end he found it easier just to say *thank you*. As it happened, it seemed that likewise many people didn't really know what to say to him either, which meant many conversations were uncomfortably short, painfully awkward, or sometimes both.

When the bell rang to signal the morning break, Caspian was relieved to get away from the swarm of sympathisers and keen to continue his intriguing conversation with Clarissa.

'How did your grandfather know about the Geldrin Blade?' he asked her as soon as they found a secluded corner of the already quiet library.

'I don't know,' she replied with frustration. 'I thought it was a story, like a fairytale. My grandparents told me many fairytales when I was a child, but I never once thought to ask them how they knew about Cinderella's glass slipper, or whether they knew Hansel and Gretel – you just take it as a *story*, nothing more.'

'But he knew about it,' Caspian continued. 'He must have heard it from someone.'

'Yes, you are right,' Clarissa replied, 'but I don't know from whom. He only ever told us the story once, and it certainly wasn't the most interesting tale.'

'Can you remember it?' Billy asked.

Clarissa scowled for a moment, but eventually gave in. 'The Geldrin Blade was supposed to have been forged by the most evil being to have ever existed. Grandpa described him as a sorcerer who conjured up the darkness and in it created a weapon that was so powerful it could even defeat light.'

'What did he say happened to the blade?' Caspian asked.

'He said that the sorcerer created the sword to rid him of his enemies who had joined to form a powerful opposition. Before he could use the blade, one of his own servants grew fearful that his master would not stop at ending his enemies but would try to destroy the entire kingdom. To prevent this, the servant stole the blade and smuggled it to the opposition, on the condition that the blade would never be used or fall into the hands of mortal men.'

'And what happened to the sorcerer?'

'It turned out that the Geldrin Blade was all that sustained the sorcerer's fading life, and that once parted from it he faded away to nothing.'

'Until now,' Billy said.

'Do you really think a sorcerer has returned for his magic sword?' Clarissa asked in a tone that suggested she thought flying pigs were a more likely outcome.

'But this has to be who both Smeelie and that shopkeeper Caspian spoke to were talking about, right?'

'I think so too,' Caspian added, 'although I'm not sure I agree about him being a sorcerer.'

For a moment Billy looked thoughtful. 'Do you really think he can come back from the dead?'

'Don't be ridiculous,' Clarissa replied. 'We know that sort of thing is impossible.'

Caspian thought back to his conversation with his father. He had asked him whether the blade could bring the dead back to life, but now listening to Clarissa snubbing the fantastical he felt foolish for even considering it a possibility. *Of course it can't!*

'Anyway,' Clarissa said. 'We will never know if it truly is a Geldrin Blade unless we work out *where* it is.' She opened a large dusty old book on Roman Britain, its pages were yellow from age and doing a very good job of distancing themselves from the book's spine. 'The first line of the passage is "At the heart of Londinium, look for the half-moon renewed." *Londinium* is the Roman name for London, so it is the heart of Roman London we should be starting from.'

'Same difference,' Billy shrugged.

'No, actually,' Clarissa corrected him. 'Londinium was by far the largest town in Roman Britain, but it didn't progress further than the defensive wall that limited city growth for over a thousand years. Nowadays, London is comprised of thirty-two London boroughs that far exceed the boundaries of the City's centre.'

Clarissa found a page in the book that showed a plan of how Roman London would have looked, and then beside it she laid a map of Greater London. 'If we use London Wall as a perimeter, then we should be able to establish where the centre of Londinium can be found today.'

Using a red pen, she began to mark on the modern map where the original London Wall had stood. 'Starting at Tower Hill, it would have run along Minories and then onto Bevis Marks.' She pointed at a road in the city called London Wall. 'This road was named after the course the wall used to run, leading up to the Museum of London.'

Caspian recalled seeing a still standing section of the wall through a window at the museum during their visit. He had learnt that the Roman's had spent almost thirty years completing the mammoth task of the wall's construction, building it from eighty-six thousand tons of stone (roughly the same weight as two-hundred and twenty Boeing 747's).

Once Clarissa had drawn the boundary of Londinium on the map of modern London, the centre was quite easy to find. All of the roads seemed to flow towards it, just like arteries leading to the heart.

'That's Bank,' Billy said, putting his finger in the centre of the area created by the wall. 'That would be the heart of London, especially as that is where all the money is.'

'Yeah…' Caspian agreed, but something was nagging at him.

'What is it?' Clarissa asked.

'I don't think Bank is the correct place.' He turned to Billy. 'I agree with your suggestion, but it isn't the heart of *London* we are looking for. Do you remember the Roman exhibit in the museum?'

'Yes,' Billy replied.

'There was that model of the Roman Basilica.'

'You don't think the phrase refers to the geographical centre,' Clarissa realised, catching Caspian's drift.

'No. The Basilica would have been the place where all trading and other important activities took place. It was their centre of commerce. That would have been *Londinium's* heart.'

Both his friends mulled over what he proposed.

'I think you might be onto something there,' Billy said after a while.

'But the Basilica was demolished over seventeen hundred years ago,' Clarissa commented. 'I'm presuming you don't think your father's riddle refers to the model Basilica in the museum?'

'No,' Caspian said, 'that wouldn't make sense. I think we need to find the place where the Basilica would once have stood. Maybe there we will find clues as to what is meant by "a half-moon renewed." '

Clarissa checked the plan of Roman London, and then pointed to the place on the map of modern London where the Basilica would have stood. 'It would be there, on the spot where Leadenhall Market stands today.'

'We need to check that out,' Billy said eagerly.

'What about the rest of the riddle?'

They looked at the strange passage that had been decoded with the Vigenère cipher. 'Follow it beneath water and stone... Follow what? The half-moon?' Caspian couldn't fathom how a half-moon could travel beneath water and stone. 'Follow it "unto" the Guardians tomb. Any ideas what that means?'

Clarissa and Billy looked at him blankly.

'Well, we need to figure it out and before the hooded man does,' Caspian said. "*The secrets they sought, to their graves did they take. In this subtle place, a message is hidden in a hidden keepsake.*" The rest of the riddle seemed to depend on knowing who the Guardians were. 'Clarissa, maybe you can do a search on the internet for any "guardians" buried in the city. Billy and I will look into any folklore and legends referring to guardians, but I suspect there is going to be quite a few.'

'Caspian?' a voice asked from across the library, derailing his train of thought. 'I didn't know you were back.'

To Caspian's uttermost surprise he found himself looking at the last person he expected to care that he had returned, let alone even notice that he had been away. But, seeing her standing in this very library where he had first set eyes on her, his heart still palpitated with joy.

'I hope I'm not interrupting,' Rose Wetherby said. Beside her stood Julie McFadden who, equally surprisingly, actually seemed rather pleased to see Caspian.

Clarissa packed up the books. 'Come on Billy, we better get started,' she said as she walked off, giving Caspian a conspiratorial look. Billy followed behind, giving Caspian the subtlest of winks before disappearing round the corner of a large bookcase.

He shook his head at the pair of them.

An awkward silence fell after their departure, but to his surprise, and somewhat disappointment, it was Julie who broke it rather than Rose.

She looked at Caspian sheepishly, her dark hair tied behind her head today in a slick ponytail. 'Caspian, I didn't know what you were going through with your mom. I'm so sorry; I'd never wish anybody to go through that.'

'Thanks,' Caspian muttered, feeling uncomfortable.

'I guess what I'm trying to say is, I owe you an apology for the way I've treated you since what happened with my diary.'

'It's okay,' he replied, feeling astonished that *she* was apologising to *him*. Maybe this wasn't going to be such a bad week back after all.

However, Julie continued and Caspian realised his optimism had come slightly too soon. 'I mean, now I understand why you've been acting out the way you have.

With your mother being ill and you sent away, you must have needed to be noticed to help you through it.'

What!? Caspian was furious. It was bad enough that he was still being blamed for everything that Hayden Tanner had done, but the idea that he was using his mother's illness as an excuse for attention seeking behaviour made him outright livid.

He was about to open his mouth and say something when a thought crossed his mind. *What will Rose think of me if I reject her friend's apology?* Were it anyone else he wouldn't have cared, but in the eyes of Rose Wetherby he found himself wanting to be seen in a different light.

Arguing that Julie was wrong would certainly not grant the positive image he desired, regardless that there wasn't a single ounce of accuracy in what she had said. In a battle of opinions it seemed better to lay aside his pride and concede defeat, allowing him to return and fight another day. Better that than fight a losing battle till his dying breath.

'So, no hard feelings?' Julie asked.

Caspian stared at her for a moment, and then swallowed hard. He found his voice and, working hard to sound as relaxed as he could, he answered, 'None at all.'

'Also,' Julie continued, oblivious to the deep level of offence she had just caused him, 'I want to thank you for letting me write that article about you when you started at the school.'

Caspian recalled being quizzed by Julie on his first day, but certainly didn't recall giving her permission. If anything, he'd felt pressganged into answering her questions.

'It was because of that piece,' Julie said, 'that I have been accepted onto the school paper as a journalist. I'm the first ninth year to make it onto the paper in the last six years.'

'They're not going to publish it, are they?' Caspian asked. He couldn't think of anything more humiliating than having his peers read his first impressions of the school.

'Unfortunately, they felt the moment had passed and that the piece was better suited for the first term of school, not the spring term.' Caspian could hear the disappointment in Julie's voice, but couldn't help feeling relieved. 'Anyway, we'd better go,' she said, turning to Rose. 'We have Chemistry next.'

'You go ahead,' Rose replied, 'and I'll meet you there. I want to have a word with Caspian.'

Julie hesitated, then with a look of bewilderment she turned and left the library, heading in the same direction Billy and Clarissa had taken minutes before.

Rose took a seat beside him, and suddenly Caspian felt uncomfortable. The feeling was not too dissimilar to stage fright, which was ridiculous considering he only had an audience of one. His heart beat rapidly in his chest, his mouth dried up, and for the strangest reason he became acutely aware of his own smell. *Do I smell bad? Can Rose smell me?* She was certainly sitting close enough to. *I can smell her, but she smells wonderful. Why can't I stop thinking about smells?*

'I'm really sorry about your mom,' Rose said, interrupting Caspian's current line of thought – to which he was grateful. There was a sincere look in her eyes that no one else had mustered, even though so many of his classmates had said to him the very same words all morning. 'I was really close to my Grandma. She used to come visit us a lot. She died last year and it really affected me, but I cannot even begin to imagine what you must be going through.'

He gave her a weak smile and shrugged. 'You just get on with it, I guess.' He couldn't keep looking into her eyes; she had this strange power over him that made him feel uncomfortable to stare at her, as though she were something forbidden to be gazed upon. But as soon as he looked away he found himself yearning to look on her forbidden beauty once again.

'I just want you to know that you are not alone with what you are going through, and if you ever want anyone to talk to...'

'I'm not sure your boyfriend would like that very much,' Caspian replied before he could stop himself.

'Oh, you don't know?' Rose said sounding surprised. 'But then why would you care? Rob and I split up a few days ago.'

'Really?' Caspian asked, a little too cheerfully. He cleared his throat and tried to appear sorry to hear the news. 'Why? What happened?'

Rose absently played with the bracelet on her wrist, and Caspian noticed it wasn't the same bracelet he had found in Mrs Plumb's Biology lesson. 'I don't really want to go into it, but he wasn't very nice to me. I don't think he ever really cared about me, but instead he treated me like I was an object, like something he owned, or worse like a stupid sports trophy he had won.'

'I'm really sorry to hear it didn't work out.'

'Are you?' Rose asked suspiciously, raising an eyebrow playfully.

'I am,' Caspian replied, trying to ignore her suspicion. 'But I think you deserve someone better.'

Rose smiled at him. 'Thank you, Caspian. I certainly think I need to find someone more intelligent. Rob isn't very smart.'

'Smart?' Caspian mocked. 'If you gave him a penny for his thoughts you'd get change!'

Rose burst out laughing and he found it infectious.

'I'm sorry, I didn't mean to make fun,' he said, still giggling but trying to control himself.

'You don't need to be sorry. You are right.'

'What did you see in him anyway?'

'I don't know,' Rose shrugged, playing with her bracelet again. 'I always seem to end up being attracted to bad boys.

'Well,' Caspian said, deciding to take a risk, '*I'm* a bad boy – the evidence certainly points that way.'

Rose looked at him curiously and smiled a heart-melting smile. 'Yeah, I guess it does,' she replied. 'But deep down, I don't really think you're really as bad as you come across.'

Caspian felt his cheeks redden. He wasn't sure whether that was a compliment or a turn down, but either way he couldn't stop himself from smiling.

XXIII:
A HEART AND HALF MOON

The weekend presented the group's first real opportunity to visit Leadenhall Market to try and interpret the meaning of the riddle. The more they had looked into the history of the Roman Basilica, the more sure they had become that this was the heart of Londinium they were supposed to start from, but anything other than that was much less than certain.

It was the first weekend in February and the weather was abysmal. The dark sky above was black and bruised, and in its agony it wept in torrents that filled the gutters like fast flowing streams, the drains struggling to manage the amount of rainwater they were forced to usher inside. Puddles grew in the streets and on the sidewalks, a multitude of innumerable umbrellas and waterproof jackets were all that could be seen.

Billy had arrived wearing a backpack, containing various things he thought they might need for this expedition. The one thing it didn't contain was an umbrella.

The small group ducked from cover to cover, sheltering under shop fronts and café canopies, hoping for a break in the downpour, but by the time they reached Leadenhall Market from Lime Street Passage the rain had not relented. They joined the hundreds of tourists that had shared the similar idea to take cover under the Market's ornate glass roof to wait out the storm.

'It's a bit busy,' Billy observed to Caspian and Clarissa as they worked their way through the crowd that had congregated near the entrance.

Caspian nodded. These were not ideal circumstances to be surreptitiously searching for secret clues, but on the other hand there were so many people here today they could probably move about unnoticed.

Lightning flashed overhead, quickly followed by a loud clap of thunder that made a few people jump, as the storm passed directly above. His eyes were drawn up to the vaulted ceiling of the market building, originally constructed for the purpose of rehousing the unruly and overcrowded stalls of the Victorian poultry market in a neat and respectable arcade.

The butchered meat and poultry that had once hung from large hooks at the shop fronts were no longer on display, giving way to the demand of retail shops. A vibrant paint scheme of rich burgundy, soft cream, dark green, and opulent gold gave the entire façade a festive feel, or the sensation of stepping into the world of Willy Wonka's chocolate factory.

Apart from sheltering the waterlogged and the rain sodden, Leadenhall Market attracted a number of sightseers who came to admire the striking design of the market and its numerous shop fronts that lined its passageways, each adorned in matching Victorian joinery to suite the theme and coated with the same colour scheme as the rest of the arcade.

Eventually they reached the centre of the market where the four passageways of its cruciform structure met beneath an octagonal crossing, supported by giant cast-iron columns. A large lantern hung from the pitched roof giving off a golden glow in contrast to the bleakness outside.

'We still don't know what we're looking for,' Billy said, looking around.

The week had been spent staring at the four lines of text that made up the riddle, and arguing over their meaning during morning and lunch breaks. The general consensus was that they were looking for a hidden passage that probably went underground (*beneath water and stone*) until it reached the Guardians' tomb. Who or what the Guardians were was still up for debate, but Clarissa was certain it referred to a medieval legend of the descendants of mythical pagan giants.

'Giants!' Billy had scoffed at hearing the idea. 'So we should be looking for a tomb built at the bottom of a beanstalk.'

'I'm not saying it is a true story,' Clarissa had said defensively. 'But these two giants are the traditional guardians of the City of London: Gog and Magog.'

'Any idea where they were supposed to have been buried?' Caspian asked.

'No, that's where it falls flat,' she conceded. 'The stories of Gog and Magog are so old that there are inevitable discrepancies between differing versions. Some stories even refer to them as one singular giant, called Gogmagog, rather than as two. The place from where Gogmagog was supposed to have fallen to his death is called Langnagog, The Giant's Leap, but there is no clear answer as to its geographical location.'

'What options are there?'

'Debatably, either Ireland or Cornwall.'

'Great,' Billy said mockingly. 'I'll go buy the tickets.'

But truthfully, to whom the tomb belonged, and where their resting place was located, was the least of their worries if they could not find the entrance to the passage. And anyhow, the meaning of the phrase "the half-moon renewed" really was the crux of the matter.

A throng of people congregated outside a café where there were presumably no further seats within. Tables and chairs had been set up outside the café, but still sheltered by the market's roof, to accommodate their sizable clientele.

'It's so crowded,' Clarissa said, seeing people every way she turned. 'How are we going to find the entrance with all these people around?'

'I'm not sure,' Caspian admitted. 'But there might be a symbol that marks it.'

'Why would you think that?' Clarissa asked.

'Do you remember when we were sat in that café after we'd been to the museum?'

'That museum trip will be pretty hard to forget,' Billy said.

Caspian continued. 'I told you about the letter that Smeelie had sent my father. What I didn't mention was the peculiar way the envelope had been sealed.'

Billy and Clarissa looked at him intrigued.

'It had been sealed with red wax like a letter from medieval times.'

'Or *Game of Thrones*,' Billy added.

'And to mark the wax, a seal had been used with a unique design,' Caspian explained, wondering how to describe it. 'It looked like it had been drawn with one continuous stroke, however at a glance it resembled two figure-eights laid over each other; one vertically, and the other horizontally – like the symbol for infinity.'

'I know what that is,' Clarissa said at once.

'How?' Billy exclaimed. 'Another one of your Granddad's stories?'

Clarissa rolled her eyes. 'No, not this time. I know what it is because I *read.* It's called an ouroboros knot.'

'An arberus what?' Billy frowned.

'Ouroboros knot,' Clarissa confirmed. 'You must have seen the symbol of a snake biting its own tail?'

Caspian recalled the golden symbol that had been displayed on the Armada Door leading into the reflectory. It was made of two snakes, each biting on the other's tail.

'It symbolises the cycle of constant regeneration, of the eternal return,' Clarissa continued. 'Sometimes the symbol for infinity is included in this to reinforce the meaning behind it of everlasting. What you have described is just a more flamboyant way of showing it.'

'What do you read?' Billy muttered. 'Dan Brown?'

Clarissa answered that remark with a scowl.

Caspian glanced around, looking for anything that might resemble the ouroboros knot, or lend meaning to the phrase about "the half-moon renewed," but all he could see were the normal shops he would find on any high street. 'I'm having doubts this is the right place,' he finally admitted.

'No,' Clarissa said adamantly. 'Even though the Basilica would have covered an area four times the size of this, this is the only part of the area that remains true to the original use of land as a centre of commerce. This *has* to be the place.'

Caspian shrugged and continued searching. Eventually his eyes drifted up towards the ceiling where the dark clouds lingered.

Up on the pitched roof that covered the octagonal crossing directly above him, behind the riveted cast-iron vaults, the panels had been painted to give the illusion that, just like the rest of the market's ceiling, these too were windows. They had been painted with a deep twilight blue, and each of these false windows had been decorated with a sprinkling of golden stars. The only real window in this crossing sat right in the centre of the eight-sided recess.

'Hmmm...' Caspian said, still looking up.

'What is it?' Clarissa asked.

'Above us, that's an octagon, right?' he asked, referring to the very centre of the pitched roof where a small eight sided window had been placed – the only real window in this part of the ceiling.

Clarissa looked at him as if he were stupid. 'Yes...' And then it dawned on her what he was implying. 'Octagon – *eight*. Do you think it represents the eight in the ouroboros knot?'

'Yes,' Caspian nodded. 'And what particular celestial shape do you notice is missing from that representation of a night sky; something that would go right where that window is?

'The moon,' she grinned.

'Exactly,' Caspian grinned back, feeling like he was on to something. 'What if the entrance to the passage only becomes clear when the moon shines through that window?'

'And reflects the light somehow to show the path...' Clarissa added.

They both stared up at the little golden stars in wonder.

'Have you two lost your bleeding minds?' Billy asked bluntly, looking at his friends like they were a few pieces short of a chess set. 'If you think that just because someone painted stars on a *ceiling* it must have something to do with a secret passageway, then you have both clearly given Reason a day off!'

'And I suppose you have a better idea, do you?' Caspian asked.

'Actually, I do,' Billy winked. 'Clarissa, you said the Basilica covered this area. Where would the entrance of the Basilica have stood?'

Clarissa pointed down the passageway that led to Gracechurch Street. 'It would have been in the very same spot as the main entrance to Leadenhall Market.'

'Ha! Just as I thought,' Billy said whimsically, clearly enjoying himself.

'Okay, Billy,' Clarissa confronted him. 'Where do you propose we look for the half-moon renewed if not beside the stars?'

'In that pub,' announced Billy, nodding in the direction of where Clarissa had just pointed.

Caspian looked in the direction Billy had gestured, and to his surprise he saw the sign of a tavern hanging from the wall, its name written in gold against the black of the sign: *The New Moon.*

'You've got to be kidding me,' Clarissa said, rolling her eyes. 'You thought our idea was ridiculous, but this...'

Billy shrugged and began marching towards the pub's entrance.

'You're not seriously going to look inside, are you?' Clarissa called to him.

'Beats standing around like an idiot, waiting for the moon to shine through a small window above my head!' he called back.

'He has a point,' Caspian shrugged and followed him.

They caught up with Billy by the main entrance. 'Now what?' Clarissa asked. 'You can't just walk in there. None of us look old enough to buy a drink.'

Billy looked at her and grinned, mischief dancing in his eyes. 'A good thing I'm not thirsty, then,' he laughed, before slipping in through the pub's door as a smartly dressed gentleman came out.'

Caspian and Clarissa exchanged looks, hesitated slightly, and then ducked inside following Billy's assertive lead.

As they entered The New Moon a woman turned and gave them a strange look, before returning to her white wine and the conversation she was having with a tall man in a tailored suit. Apart from that, nobody seemed to have noticed them enter, or if they had they didn't seem to care.

They moved through the bar looking for where Billy had gone, and eventually spotted him near one of the walls, looking at a framed black and white picture showing the Gracechurch Street entrance to Leadenhall Market in the 1930's.

'Look at this,' Billy said as they reached him. He was pointing at the small descriptive text beneath the photo explaining some of the history of the pub. Billy read it to them, ' "With the construction of the new Market in 1881, Half-Moon Passage was lost and replaced by the main entrance at Gracechurch Street. In tribute to the lost passage, the original site was marked by the tavern bearing the name The New Moon." '

'The half-moon renewed,' Clarissa quietly echoed, staring in disbelief at the passage Billy had just read.

So that's what it meant, Caspian thought. The riddle referred to Half-Moon Passage being replaced with The New Moon tavern. What was more unbelievable was that Billy had been the one to solve it. 'How did you know?' Caspian asked incredulously.

'Other than moon being in the title?' Billy smirked. 'The number was a bit of a clue, too.'

'The number?' Clarissa questioned, sounding as equally surprised as Caspian by Billy's sudden aptitude for solving puzzles.

'Yeah,' Billy replied. 'The New Moon is number eighty-eight, Gracechurch Street.'

'What does that have to do with it?' Clarissa asked.

'It was what Caspian said,' Billy shrugged. 'He said there would probably be a symbol that would mark the way. That Arborio knot –'

'Ouroboros,' Clarissa corrected him.

'Yeah, whatever it's called,' Billy shrugged. 'Caspian said to look out for a symbol resembling two figure-eights. It turned out, it was *literally* two figure-eights – Number 88.'

Caspian had to give it to Billy. He had been so busy looking for the symbol he was familiar with that he had not considered that the symbol might have been altered so it could be hidden right under his nose. 'That's actually quite impressive.'

'I know,' Billy replied boyishly.

'Alright, Brains,' Clarissa interjected. 'What next? Where is the passageway?'

Billy looked around the busy pub. His eyes seemed to stop on the far corner where a staircase had been cordoned off with a thick length of red rope that would discourage most of the punters from crossing it.

As it happened, Billy didn't fall into that category (nor was he old enough to be a punter) and before either Clarissa or Caspian could offer a word of protest his short dark slender form had slipped over the rope and disappeared down the stairs.

'We *really* need to put him on a leash,' Caspian said to Clarissa and went to follow his friend, making sure none of the bar staff was watching.

Clarissa sighed and begrudgingly followed. 'It's like the museum all over again,' she moaned.

The sign on the staircase on the way down informed them they were entering the cellar bar, which it seemed was closed this afternoon whilst it was being set up for a function. Thankfully the only person they found standing in the bar was Billy.

'Will you stop doing that,' Clarissa said to him sternly, but not raising her voice for fear of attracting attention from upstairs.

'Doing what?'

'You keep diving in head first, rather than taking a moment to stop and think.'

'It's worked well for me so far,' Billy shrugged. 'You've just got to take a leap of faith, like that giant you were talking about.'

'The Giant's Leap was not a leap of faith, you idiot,' Clarissa hissed. 'That's where Gogmagog was supposedly thrown to his death.'

'Well,' Billy grinned up at her wryly, 'at least I'll be alright. They'd never mistake me for a giant.'

Clarissa groaned with frustration. 'You're impossible.'

'Hey,' Caspian interrupted. 'If you two could save your tiff for later, maybe we can focus on finding the passageway before we get caught for being underage in a bar that is closed to the public? Why are we down here, Billy?'

'I assumed that the secret passage would be underground, if it is to pass beneath water and stone like the riddle said.'

'But presumably Half-Moon Passage was on street level,' Clarissa added. 'We are in the basement of a pub named after the passage. And in a dead end, I might add.'

Caspian suddenly held his finger to his lips to signal for his friends to be quiet. He'd heard something coming from the staircase, and their only exit from the cellar bar.

'What is it?' Billy whispered.

Caspian heard a click of a heel on the wooden step, and then a female voice said, 'Hang on, I still can't hear you. Reception is really bad here but it's too noisy in the main bar.'

Someone was coming down the stairs!

'Quick,' Caspian hissed, looking for somewhere to hide, but the cellar bar didn't offer many places where three teenagers could hide from sight.

The clicking of high heels grew louder. Caspian and his friends dove behind the bar where they hoped the woman on the phone wasn't heading, and to their surprise they found an open trapdoor.

Billy pointed down the open doorway and Caspian nodded. Scrambling on their hands and knees, they quietly dropped down the steps, hearing the woman enter the cellar bar, talking loudly on her phone with nothing but the bar to conceal them. 'No, I'll be working late tonight,' she was saying. 'We have a function booked in the cellar bar and I need to set up...'

A light had been left on below, and although dim it gave enough light to illuminate the dark brickwork of the large vault they found themselves descending into. There was a dramatic change in temperature inside the vault, which was much colder than the other rooms in the building. Large beer kegs were stacked to one side; some of them had pipes attached feeding up into the bars above. Large metal cages filled the small room, stacked high with bottles of wines, spirits, and various soft drinks.

Caspian, who was the last to descend the steps, cautiously pulled on the handle of the trapdoor. It was surprisingly heavy, but thankfully made very little sound as he carefully lowered the door shut above him. The last thing they needed was an unsuspecting bartender coming down into the vault without warning to collect stock or change a beer barrel.

As the door closed they suddenly seemed isolated, the sound of the bar muted to nothing. They stood alone in the cellar wondering what to do next.

'Well, this is great,' Clarissa whispered sarcastically.

Caspian remained on the steps, straining to hear the woman's voice in bar above him.

Suddenly, a loud hiss from behind took him by surprise and almost cost him his balance on the steps. He spun to find Clarissa, her hand clamped over her mouth, and even Billy looking startled. The shock quickly passed and his senses returned: someone had operated the beer taps in the upstairs bar, causing some of the gas used to keep the beer pumps pressurised to make the loud hiss sound. This pump in particular was making a gentle chugging and clicking noise as it settled.

'How long will we be stuck down here?' Clarissa asked. In desperation to find a place to hide she had failed to notice how dusty and dirty the bar's cellar was. Now she was taking in her surroundings with a look of disdain.

Caspian was wondering the same thing, and the longer they stayed here the more miserable Clarissa would become. 'Let's give it a couple of minutes, then I'll open the trapdoor and see if she's still there.'

'Guys…' Billy's voice came, hushed but with a sound of urgency, from behind a large rack of bottled red wine where, for reasons known only to Billy, he had decided to climb. Only his backpack was visible, which he had removed and set on the floor before beginning his latest escapade.

'What is it?' Caspian whispered tensely, not wanting his friend to further escalate their already problematic situation.

'You should see this…'

'This really isn't the time, Billy,' Caspian replied sharply.

Billy's head appeared from behind the racking. 'It really is,' he retorted. 'It's now or never in fact. I think I've found something that would put us right at the entrance of the passage.'

'Behind a rack of wine in a pub's cellar?' Clarissa sneered. 'Stop messing about, it must be filthy behind there.'

'Seriously,' Billy continued. 'Just come have a look.'

Caspian rolled his eyes relenting, came down the last few steps, and made his way to where Billy had set the rucksack. His friend had once again disappeared behind the wine racking and he was signalling for Caspian to follow.

There was barely enough space for him to squeeze through sideways. His back brushed against the wine rack, which was thankfully sturdily built and did not budge or rock. Billy was not deep behind the rack, and Caspian quickly found himself beside him.

'Look,' Billy said, awkwardly lifting his arm up to point at a rusted piece of metal engraved into the stone wall of the cellar. 'Is this what you were talking about?'

The rusted piece of metal was in the shape of the four looped ouroboros knot. It had been bolted to the wall over the place where a hole had been drilled into the stone – roughly the width of large coin – so that it was at the very centre of the knot. This little cranny seemed to tunnel quite deep into the wall.

'How did you know this would be here?' Caspian asked, befuddled that his friend had solved so many of today's puzzles.

'Didn't,' Billy answered. 'In honesty, I was looking for a place to hide so I wouldn't get caught. I couldn't see us getting out of here unseen.'

'That's good to know,' Clarissa's voice came sulkily from the other side of the racking. 'What did he find?'

'It's an ouroboros knot,' Caspian confirmed. 'Just like the one I described, except there is a hole in the middle.'

'Do we need a key?' Clarissa asked.

'It would have to be a bloomin' big key,' Billy replied. 'It seems quite deep though. I can probably fit my finger inside.'

Before Caspian could advise his friend against it, Billy promptly stuck his index finger into the hole. Just as promptly, Billy's facial expression changed to one of horror. 'Hey! My finger's stuck!'

'Sshhhh…' Caspian hissed, hoping no one had heard Billy's rather loud announcement.

Billy tried to pull his hand back but it wouldn't budge. 'Serious, it really is stuck.'

'Stop messing around,' Clarissa said from the other side of the racking.

'I don't think he is,' Caspian said, trying to get a better look at the contraption that now held Billy's finger. 'If you got it in there, you must be able to get it out.'

'It feels like something is squeezing it,' Billy said, his voice getting a little higher as panic set in. 'Wait, something's happening.'

The entire knot of metal began to slowly rotate in a clockwise direction around Billy's finger, turning slowly like a carousel with his singular digit as an axis. At the same time a deep vibration could be felt across the entire wall as if the cellar itself was trembling. Bottles clinked and chinked as they rattled and juddered.

276

Behind him, Caspian heard Clarissa gasp from where she stood on the other side of the wine racking. 'You found it!' she exclaimed.

'Found what?' Caspian said, edging out from behind the rack to take a look.

'Hey, where are you going?' asked Billy, his finger still wedged in the hole.

Caspian glanced back, 'I won't be a minute.'

As he squeezed out of the small gap covered in dust and cobwebs he found Clarissa looking at the section of wall in front of her. Where once there had been a solid wall of stone there was now an opening that led off into a dark passageway. The dim light of the cellar did not stretch far into the darkness, but Caspian could clearly read the old road sign that had been fixed to the wall just inside the entrance: *Half-Moon Passage*.

'Clarissa's right,' Caspian whispered to Billy. 'You've found it.'

'Oh, I'm so happy. Hooray for me!' Billy replied sarcastically. 'Well, do have fun on my behalf. Let me know where the passage leads. I'll just wait here and hope someone is able to release my finger before I starve to death!'

'Hang on…' Caspian edged back down the gap towards his friend. 'There has to be a release catch or something.' He checked the ouroboros knot, unsure of what he should be looking for. A lot of the detail had faded over time and with the rust the surface had become coarse and uneven.

Just like on the Armada Door, two snakes were entwined to create the shape of the knot. There were two raised bulges in the metal, which Caspian supposed were probably once their head's. He ran his finger over these, feeling the smaller bulges where the eyes were, pushing down as he did so. All of a sudden there was a *click* as he pushed one of the eyes and it retracted inwards.

For a moment nothing happened, and then the low rumbling began and once again the ouroboros knot began to turn – this time anticlockwise. There was a second click and Billy, who looked rather relieved, pulled his finger from the hole.

'The entrance is closing!' Clarissa said quietly but urgently from near the opening. 'Hurry up!'

Caspian and Billy shimmied out of the gap as quickly as they could. Clarissa grabbed the rucksack and stepped into the doorway, gesturing for her friends to follow and looking frightened that she might be trapped inside and alone. The opening was now half the width it had been before as the stones of the wall slid back into place.

There were footsteps above them on the trapdoor. Someone, maybe the woman on the phone, had either heard or felt the vibrations of the wall moving and was now painfully close to discovering the three of them in the pub's cellar.

Caspian pushed Billy through the gap and with a final look up at the trapdoor he slid through himself. Behind him he saw the hatch begin to open, the light from the bar above poured into the dusty cellar, and then the secret entrance to Half-Moon Passage sealed shut and they were swallowed by the complete and absolute darkness.

XXIV:
RITE OF PASSAGE

As the pitch-blackness closed oppressively around them the three friends tentatively held their breath and strained to hear what was happening beyond the wall that had sealed them inside. The cellar's trapdoor had opened just as the passage entrance had closed, but had anyone seen the wall move as they'd peered down into the dimly lit room below?

They could hear the clinking of bottles being moved about, and the occasional hissing and clicking of the gas bottles and beer kegs. Two different voices could be heard but they were both muffled, the words indistinct. After a few tense seconds the voices faded away and soon the infrequent hiss and click were the only sounds.

'Phew!' Billy gasped, letting out a deep expulsion of air.

Caspian and Clarissa sighed with relief also. That had been *too* close.

'Well, here we are,' Billy continued.

'Here we are, indeed,' Caspian agreed. 'Any idea where "here" is?'

There was a muffled sound and then Clarissa yelped. 'What are you doing!?'

'I packed a torch in the bag,' Billy explained.

Clarissa had grabbed the rucksack as the passage door had begun to close and was still clutching it tightly. 'Then just ask for it, don't try and feel for it in the dark.'

More rustling as someone rummaged around in the rucksack. Then a dazzlingly bright beam of light hit Caspian in the face forcing him to shield his eyes with his hands.

'Found it!' Billy said.

'Well done,' Clarissa snapped, 'now get it out of our faces!'

As Caspian's eyes adjusted he saw that Billy now held the rucksack which he shouldered as he shone the torchlight up and down the long passage they now occupied. The passage walls seemed incredibly old, made up of a hodgepodge of different bricks and stones, in some places crooked and unbalanced so that the passage seemed to twist, contract, and contort. An irregular combination of large wooden beams and dark metal girders of varying width supported the ceiling at uneven points along the patchwork of wall.

'I have to admit,' Billy said, shining the torch at part of the wall where a large crack reached from top to bottom, 'I didn't imagine this secret passage looking so shoddy.' He looked back at Clarissa. 'It's pretty filthy down here. Are you going to be okay?'

'Of course I'm going to be okay,' Clarissa shot back at him. 'Why wouldn't I be?'

'You're a little bit anal when it comes to cleanliness,' Caspian said, as diplomatically as he could.

'And what? It doesn't mean I'm scared of getting dirty, even though I'd rather avoid it. Anyway, what other choice have I got? I can hardly go back the way we came, can I?'

That was a good point, Caspian thought. None of them could go back now. 'I hope that isn't our only way in and out,' he thought out loud, looking back at the dead end behind them. There was no obvious way to open the passage entrance again from this side of the wall. 'I guess we have no choice.'

He took the torch from Billy and led the way, the other two staying close behind him. The passage had been built with the slightest gradient, so with each step they took a little further underground they went.

'Which direction are we heading in?' Billy asked after a while. It was difficult to imagine what part of the city they were beneath without any kind of landmark to appoint to their location.

'I don't know,' Caspian answered.

'How's your finger?' Clarissa asked Billy behind him.

'It's okay,' he shrugged. 'Doesn't hurt, just a little sore.'

'Maybe that will teach you not to go round sticking your fingers in dirty holes.'

Billy laughed. 'My mum would say the same thing about me picking my nose.'

They continued on and on into the darkness, soon they were so far along that they could no longer see where the passage's entrance had been, let alone where it ended.

'How far do you think this passage goes?' Billy asked.

They hadn't expected the passage to be this long, but Caspian didn't have an answer for his friend. 'I really don't know,' he said, and then stopped where he stood, listening intently and pointing the torch light at the floor just ahead of him.

The floor in this area of the passage was covered with what looked like fine sand and plaster chippings. In the centre there was a clear trail of footprints, although a light dusting of sand had fallen since the prints had been left.

'Someone's been here before us.'

'Three guesses who,' Billy said, looking down at the prints.

'He worked it out before us,' Clarissa said, a little downbeat. 'I thought we were a step ahead of the him.'

'Clearly the hooded man is a few steps ahead of us,' Billy said, pointing at the trail of footprints. 'Pun intended.'

From beneath Caspian's feet, he suddenly became aware of a very subtle rumbling in the ground. 'Can you feel that?'

'Feel what?'

The rumbling seemed to have subsided as quickly as it had come. 'I felt a rumbling in the ground beneath us, I'm sure of it.'

'Sure it wasn't your tummy,' Billy quipped.

'No, really,' Caspian said, pointing the torch down either end of the passage as if expecting to see something rolling towards them; maybe some kind of deadly contraption designed to crush, pulverise, or maim any trespassers who managed to find the entrance to the passage. If something happened to them down here, how long would it take anyone to find them, if at all?

'I can feel it,' Clarissa said from behind. 'I couldn't before, but I can now.'

'Yeah, me too,' Billy agreed.

Caspian could feel it again also, growing stronger beneath his feet. Then they could hear it too, growing louder and louder until it was a deafening sound vibrating through the walls, ceiling, floor of the passage around them. Billy clapped his hands to his ears and Clarissa screamed as the passage shook, dust and debris dropping on them through cracks in the ceiling above.

'WHAT … IS … GOING … ON?' Caspian shouted over the thunderous roar. The air became thick and powdery, making the torchlight materialise into a distinct beam.

'EARTHQUAKE?' Billy shouted back, coughing in the choking dust.

And then the rumbling began to subside, fading as quickly as it had come.

'What *was* that?' Caspian coughed, patting dust off his clothes and hair. All three of them were now covered from head to foot with the dirt and grit that had rained down from above. 'Is everyone alright?'

'Yes,' Clarissa replied, and to Caspian's surprise she was laughing.

'What's so funny?' Billy asked, his voice still husky from all the dust in the air.

'You should have seen your faces,' Clarissa laughed. 'You both looked like you thought the roof was caving in.'

'And I suppose you weren't scared at all?' Caspian asked.

'I distinctly recall hearing you scream,' Billy added.

Clarissa folded her arms and raised her eyebrow. 'It was so loud it hurt my ears. Unlike you, I chose to cover my mouth instead. Anyway, come on, let's move on before the next one comes.'

'The next one?' Billy repeated. 'Next *what*? Do you think there is going to be an aftershock?'

'That wasn't an earthquake, Billy.'

'It bloody well felt like one,' he replied.

The dust was beginning to settle now and it was becoming easier to see again.

'Think about it,' Clarissa said. 'We're under the streets, moving beneath central London. What else moves beneath the city that could explain that kind of noise?'

'Are you telling me *that* was an Underground train?' Caspian asked.

She nodded. 'We must be very close to part of the Tube network. It might even have passed directly over our heads.'

'Any idea which line it was?' asked Caspian.

'If we are moving towards Bank, then that could have been either the Northern, Central, or Waterloo and City line,' Clarissa explained. 'If we're moving south, although I doubt we are, that could have been the Circle or District line.'

'Well, I'm not hanging around for the next one, that's for sure,' Billy said.

Caspian agreed. He pointed the torch back at the trail of footprints, still easily visible in the dirt, and he followed them deeper into the passage.

A few minutes later the small underground expedition was greeted by a different sound. Instead of the treacherous tremors of a train passing close by, they heard the sound of water trickling and dripping inside the walls beside them. Up ahead the passage rounded a corner, beyond which a dim light flickered appealingly, as a flame does to a moth.

As the group saw what lay ahead they came to a halt.

'Do you think it's safe?' Caspian asked, shining the torch light before them.

Clarissa shrugged. 'At least we know we are on track,' she said, looking at the obstacle before them. ' "Beneath water and stone." '

Around the bend Caspian had found himself standing on the edge of a gaping chasm, a massive rupture that had opened up in the ground and dropped away into the deepest darkness below. Painted in a stencilled yellow design to imitate that found in the London Underground was a three worded warning: *Mind The Gap.*

In the ceiling above, the crack exposed numerous pipes, electrical cables, and structural supports. A large conduit leaked water that fell like rain into the darkened abyss, illuminated by the flickering of an exposed wire which popped and fizzled, expelling sparks and flashes of light, as droplets dripped over the live current.

'Where's all that water coming from?' Billy asked. Even the downpour on the surface above them couldn't account for this much water.

Clarissa gestured for Caspian to shine the torch up to where the spray gushed from a leaking conduit. 'I think we are passing beneath the Walbrook, one of London's lost rivers.'

'How can a city lose a river?' Billy asked, still looking up.

'As the city grew, some of the courses of the smaller rivers that fed the Thames had to be altered. In the case of the Walbrook it was essentially paved over so that streets could be built on top of it, but not before it was made flow through that large conduit you can partly see up there.' She looked thoughtful for a moment. 'If that really is the Walbrook, then I'd guess we must be heading for Bank. We might even be right beneath the Bank of England right now.'

Crossing the chasm, passing through the shower of rain and sparks, was a narrow bridge – however bridge would need to be used in the loosest possible terms as a noun in this particular case. This "bridge" lacked any kind of rail for support and was really nothing more than a length of grated metal that stretched precariously out over the void.

Caspian edged forward and tested the metal walkway with his foot. The water made it very slippery, and the erratic and inconsistent electrical bursts and flashes had a destabilising effect on the walkway that seemed to shift and shimmer with each flicker of light.

'I'll go first,' he said, swallowing hard and focusing the torchlight on the path ahead. 'Then I'll shine the torch back so you can come across.'

'Be careful,' Clarissa said.

'I'm pretty sure he already knows that,' Billy retorted, but there was a tension in his voice that could be attributed either to fear for his friend's life, or anxiety that he would eventually have to cross the walkway himself.

Taking each step slowly, one and then another, Caspian edged forward. He tried to keep his eyes focused on the walkway, rather than the sheer drop below. He tried not to be put off by each explosion of sparks overhead. He wasn't sure whether it was the shower of the Walbrook that made his back moisten, or whether his concentration was making him sweat profusely. Nevertheless, after a terrifyingly tense minute (that felt ten times longer) his left foot touched the hard stone where the passage continued and he stepped fully onto the other side.

He pointed the torchlight back across the walkway, keeping it pointed at Clarissa's feet as not to dazzle her. She crossed the walkway even more cautiously than Caspian had, and there was a brief moment of tension when a large crackle of electricity almost caused her to lose her balance, but she too made it safely to the other side.

'Come on then, Billy,' Caspian called, shining the torchlight back to the start of the walkway. 'Last one to cross.'

'Yeah … okay …' Billy replied. He stepped out onto the walkway and his foot instantly slid forward. He kept his balance but looked extremely uncomfortable. 'It's … errr … a bit slippery.'

'Just take it slow,' Clarissa called with encouragement.

The initial slip seemed to have stripped Billy Long of all the fearlessness and confidence he usually portrayed, leaving him very nervous and noticeably tense and uneasy as he began to edge forward onto the bridge.

'Keep coming, mate,' Caspian cheered him on, 'you're doing really well.'

A great snap of sparks fizzled from over his head, making him momentarily freeze, but then he continued.

'Come on, Billy,' Clarissa said. 'Careful, you're already two thirds the way across.'

Billy nodded, but his eyes remained so tightly focused on the walkway it was as if they were clinging to it in place of his hands. 'I'm okay,' he said unsteadily. 'I think I've got it n–'

As he took another step his back foot slipped and he came down heavily onto his left knee. His hands scrambled wildly for purchase on the slippery metal walkway as his body lurched uncontrollably over the side.

Without a thought Caspian shoved Clarissa the torch and before he knew it he was scrambling across the walkway to Billy, whose legs and hips now dangled freely into the darkness below.

'Hold on!' Caspian said as he knelt down and grabbed Billy by the straps of his backpack.

'Obviously!' Billy replied as terror took a hold of him.

The walkway let out a loud creak as it strained under the weight of both the boys. The torchlight was dancing all over the chasm as Clarissa shook hysterically with horror.

Caspian reached down and grabbed his friend by the material of his trousers and heaved with all his might to bring him back up. Billy pulled himself forward too, assisting his own rescue.

The walkway moaned again, louder and higher in pitch than before.

Billy was laying down now, both legs back on the bridge. Caspian began to edge carefully backwards towards where Clarissa stood, outstretching his hand to help guide Billy.

A loud *Pang* echoed from the far side and the walkway shifted ever so slightly, threatening to tip both boys into the deep below.

Clarissa grabbed Caspian by the shoulder and pulled him backwards, the torchlight swinging from floor to ceiling, left to right. There was another loud *Pang* and a loud creak, and then the walkway began to fall away.

Billy placed a foot on the stone of the passage, and Caspian grabbed his friend's arm and pulled him towards him. At the same time the walkway dropped away, clanging, clanking and clattering as it banged and crashed its way down, down, down.

All three collapsed to the floor suddenly feeling exhausted, panting and shaking as a potent cocktail of shock and relief began to settle in.

Billy's senses returned first, particularly his sense of humour.

'Well, that was tense,' he said, but no one felt like laughing.

XXV:
IN THIS SUBTLE PLACE

The passage stretched out before them, as though they were staring down the gullet of a long outstretched snake toward the dark pit of its gut, each wondering how much further they were to travel, and what obstacles they were still to overcome before they reached the belly of this beast.

They had been treading carefully through the dark tunnel, illuminated only by the light of their flashlight, for five or six minutes since leaving the chasm that had nearly claimed the lives of the boys. There was definitely no going back now: the narrow bridge had plummeted innumerable feet into the gloomy fissure that greedily swallowed it whole. Their only hope was that a way out awaited them wherever this passage ended.

'I can see something,' Caspian said after a while. The torchlight caught something not far ahead from where the group were. He squinted, straining to see in the darkness. He couldn't see much, but there appeared to be a row of steps. 'I think it's a staircase.'

He felt both Clarissa and Billy breath a sigh of relief. No one had said much since the incident at the walkway, but it was a safe assumption that everyone was looking forward to escaping this dark warren beneath the city.

As he got closer, Caspian was pleased to see he was right. The passage finally drew to an end, meeting a staircase that spiralled upwards. Even after crossing the chasm, the passage had continued its decent at an ever so slight gradient, making it impossible now to estimate how far underground they really were. Whatever lie at the top of this staircase could still easily be very deep below the city surface.

'Look at the design of this opening,' Clarissa said, referring to the portico before them where the staircase began its ascent. It was clearly of the same architectural design as the staircase beyond, however it was of a much grander and sturdier design than the patchwork style of the passage they had just passed through. 'It seems much older than the rest of the passage.'

Caspian had to agree. It was almost as though this staircase had been built deep into the earth long before the passage was built. Had someone known about this entrance and built the secret passageway to connect it? If so, who – and more importantly, why?

Staying in single file, Caspian led the way with Billy at the rear of the group. Round and round the staircase went, completely throwing any sense of direction they had retained whilst being so deep below the ground. Up and up, and round and round. They were grateful to finally reach the top where the staircase opened up in another, albeit much shorter, passageway. Another portico greeted them here, signifying the entrance to a vast chamber beyond, devoid of any light other than the beam that the torch emitted.

'What is this place?' Billy asked, staring up at the ancient entrance before them.

'My guess,' Caspian said, 'is that this is the Guardians' tomb.'

'Do you think it's safe to go inside?' Clarissa asked. 'What if there are traps in there?'

'We don't really have a choice,' Caspian replied, recalling the memory of the walkway dropping away whilst he clung on dearly to Billy's arm. 'Let's just be very careful.'

The passage led into a large circular subterranean chamber. Stone blocks arched smoothly down from a vaulted ceiling to meet the large supporting stone pillars that filled the chamber like a fossilised orchard buried beneath the earth.

In the centre of the chamber, in a circular clearing, two large stone figures lay on their backs atop huge box tombs. The figures were of two large men who, even though depicted in granite with closed eyes, still looked barbaric and harsh with their long unkempt hair and lengthy wild beards. They were positioned side by side but pointing in opposite polar directions. Crowns of leaves, thorns, and bracken were carved above their mighty heads, like pagan kings of old.

As the torchlight poured over these statues, Caspian realised he recognised these odd individuals. He had seen them both before, except the last time he had come across these two bearded figures they had been standing with powerful authority.

On the very same bookshelf he had discovered his family crest, two small figurines had stood. Now he understood that they were representations of these same great men: the Guardians of the City of London.

They were not 'giants' by any means, but it was clear that if these effigies bore any likeness to the men they represented, then these men had both been of admirable stature. One held across his torso a long sturdy looking weapon that was topped with a spiked ball and chain. The other clutched a shield across his chest, emblazoned with a bird spreading its wings.

'Are those what I think they are?' Billy asked, looking at the statues.

'That depends what you think they are,' Clarissa replied.

Billy tentatively put his hand on the rough stone of the nearest figure. 'Are these the tombs of the giants?'

'I doubt they are really buried here,' Clarissa said. 'These statues were probably just put here to represent Gog and Magog to pay homage to their legacy.'

'And where do you think *here* is?' Caspian asked, looking at the strange chamber they had found themselves in. 'This is a crypt, isn't it.'

'It's probably more likely a sub-crypt,' she replied, 'and I have my suspicions where it can be found.'

'Really?' Billy asked.

'Absolutely,' Clarissa smiled. 'I suspect we are right beneath the Guildhall, or to be more precise, beneath the crypt of the Guildhall.'

'Can that really be possible?' Billy asked, looking astonished. 'The Guildhall is quite a walk from Leadenhall Market.'

'No, I think she might be right,' Caspian said, considering the possibility. 'I'd guess it's about a fifteen or so minute walk at street level, however the passage took a reasonably straight course from The New Moon Tavern to here.'

'Give or take the odd deadly drop,' Billy added.

'But what makes you so sure we're beneath the Guildhall?'

Clarissa pointed to the two stone giants lying on their backs. 'I had a feeling that the riddle's "Guardians" were Gog and Magog. They have featured as the Guardians of the City of London since the reign of King Henry V. As it happens there are only two places throughout the city where these figures are commonly seen; the most common being at the Lord Mayor's show where wicker effigies of them are carried along the procession.'

'And the other is at the Guildhall?' Billy asked.

'Yes,' Clarissa nodded. 'There are two statues standing in the Guildhall to represent them as a symbolic link between the modern business establishments of the City and its historic past. It would be logical that their figurative tombs are here, beneath it.'

Caspian moved around the two large stone figures, examining them closely in the torchlight. How had the riddle continued? *The secrets they sought, to their graves did they take.* He passed the feet of the figure with the weapon, but he could see no place to hide a message.

'A message is hidden in a hidden keepsake…' he repeated out loud to himself.

'Which is which?' Billy was asking Clarissa.

'Gog is the one holding the long-handled flail,' she replied. 'Traditionally he always stands to the north, whilst Magog to the south. I'd put money on that being the direction they have been positioned, their feet pointing to those same directions.'

'Not that we can tell all the way down here,' Billy added with irreverence.

'You see the bird on Magog's shield?' Clarissa continued. 'That's supposed to be a phoenix, representing rebirth: quite a poignant symbol for the City?'

'How so?' Caspian asked, coming over to examine the shield more closely with the torch.

'Consider the history of London,' Clarissa said. 'This city has fallen so many times, be it at the hands of invading countries, plagues, fires, and war. Each time it fell it arose again from the ashes – quite literally in the case of the Great Fire.'

'What's he holding in his other hand?' Caspian asked, shining the torchlight down at Magog's right hand where it gripped a cylindrical shaped object. Whatever it was, the cylinder was unsealed. It looked like it was supposed to be a scroll case, once elaborately decorated but the detail had deteriorated with time.

A message is hidden in a hidden keepsake.

Caspian wondered whether this was the keepsake that contained the message? It would make sense with the riddle, after all a scroll case would normally contain a communication of some form. He directed the beam of light into the cylinder to see if he could see anything hidden

292

inside. At first he thought it was empty, nothing more than a hollow stone case, but then his mouth fell open.

'Billy, take the torch,' he instructed, pointing for him to shine the light as he had done, but from the other end of the case.

At first Billy and Clarissa couldn't understand what he had seen, but when he let the light hit his hand after shining through the case, it all became clear. There on his palm, written in distinct letters of light, was the next part of the riddle.

the lilies and roses denote my day
a wall gone can unveil the way
join the place a cursed knight's bones fell

'Whoa,' Billy said with amazement, trying to keep the light steady.

Clarissa was excited too. 'The lilies and roses,' she said with glee. I think I know what that means.

'Really?' Billy asked.

'Yes, and I'm surprised you don't also.'

Both his friends were talking quickly with excitement, but Caspian barely heard a word. As his eyes passed over the letters inscribed in light on his hand he suddenly felt a wave of convulsion pass through him. For a moment he thought he was feeling the repercussions of touching the cursed ring back in Artemis Grieves' shop.

Clarissa noticed something was wrong first, stopping mid sentence. 'Caspian? What's wrong?'

His hand dropped away, shaking, the illuminated words slipping from his palm.

'Are you alright, mate?' Billy asked. 'You look like you're about to hurl.'

Quickly, Caspian fumbled in his pockets until he found what he was looking for: the small bottle Artemis Grieves had given him labelled *Sauerpott's Sore-Bone Remedy*. He was about to unscrew the top and take a swig, but this spell of dizziness and nausea were not like the agonising pain the Ouanga ring had induced before.

Instead, he crouched down and held his head. 'I just feel really dizzy,' Caspian answered. What was causing this? His head spun wildly. He took deep breaths and put his back against the hard stone of the tomb as he recovered. His back felt cold with sweat, but after a few minutes he began to feel better.

'What was *that* about?' Billy asked, concerned. He took the bottle from Caspian's hand. 'I didn't know you are on medication. What is this stuff?' He unscrewed the lid and took a sniff. 'Eww, yuck!'

'The taste isn't much better,' Caspian informed him.

'But what made you feel dizzy?'

'I don't know. I was reading the words and I felt … weird.'

'Are you sure you are okay?' Clarissa asked.

'I'm fine,' he reassured them. 'What were you saying about the lilies and roses?'

'It's a clue as to where we have to go next, and also when.'

Billy shrugged. 'I still don't get it.'

'Don't you ever listen?' Clarissa said, incredulously. 'Remember the trip to the Tower of London?'

'Of course I do! It was only a few weeks ago, I'm not senile.' Billy snapped, but it was obvious he didn't know what the school trip had to do with the words hidden in the scroll case.

'The guide who took us around the Tower told us that King Henry VI was imprisoned in the Wakefield Tower,' she said, mainly for Caspian's benefit. 'Supposedly, he was knelt in prayer when someone crept up behind and murdered him, on the night of the Vigil of the Ascension.'

'Hang on,' Billy shook his head, 'the Vigil of the what?'

'Ascension,' Clarissa replied. 'The ascension of Jesus Christ to Heaven.'

'Okay,' Billy replied. 'But what's a vigil?'

'If you'd been paying attention rather than messing around…' Clarissa gave an audible sigh. 'A vigil is a ritual that takes place before a holy day. The devoted are supposed to stay awake in a state of watchfulness.'

'*Watchfulness!*' Billy scoffed. 'So much for that if someone snuck in and killed him.'

'No, not that kind of "watchfulness," ' Clarissa exasperated, her patience beginning to show strain. 'He would have been reading psalms or prayers, or have been in a state of religious thought or meditation. A common vigil is a funeral wake, which originally was when prayers would be said to watch over the dead so the body would not be left alone before being buried.'

'How do you know all that?'

'Because I *listen.*'

'What has any of this got to do with lilies and roses?' Caspian interrupted, slowly getting up from the floor. Billy went to return the bottle of Sore-Bone Remedy to him, but Caspian gestured for him to put it in his rucksack for safekeeping: it didn't seem like he needed it after all.

'Henry VI was the founder of both Eton College and King's College Cambridge,' Clarissa continued. 'The students of both colleges participate in a ceremony commemorating the death of their college's founder. Each year they gather to lay the flowers associated to their respective colleges – lilies for Eton and white roses for King's College Cambridge – on the spot where the King died.'

'And when does this ceremony take place?' Caspian asked.

'On the twenty-first of May: the anniversary of Henry VI's death.'

'May?' Billy said, his disappointment showing. 'That is still months away.'

'Yes, but the Tower of London is huge and by the sounds of it we need to be in the right place at the right time. Remember what the hooded man and Smeelie discussed? They said an anomaly will take place in May. We could do with the time to work out the rest of the riddle.'

Billy didn't seem to agree.

'What about the rest of it?' Caspian asked. 'Any idea what it means?'

'Hmmm…' Clarissa said thoughtfully, gesturing for Billy to shine the light through the scroll case again. She held out her hand as Caspian had, so the words appeared once more.

As Caspian read the words some of the letters began to fade away.

'Hey, keep the light straight,' Caspian said to Billy. 'Some of the letters have gone.'

'I am,' Billy said.

'The letters are all there, Caspian,' Clarissa confirmed, but they weren't.

Caspian tried to read the phrase with the letters missing from some of the words. He felt the nausea return, creeping up inside him. What was happening?

the lilies and oses enote my ay
a   all gone can unve l the wa
join the place a c   sed knigh 's bones fell

As he watched, to his disbelief, the words broke apart before his eyes into their component letters and began to move around, creating new words and sentences entirely.

'Are you seeing this?' he asked in wonder.

'Seeing what?' Billy asked.

The letters stopped moving. The sentences they spelt out were now completely different to what had been there but a moment before.

only a saoul may see all is concealed
between the line of kings
and john the evangelist's chapel

He read the message out loud.

Clarissa gasped. 'It's an anagram! Caspian, how did work it out?'

'Work it out?' Caspian asked. 'I just read it.'

'But that isn't what it says.'

'What?' Caspian asked, confused. 'You mean you didn't see the letters move?'

'No,' Billy frowned. 'It still says the same thing. You should go on TV though. You'd make a killing on Countdown.'

Caspian stared in bewilderment at the message before him: a message hidden within a hidden message. But why was he the only one who could see this? And what did it all mean? He had never heard of a Saoul, whatever that might be.

'Between The Line of Kings and John the Evangelist's Chapel,' Clarissa repeated. 'Both of those are in the White Tower in the Tower of London.'

'What about the rest of it?' Billy asked. 'The wall gone, the cursed knight's bones, the Saoul that can see where it is all concealed? I mean, what's a Saoul? Where are we going to find one of those?'

'It's going to take time to work it all out,' Clarissa conceded. 'And we really should first work out how we are going to get out of here.'

'I agree,' Caspian said, looking around the murky chamber. Without pointing the torch he couldn't even see the walls surrounding them, it was that dark. He took out his mobile phone and pressed a button so the screen illuminated, giving off a little more light. Clarissa did the same. 'Let's spread out and search the chamber. There must be another way out.'

'If not, all that fancy anagram solving will have been for nothing,' Billy said.

They split up, each heading for a different section of wall and scanning it with whatever light source they had. Billy stood in the middle of the chamber and slowly rotated like a lighthouse, shining the beam of light around the entire space. There was only one passage into this room, and they all knew they couldn't go back that way.

Caspian searched the wall, feeling along the old brick blocks for any sign of a hidden switch that might open another exit. There had to be another way out. This couldn't be where the passage ended. To have come this far only to be trapped inside, too far underground to get a phone signal and with no hope of anyone finding them for weeks, maybe years. Maybe never.

'Hey, come here,' Clarissa said from her spot by the wall. 'I can feel air moving.'

'So what?' Billy said. 'What does it matter if we have air, but nothing to eat or drink? We'll still be dead.'

'That's not what she means,' Caspian interjected. 'For there to be a draft, there must be somewhere for the air to come from, and somewhere for it to go. There might be an exit on this part of the wall.'

All three searched Clarissa's part of the chamber wall, combing with their hands and lights.

'What are we looking for?' Clarissa asked.

'Probably another switch, hidden in the wall.'

'Well, this time one of you can put *your* finger in it,' Billy said.

'That's if we find it,' Caspian replied, stepping back to look at the wall from a distance. There was nothing like there had been in the cellar of The New Moon Tavern – no ouroboros knot to show the way.

'This is hopeless,' Billy said.

'It has to be here. Billy give me the torch a minute.'

Caspian took another couple of steps back, sweeping the wall with the torch from top to bottom, then left to right, slowly and methodically searching the surface of the wall. Where was the switch? It had to be there.

He took another step back, still scanning the wall. Then another. And then he almost fell onto his backside as his heel slipped on a slightly raised block on the floor. Trying to keep his balance, the torch waved around wildly as his arms swung out. He staggered with his full weight onto the raised block, which to his surprise began to sink into the ground with a low rumble. At the same time the wall before him folded open like interlinked fingers on a pair of hands sliding apart.

'You found it!' Clarissa shouted happily.

Caspian stayed where he was, looking with astonishment at the newly appeared exit. He *had* found it, but nearly sprained his ankle in the process.

'What are you waiting for?' Billy asked, looking back at Caspian as he made for the newly opened passageway. 'Aren't you coming?'

But Caspian stayed rooted to the spot until both Billy and Clarissa were beyond the opening in the wall.

'What is it?' Clarissa asked.

'I have a hunch that as soon as I step off this block the wall is going to close.'

'What makes you think that?' Clarissa asked.

'It'd be too easy to just walk out of here,' Caspian said, thinking about how difficult they had had it so far.

'It's not that far,' Billy reassured, 'you can make it.'

'Even so, give me some room,' he said, getting ready to dart for it. He knew that as soon as he stepped off the weighted stone it would rise back into place sealing him inside the chamber, and he was determined he would not be left inside to remain a permanent guest of the Guardians of the City of London.

'Okay,' Billy said. 'I'll count you down.'

Like that will help! Caspian thought.

'Ready? Three … two … ONE!'

Caspian sprang off the block going straight for the exit. He felt the block rise almost immediately as he stepped off it, confirming his suspicions, the exit closing much quicker than it had opened. It wasn't far to travel, but he had to make it just right as otherwise the closing stone would crush him like a tomato in a trouser press.

Two more steps … one more step … the gap was so small. He swivelled and flew through sideways, feeling the rough stone brush against his clothes, his skin, and his shoes. The torch clanked against the hard brick. He yanked his foot out of the way just as the exit snapped shut, as though it were a hungry dog's mouth.

'Are you okay, Caspian?' Clarissa asked.

'I think so,' he replied, between gasping breaths.

'I told you you'd make it,' Billy pointed out.

Clarissa turned on him, 'Oh, shut up, Billy.'

XXVI:
ARISE FROM THE ASHES

Despite the impression that motion pictures have given over the years of long straight staircases ascending high into the mountains, where a solitary Tibetan monastery awaits only the most perseverant initiate seeking enlightenment, the longest known straight staircase in the world can actually be found on the remote tropical island of St Helena. At a formidable six hundred and ninety-nine steps, the straight stair, named *Jacob's Ladder* (in biblical reference to the ladder from Jacob's dream that stretched up from the Earth to the Heavens), allowed for the transportation of supplies up the island hillside to the fort on top.

Even the longest escalator on the London Underground, found at Angel Tube Station, is only a third of the length of this staircase. To match it, one would have to climb *up* the down escalator at a consistent pace of one and a half times the speed that the escalator moves – and that would mean no stopping to catch your breath, nor would it take into consideration the flow of angry commuters trying to barge their way passed you onto the platform.

All that being said, the long straight staircase that Caspian, Billy, and Clarissa were now climbing from the Guardian's tomb seemed to endlessly stretch upward with the potential of beating the length of Jacob's Ladder.

'Three hundred and thirty … three hundred and thirty one … three hundred and thirty two …' Billy counted with each step.

'Do you really need to count?' Clarissa asked with frustration.

'Three hundred and thirty three … Yes, this has got to be … three hundred and thirty four … some kind of record.'

'It would be a record if you could make it to the top without saying anything.'

'Now, now, Clarissa,' Billy replied. 'There's no need to get all catty. And anyway, we don't know how far – ah, damn it! I lost count!'

'Come on,' Caspian said from the front, 'stop messing about. We don't know where this staircase leads nor whether it ends in a way out.'

'It has to lead somewhere.'

And sure enough it did. After seven hundred steps in total (had Billy managed to maintain his count) the staircase abruptly ended at a flat ceiling. A heavy square stone tile covered their only way out from the underground tomb.

Clarissa held the torch and both Billy and Caspian pressed their shoulders against the cover stone and lifted it an inch. Instantly, light poured in through the crack. The room beyond was high-ceilinged, white walled, and huge. What was this place?

A couple of hours had passed since they had first arrived at Leadenhall Market and begun their journey into the tunnels beneath the city. They carefully slid the cover stone aside and cautiously peered into the ginormous room making sure no one else was there.

Each great window had been dedicated to a saint, recreated in stained glass, which must have shone with a cherubic glow when sunlight passed through the transparent colours. The late afternoon light had diminished and given way to eve; only raindrops bounced off the windows this evening.

Lined up along the sides of the room were white pillars with elaborate gold trimmed capitals that created an elegant transition from pillar to arcade base. More of the rich trimming underlined the clerestory above the arcade, where smaller windows were positioned to illuminate the interior from high above. The floor, up through which they had poked, was polished white marble. Varnished dark wooden pews and panels lined the room, again adding to the richness and sense of prosperity this great room held. This clearly was no ordinary church they had found themselves in, or more precisely: under.

Billy and Caspian helped Clarissa into the room and then carefully they slid the square tile back into place. As they lowered it they had to be careful not to catch their fingers, and it dropped with a loud *thump* that echoed around the room.

'Shhh…' Clarissa protested.

'Are you saying that to us, or to the noise?' Billy asked. 'Either way, it won't make any difference.'

Now the cover stone was back in position, level with the surrounding marble floor and sealing the opening to the staircase, there was no way to open it again.

'Do you know where we are?' Caspian asked her. So far Clarissa had been the most adept at recognising their geographical location.

'Yes,' she replied, still scowling at Billy's retort. 'This is the St Lawrence Jewry.' She turned and pointed in the direction the staircase had descended. 'The Guildhall is over that way, a short walk across the courtyard. We *were* beneath the crypt.'

'The passage leads to a church?' Billy stated surprised. 'I wonder what the clergy would make of a staircase leading down into the dark depths beneath?'

'I'm just glad we are out of the ground,' Clarissa said.

Suddenly, a strict voice boomed across the room, 'What are you up to!' It belonged to a very stern looking priest who had a look on his face that suggested a suspicion of devious activity afoot in his church. 'You three should not be in here. We are now closed to the public.'

The priest was an older man with greying hair and a wrinkled brow. His eyes darted around the room, clearly scanning for anything these three young intruders might have damaged or put out of place.

'Really?' Clarissa asked politely. 'We thought it was open until six?'

'It isn't,' the priest replied. 'Now come, I should have locked the door. Out with you so I can lock up.' Suddenly he stopped and his eyes widened as he took in the three of them properly, covered from head to foot in dust, dirt, cobwebs, and who knew what else. 'You are filthy,' he said, his mouth open.

'Of course we are,' Billy agreed. 'We're teenagers.'

The priest promptly marched them to the door as if hoping to prevent their filth spreading to his immaculate place of worship. Outside the Jewry the three friends found themselves standing in the rain at the edge of a large courtyard, the Guildhall standing opposite them with its proud and powerful architecture, windows illuminated by the lights within.

They took shelter beneath the ambulatory (a covered walkway to the left of the Guildhall's main entrance) and took a moment to collect their thoughts. In the last hour they had successfully found the secret passage that only a very few knew existed, linking Leadenhall Market to the St Lawrence Jewry. Not only that, they had found the tombs of The City's Guardians, hidden deep below the Guildhall in a sub-crypt that had probably been long forgotten.

'Has anybody else noticed the theme that seems to be running through this mystery?' Clarissa asked after a while. Billy and Caspian shook their heads, not knowing what theme she referred to. 'There seems to be a repeated theme of rebirth, or regeneration within the clues and locations we have seen.'

'How so?' Caspian asked.

'Firstly, there was the ouroboros knot,' she explained. 'The snake devouring its own tail is a well known sign for an infinite cycle of recreation and regeneration.'

Billy involuntarily held his finger at the mention of the knot, remembering the switch that had opened the Half-Moon Passage but clamped shut on his digit.

'The half-moon was renewed as a new moon,' Clarissa continued, 'and in the Guardian's Tomb there was Magog's shield.'

Caspian recalled the phoenix emblazoned on the giant's stone shield and the explanation Clarissa had given. The phoenix symbolised rebirth, rising afresh from its own ashes.

'Even the myth of the Geldrin Blade hints at regeneration, although the stories are contradictory. Whilst some say the sword can absorb energy from all it touches, others believe that it could transfer this energy to its master.'

'And the latter must be what the hooded man believes too,' Caspian surmised. He obviously intended to use the blade to resurrect his own master, the sword's creator.

'Presumably,' Clarissa agreed, 'but why this underlying theme? Do you think it means anything, or is it just coincidence?'

The boys shrugged noncommittally; there was really no definitive answer.

'What now?' Billy asked.

'I guess we head home,' Caspian shrugged. He had begun thinking about the message hidden in the text that only he had been able to see. He still wasn't sure how that had happened and it troubled him, but if Clarissa was right about the ceremony of the lilies and roses they would have plenty of time to work it all out. 'We know the next part of the puzzle, and we have until May.'

'And what about the hooded man?' Billy asked.

They had seen footprints down in the tunnel and, even though there was no way of knowing whether they belonged to the man in the dark cloak or not, they knew it was a possibility they could not ignore. 'If he did find the tunnel before us, we don't know whether or not he saw the hidden message.'

'But what if he did?' Clarissa asked.

'Then we may not be the only ones searching the Tower of London for a secret passage, come May the twenty-first,' answered Caspian.

XXVII:
PREPARATIONS

Hayden Tanner returned to school the following week, regaling his gaggle of followers with tales of his mountain top feats. It was difficult to know whether Hayden was either a particularly accomplished skier or a particularly accomplished liar, however it was plausible that his self-confessed skills on the ski slopes were true – after all, he seemingly excelled at everything he set his mind to.

In the wake of the weekend's excitement, Caspian had become increasingly anxious about his foe's return; after all, what better ammunition to give someone with the spite and malevolence of Hayden Tanner than his target losing a family member? It was like welcoming an infection into an open wound.

This anxiety was heightened by the fact that the last time they were in the same room as one another they had done battle with accusations of fraud over their history reports.

Caspian had dodged a bullet that day having been called out of class before his nemesis' master plan could be fully realised. Surely that would have been hard for Hayden to swallow, to have had that victory snatched away from him by an ill-timed visit from the Headmaster when it was right within his grasp: Now he would be out for blood.

However, as it happened, Caspian couldn't have been more wrong. Hayden spoke to everyone come his return. He moved around the classroom with the easy charm he naturally oozed in the same way a tree drips with sap. He shared jokes, swapped stories, and acted in his general likeable manner.

The only person to whom he did not speak was Caspian. He drifted passed him without a single acknowledgement, and when he looked with his ice blue eyes in Caspian's direction his gaze passed through him with the ease a shark cuts through water. It was almost as though he had ceased to exist in Hayden's world.

Whether or not the intent of ignoring Caspian's existence was malicious, Caspian could not have been happier. No further tricks were played on him and no mean words were sent his way. Even Rob Harper left him alone. He was happy not to exist in Hayden Tanner's universe, especially as it gave Caspian, Billy, and Clarissa the time they needed to focus their energy on solving the mystery of the hidden message.

Unfortunately, the ceremony of the lilies and roses was not the only date in May they were on a deadline to meet. The twenty-first of May fell right at the end of their end of year exams when the trio were due to sit their SATs.

'What does SAT mean anyway?' Billy asked one morning after they had sat through a mock exam. 'That's an absolutely rubbish name if you ask me.'

Clarissa shrugged, not wanting to comment.

'But do you know what SAT stands for?' he persisted.

Clarissa sighed. 'It's either "statutory aptitude tasks," "standard assessment tests," or something like that.'

'How about "superfluous acronym tests?" ' Caspian joked.

'More like, "stupid and trivial," ' Billy added.

Whatever SAT stood for, there was no escaping the fact that the amount of additional homework and revision they had been set for March and April would consume a lot of the time they had hoped to spend making progress with the next part of the riddle. Regardless, they still found time to discuss and analyse the possible meanings the sentences held.

Whilst they were at school, the library became their fortress of solitude, allowing them the peace and the privacy to decipher each phrase's meaning. They sat around the table – the very same table where their friendship had formed with the help of a particularly curious clockwork spider.

One mid-morning break, Caspian removed from his bag a white plastic ice-cream tub. Slowly, and with the gusto and theatricality of a seasoned stage magician, he rotated the tub so that the container was upside-down and the lid was on the bottom.

He placed it on the table, his hand poised on top, and smiled at the confusion that crossed Billy and Clarissa's faces.

'Er...' Billy asked. 'What you doing, mate?'

With his other hand he loosened the container from the plastic lid and then, like a waiter removing a cloche to reveal some glorious gastronomic wonder beneath, he swiftly raised the container away from the table, leaving the lid and contents behind.

Billy and Clarissa both drew a breath. A reassembled golden spider stood perfectly still.

'You fixed him?' Clarissa asked. 'When?'

It had taken Caspian a great deal of time to repair the little spider, but he had kept his word and worked diligently at putting him back together. Whenever he had reached a point where he was unsure, or a part just didn't seem to fit, Caspian had visited his father in his study to seek his advice. Apart from that, he had essentially rebuilt the little device on his own.

The tensest moment came when he was tightening the final of Sprocket's pieces into place. Caspian had turned the miniscule screw with a tiny screwdriver used to fix watches, and then had carefully turned the spider over and stood him on all eight legs.

Then he waited.

Sprocket didn't move.

He held his breath.

Sprocket didn't move.

Had it worked?

Sprocket didn't move.

Maybe he had put something back in the wrong place? Maybe a part was missing? Rob Harper had made a mess of him, after all.

Come on! Caspian had willed the little spider.

Still, Sprocket didn't move.

Please! Caspian persisted. But still, Sprocket didn't –

A leg twitched. A cog stuttered. A minute piston moved a millimetre. A gear began to turn. Another leg twitched. Something deep inside gave a low *whirr*. And then the spider collapsed into a deflated heap on the table.

Caspian let out a sigh of despair. He had failed.

But the little spider was not yet ready to throw in the towel. Slowly it rose to its feet – all eight of them – and gave the slightest little whirr. Caspian gently placed his hand beside it, which it approached with caution. It seemed to examine his hand like an alien object, unsure of what to make of it.

The spider froze, and the moment seemed to drag on and on. Then, finally, with a joyful chirp, Sprocket happily nuzzled his face against Caspian's skin.

'Hey, boy!' Caspian said happily. 'You're okay!'

Sprocket had chirped in agreement.

Now, waiting obediently on the lid of the container as though it were a stage, the little golden spider took an elegant bow – which for an eight-legged creature was quite a feat on its own.

'Oh, Sprocket!' Clarissa beamed, giving the clockwork spider a polite round of applause.

'Good idea,' Billy said, referring to the tub Sprocket had been transported in.

Caspian smiled, 'the benefits are two-fold: firstly it offers a bit more protection than my bag's pocket, and secondly it prevents any curious wandering.

Sprocket gave a guilty whine, as though he understood every word they were saying. The group laughed, happy to be reunited again.

'I've been thinking,' Clarissa said, thumping a great big book of Arthurian legends onto the table and causing Sprocket to scramble for cover. She fingered through the pages until she found what she was looking for. 'Ah, here,' she said, pointing to a short passage of text. 'It could refer to the story of Sir Balan?'

When it came to the matter of deciphering the clue they had found hidden in Magog's scroll case, they were pretty certain as to the meaning of the first line. "The lilies and roses denote my day" seemed in all likelihood to refer to the ceremony of the lilies and roses on the twenty-first of May, just as Clarissa had deduced. Likewise, they were sure the entrance could be found where a wall had once stood but had been removed: "a wall gone can unveil the way."

They had tried to find out whether a wall had been removed from between the Line of Kings and St John the Evangelist's chapel – both of which could be found within the Tower of London – however there wasn't anything on the internet that was helpful, and searching for specific information in the vast volumes of text written about the Tower was like looking in a haystack for a needle without the luxury of a very strong magnet.

However, the line that was causing them a real headache, and long debates over the ambiguity of the sentence, was in fact the line that referred to a cursed knight and his bones.

'Listen to this.' Clarissa read; 'Sir Balan came across an island castle, but he found it guarded by another knight who was bound by a curse. The cursed knight refused to let him pass, unless he beat him in a battle to the death. There,

Sir Balan fought him and won but, in killing him, freed the knight of his curse and unwittingly fell under it himself. From hence forth he was held under the same curse, forcing him to stand guard over the very island castle he had hoped to pass.'

'Who was the cursed knight Sir Balan fought?' Billy asked. 'Is it *his* bones the clue refers to?'

'It could equally be Balan's,' Caspian said. 'He too was a knight who fell under the curse. But is there anything to tie this to the rest of the puzzle?'

'The island castle?' Clarissa suggested. 'Maybe it is indicating the Tower of London?'

'It's not really on an island though, is it?' Billy challenged.

'The United Kingdom *is* an island.'

'It does seem a bit of a stretch,' Caspian added.

'And why go to the bother of saying a cursed knight's bones when they could have just said Balan's bones?'

'Because then the anagram wouldn't have worked,' Clarissa pointed out.

The other line that was causing them confusion referred to the "Saoul," and they were no closer to uncovering what this actually was, despite Billy's ludicrous theories.

'*Saoul* is the French word for drunk, if I'm translating it correctly,' Billy had discovered after typing the word into an online universal translator. 'Maybe only a *drunk* may see all is concealed? That might explain why the entrance to the Half-Moon Passage can be found in the cellar of a pub, behind a rack of wine no less!'

'I'm not sure getting inebriated is exactly what the clue suggests,' Clarissa said, shaking her head. 'We didn't need to be drunk to find the entrance last time.'

'It might have helped,' Billy grinned.

'You almost fell off that bridge on your own, without the assistance of alcohol.'

'You never know, might have calmed my nerves.'

'Might have upset your stomach,' Clarissa countered.

Frustratingly, the one person who could easily define a Saoul was the one person they couldn't ask – Caspian's father. In asking him, they would not only give away their discovery of the secret passage but also their intention to uncover where the riddle would lead them.

'There's one thing we haven't considered,' Clarissa pointed out.

The boys looked at her expectantly, but neither offered any guesses or conjecture as to what consideration she referred to.

'The Tower of London,' she continued when it became clear her listeners had nothing to contribute, 'is a guarded fortification. It's not like we can just walk in, can we?'

'We'll just buy tickets,' Caspian shrugged, not seeing this as a concern.

'The Tower closes early on the evening of the ceremony.'

'We can go earlier, then,' Billy chipped in.

'Er … no, we can't,' Caspian said. 'We have our English exam on that afternoon. By the time we get across London to the Tower it will be close to five.'

'Hey,' Billy said reassuringly, 'don't worry about getting in.'

Clarissa, however, was far from reassured. 'What do you mean, "don't worry?" ' she said crossly. 'If there is one place in this whole endeavour where we need a plan, this is it!'

Billy simply grinned. 'I know that,' he said. 'I meant, leave it with me.'

'Leave it with *you*?'

'Yeah, leave it with me. You two are much better at this code breaking stuff than I am, but when it comes to reckless rule breaking and all manner of mischief, then I'm your man.' There was a familiar gleam in Billy's eyes.

Clarissa didn't say anything. She just looked at him with her mouth slightly ajar.

'You've got to admit,' Caspian smiled, 'he has a point.'

Caspian woke with a start.

It was just after five in the morning on the twenty-first of May, and his sheets were clammy from sweat, his heart pounding in his chest. Sprocket must have sensed something was awry and had climbed onto his lap with a worried chirp.

'I'm okay,' Caspian muttered wearily. 'Just that dream again.'

As the ceremony of the lilies and roses had drawn closer, Caspian had been plagued by the same reoccurring nightmare. In the dream, he found himself running down a dark unending passageway – not too dissimilar to Half-Moon Passage. In front and behind him was darkness, but he kept running because he knew somewhere in the blackness the hooded man pursued him, one half of his face twisted and scarred, the other concealed by that horrid metal mask.

No matter how hard he ran he could not escape. Out of the shadows his hand reached out and clasped at Caspian's shoulder, pulling him to a halt. Then, the monstrous wraith of a man was bearing down on him, his one visible eye looking into Caspian's.

'*Saoul*,' the hooded man said, his voice as horrid as his face.

Then he would let Caspian go, letting him fall, plunging into a hole, falling, falling, *falling*. His arms would fly out, and he would awaken disorientated in a startled sweat. Always the same dream, always the same torment.

The ceremony of the lilies and roses could not have come at a more inconvenient time. He had so much on his mind, and the restless nights as a result of this recurring nightmare were certainly not helping. The SATs were now fully underway and even the exams he thought he *had* been prepared for were more difficult than he'd anticipated.

Hayden was now not the only one giving Caspian the silent treatment. Ever since their subterranean adventure beneath the city, Jessica had become increasingly distant. It had now reached the point that his once closest friend would not even return his calls.

Clarissa, who had stayed in touch with Jess since they had met after Christmas, said that she was feeling excluded from the group's adventures. This frustrated Caspian as there was nothing he could do about that. After all, she lived a long way from London so of course she was going to miss out on things. He wanted to talk to her about it and make amends, but there was little he could do when she wouldn't answer the phone.

He lay in bed and looked at the ceiling, his mind busily whirring away like the mechanism inside Sprocket. By the time the sun rose at half passed six, Caspian had moved to his bedroom window and sat looking out onto the small graveyard beyond. The branches of the Bloodgoods that sheltered the graves were crowded with dark red leaves whence they were named. The early dawn sunlight danced across the leaves, illuminating their rich vibrant shades of red, crimson, burgundy, and maroon.

His mind drifted briefly to his mother, as it did from time to time. Whenever he felt a quietness in his heart, he thought of her. Looking out at the tranquillity of the graveyard at sunrise, he found a peculiar peacefulness fall upon him, like the way a calm falls just before the coming of the storm.

XXVIII:
AB LIBITUM

There was a gentle knock on Caspian's bedroom door. 'Are you up, Dear?' the kindly voice of Mrs Hodges asked from the other side.

'Yes,' he replied, having been up for hours. As this day had drawn closer and closer, he had become increasingly concerned as to whether he should inform his father of what was going on. After all, perhaps now there was too much at stake to worry about getting in trouble for all that he had done behind his father's back.

But a few days ago, the decision was made for him.

Tuesday morning Caspian had come down to the kitchen to have his breakfast. Mrs Hodges was busy cleaning in the living room, but his father was nowhere to be found. At first he had assumed that Father was out, dealing with a business errand early that morning, but when he finished the last of the cereal and went to throw away the packaging he noticed something lying in the waste bin.

An open envelope had been discarded after its contents had been removed. It lay crumpled in the bin, its seal broken where it had been opened: a seal of red wax.

'Where's Father gone?' he had asked Mrs Hodges, shortly after.

She had kept on cleaning but answered, 'Out, Dear. He will be away for a couple of days, apparently. A client wants him to see a certain piece that he means to have valued.'

'When will he be back?'

'A couple of days, a week at the most. Oh, I wouldn't worry, Dear. He has to travel from time to time, sometimes to other countries to see these expensive antiques.'

'But, he just went,' Caspian said, still processing the information. 'He didn't say goodbye.'

'You know your Father,' she had replied, by way of explanation. But a question had lingered; did he really know his father at all?

He didn't believe that Father was really away on business. No, Smeelie had written to him again and had called him away, but why, and to what end? Caspian knew that Ponsonby Smeelie was in league with the hooded man, even if Father wouldn't see it, but with the date of the ceremony approaching he couldn't shake the feeling that his father had been lured away. Was he in danger?

Father's unexpected departure seemed ominous to Caspian; if his father was not around to protect the Geldrin Blade on the eve of the twenty-first then it would be up to him. After all his family had sacrificed to keep this thing safe, were it to fall into the hands of the hooded man it would have all been for nothing.

Mrs Hodges gave another tap on his door, a little stronger than before.

'I'm up,' he said, feigning weariness and picked up his school bag.

'I should hope so.' Mrs Hodges had taken to a parental role whilst Father was absent. 'You have a big test ahead of you today.'

You have no idea, Caspian thought to himself as he headed for the door.

The morning was consumed by a science lesson, and then geography before lunch. At the end of their lunch break the Year 9 students gathered outside the school hall, ready for their English exam.

'Is this reading or writing?' Billy asked Caspian in a whisper.

'Which have you revised for?'

'Neither.'

317

'Then what does it matter?' asked Caspian.

'I hate reading,' Billy muttered.

They entered the hall and were seated in alphabetical order by their surname, placing Caspian a long way from Billy. He was, however, close to Hayden Tanner, although separated by Susan Stroud and Ben Sutton.

The English exam was, much to Billy's dismay, a reading exam. It was not as bad as Caspian had anticipated, but when he snuck a glance over at Billy he could tell that his friend did not share his optimism.

He finished it in reasonable time, and after checking that he had satisfactorily answered all the questions to the best of his abilities, his mind meandered towards the evening's antics. Billy had been left in charge of devising a way into the Tower without being noticed, but had thus far failed to share any of his plan's details with any of those involved. Clarissa shared Caspian's concern about this particular point.

The absence of Caspian's father had been the perfect alibi for Billy and Clarissa, who had told their parents that they would be staying over at Caspian's that evening to study for their next exam. Caspian, on the other hand, had told Mrs Hodges that he would be staying at Billy's for the same purpose, and they were all safe in the knowledge that none of their parents or guardians had the other's telephone number, so there was little risk of their ulterior motives being uncovered.

The monitoring teacher checked her watch and signalled that time was up and that the exam had finished. The papers were collected and then, row-by-row, the students quietly exited the hall.

Clarissa met Caspian outside. 'That wasn't too bad,' she said.

'Yeah, I didn't think so,' Caspian agreed.

Billy came and stood glumly beside them both.

'Oh dear,' Clarissa said, looking at his sullen face.

'What was the problem?' Caspian asked.

'The problem,' Billy answered, 'was the "Reading Comprehension" section. The extracts were so dull I couldn't concentrate on what they were talking about, and I'm sure there was more than one correct answer.'

'But you answered every question?' Clarissa asked.

'Of course. It was multiple choice, so I just left it to fate and ticked whatever box took my fancy.'

'I'm not sure that's how the test is supposed to work.'

'Maybe not, but if I *do* do well on that test, perhaps my dad'll let me pick the numbers for the lottery.'

They left the school grounds and headed down the street in the direction of the nearest Tube station.

'So what's the plan?' Caspian asked.

'You'll see,' Billy smirked conspiratorially.

It took just under an hour to traverse the city to Tower Hill Underground station. Even though it was a school day, as they alighted the station they found the surrounding streets to be exceptionally busy; tourists ambled in every direction, stopping to take photos or consult maps. There was also a formidable amount of suited office workers chatting loudly on mobile phones as they walked out in front of taxicabs that honked loudly in protest.

The Tower of London stood before them, an impressive medieval castle that had somehow survived the passing of time and stood in exceptional condition in the heart of the modern city of skyscrapers, coffee shops, and clothes stores. And yet it did not seem out of place, but if anything it was an irreplaceable part of the ambiance – like a grandfather asleep in his armchair after a Christmas meal, whilst the rest of the family played board games. Tourists still flocked in their hundreds to visit the Tower of London, to see the home of the crown jewels and the Beefeaters that guarded them on a daily basis. Slipping in unseen would be a remarkably difficult undertaking.

'So?' Clarissa said, looking expectantly at Billy. 'It's too late to enter with tickets. What have you got up your sleeve?'

Billy grinned. 'I've got a way that we can get in and not have to pay a penny. All we need to do is wait over there.' He pointed to a side entrance, known as Henry III's Watergate, where a solitary guard stood outside a cabin armed with a radio and an intimidating looking rifle.

'How are we going to get passed the guard?' Caspian asked.

'Just wait and you will see.'

Knowing Billy and his flare for mischief, both Caspian and Clarissa had a feeling this would not bode well. 'I've got a bad feeling about this,' Caspian quietly admitted as they approached the side gate.

The guard only glanced at them the once, the rest of the time he stood watching the other tourists passing him by or talking to his colleagues on the radio he kept clipped to his belt. This guard was not dressed like a Beefeater but instead dressed in dark military style shirt and trousers; smart but sturdily built, much like the man who wore them.

They waited by the guardrail, a short distance from the sentry guard and his position at the guard cabin. As it got later and later, they became increasingly frustrated and impatient for Billy to reveal his plan. A red and white striped barrier was lowered across the entrance, but the group could see the tourists beyond, and the occasional Beefeater in their dark blue uniform with red trimming guarding an entrance, conducting a tour, or posing for a photo opportunity. It was curious how the duties of the Beefeater's had evolved over the centuries as the times had changed, Caspian reflected.

The Yeomen Warders, as they were formally called, had once been charged with guarding the crown jewels and ensuring the Tower's prisoners were kept in their confinements. They had been nicknamed Beefeaters by historical commentators who had observed them enjoying their right to eat as much beef from the King's table as they liked. Now, no prisoner was kept in the Tower and the Beefeater's role had transformed from guarding a main attraction to becoming attractions in their own right.

Caspian noticed that the tourists and bystanders surrounding the Tower's wall began to part to make way for a small white minibus that was carefully approaching them. Billy gave Caspian a slap on the shoulder. 'Show time,' he said.

The minibus came to a halt not far from where they stood and the travellers began to pile out. The passengers were children, most of them similar ages to the three friends, except they were all dressed in the same identical ceremonial robes. On their left breast a logo had been stitched in black and red – a dragon amongst a ring of flames.

'Those students are from Drayston Academy,' Caspian said, recognising the logo. 'What are *they* doing here?'

'They are the Drayston school choir,' Billy explained. 'They are renown for being the best school choir in the London borough, but considering how strict their teachers are I'm not surprised. They are singing at tonight's ceremony.'

Drayston Academy – or to use its full name: Drayston Academy and Institute of Correctional Castigation – was a boarding school in the same area of London as Hogarth House High, although it was more like a prison for young offenders than an educational establishment; the school motto was "Disciplining the Disobedient."

Most of the students sent to Drayston Academy had been expelled from their previous schools, the school before, and more often than not the school before that. Some had been caught committing illegal acts and thus had been placed under the vice-like care of the Institute of Correctional Castigation.

Caspian's classmates had told horror stories about the Academy, claiming they knew of kids who had ended up there; troubled kids, disturbed kids. If there was a school ideal for breeding super villains, Drayston Academy was it. But, even though Caspian very much doubted that any of the fables he'd heard contained a modicum of truth, he was still greatly surprised to learn that out of this agglomerate of reprobates, malefactors, and miscreants a talented choir had been formed.

'Drayston Academy has a choir?' Caspian voiced his surprise.

'Yes. As I said, they're meant to be one of the best in the city.' Billy smirked as he read Caspian's reaction. 'Not the scum of the earth you were expecting?'

'No,' Caspian confessed, feeling a little ashamed he had formed this prejudice opinion of these pupils. 'Maybe the Academy isn't as bad as everyone says.'

'Oh, it is,' Billy shrugged, 'but spend enough time clawing through the dirt and eventually you're bound to find a diamond or two.'

'And how is this choir going to help us inside?' Clarissa asked, watching them unpack the minibus.

Billy took his rucksack off his shoulder and unzipped the main compartment. The other two had left their bags in their lockers, but Billy had insisted on bringing his as he had packed it with supplies he deemed necessary for the evening's activities. 'Time for the clever part of my plan,' he said.

Caspian felt the confidence he had placed in his friend's plan ebb away as Billy carefully passed around the white-cotton choir gowns he had kept surreptitiously concealed in his backpack. They were clearly not of the same quality material as those worn by the actual choir, and on the left breast a shoddy replica had been sewn of the Academy's dragon and flame logo – it more resembled an ostrich being barbecued.

'Where did you get these?' Clarissa asked, looking in disgust at the fabric she held in her hands.

'The internet,' Billy answered. 'Had to make the logos myself. I know they're not perfect, but home economics was never my strongest suit.'

'I'd rule surgeon out as a career option, if were you,' Caspian said, thumbing the stitching around the "dragon," some of the thread came out as he touched it.

Clarissa looked thoroughly unimpressed – and not only by Billy's crochet. '*This* is you're plan?' she exasperated. 'We're not going to make it passed the choirmaster, let alone by the Tower guard.'

'Oh, ye of little faith,' Billy said and rolled his eyes as though she was being unreasonable. 'Just stick with the group and keep your head down. They'll never even notice.'

Clarissa looked at Caspian in desperation.

'I don't think we have any other choice,' he shrugged, apologetically.

'That's the spirit,' Billy enthused, and slung his own gown over his head.

Dennis Harlington had been the choirmaster for the Drayston Academy choir for almost fifteen years. He was a very proper man and he didn't take jip from anyone, no, siree! That was what a military background did to you. It made you worth your salt. It made you *disciplined*.

True, being in the army reserve band, Dennis Harlington had never actually seen combat, nor had he ever undergone any military training, but that trivial little datum had never deterred him from commanding his choir in any manner other than that a sergeant does his troops.

Now in his late fifties, Dennis Harlington was tall, thin, and wore a pair of thick-framed glasses. He was an appallingly vain man who took a tremendous amount of care in his appearance. His brilliantine moustache always neatly trimmed, his chin clean-shaven. His suit ironed and pressed, not a crease in sight or a fibre out of place. And so, when his full head of hair suddenly thinned and a bald patch emerged (coincidentally, correlating with his first month at Drayston Academy) he was utterly mortified. Now, the slightest implication that he wore a toupee to cover the desolate spot his follicles had abandoned was terrifically taboo.

He watched the students in his rear view mirror as they disembarked the minibus. Then he took the key out of the ignition, climbed out of the driver's door, and breathed in the sight around him. It was places like the Tower of London that made him feel proud to be here in good old Blighty. Here he was, leading the choir on the ceremony of the lilies and roses, in the very same historic building that held the crown jewels. He took a deep breath and puffed out his lungs in self-importance.

Dennis Harlington marched the choir over to the gate, keeping a watchful eye that none of them put a foot out of place. A sentry guard peered at him from his small guard cabin.

'Dennis Harlington,' Dennis Harlington announced, 'with the Drayston Academy choir.'

The guard looked at him for a moment, and Dennis could not help the subconscious feeling that this guard was looking at the top of his head.

The guard's mouth twitched in the slightest of smirks.

'Is there something funny here?' the choirmaster demanded sharply.

'No, sir,' the guard quickly replied, 'there's nothing funny hair.' He coughed, 'I mean here. Nothing funny *here*.'

Dennis Harlington felt his cheeks flush. He was certain he had heard a few members of the choir giggle, but when he turned to look they were all standing still and behaving.

The guard was speaking on his radio, and then raised the barrier and waved them through. The choirmaster made a mental note of the guard's badge number – he would put in a complaint about how he had been treated. *I was in the army for Christ's sake.*

His bitterness quickly abated when he spotted a reporter standing beside the entrance of St. Thomas' Tower. He told the choir to halt and waved the reporter over. If he was going to appear in a newspaper he wanted to ensure that they spelt his name correctly.

At the back of the group of gowned choir members, Caspian, Billy, and Clarissa stood silently huddled with their heads down. Billy held his rucksack close to his chest and his friends had huddled close to help him smuggle it inside. The choirmaster had been preoccupied with the sentry guard smirking at his obvious toupee. So much so, he had not noticed the three extra choir members join his troupe, although Billy had almost given them away after the guard accidentally said "hair" instead of "here," and had to suppress a laugh.

They stayed with the group as the choirmaster led them on a procession, turning left and passing under an archway. The guards waved cheerily to them as they passed, whilst other guards had begun guiding groups of tourists towards the exit. The general public were not permitted to attend the evening's ceremony and the Tower was beginning to close.

'Just keep hanging back,' Billy had whispered as the choirmaster stopped them and spoke to a man with a large camera around his neck. 'We'll slip away when we get a chance. It isn't like anyone is looking at us.'

'Your attention, everyone,' the choirmaster said addressing his troupe, still stood beside the man armed with a camera. 'Get into your positions,' his voice was sharp and rushed. 'Quickly. Quickly. This gentleman is from the *Standard* and he is going to take our picture.'

Billy gaped at Caspian, horrified. 'My father reads the Standard,' he said, 'as do my brothers. I'll never hear the end of it if they think I've joined a choir!' The Standard was one of London's tabloid newspapers given away for free across the city, and many of their peers also read the paper for its sports pages, celebrity gossip, and occasionally the news.

They formed ranks against the wall opposite St Thomas' Tower whilst the reporter clicked away behind his camera, taking picture after picture in quick succession, many of which Caspian couldn't be sure he had avoided being in. Then, the reporter said to the choirmaster how nice it would be to hear a quick song.

'Oh, you've got to be kidding,' Billy gasped in protest.

The choirmaster agreed with enthusiasm, keen to show off what his group were capable of, and moved to stand before them. Caspian, Billy, and Clarissa, meanwhile, tried to work their way to the back of the ensemble, however, as they were positioned by height poor Billy ended up being moved to the front.

Caspian felt his palms grow clammy as he suddenly became very nervous. He was not particularly musical – Herr Trommel, his music theory teacher, would certainly vouch for that – but singing alongside the best school choir in London he would stick out like an elephant in an ant's nest.

'I think *The Maiden's Song* will be appropriate,' the choirmaster mused, and raised his skinny arms theatrically. He clicked his fingers to set the tempo, and after the forth click he made a waving motion for the choir to begin. All around them voices sung out confidently.

The maidens came when I was in my mother's bower
The maidens came when I was in my mother's bower
I had all that I would

The bailey beareth the bell away
The lily, the rose, the rose I lay

The harmonious sound of the choir's singing drew the attention of several groups of tourists who were being herded out of the surrounding area, many of which took further photos of them.

Caspian felt his cheeks burn red as he blushed. Billy, however, seemed even more uncomfortable than he was. He stood at the front, opening and closing his mouth at what he hoped were the appropriate moments as he attempted to mime along with a song to which he did not know the words. Quite a few times he was caught with his mouth open when no one was singing, giving him the appearance of a dehydrated goldfish.

Eventually the song came to the coda with a final reprise of the chorus and the crowd, including a couple of beefeaters, burst into applause. At the front of the choir, the choirmaster turned appreciatively to the crowd and spread his hands, clearly enjoying his moment in the limelight. The crowd clapped even more fervently, and the choirmaster placed one hand across his waist and gave a low grateful bow.

It was only as he was tipped over that the choirmaster realised his mistake.

The problems with overcoming partial baldness with a replacement hairpiece are threefold:

One - windy weather must be avoided at all costs.

Two - movements encouraging the natural pull of gravity are advised against as a precautionary measure.

Three - once discovered to be false, others may find your hairpiece looks ridiculous.

Dennis Harlington may have taken into consideration point one, but caught up in the moment he completely forgot about the second point. Bent over in a low bow, his toupee slipped from his head to the floor resulting, almost instantly, in point three.

The crowd suddenly roared with laughter.

The poor embarrassed choirmaster snatched up his wig from the floor and hastily replaced it atop is bald bonce, albeit slightly skewwhiff.

Caspian saw this as their moment to scarper and tugged at Billy and Clarissa's gowns. They ducked out of the choir, who by now had also collapsed into a fit of sniggering, and headed under an archway nearby. There they found an open door and slipped inside: a sign above the doorway informed them, ominously, that this was The Bloody Tower.

There they discarded their gowns and watched through a small window as the choirmaster, trying to recoup what little was left of his dignity, marched the choir into St Thomas' Tower whence they would slowly cavalcade into the adjoining Wakefield Tower where the ceremony of the lilies and roses would take place.

The rest of the crowd began to depart and soon the chatter outside had died away. Once they were sure it was safe to continue, the three friends turned their attention toward the White Tower, and the next challenge they faced.

XXIX:
LINE OF KINGS

The White Tower stood solitarily at the heart of the castle, a 90ft tall, virtually impregnable keep. William the Conqueror had ordered its construction shortly after he had taken the city. It would prove to be a formidable fortress against any attacking or invading force, as well as acting as a residence and a venue for great ceremonies. The great tower's real purpose however was as a reminder to the city's population, living beneath it in their modest buildings. They would have been unable to ignore this impressive monument symbolising the power and presence of the Norman monarchy that had conquered them.

The corners of its western facing wall were reinforced with square turrets that extended up above the battlements. A round tower housing the main staircase formed the corner to the northeast, whilst a round projection was built to the southeast that housed the chapel apse – this was where the Chapel of St. John the Evangelist could be found.

The Chapel was located on the second floor, whilst the Line of Kings lay in the room to the east on the floor below. Unfortunately, as the White Tower stood alone and unattached to any buildings, were they to cross the exposed courtyard and open green there was little to shelter Caspian, Billy, and Clarissa from onlookers.

The Tower of London had not always been detached from the numerous towers, walls, gates, and halls that formed the castle in its entirety. Now all that remained of these connecting structures were the ruins of Coldharbour Gate and the Wardrobe Tower, both of which amounted to little more than foundations in the tower green.

As daylight faded, Caspian lurked in the shadow of the Wakefield Tower. Up above him, through the open window of the tower, he heard the Drayston choir start to sing: the ceremony of the lilies and roses was beginning.

They kept low as they made their way along the ruins of an old wall. Ahead of them a pair of guards stood, backs turned. The wall beside them had dropped to waist height so they quickly climbed over it before they could be spotted.

A loud *squawk* made them all jump as they planted themselves against the other side of the wall. A huge raven watched them with beady eyes, behind it a row of cages stood where more of these big black birds hopped about.

'What on earth?' Caspian whispered when he saw the big birdcages.

'Raven's lodgings,' Clarissa whispered back.

They were now not far from the White Tower. The entrance was before them on the southern wall atop a large timber staircase that climbed up to the ground floor – the ground floor was raised as part of the Tower's defensive architectural design and there were no entrances below. The wooden staircase was the only way in and out.

Large blocks of stone from the ruins of previous structures slightly concealed them where they hid, but they could not remain there for long without being discovered. Spotlights illuminated the Tower; they watched it and the surrounding courtyard for a moment longer, but there was no sign of movement.

'We can't stay here,' Caspian said quietly, 'we're very exposed.'

'Can we get to the entrance?' Clarissa asked.

'Most of the guards must be attending the ceremony,' Billy surmised. 'They probably have a limited patrol watching the Tower at the moment. We're going to have to risk it, before the ceremony ends.'

For a brief moment Caspian felt a wave of paranoia wash over him. His eyes were drawn to the rooftops of the encircling buildings, black silhouettes in the dying light. He wondered when the hooded man was planning to strike. Was he already inside the castle walls, or waiting for the light to completely depart to conceal his entrance? 'Let's go,' Caspian said, not wanting to give their masked enemy further opportunity to beat them to the Geldrin Blade.

When they were certain the way was clear, the three friends darted across the courtyard separating them from the sheer wall of the White Tower. Keeping as low as they could, they slinked under the timber scaffolding of the entrance staircase to regroup and temporarily survey for watchful eyes. Confident they were safe to continue, Caspian led them as they crept up the wooden staircase.

About halfway up he suddenly froze. The abruptness of his halt caused Billy to bash into him and almost knock him over.

'What is it?' Billy mouthed silently, once he had regained his balance.

Caspian held up his hand as he listened, unsure what it was that he had initially heard to bring him to a stop. Then his eyes widened and he frantically waved them all back down the staircase. 'Quick! Quickly!' he hissed as they slipped down the staircase and ducked back under into the shadowy cover of the scaffolding.

Above them they heard heavy boots step out of the Tower. From what Caspian could hear, there were two of them, they sounded like guards. He distinctly heard a heavy door close and then the jangle of keys.

Billy looked at him unhappily, and Caspian knew why – the guards must have just finished their sweep of the Tower and had locked up for the evening. How would they get inside now?

The guards began to descend the timber stair, their boots thudding loudly as they made their way down. Hidden in the dark recess beneath them, Caspian became increasingly nervous. He waited anxiously, as it would only take a passing guard to glance in their direction and all would be lost.

Once the guards were at ground level Caspian could see them more clearly through the gaps in the steps. They were dressed differently to the other Beefeaters they had seen around the Tower who wore a dark uniform with a red trim. These were dressed in a vibrant red uniform with a gold trim, large faux bearskin hats atop their heads. They much more closely resembled how Caspian imagined the royal guard to look.

Thankfully, the guards did not look behind them as they reached the bottom of the staircase. One of them made a comment that the other grumbled at, and then they headed away from the Tower.

Clarissa breathed a sigh of relief. 'That was lucky,' she whispered nervously.

'Not really,' Billy replied. 'Now we're locked out.'

'Better locked out, than thrown out.'

'Same difference,' Billy hissed. 'Either way, we can't get inside.'

Caspian wasn't so sure. They had come so far, and he wasn't willing to be stopped by a locked door; the hooded man certainly wouldn't be. He said to his friends, 'those guards can't carry those keys with them all the time. They must leave them somewhere once they have locked up.'

By using a large tree for cover, they were able to follow where the guards went. They didn't go far from the Tower and eventually stepped inside a guard post that doubled as an information point just between the edge of the green and Lanthorn Tower to the southeast.

Moving slowly across the dark stretch of grass before them, they were able to get close enough without being seen and yet still see inside the guard post. It was only large enough for two guards, but two chairs had been squeezed in so they could sit down. Behind them was a wall with hooks from which keys were hung, including the keys to the

Tower. Both guards were sat inside looking northerly with their backs to the guard post door.

'What now?' Clarissa asked, observing the hopelessness of the situation.

'We're going to have to sneak in and steal the key,' Caspian said, although he wasn't entirely confident that this was going to work. He looked at Billy beside him and saw that his friend was grinning – that was not a good sign.

'I'll give it a go,' he said, 'but you better come with me as a lookout.'

Caspian nodded. As Billy was about to sneak off Caspian caught his arm. He whispered, 'you really need to make sure that you don't get caught.'

'Don't worry about me,' he whispered cockily with a smirk, 'I'm the *Solid Snake* of stealth.' And he crept off, keeping close to the wall and moving silently in the shadows towards the guard post.

'Solid Snake?' Clarissa questioned.

'More like Secret Squirrel,' Caspian answered wryly. 'Stay here and watch our backs. If someone comes, make a noise.'

Clarissa looked at him, concerned. 'What sort of noise?'

'I don't know,' Caspian shrugged. 'What noises can you make?'

'I can do a pretty convincing cat sound.'

'Okay,' Caspian encouraged, 'if someone comes, *meow*.'

Caspian followed the same route Billy had taken, pausing from time to time, ensuring that the guard's in the guard post had not noticed him approaching from the side. He found Billy already in position a few feet from the guard post door, hiding behind a small shrubbery. It was a mild evening and the door to the guard post had been left open. They could hear the guards talking to one another inside.

'Thank goodness we ain't gotta wear this everyday,' one guard was moaning grumpily. 'I'd be more comfortable in a pair of burlap breeches and a dog-hair doublet.'

'If it's a life of comfort you were after you shouldn't 'ave become a Beefeater,' the second guard replied.

Billy edged slowly forward so that he was right beside the open doorway and ready to enter.

'Beefeater, eh? Now there's a misconception in terms,' the first guard said. 'Those ruddy birds get served more beef on a daily basis than I get in a week. *They're* the real Beefeater's in this place.'

Caspian bit his lip as he watched Billy lean into the guard post. He was directly behind the seated guards, were they to turn around he would be caught red handed.

The first guard continued his rant. 'Twenty-five years I served in the army; I was awarded medals for long service and good conduct, I was. And where has that got me? Stuck in 'ere' with you, guardin' the keys to the stinkin' toilet and whatnot.'

'Don't you *ever* stop moaning,' the second guard said with exasperation. 'You're always going on and on: "My feet are sore! It's raining again – I hate the rain! God, It's hot, when will it cool down? We've got nothing to do! They're working us too hard!" Moan, moan, moan, moan, moan!'

Billy had wrapped his hand around the keys where they hung to prevent them from jangling as he unhooked them. Very slowly he started lifting them. Caspian couldn't see what Billy was doing, but his palms were getting sweaty. He hoped Billy's hands were not as slippery as his were.

'I was just speaking my mind,' the first guard whined defensively. 'Hey, did you hear that? I thought I heard a cat?'

Caspian's heart pounded. He too had heard a cat meow. He glanced over at the tree where Clarissa was hiding and saw her waving frantically to him. Someone was heading in their direction.

He tried to catch Billy's eye, but Billy was concentrating hard on the task in hand. Slowly, he leaned away from the door and with a smirk showed Caspian the keys held tightly in his hand.

Caspian mouthed the word 'cat,' but Billy simply frowned and shrugged his shoulders. Then it dawned on him that Billy had missed the decision that a cat meow would be the warning sound.

'So what?' the second guard asked inside the guard post.

'What if it tries to get at the ravens?' the first guard said, getting up.

Billy slipped over to Caspian and they both climbed behind the shrubbery.

'I didn't think you much cared for them?'

'I don't, but if it gets its claws into any of those ruddy birds they'll have our guts for garters. Come on.' Both guards smartly marched out of the guard post and started walking towards the raven lodgings. Caspian was relieved to see that Clarissa had had the sense to fall back to their hiding place beneath the timber staircase.

'We haven't got long,' Caspian said to Billy. 'Once those guards find no sign of a cat by those bird cages and turn around, they will have a full view of the Tower, its entrance, and the scaffolding beneath the staircase.'

Billy nodded in understanding. Keeping their distance, the two boys crept behind the two guards, following the same path they had taken. Once the guards were level with the timber staircase, Billy and Caspian deviated from their path and began ascending the steps.

'The procession is coming this way!' Clarissa said anxiously as she slipped out from beneath the stairs and joined them. Billy picked a key from the set he held and tried it in the lock. It wouldn't turn.

The guards were by the raven lodgings now, looking around the cages.

Billy tried the next key. His brow was beginning to sweat. Caspian and Clarissa watched with bated breath. Billy tried the key, but again it would not turn.

'Come on,' Clarissa urged, rather unhelpfully.

There was one key left on the key ring. Caspian sincerely hoped that Billy had not stolen the wrong bunch, but it was too late now if he had.

The guards were giving up their search as Billy put the key in the lock and turned it. Clarissa squealed anxiously as the ceremony procession rounded the corner. Caspian helped Billy heave the door open and all three slipped inside and gently closed the door, hoping nobody had seen them.

'That was too close,' Billy observed once the door was shut.

'You are not wrong,' Caspian responded.

The Tower interior was dimly illuminated by emergency lighting, which gave the vast stone chambers a cold and eerie feel. Large suits of armour were displayed nearby, mounted on featureless mannequins whose faceless expressions sent a shiver up Caspian's spine.

'I forgot how big this sword is!' Billy gawped as he stood before the colossal battle sword that was on display near the entrance. He was in his element, surrounded by displays of medieval weaponry and armaments. 'I didn't get to have a good look at these last time we came. It was really busy.'

'Well, *we're* too busy for that now,' Caspian said. 'Which way should we go?' This was the first time he had set foot in the White Tower, whereas the other two had had the benefit of a tour during the school trip.

'The White Tower has the same layout on all four floors,' Clarissa explained as she led the way. 'This massive chamber takes up the entire west side of the keep. Then there is a medium sized room to the northeast corner, and the chapel and spaces beneath it occupy the smaller room to the southeast.'

Every five years or so, the displays within the White Tower were rearranged to revitalise the visitor experience or to make way for a new part of the exhibition. The royal storehouses had always attracted the visitors of London to come and marvel at its magnificent displays; be it the Armouries festooned with weaponry to infer the invincibility of the English, or the celebration of the ruling monarchy represented by the impressive Line of Kings.

The Line of Kings was the first stop for the small group. Their interpretation of the riddle had implied that they sought the place where a wall had once stood, somewhere between the Line of Kings and the Chapel of St. John.

They turned the corner and Caspian saw before him the grand display of suits of armour, swords, and large wooden horses.

'The row of figures represent each of the kings of England,' Clarissa said. 'Each king has a unique carving of his head and their own full-size wooden horse. The display was built to remind those who viewed it of the monarch's God-given right to rule and the rewards of noble kingship, but it is in essence – '

'All the king's horses and all the king's men,' Billy interrupted.

'That's not exactly correct,' Clarissa said reproachfully.

'But what are we *looking* for?'

'Anything that could be the entrance to a secret passageway,' Caspian said to Billy. 'You're usually good at finding that sort of thing,' he wryly added.

They set about searching the display for any clues that fitted with the riddle. 'The lilies and roses denote my day, a wall gone can unveil the way,' Caspian contemplated the phrase out loud whilst he searched. 'Perhaps the entrance is quite literally marked with a lily or a rose?' he speculated.

Billy moved around the display, looking in the spaces behind the horses, on the stone flooring, and the walls beyond. Nothing.

'Only a Saoul may see all is concealed between the Line of Kings and John the Evangelist's chapel,' Clarissa pondered, looking at the wall. 'A wall gone can unveil the way.'

'What are you thinking?' Caspian asked her.

'Maybe we are not in the right place. The riddle said *between* the Line of Kings and the chapel.'

'Okay. Well, where is that?'

'That's where I'm stumped,' Clarissa admitted. 'The Line of Kings is on this floor, whereas the Chapel of St. John is above the room next door. So, between them is this wall, but it certainly hasn't *gone* anywhere.'

'Let's try the chapel,' Caspian suggested. 'Maybe we are looking at this from the wrong angle.'

They took the staircase up to the first floor. On the way up, Billy took great pleasure in pointing out to Caspian that there were latrines built into the walls of the Tower, known as garderobes. Incidentally, the term 'garderobe' was derived from the French word 'garder,' which meant to keep, and 'robe' as in clothes. The reason for the odd choice of storing clothes nearby the medieval toilet was that the pungent odours deterred cloth-eating moths (although they probably attracted all manner of other insect) and is from where the modern term 'wardrobe' originated.

Latrines constructed within the Tower walls were considered a sophisticated building feature in the time it was built. Waste was expelled through an opening halfway up the outer wall.

'Most of the gardrobes are built into the northern wall so that the dropping excrement couldn't be seen from the entrance side of the Tower,' Billy explained. 'I bet people on that side didn't refer to it as the *White* Tower!'

'They did construct a wall so that the waste wasn't visible,' Clarissa said, shaking her head in disapproval at the direction conversation had taken as they ascended the staircase. As they reached the second floor she led them towards the Chapel of St. John the Evangelist.

The chamber that contained the chapel was the smallest of the three chambers within the White Tower, although it was also the tallest. Sturdy stone columns plotted a narrow arch towards the semi-circular protrusion of the chapel's apse, each column supporting an archway of its own. Above, another row of arches peered down from the gallery level turning the chapel into a grandiose Romanesque architectural statement.

A few rows of wooden chairs had been lined up facing the altar at the apse end of the chapel where a large circle-top window framed the golden crucifix positioned before it. A thick red cordon roped off the area to deter visitors from stepping into the sanctuary beyond.

'When will they learn that a cordon doesn't stop anyone?' Billy asked rhetorically as, without hesitation, he stepped over the rope barrier; much in the same way he had done in the New Moon Tavern, and in the Museum of London before that.

'I'm not sure they anticipated anyone as impulsive as you,' Caspian said, following him. Once again they began to search for any sign of a secret entrance, or anything that the riddle might have referred to.

Caspian found his attention drawn to a doorway on the northern wall of the chapel – the same wall through which they had entered. 'That's odd,' he thought out loud, and then went back into the room before the chapel.

The door he had seen should have led into this room, but where the door should have been a solid wall stood with no indication a doorway had either been there or had been covered up. He went back inside the chapel and returned to the door again, counting his steps to make sure he had not miscalculated. No – the door should lead into the northeast chamber.

He turned the handle. The door opened.

The open door revealed a space within the wall between the two chambers. Inside, a staircase descended, heading east and utilising the inner wall space in the same way the gardrobes had been built within.

'Look here,' Caspian called to his friends, excited by his discovery. The staircase would descend right between the chapel and the Line of Kings, this had to be it, but why was it so easy to find? Not only that, but why was it open? Surely this door would be known to anyone who worked at the White Tower, and countless people must have opened it and gone down to see where the staircase went. Why did all the mysteries and riddles lead to such an obvious entrance?

'What have you found?' Billy asked, coming to stand beside Caspian and looking at the open doorway.

'This,' Caspian frowned.

'What?' Billy asked, frowning also.

'Don't you think it's a little weird?'

'Not really, mate, no. I think *you're* a little weird.'

'What?' Caspian asked, wondering why Billy of all people, the more excitable of his friends, was not interested in where this staircase went. 'But it matches the riddle exactly: Between the Line of Kings and John the Evangelist's Chapel.'

'I don't get it?' Billy said, looking over to Clarissa for support as she came to join them.

'Why else would it be *here*?'

'The wall?' Clarissa asked.

'To hold the roof up I expect,' Billy said, deadly serious.

340

'No.' He could feel himself becoming frustrated. Why were his friends not taking this seriously? 'Not the wall, the *door*.'

Clarissa and Billy exchanged a look. 'There isn't a door here, Caspian,' Clarissa said.

'Are you alright, mate?' Billy asked.

Caspian looked at them both blankly. Could they really not see it, right here on the wall in front of them? 'Alright,' he said. 'If you don't believe me, watch this.'

He walked over to where the door stood open, and reached his arm across the threshold and into the passage beyond. Clarissa's eyes widened and Billy's mouth almost hit the floor.

'*That* is bloody amazing!' Billy declared.

'You can see a doorway?' Clarissa asked.

Caspian nodded.

Clarissa gasped. 'A wall gone can unveil the way.'

'Wow,' Billy said. 'That must mean you are a Saoul!'

Only a Saoul may see all is concealed. The line of the riddle had crossed Caspian's mind also and it troubled him. He didn't know what a Saoul was, let alone if he wanted to be one. And if he truly was, why was he chosen to be able to find the doorway when others could not.

'That's why you could see the letters move in the Guardians' tomb,' Hearing Billy say it out loud made Caspian uncomfortable. He didn't want to be different, or see things differently. He stepped into the passage and watched his friend's faces return to surprise, and then he helped guide them in after him.

Clarissa was the last to step through the secret door, tentatively reaching forward with her arms and shutting her eyes as she passed through what she perceived as solid stone.

They were about to start descending the passage when Clarissa froze and grabbed at Caspian's arm. 'What was that?'

'What was what?'

Clarissa looked over her shoulder and stayed perfectly still for a moment whilst she listened. When she spoke again, her voice was hushed and trembling. 'I think I heard something,' she whispered unsteadily. 'Somebody else is in the Tower.'

XXX:
THE KEEPER OF THE WHITE TOWER

'Tell me you locked the door,' Caspian whispered harshly at Billy.

'Err…' Billy hesitated. 'I didn't think I needed to.'

'You didn't think you *needed* to? Why on Earth not? We're not the only ones trying to get in here tonight!'

From within the wall, Clarissa and Billy were now able to see the door that previously only Caspian had seen. Clarissa reached out and closed it behind her, hand shaking as she nervously tried to shut it without making any noise.

'Better lock it,' Billy whispered to her when she turned back to him.

'There isn't a lock on *this* door,' she hissed venomously. 'Idiot!'

'Do you think it's *him*?'

'Shush!' Caspian silenced them. He couldn't be sure whom Clarissa may have heard, but he took it a sign not to wait around to find out, and gestured for them to follow him.

Billy's torch came in handy as once again they descended a darkened staircase. The space to move was narrow, and the stair doubled back on itself a couple of times to stay within the confines of the inner wall. Down and down they went until they were certain they were beneath even the lowest levels of the White Tower. The stairs ended at a large doorway that was so old it was almost conceivable that this door was the surviving original from when this part of the Tower had first been built.

'Caspian?' Billy asked as they reached the final step. 'How does your father know about this place?'

'I don't know?'

'Well, one thing's for sure. He certainly has a lot of skeletons in his closet.' Billy pushed on the door and budged it open, a haze of dust moving with it. 'Oh,' Billy said sheepishly when he saw what lay in the room before them. 'Maybe forget the closet!'

Low hanging lamps with small and delicately crafted octagonal frames, glass on each of the eight sides, illuminated the room. They reminded Caspian of Victorian style gas lamps, but instead of a small wick dipped in paraffin, these lamps contained a metal filament that glowed a golden yellow.

As the golden light cascaded across the room their attention was drawn to the crumpled heap of an old skeleton collapsed against the side of the room.

'Who do you think this was?' Clarissa whispered, unnerved by the way the empty sockets of the skeleton's skull seemed to watch her wherever she stood. Beside the skeleton was a large shield. It was still gripping an aged sword with its right hand, although the entire left arm rested a couple of feet away from the torso, detached at the shoulder.

'A better question,' Billy replied, 'is what happened to him?'

They cautiously entered the room and moved closer to the skeleton. Billy went over to touch the severed left arm. 'Wait!' Clarissa cautioned him. 'Cursed bones.'

'Cursed bones?' Billy snubbed. 'Yeah, right. What have we got to be afraid of?' He turned and kicked the bony arm, which rolled and stumbled across the floor, still held together by pieces of sinew, until it came to rest in a twisted heap.

'Don't *do* that,' Clarissa said nervously.

'Why? You afraid?' Billy jested.

'No, I'm not afraid,' she said, clearly uncomfortable but not willing to admit it.

'Guys?' Caspian interrupted, pointing to the skeletal arm where it lay. Slowly, before their eyes, it rolled over and its gaunt fingertips gripped the floor. As they watched, it pulled itself forward with its fingers until its hand made a fist, then extended its fingers again and repeated the movement, pulling the rest of its arm in tow.

Billy leapt back in fear as the arm made its way toward him.

The severed arm moved on with creepy determination.

Then a raspy sound from behind filled them all with dread. Behind them, the skeleton turned its head. Slowly, and with great effort, it began to heave itself to its feet.

The severed arm scuttled over to join the rest of its body. With its index finger, it tapped on a foot to get its attention. The bony figure bent down and picked up the arm, twisting it back into place with a loud *click*. Then it picked up the shield at its feet and turned to face the three friends, making a loud, guttural sound. 'Gwwaaaagggghhh!'

'That's not good,' Billy murmured.

The skeleton raised the sword it still held and started stomping towards Billy.

Billy turned and ran, lunging left, and then right, as the monster swung the sword in wide arcs in his general direction. Quickly, he doubled backed and ducked under its arm, and made his way to the other side of the room.

The skeleton turned, its gaunt white head moving from side to side. 'Gwwaaaagggghhh!' it cried again, seething with rage. The noise made Clarissa shriek, and now the cursed bones were bearing down on her.

'Get away from her,' Caspian yelled, jumping on the skeleton's back and making it drop its shield in surprise.

'Gwwaaaagggghhh!' it responded, and thrashed about wildly, its arms flailing.

Caspian couldn't keep his grip for long. His fingers slipped and he was thrown from its shoulders, landing heavily on the hard floor. He didn't have time to acknowledge the pain as the skeleton had started towards him, sword raised above its head.

It came crashing down, just as Caspian rolled out of the way and heard the ear-piercing *clang* of it smashing into the floor where moments earlier his head had been. He lifted his leg and kicked at the skeleton, sending it stumbling back a couple of steps.

This only seemed to enrage it further.

It roared loudly and raised the sword again. Caspian shuffled backwards, his shoes scraping against the dusty stone floor.

Then an almighty *crack* sounded from beside the skeleton and sent it tumbling to the ground. Billy had picked up the shield and had swung it into the side of the monster.

Caspian took the moment's hiatus to get to his feet and move away from the toppled bones.

It didn't stay down for long.

From the floor it swung its sword towards Billy, who reacted just in time to block it. The blow clonked heavily against the old shield, the force of it threatened to knock him over. Billy kept his footing, but by now the skeleton was standing again and swinging the sword back at him with its full might.

Billy blocked the next blow, and the next, but he was quickly tiring whilst the skeleton carried on with its relentless attack. Then, out of nowhere, it raised its foot and kicked Billy, taking him by surprise and knocking him stumbling for balance. At the same time it swung the sword heavily from its right side and narrowly missed Billy's head.

The sword rang against the shield with such force that it liberated it from Billy's grip, sending it clanging noisily across the floor. Billy fell backwards and landed heavily on his backpack. He rolled just in time to miss the sword skewering him, but it instead tore through the material of his backpack and spilled the contents all over the floor like the intestines of a gutted animal.

Seeing Billy lying on the floor in peril made Clarissa scream out.

The skeleton stopped. It turned to look at her.

'Gwwaaaagggghhh!' it roared, and headed directly for her.

Clarissa screamed again and backed away from it. She was caught in a corner with nowhere else to go.

Caspian had been watching from the side of the room not knowing what to do. There was something odd about the way that the skeleton was attacking them. He had a theory, and unfortunately there was only one way to test it. 'Nobody make a sound,' he instructed his friends, and then to ensure he had the skeleton's attention he added, 'Oi, Bony! I'm over here!' He picked up a loose stone from the floor and hurled it at the skeleton's head for added affect.

It worked. Caspian now had the skeleton's full attention. He ran to the other side of the room, away from where he was standing before, and shouted again. 'I'm over here!'

The skeleton changed direction and came after him.

Quickly and as quietly as he could, Caspian returned to the other side. Once again the skeleton changed direction, but only after Caspian called to him.

He can't see! Caspian realised. That was why it went for whoever made a sound. He gestured for his friends to stay quiet, and then he quietly began to approach the skeleton.

The skeleton had reached the spot it thought Caspian was and swung its sword around wildly. 'Gwwaaaagggghh!' it roared in frustration when its blade came up short of maiming anyone.

Caspian was only a couple of feet away, and he didn't really have a plan. Maybe he could dislodge a bone somewhere in the skeleton that would cause it to collapse? He tried to think back to biology with Mrs Plumb. Maybe he could attack the monster's spine – would that stop it? He wasn't sure.

As he approached his foot knocked a small glass bottle that had rolled out of Billy's backpack when it had split. Caspian froze. The *clinking* of the glass on stone seemed to echo loudly in the chamber.

The skeleton stopped swinging its sword randomly and slowly turned to face Caspian, its white eyeless skull in a permanent sinister grin.

'Oh no,' he heard Clarissa whimper from far away.

The sound was not enough to distract him from Caspian; he knew he had him now. 'Gwwaaaagggghh!' the skeleton rasped so close to Caspian he could smell the dust and rot of the bones.

Deliberately the skeleton raised its sword, preparing to perform the coup de grâce on its hapless victim. Clarissa and Billy were shouting now. Billy was running toward them. It made no difference. It was transfixed on Caspian.

Caspian caught sight of the offending bottle at his feet. *Sauerpott's Sore-Bone Remedy*, the label read. He had forgotten to retrieve it from Billy's backpack since their trip beneath Leadenhall Market and it must have remained there until the bag had been dissected.

With nothing to lose now, he snatched up the bottle and in one swift movement he leaped onto the skeleton, plunging the glass vial in its mouth whilst using the flat of his palm to force its jaw shut. The bottle shattered.

The skeleton froze, sword still poised above its head. It seemed bewildered by what had happened, opening and closing its mouth as though it were trying to ascertain what it were tasting.

Then the sword dropped from its grip and clanged against the ground. Caspian was knocked over, and the monster started to violently convulse, doubling over and heaving as though trying to retch. It dropped to its knees, grabbing at its throat, screaming a horrible scream. The scream turned to sickly gargle, and then it fell onto its hands and shook so violently that all its component bones rattled like an overly enthusiastic percussion section.

'What is that stuff?' Billy asked, helping Caspian back to his feet.

'Sauerpott's Sore-Bone Remedy,' Caspian answered. 'It provides relief to aching bones.'

'How did you know it would stop him?'

'I didn't,' Caspian admitted.

The skeleton was still on its hands and knees, but had stopped shaking. With an unnatural suddenness, it coughed once and, much to their surprise, cleared its throat.

'Ah, zat is *much* better,' the skeleton declared with a heavy French accent, steadily getting to his feet. 'Although, it does have a peculiar taste; grasshopper and herring, if I am not mistaken.'

'With almonds and dog's milk,' Caspian confirmed, once he was confident the skeleton was not going to attack them anymore.

'Hmm… Yes, you know it *did* taste a zittle nutty,' the skeleton decided, and then stretched its bony limbs. 'For nine 'undred years I have been at zee mercy of zat agonising curse. Sorry if I came across a zittle bit grumpy, but see if nine 'undred years of torture doesn't make you a touch grouchy.'

'*Grouchy*!' Clarissa exclaimed with some annoyance. 'You tried to kill us.'

'Those are zee terms of my employment, Mademoiselle,' the skeleton answered courteously, 'I am just doing my job.'

'Hey, you're French,' Billy blurted out.

'Zat I am,' the skeleton confirmed. 'I am zee keeper of zee White Tower. I am supposed to be stopping anyone who comes down here. How many of you are there?'

'Three of us,' Caspian said.

'Can't you see us?' Billy asked.

'No, he can't,' Caspian explained. 'That's why I told you both to be quiet when he was attacking us. He's blind.'

'Zat's the truth. I 'ave no eyes,' the skeleton said, pointing at his empty eye sockets to help establish this point. 'Zey went long ago. Either zey rotted away or were eaten by worms; it's 'ard to remember which.'

'He hasn't got vocal chords either, but that doesn't stop him talking,' Billy whispered to Clarissa.

'I heard zat!' the skeleton snapped, which only raised further questions.

'But, how did you come to be like … this?' Caspian asked. 'Cursed for nine hundred years…?'

For a moment the skeleton's face seemed to sadden, which was quite an achievement considering his skull had been stripped of any facial muscles. 'I wasn't always like zis.' He lifted a bony hand and lightly tapped a finger on the side of his cranium.

Clarissa gingerly stepped forward and placed a hand gently on the skeleton's shoulder. 'What happened,' she asked softly. 'You don't seem to be evil … not since you've stopped, you know, trying to kill us and all that.'

'EVIL!' he bellowed so loudly that Clarissa leapt away from him, letting out a tiny shriek of fear at the same time. 'Even after nine 'undred years of persecution, I am still bound by zis 'orrible label.'

He slumped back down onto the floor and shook his head sadly. 'Once, I was a great knight. My name was Jacques, Grand Master of zee Knight's Templar. Zat was before King Philip had zee lot of us charged with 'eresy.

'Heresy?' Clarissa said with disgust. 'I thought the Templar Knights served the Church.'

'As did we,' Jacques replied sourly. 'We fought many campaigns for him and zee Church, but our services were not cheap. King Philip owed us a great debt, one he was reluctant to pay. He could not disband my Order; doing so to avoid paying a debt would turn him into a greedy tyrant in zee eyes of his subjects. But by charging us with 'eresy, his plight became something greater than his petty avarice – he was defending God.'

Caspian recalled that Grieves had mentioned King Philip when telling him about the Ouanga ring. King Philip the Fair of France, he had called him. 'Couldn't you appeal to the king and prove yourselves innocent?' he asked.

Jacques gave a bitter laugh. 'How do you prove you are not a heretic, when your own king has labelled you so? One by one my Templar Knights were caught and forced to confess to zis 'orrible sin.'

'But why confess?' Billy asked. 'If it wasn't true, why agree to their accusations?'

Jacques turned menacingly towards the sound of Billy's voice. 'Our wrists were bound behind our backs, and by zem we were hung. Our persecutors would heave us up, then let us drop, and do zis over and over again.'

Caspian noticed hairline fractures on the skeleton's shoulders and arms – probably from where the repetitive sudden stops after short drops had caused strain on his limbs. He couldn't imagine how painful that kind of torture must have been.

'Believe me,' Jacques continued, poking a bony finger in Billy's direction. 'Zey would 'ave you singing whatever song zey wanted just to make zee punishment stop. Fires were built and we were burnt as a public spectacle – zey all cheered as zee flames rose around my companions.'

'And what about you?' Clarissa asked gently.

'I was the last to be burnt. As they tied me to zee stake I looked zem all in zee eye and I said, "Zee only thing I am guilty of is betraying my Order by giving in to torture and confessing to zee false charges *you* 'ave laid upon us." I warned zat if zey used false claims against God as reason to kill me, zey would suffer 'is wrath.'

'What did they say to that?' asked Billy.

'Say?' Jacques repeated. 'Not a word. Zey lit the kindling at my feet and watched zee flames rise higher. Unbeknown to me, zis fire had been conjured by witchcraft, and as I burnt zee flames licked against by skin and cursed my bones. Even in death I would never know peace.'

Caspian felt sorry for Jacques. He knew only too well what it was like to not have anyone believe you when you are innocent, but to have suffered for nine hundred years in the grip of a curse was unimaginable. 'How did you end up down here?'

'Not many people will employ a skeleton cursed to suffer unrelenting pain and reduced to going "Gwwaaaagggghh!" all day long,' Jacques explained. 'But zee man who gave me zis job down here took pity on me.'

'Edgar Stone?' Caspian asked.

The skeleton was silent for a moment. He began to get up, and picked up his sword. 'What do you know about Edgar Stone?' Jacques asked darkly.

'He's,' Caspian began, wondering whether their friendly chat had come to an end. 'He's my father.'

'Your father?' Jacques said surprised. 'Are you truly zee son of Stone?'

'Errr … yes,' Caspian replied, 'although I never call myself that.'

'And zee others?' Jacques asked, using the tip of his sword to gesture at where Billy and Clarissa stood.

'My friends.'

'You should not be down here, son of Stone,' Jacques warned him. He no longer sounded sorry for himself but instead much more knightly. 'Zis night brings great danger.'

'We know,' Caspian said. 'I think my father is in danger too. We have to protect what you are guarding.'

'Danger?' Jacques repeated. 'I would not see Edgar Stone come to 'arm.'

'Then let us pass,' Caspian pleaded. 'We have to help him.'

Jacques considered this for a moment. 'Okay,' he said. 'Which way is zee door?'

'Behind you.'

'What you seek lies beyond zat wall,' the skeleton said, pointing to the opposite end of the chamber. 'But you should be warned…'

They waited to heed a warning, but it never came.

'What should we be warned about?' Billy asked.

'I cannot remember,' Jacques said solemnly. 'I believe zat old age is finally catching up with me.'

The far wall of Jacques' chamber terminated in a dead-end: There were no doors, openings, or any access ways obvious to Caspian for them to pass in order to get "beyond" the wall.

Caspian turned to Jacques, 'Which way?'

The old skeleton raised a finger and pointed directly at the wall.

'It's a dead-end,' Caspian said. 'How can we go *that* way?'

'You, son of Stone, may pass *through*.'

Caspian approached the wall. Was this like the hidden doorway in St. John's Chapel, except this time he couldn't see the doorway either? He held out his hand and slowly approached. Billy and Clarissa were close behind him.

His hand reached the wall and his fingers passed right into the stone as though it were liquid. Next his wrists disappeared, and then his elbows. 'This is weird,' he said out loud.

'You're telling us,' Billy said.

Caspian felt foolish, but he couldn't help himself. Before pushing the rest of his body through the wall he took a breath and shut his eyes.

Clarissa watched as Caspian vanished into the solid stone.

'Come on,' Billy said clutching the torch. His rucksack was in too poor a shape to be of any help, and so he had abandoned it along with most of the contents. The torch seemed like the logical thing to take into the next chamber. 'Don't look so nervous,' he was saying. 'I find it's easier if you do it at a –'

Thwack!

Billy took two steps back from the wall and fell onto his backside rubbing his head. There was a nasty gash across his brow. Something had gone wrong. He was mid-sentence as he met the wall, but rather than pass through like Caspian had, Billy instead slammed against it as he would a regular wall.

'Ouch,' Billy said, amongst other things, from where he sat.

Clarissa also attempted to pass through and pressed her hands against the wall. She felt the cold stone beneath her fingers and, just like Billy, could not follow Caspian. 'We can't get through,' she said to Jacques, wondering what they were going to do.

The skeleton did not look surprised. 'Well, of course not. Only a Saoul may pass.'

She turned back to the wall and cupped her hands over her mouth. 'Caspian!' she shouted. 'Can you hear me?!'

She waited, but there was no response.

'*Caspian*!' she shouted again. Still nothing.

'He will not be able to hear you,' Jacques said softly.

She looked at Billy, sat on the floor in a sorry state, and then at the skeleton who stood there shrugging. 'So, he's on his own?'

Jacques snapped his fingers as if struck by an epiphany. 'Zut alors! Zat was it!' he exclaimed, suddenly remembering. 'I needed to warn you zat another had entered zat chamber tonight.'

Clarissa marched over to the skeleton, grabbed his little finger and twisted it. 'Gwwaaaagggghh!' he responded in agony.

'It only *just* crossed your mind to tell us! Who, other than Caspian, entered there tonight?' she demanded.

'I do not know,' Jacques whimpered and at the same time sounded ashamed. 'He was quiet and caught me off-guard. Before I knew it he had disarmed me – literally.'

She bent his little finger back until it was close to snapping and quietly asked through gritted teeth, 'Jacques? Is that person still inside?'

XXXI:
His Father's Secret

The cold, dry air had to it an earthly taste. Cobwebs caught lightly on his hair and face – languidly he brushed them away. Stillness smothered this place, as though it had not been disturbed for a very, very long time.

Caspian was stood in a corridor paved with white marble and built of white stone. Ahead of him the corridor turned left and steps descended to where the warm glow that lit this secret place emanated.

'Where are we?' Caspian wondered, but no answer came. In fact, no one other than he had passed through the wall from Jacques' chamber. What was keeping them?

He turned back to the wall, but when he tried to pass through to find his friends he found that his ability to traverse the solid wall was spent. 'Clarissa? Billy?' He said, slapping his hand against the rigid surface. They seemed unable to hear him. He was alone here.

Turning back to the corridor, he looked upon the descending steps. With no other way to go, he began towards them. Nearing the corner, he saw that they descended into a large room built entirely of white stone beneath a vaulted ceiling, similar to that which adorned the tomb of the Guardian's.

This appeared to be a lost undercroft beneath the Tower of London, but the use of white stone in every aspect of its construction obliged the room's ambience to exude something aesthetically otherworldly.

The corridor ended and the steps widened as they entered the room, like the mouth of a river rolls into the ocean. A statue of a woman knelt in the chamber's centre, her head bowed.

He passed between two white trees, carved from smooth white stone that reached with leafless branches up to the arches of the curved ceiling. Embedded in the trunks, large amounts of a rough looking, peach coloured, mineral oozed. Light radiated from this honey-tinted quartz, glowing from its core to illume the space around it. Somehow, Caspian felt that this light was drawn to the statue in the centre of the room, as was he.

He reached the final step and approached the kneeling woman. She was sculpted of white marble, and the work was exquisite. An illusionistic veil was draped over her head; through it he could see the sad expression frozen on her face as she looked down at her hands. There, across her spread palms as were it her burden to bear, lay a sword unlike any Caspian had ever seen. Here lay the Geldrin Blade.

The hilt was black as a starless night, like the depths of space further out than the edge of the universe that has never known light. Four spiky quillons protruded from it, their sharp looking tips curved in toward the long blade of the sword that held dominion over them.

The blade itself was of a grey-silver, the colour of an overcast sky on a gloomy day. It did not shine or reflect any of the light that the glowing trees gave off, but instead seemed to dismiss the existence of light altogether. As Caspian watched he saw something flicker across the blade and vanish into the edge, a dark glimmer of a black flame, like a curl of smoke it had come and gone.

As he reached down toward it he felt the air around the metal go cold. The dormant blade lay feeding on the warmth, the light, and all that was good in the world. He stopped his hand above the hilt, and hesitated.

The dark glimmer flickered across the blade in hungry anticipation.

'Try and take it,' a voice beside him hissed bemusedly, making Caspian jump and spring away from the statue to face the direction it had come. The hooded man was pressed against a pillar and had been watching him through his half-mask and hood. 'Go on,' he encouraged. 'Reach down and take it.'

'No,' Caspian said uncertainly. He felt it was a trick, or otherwise it would already be in the hands of his tormenter.

'No? But if you have not overcome all those obstacles to claim it, then what is your purpose for being here?' he mused, his words slithered like a snake from his half deformed mouth. 'Ahh, to protect it from *me* perhaps? Is that the plan?'

Caspian nodded, feeling foolish. He had nothing to fight off the cloaked man. He was trapped in here with him, alone. 'What did you do to my father?' he demanded.

'Nothing,' the hooded man replied, before adding, 'yet.' He pulled back his hood and long greasy locks of hair fell onto his shoulders. 'But you needn't worry. I promise that his dues are long deserved.'

Caspian looked horrified at the face of the enemy, now finally revealed to him in the mineral light of the white marble trees; the flesh on the unmasked side of his face that was warped by fire and scarred by who-knew-what-else, and the grotesque contortion of metal that covered the other side was not any more appealing.

'How did you get in here?' Caspian asked him, wondering how he had made it passed Jacques and through the wall into this chamber. His friends had not even made it this far.

The half-masked man tilted his head so his mouth formed a grin. 'You and I are more similar than you realise.' He reached up and gripped the mask and slid it from his face.

Caspian didn't want to see what he kept beneath, but he also couldn't look away. As soon as the skin beneath was revealed he gasped.

Beneath the mask, the cloaked man's skin was not burnt, scarred, deformed, or blistered. It was in fact perfectly normal, albeit rather pale. But it was not his unblemished skin that really made Caspian's mind spin in surprise, it was the colour of his eyes that came as a real revelation.

His left eye, the eye that had been visible on the scarred side of his head, was dark green in colour. The concealed eye, however, was a golden hazel – just like Caspian's. The hooded man shared the same hereditary trait as he; both eyes were different colours.

'I am a Saoul, like you,' he hissed, fitting the mask back over the right side of his face. This was the first time anyone other than Caspian and his friends had said this word, and he pronounced it *Sa-ool*.

'I don't know what that is,' Caspian admitted, 'but I'm nothing like you.'

The masked man stifled a laugh. 'Oh, you and I are more alike than you dare imagine. I just did not conceive that Edgar Stone could be stupid enough to father a child. Now it seems, you will be his undoing.'

'Who are you?' Caspian asked, trying to buy more time and wondering how much more he could afford. 'What do you want with my father?'

'I am Kyeir,' he growled through his mask, 'and my master wishes your father to *suffer*.'

At that Kyeir lunged toward Caspian.

Caspian ducked backward, narrowly missing being grasped by Kyeir's hand. He looked around, but there was nowhere to go: the kneeling woman would provide little cover, the pillars circling the centre of her chamber would not provide much defence, and returning up the steps to the corridor would result in him certainly being caught.

Without any further thought he bent down and reached for the hilt of the Geldrin Blade, but as his fingers touched the cold air before the sword's grip the blade vanished before his eyes, leaving the kneeling lady empty handed.

'What?' Caspian spluttered in surprise, but Kyeir turned his head upward and roared with laughter.

'Foolish *boy*,' he snarled. 'Your father sentences you to death.'

Kyeir again came for Caspian, and this time he grabbed him, lifting him easily off the ground. Caspian flailed helplessly in his strong grip, struggling and beating at the arm that held him. He felt fingers close around his neck and soon he was gasping, unable to swallow, unable to breath. His head began to burn, starving for oxygen as though it might suddenly *pop*. In his barely conscious state he thought he heard someone call his name.

The hand began to release.

Caspian was dropped onto his knees where he grasped his wrung neck and gratefully gulped air into his lungs. His eyes watered, but quickly he wiped them dry as he tried to see what change in circumstance had freed him from death's embrace.

'Step away from him,' the voice commanded loudly, as if coming from above.

Caspian turned and looked to the steps where his father stood. In his hand he held the Geldrin Blade, its subtle tip pointed in the direction of Kyeir.

'Give me the blade,' Kyeir demanded, 'and your son lives.'

'You hurt him, and you die,' Father fired back.

'Death?' Kyeir said with dark amusement. 'You threaten me with a concept you do not know. Not a man of your ... condition.'

'I know death,' Father replied. 'And just because I do not fear it, do not suppose that I have not felt its bitter sting. No one need die tonight. You have no endgame here: you might kill my son and take the blade, and then what? You will still be trapped in this chamber until death comes for you also. What have you accomplished?'

'You will not allow your son to die,' Kyeir snarled, sensing a bluff. He pushed something cold and solid against the back of Caspian's head.

It was only then that Caspian realised a gun was being pointed at him.

'Come down from the steps,' Kyeir instructed.

Father descended slowly. Caspian watched from where he knelt – he had assumed the same position as the veiled lady. 'Don't give him the sword,' he said, but was rewarded with a knock on the head from the barrel of Kyeir's gun.

'All this for an old sword,' Father said as he slowly circled Kyeir. 'You realise the myth surrounding this blade is simply that: a myth.'

'Don't move any further,' Kyeir snapped. Father was to his right now, Caspian had to turn his head to see what was going on.

'I'm just saying,' Father continued, weighing his words carefully. 'Sometimes the secret is just not worth the knowing.' Suddenly, he turned and hurled the sword to the back of the chamber where it clanged loudly against the marble floor. Simultaneously, a single blast fired from Kyeir's gun, making Caspian's ear ring painfully – for a moment he thought he had been shot.

It took him a moment to comprehend that the gun had not been pointed at him when it went off, but instead had been aimed at his father. As Kyeir abandoned his captive to dive after the flung blade, Father doubled over and clutched at his chest. The deep red of blood had already begun to coat his hand.

'Caspian!' Father spluttered, and gestured to the steps.

Kyeir was almost where the blade had landed. Father, still on his feet, made for Caspian.

'Father?' Caspian said in shock as realisation took hold – Father had been shot. He didn't know what to do.

'Come on,' Father said, and with his other hand heaved Caspian off his knees on to his feet.

From the dark recess of the chamber Kyeir roared with rage. Caspian helped Father up the steps as fast as he could go. They turned the corner just as a shot rang off the wall beside them.

Not stopping, they staggered towards the dead-end through which Caspian had entered. 'How are we going to…?' Caspian began to ask, remembering how he had found himself trapped after passing into this chamber. But Father, leaning on his shoulder for stability, gripped his arm around his waist and threw them both forward.

'STONE!!!' Kyeir yelled, his footsteps heavy behind them. Another shot fired with a tremendous *bang*, but before the bullet had reached the solid wall Caspian and his father had already passed through.

'Caspian!' Clarissa's voice was shrill. 'Oh my *God*!'

By this point Caspian was covered in so much of his father's blood it was difficult to tell to which of the two of them it belonged.

'It's his,' Caspian explained, carefully lowering his father to the ground so he could sit him with his back against the wall. 'He's been shot!'

'Oh, thank goodness,' a calm voice said slowly in a melancholy tone.

Caspian looked in surprise at the gangly figure of Artemis Grieves who stood beside them. 'What do you mean, "thank goodness!" ' Caspian roared incredulously.

'It's okay,' Father said softly from where he sat.

'No it isn't. We need to get you to a doctor, to a hospital.'

'Caspian. Let Artemis examine me first,' Father said sleepily. 'He is used to seeing a lot of blood.' Father had bled profusely and Caspian was worried he was drifting into shock.

Clarissa and Billy directed Caspian away as Grieves knelt down and took a small leather pouch – a surgical kit – out of the inner pocket of his long coat. He carefully selected a long set of forceps, examined them, and then began to open Father's shirt to inspect the wound.

'What happened in there?' Billy asked Caspian.

'I don't know?' Caspian answered, still trying to comprehend what had taken place. Then he noticed the bandage around Billy's head. 'What happened to you?'

'Who? Me?' Billy replied, a little confused. 'I was following you through the wall, except when I got there I couldn't get through.'

'We tried to follow you,' Clarissa added. 'Then your father arrived with Mr Grieves.'

'That's right,' Billy said, raising a finger, and then he frowned. A moment later he remembered what he was going to say. 'That Grieves fellow bandaged my head, and you know what? He *does* resemble a vampire.'

'I think Billy's got a concussion,' Clarissa suggested.

'That's what I just said!' argued Billy.

'How did we get out of there?' Caspian asked. He had not been able to leave on his own, but when he and Father were running from Kyeir they had passed straight through the wall. At the time he didn't really have the chance to question it; after all, being chased by a maniac firing a gun at you presents higher priorities to be concerned with rather than the permeability of a solid stone wall.

'That would be because your father had this on him,' Grieves said from his knees, where he presented a dark polished ovoid from Father's pocket. 'That is a Weystone. It allows the holder, with some practice, to alter the state of solid objects; in this case walls.'

Caspian inspected the Weystone, which was formed from a sculptured piece of dark green aventurine and carved with a beautifully intricate pattern of swirls, twirls, eddies and churns, as though its entire surface had once been covered by a wavering watercourse that couldn't quite decide which way to flow.

'As you were in contact with your father,' Grieves went on, 'who in turn was in contact with the Weystone, both of you were granted passage.' He gave the forceps in his other hand a stiff yank.

'Yaaagghhhh,' Father cried as Grieves retracted the forceps, clutching the bullet between them.

Caspian returned to his father's side and helped Grieves apply a dressing. 'Can you save him?' he asked desperately. He could not contemplate losing his father. His father was all he now had left of his family.

'Save him?' Grieves said with some confusion. 'Your father does not need saving?'

'But he's been *shot*! He's lost a lot of blood.'

'Yes. But this is not a mortal wound.'

Caspian wasn't entirely sure Artemis Grieves grasped what constituted as a mortal wound. After all, this was a man who spent most of his time communicating with an urn that contained the remains of his business partner.

Father was terribly pale and it looked like he might lose consciousness at any moment. 'We need to get him some help,' Caspian said, looking about the room at the motley crew that accompanied him: the vampire-like, Artemis Grieves, solemn as a slab of granite – Jacques, the blind skeleton knight, tenderly holding his little finger and sheepishly avoiding Clarissa – Billy Long, head swathed in a bandage, looking rather confuddled in the company of both Grieves and Jacques alike.

Clarissa seemed to be the only one amongst the lot of them bestowed with any real normality at all. Caspian turned to her for help. 'You must go and get some of the Tower guards. Tell them we are down here. We might still be able to get to a hospital in time.'

She turned to follow his instruction when Father told her to stop.

'You can't worry about this place being found,' Caspian told his father, wondering why he wasn't more worried about having been shot. 'If we don't get help you will die.'

'You cannot be certain of that,' Father said hoarsely. 'Artemis, help me to stand.'

'I don't think you should,' Caspian said with concern. He looked at the bandage across his father's chest. He knew his father should have died, or at least have been fighting for his life. Yet Father, although in pain, did not seem as worse off as he should. There was something not quite right about all of this.

'We cannot stay down here,' Father replied weakly. Once on his feet, and using the wall for support, he allowed Grieves to place his long coat over his shoulders to help conceal the bloody wound on his chest.

'But we can hardly just walk out of here,' Caspian protested. 'The three of us were able to sneak in without getting caught, but only just. There is no way we can get you out without any of us being seen.'

'Who said anything about not being seen?' Father answered. 'How do you think *I* came to be in here tonight? By *sneaking*?'

Caspian hadn't even thought about *how* his father had come to be here. That had been the least of his worries. He shook his head, uncertainly.

'As an expert on antiques and relics, my services have often been called upon here at the Tower of London,' Father explained, strength returning to his voice. 'The guards here are familiar with my presence during off limit hours, and I have a pass that allows me access.'

'Not to mention a talisman that allows you to walk through walls,' Clarissa pointed out.

'Admittedly, that does help,' Father said, giving the slyest of winks. 'Tonight though, I feel we should take our leave in the manner that the architects of this fine castle intended: through the front door.'

'And what about getting to the hospital?' Caspian asked.

Father put his arm over Caspian's shoulder for support. He winced as he let Caspian take some of his weight. 'We cannot go to the hospital. Too many questions will be asked,' he stated, and gave Caspian shrewd look. 'Let's instead go somewhere where we can reflect on all that has transpired this evening. As it is, I believe I already have enough questions to answer.'

XXXII:
Vɪᴠᴇ ᴜᴛ Vɪᴠᴀs

Billy Long was quivering with excitement. During the cab journey across London he had regained his senses following the blow he had suffered to his head. Now, sat in the mirrored octagonal room of the reflectory, anticipation threatened to overwhelm him. The moment the circular lift had begun to descend, his mouth had opened wider than the most ambitious of pythons.

Caspian and Clarissa sat beside Billy at the table, whilst Sprocket, whom Caspian had collected from his bedroom whilst Father re-dressed his wound, scuppered about across the polished metal surface. Leaving the Tower of London had been as easy as Father had said. The group had left together and simply walked out of the castle through the main entrance arch, whilst Mr Grieves had stayed behind to assist Jacques in filling out a prescription for a year's supply of Sauerpott's Sore Bone Remedy. Any guards they met on their way out simply waved to Father or wished them a good night, none the wiser to their purpose for being there that evening.

Father gradually lowered himself into a seat opposite them and gave them all a long, hard look. 'Do the three of you realise exactly how much trouble you could have been in?' he said after a long silence.

'Trouble?' Caspian exclaimed. 'We were trying to help. We thought you were in danger.'

'And so you decided that the best course of action in "rescuing" me was to plunge head first into something you didn't fully understand, bringing your friends along for good measure,' Father said frankly. 'I am only surprised that you didn't give Jess a call and drag her into this mess also.'

'She couldn't come,' Billy said, rather unhelpfully, and earned himself a kick in the shin from Clarissa.

'I specifically told you to leave this alone, did I not?' Father said to Caspian. 'But here we all are, having this discussion.'

This isn't fair, Caspian thought. They really had been trying to help. 'If you had been honest with us from the start then we wouldn't have ended up at the Tower of London,' he blurted out before he could stop himself. 'But you are so concerned about protecting the Geldrin Blade that you don't think about anyone else.'

'Caspian,' Father said plainly. 'It is not the Geldrin Blade that I am worried about protecting. A sword can be lost and found, stolen and reclaimed. You, on the other hand, are far more precious to me. It is *you* that I am worried about losing.'

'But...' Caspian floundered, realising that his father had indeed tossed aside the weapon he had been charged with protecting to save him from Kyeir. 'The blade? Kyeir has it now.'

'Kyeir...' Father said slowly, digesting the name of the hooded man. This was obviously the first time he had heard it. 'Kyeir does not have the Geldrin Blade.'

'I saw it,' Caspian said, first thinking about the statue of the kneeling woman, and then seeing it in Father's hand.

'No,' Father said patiently. 'What you saw was an illusion, designed to vanish when someone tried to remove it. Similarly was the blade I carried into the undercroft a decoy, with a singular purpose of deceiving Kyeir and whomever he might be working for. I imagine that was what instigated his howl of rage as he discovered that *that* blade was also a counterfeit. It was an illusion, much in the same way the entrance to the undercroft appeared to be a solid wall.'

Billy tentatively touched his bandaged brow. 'It felt pretty solid to me,' he muttered.

'So you knew Kyeir was going to steal the Geldrin Blade?' Clarissa asked.

Father nodded. 'I knew he would attempt it. In fact, I was counting on it as it presented the most viable opportunity of capturing this shadowy villain.'

'How long have you known about him?' Billy asked.

'For some time,' Father conceded. 'The mystery of who Kyeir, as he calls himself, truly is will soon be resolved. He will be taken away and interrogated, and then we can try and discover who it is pulling his strings.'

Billy looked at Clarissa and Caspian. 'The sorcerer.'

Clarissa put Billy's comment in context for Father. 'My grandpa told me stories when I was younger about the Geldrin Blade. He said it was forged by a sorcerer intent on destroying the entire kingdom.'

'We thought it sounded similar to the story you told me,' Caspian added, 'about the blade being forged in the dark flame by a mysterious master.'

Father looked at them for a while before answering. 'These are two versions of the same tale,' he agreed, 'although I would discourage you from thinking of him as any kind of sorcerer, mage, or wizard. These are all elements of fantasy, but the man who wielded the blade, the Master as he was known, was of no fairytale.'

'Artemis Grieves described him as pure evil.'

Father looked down for a moment, his golden eyes watching Sprocket clamber over the table without a care in the world. 'The three of you will find as you grow in this world that good and evil are not as easy to distinguish as black and white. We all have elements of both in us; we are all different shades of grey, capable of doing both good and bad. Take this little fellow,' he gestured to Sprocket. 'You wouldn't consider him a device built for evil, would you?'

They all shook their heads. Sprocket certainly wasn't evil.

'Then you might be surprised to learn that the same man who forged the Geldrin Blade gave life to Sprocket.'

'What?' Caspian frowned, thinking he had misheard his father. '*He* created Sprocket?'

Father nodded. 'Not all of his actions in life resulted in the creation of evil. It were only those actions he administered with evil intentions that were his true acts of darkness.'

'But you don't think The Master exists anymore,' Caspian said, thinking back to his previous conversations with Father on this subject. 'You don't think that Kyeir was planning to use the Geldrin Blade to resurrect *Him*.'

'Not at all,' Father answered openly. 'The Master perished a very long time ago. As for the real Geldrin Blade, it *is* capable of killing any living thing; the properties of the dark flame folded into the metal will draw the energy, the life force, out of all it touches. I would even concede it possible that the blade could transfer the energy it absorbed to its master, as this was most likely his purpose for creating such a weapon – to sustain his own life.

'It cannot, however, be used to revive the dead. Once life has passed from a living thing, no matter how much energy you put back into it, life cannot return. Kyeir's intentions for the blade are still to be realised, but I stand by my belief that he is not trying to bring back the original Master. I am more concerned by the intentions of whomever it is that has power over Kyeir: he who has assumed The Master's mantle.'

'Do you really think someone out there is trying to continue what *he* started, all those years ago?' Clarissa asked.

'I cannot be certain,' Father replied. 'These are questions still to be answered.'

'I'll tell you what is certain,' Billy said. 'Kyeir is definitely out of his mind.'

Caspian looked down at his hands. The thought that Kyeir was "out of his mind" troubled him, especially because of the inescapable similarities between Kyeir and himself. *You and I are more alike than you dare imagine.*

'What is it, Caspian?' Father asked him kindly. There was concern in his voice, and both Clarissa and Billy were looking at him now.

The nightmare he had repeatedly experienced leading up to the ceremony of the lilies and roses replayed in his mind. Kyeir reaching out of the darkness for him, his twisted mouth saying *Saoul*, although he now pronounced it the way he had in the undercroft. It bothered him now more than ever. Why was he different? Was he really just like Kyeir? Was he really a…

'Saoul.' Caspian said quietly. 'Kyeir said that he and I are the same. His eyes are different colours, just like mine.'

Clarissa couldn't contain her gasp at this revelation. Billy took a double take.

'It's true,' Father said slowly, 'you and he are both Saouls. That is how you both could see things hidden that the others could not.'

'If that is true,' Clarissa said warily, 'then you knew Kyeir was a Saoul. You knew he would be able to follow the clues.'

'You are partly right, Clarissa,' Father agreed. 'However, the clues were left as a failsafe, just in case something were to befall me. The clues were left for Caspian, for my son to follow. But when it became apparent that Kyeir possessed a Saoul's eye an opportunity arose and I left the trail in place, unaltered.'

Caspian shook his head, incapable of finding the answer he wanted, the answer he needed. 'But why me?' he asked. 'Why am *I* different?'

Father looked him in the eye, his hazel eyes reaching deep into Caspian. They took hold of him, hypnotised him, mesmerised him. He felt them searching him, trying to read his thoughts, his feelings. He felt the unfathomable age of them wash over him, and for once he did not resist.

'Because of me,' Father's solemn words bringing him back from the brink. Back from wherever he had drifted.

'What do you mean?' he asked, confused.

'You are different,' Father said, 'because I am different. You see things differently for the same reason that I did not die tonight.'

'I don't understand,' Caspian said, trying to follow.

'Caspian, I have been on this Earth a lot longer than you imagine,' Father said carefully. He took a moment to gauge the reaction of his young audience before continuing. 'There are only a few like myself who do not age, and cannot die at the hand of any mortal weapon. I am both blessed and cursed with a life eternal.'

'You are *immortal*?' Clarissa said slowly. 'You cannot mean that.'

Father simply gave a nod. 'A handful of us have long lived amongst the mortal men and women of this world without anyone becoming the wiser, usually because we outlive anyone who becomes suspicious of our longevity.' He looked at Caspian, sadness in his eyes. 'I am sorry I did not tell you, but you understand how ridiculous this sounds?'

It *did* sound ridiculous, but somewhere, nagging at the back of his mind like a memory he couldn't quite place, he couldn't help feel that this answered a lot of questions.

Prior to him moving to London, long periods of time would pass between his father's visits. Father had never seemed to change from how he had remembered him, but nobody really expects someone to change in the time since they last saw them. Now he thought about it, Father had not changed at all.

'Immortal?' Caspian said quietly, almost to himself.

Father nodded. 'I've learned to move with the times, but in many ways you must have noticed that I am exceptionally old fashioned.'

'To be fair,' Billy shrugged, 'we all see our parents that way.'

Caspian thought about the observation Clarissa had made whilst on the trail for the Geldrin Blade. There had been an underlying theme throughout the riddles – rebirth, regeneration, everlasting. But immortality? That wasn't really possible, was it? That was the stuff of children's books; the fountain of youth, the philosopher's stone, the Holy Grail.

Under this new perspective, the slight Kyeir had made at Father seemed to suddenly make sense. *Death? You threaten me with a concept you do not know*, Kyeir had said.

An obscure thought suddenly struck him. 'Does Mrs Hodges know?' It sounded silly after asking, but he found himself strangely worried that poor Mrs Hodges was unaware of all of this.

Father smiled warmly. 'She may be old, but she is not daft. And besides, she has been in my employment since the age of sixteen. As the years slipped by I had to make a choice to either let her in on my secret or let her go. I opted on telling her: believe me, good housekeepers are hard to find.'

'What does all this mean about Caspian,' Billy asked. 'Is he immortal too, or *half*-immortal. How does that work, him being a Saoul?'

'A Saoul is the progeny of an immortal and a mortal,' Father explained. 'The child will always take the mortal parent's tendencies, although they are distinguishable by their dual eye colour, particularly a golden eye – the Saoul's eye – that they inherit from their immortal parent.'

Caspian was processing all of this as fast as his mind could make sense of it. 'If that is the case, then Kyeir must be the son of *another* immortal.'

'Without a doubt,' Father said very seriously. 'Either someone has deliberately employed a Saoul to work for them, or worse, someone within my own Council has a clandestine motive. It would seem that the circle of those I can trust is growing tighter.'

'Ponsonby Smeelie,' Billy suggested. 'It has to be.'

Clarissa interrupted. 'That doesn't make sense. We saw Smeelie being tortured by Kyeir in the museum.'

'But the guy's a creep,' Billy argued. 'He had that file too, that Jess found. He has to be in on it.'

'I agree,' Caspian said to his Father. 'Mr Smeelie may not be the mastermind behind all of this, but he is definitely involved. He wrote to you, didn't he? Just before you went away.'

'He did,' Father confirmed after giving Caspian another long look. 'Ponsonby thought he had discovered the identity of Kyeir. The location of this particular piece of evidence was far from here, so I travelled there to meet him.'

'Isn't it a bit coincidental that he uncovered this "evidence" a couple of days before the evening of the ceremony?' Caspian asked sceptically. 'Just at the right time to draw you away from the Tower on the night Kyeir would try and steal the blade.'

'You are forgetting that the blade was not in the undercroft,' Father reminded them. 'Let me explain: Mr Smeelie and I have been collaborating for some time in trying to uncover the mysterious plans that have been unravelling concerning the Geldrin Blade and the hooded man, whom we now know as Kyeir. Smeelie found his way into the employment of Kyeir as an inside man, but in fact he was really *my* inside man. As soon as we discovered what Kyeir was after I moved the Geldrin Blade to another location, but once the blade was safe we decided to stay the course and see whether we could bait him in. Artemis was keeping watch on the Tower of London. He is rather fond of the night, after all.'

Caspian had felt like he was being watched when they were outside the White Tower. It had probably been Grieves that Clarissa had heard when they were entering the passage between the walls of St. John's Chapel.

'He was supposed to alert us when the trap had been sprung – which worked perfectly until the three of you almost got yourselves split in two by Jacques, and then Caspian deciding to go one-on-one with Kyeir himself.'

'So, Smeelie is working with *you*?' Billy asked for the sake of clarity.

'Yes.'

'Then why did he have a file on you in his office at the museum?' Caspian asked.

'Because that is his job,' Father replied. 'Ponsonby Smeelie is the record keeper. He collects any documents, articles, and images of those of us that are immortal and keeps them safe. He keeps us out of history as much as possible, but with the digital age we live in it is becoming harder and harder to be avoided.'

'Is that why you haven't got a Facebook account?' Billy asked.

'I still don't think Smeelie can be trusted,' Caspian said, moving passed Billy's question.

Father smiled. 'I do not trust Smeelie, but I know he would not move against me or the others like me.'

'But how can you be sure?'

'Because,' Father said, 'he is one of us. You saw for yourself how he sealed his letters.'

'The ouroboros knot,' Caspian realised, 'it's a symbol for immortality.' That was why he had not only seen it imprinted in the wax of Smeelie's sealed letters, but also on the entrance to Half-Moon Passage, and on the Armada door entering the reflectory.

'That is right,' Father said. 'The two snakes devouring one another in their never ending cycle is the emblem of our immortal Council. Ponsonby Smeelie, like myself, is a member of this ancient order, charged with keeping the existence of the rest of us concealed from the world. You are the first three to learn of our existence in a very long time, and I expect you to keep this secret.'

'I'm not sure anyone would believe us if we *did* tell,' Billy said.

Caspian had to agree. If he started going around telling everyone his father was immortal they would probably think he had gone mad.

'I have to ask,' Caspian began. 'On our family crest there was a phrase in Latin; the same phrase that was the key to the Vigenère cipher. Is that our family motto?'

'Yes, it is.'

'Can you tell me what it means?'

Father smiled. 'Vive ut Vivas: Live that you may live forever.'

Caspian was glad he was already sitting down, as otherwise he was sure he would have hit the floor. *Live that you may live forever*. His mother's final words to him had been the key to the cipher.

'Rather appropriate, no?' Father said.

Caspian couldn't agree more. Mother had meant the words to inspire him to live every day like it might be his last, to live for the moment and have no regrets. Now in light of his father's revelation they took a much more literal form.

'Wow,' Clarissa said, astonished by the connection.

The three friends sat in silence for a moment, processing the incredible revelations that had been unveiled to them this evening; the answers to all their questions, a final destination to the mysterious journey they had climbed aboard.

Eventually Caspian broke the silence. 'So I guess, now I know *all* your secrets.'

Father gave his son an earnest smile in return. His golden eyes seemed to glow in the warm light of the reflectory. 'My boy,' he said inscrutably, 'you have only just begun to scrape the surface.'

XXXIII:
ENDGAME

In the weeks that followed, Caspian felt a vast change in the dynamic between his father and himself. It was like a smoke screen had finally lifted revealing his father for the man he really was: still a man of many mysteries, but Caspian finally understood why he was the way he was. More importantly, he had let Caspian in on his rather incredible secret.

One thing was for certain; things would certainly never be the same again.

The day following the ceremony of the lilies and roses, the Standard had indeed published an article on Drayston Academy's choir. The article entitled: *Drayston Academy Deliver Hair-raising Performance*, was accompanied by a picture of poor Dennis Harlington, mid bow as his toupee abandoned his bald spot, rather than an embarrassing picture of the choir featuring Caspian, Billy, and Clarissa.

Father's wound had taken a couple of weeks to mend, and although it was still not fully healed he had returned to his work. He would carry the scar the bullet left for the rest of his very long life. It seemed his father, although immortal, was not invulnerable.

Caspian had finally spoken to Jess, who had agreed to come and stay for a couple of weeks during the break from school, and he couldn't wait to share with her everything that they had discovered.

At school, his exams had drawn to a close, and on the final day of term he had only to survive the last few lessons and then they would break up for the long summer holiday.

The final lesson of the day was biology, and the atmosphere was electric. Mrs Plumb was struggling to keep order, as the entire class knew that once the bell declared the end of the lesson they would be released from the shackles of classrooms, homework, and education for six long weeks of doing whatever they pleased.

'Simmer down, *please*,' Mrs Plumb fretted, after taking a long swig of her obligatory mug of hot chocolate. Caspian suspected she would require something stronger than hot chocolate to survive this final part of the day.

'So what are we going to do next week?' Billy said conspiratorially from his seat beside Clarissa. 'We've got six weeks to fill. Think we should have another adventure?'

'Preferably one that doesn't involve hooded maniacs,' Clarissa smiled.

'My uncle is supposed to be back in the country. He is coming to stay,' Caspian informed them.

'Is he the one who built that car?' Billy asked.

Caspian was very much looking forward to meeting his uncle Toby. He was still impressed that his uncle had built his own car, the Calideus, all by himself. Father spoke very highly of him, and Caspian was intrigued to meet one of his father's closest and oldest friends.

'Yeah. I've never met him, but Father thinks I'll like him. From what he's told me, I think you'd probably get on with him too?'

'Why?' Billy asked. 'Does he share my witty, intelligent, sense of humour?'

'Only if by that you mean, "has an inescapable attraction to trouble," then yes,' Caspian smiled.

'You are hardly one to talk, Caspian,' Clarissa laughed.

Caspian laughed also. She was right of course.

'Hey,' Billy said to get their attention. 'What's wrong with Mrs Plumb?'

Mrs Plumb had been mid sentence when she abruptly stopped and her mouth had dropped open in horrified surprise. She tried to compose herself and continue but stopped again and held her stomach that, judging by the giggling from the front row of the classroom, must have made an audible sound.

Then, with no warning other than a very panicked expression on her face, Mrs Plumb turned and bolted for the classroom door, a loud *ppphhaaarrrrrpppp* escaping her backside.

A raucous roar of laughter quickly shattered the stunned silence as the class erupted, with the exception of Clarissa who looked absolutely appalled by what had just occurred.

Caspian laughed so hard his sides started hurting, until he realised he was being watched by the pair of ice blue eyes belonging to the boy who had practically ignored his existence for the last couple of months. Hayden Tanner now wore a smile that was truly menacing as he looked Caspian directly in the eye.

Oh no, Caspian thought. Now the moment had passed he could see clearly that this sort of incident had Hayden written all over it. Had he spiked poor Mrs Plumb with a laxative? Could he have coerced someone into contaminating her hot chocolate, calculating for an uncontrollably colossal bowel movement?

And if so, what was Hayden's ulterior motive? It would not be easy to discern as even his ulterior motives had ulterior motives, but Caspian was sure that this would come back to him in some way or form. Would Rob Harper be waiting for him at his locker after class, ready to point out the bottle of laxatives that had miraculously appeared there, just as Hayden rounded the corner with a senior member of the faculty?

Julie McFadden turned round and looked at Hayden, who gave her the slightest of nods in return. At that signal, both Hayden and Julie made their way to the front of the classroom and stood before Mrs Plumb's desk. Hayden held in his hand a sheet of paper.

'What's going on?' Billy asked, watching the peculiar pantomime unfold.

Clarissa, it seemed, was on the same page as Caspian. 'You'd better brace yourself,' she cautioned him. 'I think all of this is going to be for your benefit.'

'Could I have your attention,' Hayden said in his most charming voice, raising his empty hand to suppress the laughter and erratic chatter created by Mrs Plumb's prompt exit. The class obliged him and fell silent. 'Thank you,' he continued. 'Whilst Mrs Plumb is temporarily incapacitated, Julie and I would like to bring something to the attention of the class.'

Caspian had thought that Hayden's silent treatment had been too good to last. Now, whatever he had been scheming was about to come into fruition.

'Uh oh,' Billy cottoned on.

'As you may be aware,' Hayden chimed, 'Julie has been writing for the school paper this year, which is really great as she is the first year nine student to make it onto the writing team for a very long time.'

Beside him Julie was blushing. 'Thank you, Hayden,' she spluttered with embarrassment, 'but it was with your help…'

'No, no,' Hayden said coyly. 'You deserved to be on the team.'

'Before our SATs began,' Julie said, still blushing from Hayden's complements, 'you may recall that I offered the opportunity for others in our year to write something for the paper to give an insight into the lives and feelings of our fellow students. The uptake on this was not particularly high, which is understandable with the exams coming.'

'And that nobody likes additional homework,' Hayden added with a smile. A few of his classmates chuckled.

'However,' Julie continued, 'someone from this class *did* write something, clearly intending to squander this opportunity in attempt to blight the reputation of Hayden.'

And there it was.

Hayden Tanner looked directly at Caspian, who had not submitted an article for Julie to print. Yet, it seemed, one had been submitted on his behalf.

A few members of the class had followed Hayden's line of sight to Caspian, and were turning round now to look at him. He felt his face redden, which probably made him look all the more guilty, but he felt so uncomfortable by the sudden attention he couldn't prevent it.

'As you all know,' Julie said, 'Caspian had to take some time off earlier this year due to some unfortunate family circumstances.'

More of the class were looking at him now, a few were whispering things to one another. Caspian felt like his seat was going to swallow him whole.

'A lot of us felt sorry for him, after all he had been through. I thought that was the reason why he had acted out on so many occasions, but it seems at the root of it all it was nothing more than petty jealousy.'

Billy looked at Caspian. 'You didn't write anything, did you,' he quietly assumed.

'Not a word,' Caspian confirmed.

Julie continued from the front. 'The article he submitted was titled: The *Real* Hayden Tanner,' she announced, to the sniggering of a few people in the class.

Like a seasoned stage performer, Hayden quickly played off this. 'An *awfully* flattering title, I think you'll agree,' he smirked.

'Is it a declaration of love?' Rob Harper called out mockingly. A few more people giggled, and Julie McFadden went red again as she was struck by déjà vu of her own declaration of love being read by half the school.

'I'm not sure *love* is the right word,' Hayden hinted. He lifted the piece of paper in his hand and began to read, in a loud and clear voice, the article that Caspian had supposedly written. 'Many of you know Hayden Tanner: star pupil of

Mrs Scrudge's tutor group.' He gave his classmates a cheeky wink and wave, causing an eruption of laughter.

He's playing the crowd, Caspian realised.

'You know him to be kind, charming, intelligent…' Hayden stopped and looked at Caspian in mock disgust. 'Oh, you forgot handsome.' More laughter from the class, enjoying the spectacle. 'Basically, an all round good guy. But you have all been deceived. In this article, I intend to bring to light the true nature of Hayden Tanner: he is not the golden boy he presents himself to be, but instead a cruel and spiteful boy no better than a common school bully.'

The laughter had stopped now. A stunned silence hung over the classroom as Hayden paused for effect.

Then he continued to read the article that, fabricated as Caspian's own words, explained how it had really been Hayden who stole Julie's diary and planted it in Caspian's locker. It told how he had riled Caspian on the athletics field whilst feigning fatigue and coerced him into trying to punch him. It claimed that he had boasted about convincing their classmates that Caspian was a liar. It argued that he had stolen Caspian's history report whilst he was in detention and had reproduced it, along with his notebook, as his own work to present the following day.

Everything it claimed, every single word of it, really was the absolute truth.

And yet, despite being very well written, its affect was not to convince Caspian's peers that all of this had really happened, but instead to present it as a preposterous story that was precisely a little too tenuous to swallow. The manner that Hayden had stood before the class and explicated this fantastic account would have sown the seeds of doubt in the minds of all his listeners. They would never believe any of it was true now, no matter what Caspian had to say – which, of course, was Hayden's intention: he had successfully delivered a perversion of the truth.

'The boy you know as Hayden Tanner is nothing more than an act,' Hayden concluded. His demeanour was serious now: no more joking about for the crowd – he had them exactly where he wanted them. 'A persona he has conjured and adopted to mislead my innocent classmates into believing he is something more than he really is; something much greater, better. Kinder. In truth, Hayden Tanner could not be further from these things.'

Hayden lowered the paper and his eyes met Caspian's with grim satisfaction. This was it. This was his endgame. He had won.

There were a few murmurs in the classroom as people began to digest all they had just heard, every unbelievable accusation. Julie spoke over them all, directly to Caspian. 'What have you got to say for yourself? Or at least, what have you got to say that isn't a slanderous lie?'

Caspian didn't answer. What could he say? He stared at Hayden, sensing the pleasure he must be feeling in this moment. He could feel the rest of the class looking at him too. Rose Wetherby would be looking at him – what would she think of him now? He didn't even want to look at her for fear of what he might see on her face: disappointment? Maybe even dislike.

He could only look back into Hayden Tanner's ice blue eyes, feeling himself welling with hatred and anger. Anger that once again this boy had manipulated him into being the villain so that he could come across as the victim, or even the hero. What made Caspian feel worse was that he knew how Hayden thought; he should have seen this coming.

Then it crossed his mind: he *knew* how Hayden thought.

Caspian stood up.

Billy grabbed his arm. 'Don't,' his friend warned him, worried for what he was going to do.

'Trust me,' Caspian said calmly, and he began to walk to the front of the class where Hayden stood waiting.

Rob Harper was out of his seat too, clearly anticipating a fight just as Billy had, but Hayden signalled for him to stop. Hayden *wanted* Caspian to go for him, to justify every word he had just said by sealing it with an act of violence. He had made Caspian angry, just as he had on the athletics field, and he expected Caspian to lash out again. Only this time, the whole class would see it.

Hayden Tanner could predict what Caspian was going to do. Every move Caspian made, Hayden was already ten steps ahead. The only way to beat an opponent like that was to throw him off his game by doing something unpredictable, something he'd never see coming. It was time to take a leaf out of Hayden's book: the truth didn't matter, only the show.

Caspian reached where Hayden stood, but instead of facing off against him, he turned away from the boy that had given him so much torment and turned to face the rest of the class.

'It *is* all true,' Caspian said in a confident voice.

He could almost feel Hayden's smile in the back of his head, satisfaction that Caspian was arguing that the events the article told were the truth.

'Not what I wrote in that article, of course,' Caspian verified, 'but what Julie said about me. She is completely right.'

He met the gazes of his friends. Billy looked confused, but Clarissa was giving him a knowing smile. Renewed, he continued. 'What I said in that article was, of course, made up,' he laughed. 'Julie knows it was me who took her diary and spread it around school.'

Caspian turned and looked at her. 'I never really apologised to you for the hurt and embarrassment that little stunt caused you, but I am truly sorry.' He turned his attention back to the class. 'Of course it was Hayden's report he presented in history,' he said obviously. 'No one in their right mind would stay up all night copying not only a report, but an entire notebook as well. If anyone was to really do that we'd have to question what kind of a dull life that person must lead!'

He didn't turn to look at Hayden, but he knew that subtle blow would have hit the mark. Better still, a few members of the class smiled, or nodded in agreement. His plan might actually work, he thought to himself. He also took delight in the creased brow of Rob Harper – this was clearly not how Hayden had told him it would play out.

'I came to this school after the first term had begun,' he continued, 'and I thought it was going to be difficult making friends. As Julie has already said, you all know my real reason for having to move down here. I am not asking you for any sympathy, and I am not using it as an excuse for what I did. But, I hope you can understand how I felt being a stranger amongst you: I *needed* to be noticed, I *needed* a distraction, I *needed* your attention.'

He turned to Hayden now. 'Hayden took me under his wing in that first week. I'm sure many of your noticed how close we were back then. I shared with Hayden what I was going through, and like the truly good guy that he is, he helped me concoct this entire plan to keep me distracted from the tragedy I was suffering at home.' The look on Hayden's face was priceless. Caspian placed his hand on Hayden's shoulder in a friendly gesture and continued, 'this has all been a farce by his design, and without his help I could have never pulled this off.'

The class were blown over by this new twist. They looked at one another, trying to see if anyone else knew what was going on.

Caspian knew that this gamble wasn't entirely watertight: they might ask that if Hayden was helping him, why was he trying to publicly shame him? Would the information overload, as they tried to untangle the ruse from the truth, keep them from noticing something was amiss?

He couldn't be sure. His whole plan depended on the class accepting that he was telling the undisputed truth. And so, before Hayden had a chance to say anything that might imply otherwise, Caspian asked the entire class to give Hayden a round of applause.

Slowly applause filled the room as his classmates began their usual ritual of praising their beloved Hayden Tanner. Caspian smiled, inwardly enjoying using Hayden's own popularity against him now.

When Caspian looked at Hayden, he appeared somewhat amused by what had just transpired. He must have realised that his plan had backfired. After all, he was being publicly praised for doing something good, something entirely characteristic and plausible of his fabricated nature. He would have to go along with it, or come out worse off.

'And so,' Caspian announced with an air of finality, 'all that said, we have ten minutes left of our last day of term. I, for one, do not want to spend this evening in detention for the laxative *I* put in Mrs Plumb's hot chocolate, so I'm getting out of here.'

To his surprise, this announcement was greeted by another round of applause with cheers from many of the audience, particularly Billy and Clarissa. He caught a glance of Rose Wetherby's beautiful features and long golden hair. Dimples formed under her cheeks as she smiled at him, as though they both shared some unspoken secret.

Caspian couldn't be sure what nature this secret held, but it felt absolutely wonderful nevertheless.

EPILOGUE:
EFTERFALT

For all the stories, myths, and legends that had grown about the Nine Sabres over the centuries, no one had ever suspected that the tallest of these was actually hollow. Within the harsh rocky walls of Efterfalt, protected from the howling icy wind of the Norwegian Sea, Saoul Kyeir lit the oil lamp that hung on the wall beside him. The warm flickering glow of the flame illuminated a tunnel that cut deep into the heart of this towering seastack.

The smooth floor was moist inside the rock, the air clammy and pungent. He carefully followed the tunnel to a staircase and descended. It was not long before he found another light illuming from a large chamber ahead, a thick doorway of glass sealing it from the tunnel. He opened the door and stepped within.

The chamber at the heart of Efterfalt was lavish and warmly lit. A deep red carpet had been laid on the stone floor, antiques of incredible beauty and value lined the room. How these items had come to be here, to have made it inside without being lost to the sea, Kyeir had always wondered but did not know.

The boy, the son of Edgar Stone, disturbed him. He had not known of the boy's existence, but now that he did he wondered what it meant. He had almost caught the boy in London, following him into Covent Garden. *How much did the boy know?* How much had Edgar Stone shared with his son? Did the boy know the phrase to break the Vigenère Cipher? Did he know the location that Stone kept the Geldrin Blade?

'Dark is the night that Saoul Kyeir returns to my sanctuary.'

Kyeir bowed his head. He had not noticed his master sitting on the far side of the chamber in a large chair, his back to him. All he could see of him was his thin hand that idly traced across the cover of a leather bound book on the table beside him.

'You have not returned with the blade.' The words The Master spoke were not English, nor were they in a tongue known to any country. His voice was soft and smooth; it was not harsh or monstrous. Had it belonged to another mouth it might have been pleasant, but it did not. 'So what has brought about your premature return?'

'Something is amiss, Master,' Kyeir said in the same unusual language that his master had spoken. 'Stone has fathered a child – a boy. He is a Saoul, like myself.'

The Master's hand froze on the surface of the book. 'A Saoul? You are sure?'

'I am, Master.'

'And his abilities?'

'The boy is young,' Kyeir replied. 'I have not witnessed any abilities to speak of, but he clearly bares a Saoul's eye.'

The Master sat quietly for a moment. 'This troubles you?'

It did. Kyeir wasn't sure why. It was like the reasoning behind it had been severed from his memory, cut from his mind so that he could not comprehend the source of what unsettled him.

'You must stay away from the boy,' The Master instructed calmly. 'He is destined to play an integral part in all that is planned, but not just yet. If you must cross paths with him, let him live.'

'Live?' Kyeir said surprised. He had never known his master to show compassion or restraint, especially against his enemies.

At a gesture from The Master, a mechanical device walked across the room. It was made of complex clockwork components and humanoid in design. The automaton stopped beside The Master's chair and extended its arm to receive a small drawstring bag.

'There is something else about the boy,' Kyeir rasped.

'You feel like you have seen the boy before?' his master replied before he could speak the thought.

'Yes,' he admitted. 'A shadow of a memory clouds my mind, a memory from a long, long time ago. From a time before…' Kyeir stopped, thinking better of what he was going to say. 'The boy is familiar to me.' He had searched for the meaning to this deep within his cerebellum, straining to find the connection that was missing.

'*Familiar*,' The Master mused from his chair, and then with a flick of his hand he sent the mechanical man ambling over toward Kyeir.

The automaton handed him the drawstring bag. It was small, made of dark purple silk, and seemed to contain some kind of powder. 'What is this?'

'You will need it,' The Master answered. 'Your search for the Geldrin Blade will end in a trap, I am certain of it.'

'A trap?' Kyeir replied. 'Does Stone suspect what I am after?'

'Almost certainly. And if he doesn't, he will.' The Master did not seem bothered by this. 'He will turn whatever tricks he has in place to protect the blade into a means of capturing you. The Geldrin Blade will be moved to another location.'

'And when he does, am I to take it?'

'No,' The Master replied. 'You are to proceed as if ignorant to him having any knowledge of your intentions. Proceed as planned, and be captured. Opportunity to claim the blade will come.'

Kyeir looked at the little silk bag in his hand. 'This is your true design? Your intention is for me to end up in *their* hands?'

The Master ran his hand across the leather book cover and slid it open. 'Every thing I ask of you is as certain as the words on this page,' he said quietly. 'Just as certain as Edgar Stone's undoing will come at the hand of his own kin. Follow my instruction.'

Saoul Kyeir bowed his head. He knew better than anyone to question his master's judgement. Every day was a reminder to that, every time he caught a glimpse of his hideous face in a reflection, every waking moment when pain and discomfort coursed through his wretched body.

But the thought of his master's plan made a smile painfully turn the corner of his mouth, stinging the broken nerves beneath his lip. The thought of Edgar Stone's death – the man who had abandoned him and condemned him to become this monster – was too satisfying a thought to refuse.

'Is that clear?' The Master asked.

'Yes, my Master,' he bowed, safe in the knowledge that Edgar Stone's time was almost spent.

After all, no one can live forever.

Printed in Great Britain
by Amazon